'A surprising and sometimes delightful reading experience . . . Lindqvist manages to maintain a light touch in an otherwise bleak landscape.'
SUNDAY TIMES

'Combines an atmospheric coming-of-age story set in Stockholm in 1981 with a shocking (and very gory) thriller. His vampire is an original, both heart-breakingly pathetic and terrifying. This was a bestseller in Sweden and could be equally big here. Don't miss it.'
THE TIMES

'Gets my vote as one of the books of the year.'
ILLAWARRA MERCURY

'An energetic, noisy, highly imaginative novel that blends the most extreme kind of vampirish schlock-horror with a complicated love story, a profoundly gory sequence of murders and some rather good domestic realism about life in 1980s Stockholm . . . Lindqvist, while he seems to be mostly having fun with the idea, has also thought carefully about the issues of blood, death, infection and starvation that sit at the heart of the vampire myth; to say nothing of the close connection between vampirism and eroticism.'
SYDNEY MORNING HERALD

'Lindqvist has reinvented the vampire novel and made it all the more chilling . . . An immensely readable and highly disturbing book in which grim levels of gore and violence are tempered by an unexpected tenderness.'
DAILY EXPRESS

'Justifies its cult status in Scandinavia with its disturbing and convincing take on the banal horror of normality.'
TIME OUT

HANDLING THE UNDEAD

John Ajvide Lindqvist

THOMAS DUNNE BOOKS

ST. MARTIN'S GRIFFIN

NEW YORK

To Fritiof. Mah-fjou!

This is a work of fiction. All of the characters, organizations, and events portrayed in this novel are either products of the author's imagination or are used fictitiously.

THOMAS DUNNE BOOKS.
An imprint of St. Martin's Press.

www.thomasdunnebooks.com
www.stmartins.com

The Library of Congress has cataloged the hardcover edition as follows:

Ajvide Lindqvist, John, 1968–
    Handling the undead / John Ajvide Lindqvist.—1st. U.S. ed.
        p. cm.
    ISBN 978-0-312-60525-4
    1. Zombies—Fiction. 2. Horror tales. 3. Stockholm (Sweden)—
Fiction. I. Title.
    PT9877.22.I54 A2 2010
    839.73'8—dc22

                                                            2010029288

ISBN 978-0-312-60452-3 (trade paperback)

First published in Sweden as *Hanteringen av odöda* by Ordfront

First St. Martin's Griffin Edition: August 2011

Solidarity is always directed at
'one of us' and 'us' cannot refer
to everyone . . . For 'we' assumes
someone who can be excluded,
someone who belongs to the others,
and these others cannot be animals
or machines, but people.

SVEN-ERIC LIEDMAN,
To See Oneself in Others

All that we hope is, when we go
Our skin and our blood and our bones
Don't get in your way, making you ill
The way they did when we lived

MORRISSEY
There's a place in hell for me and my friends

Prologue

When the current reverses its course

Sveavägen 13 August 22.49

'Salud, comandante.'

Henning held up the box of Gato Negro and toasted the metal plaque in the sidewalk. A single withered rose lay on the spot where Prime Minister Olof Palme had been gunned down sixteen years earlier. Henning crouched down and ran his finger over the raised inscription.

'Damn it,' he said. 'It's all going to hell, Olof. Down, down and further down.'

His head was killing him, and it wasn't the wine. The people walking by on Sveavägen were staring into the ground too; some had their hands pressed against their temples.

Earlier in the evening it had simply felt like an approaching thunderstorm, but the electric tension in the air had gradually, imperceptibly, become more intense until it was now all but unbearable. Not a cloud in the night sky, though; no distant rumble, no hope of release. The invisible field of electricity could not be touched, but it was there; everyone could feel it.

It was like a blackout in reverse. Since around nine o'clock, no lamps could be switched off, no electrical appliances powered down. If you tried to pull out the plug there was an alarming crackling sound and sparks flew between the outlet and the plug, preventing the circuit from being broken.

And the field was still increasing in strength.

Henning felt as though there was an electric fence around his head, torturing him, pulsing with shocks of pure pain.

An ambulance went by with sirens blaring, either because it was on a dispatch or simply because no one could turn them off. A couple of parked cars were idling on the spot.

Salud, comandante.

Henning raised the wine cask to face level, tilted his head back and opened the tap. A stream of wine hit his chin and spilled down over his throat before he managed to divert it into his mouth. He closed his eyes, drinking deeply while the spilled wine trickled down over his chest, mingled with his sweat, and continued on.

The heat. God almighty, the heat.

For several weeks all the weather charts had shown enormous happy suns plastered across the entire country. The pavement and buildings steamed with heat accumulated during the day and even now, at almost eleven o'clock, the temperature was stuck around thirty degrees.

Henning nodded goodbye to the Prime Minister and traced his assassin's steps toward Tunnelgatan. The handle of the wine cask had broken when he lifted it out through an open car window and he had to carry it under his arm. His head felt larger than usual, swollen. He massaged his forehead with his fingers.

His head probably still appeared normal from the outside but his fingers, they'd definitely swelled up from the heat and the wine.

This damned weather. It's not natural.

Henning steadied himself against the railing, walking slowly up the steps cut into the steep footpath. Every unsteady step rang through his throbbing skull. The windows on both sides were open, brightly lit, music streaming from some. Henning longed for darkness: darkness and silence. He wanted to keep drinking until he managed to shut down.

At the top of the stairs he rested for a couple of seconds. The situation was deteriorating. Impossible to say if he was the one getting worse or if the field was growing stronger. It wasn't pulsating now; now it was a constant burning pain, squeezing him relentlessly.

And it wasn't just him.

Not far from him there was a car parked at an angle to the sidewalk. The engine idling, the driver's side door open and the stereo playing 'Living Doll' at full blast. Next to the car, the driver was crouched in the middle of the street, his hands pressed against his head.

Henning screwed his eyes shut and opened them again. Was he imagining things or was the light from the apartments around him getting brighter?

Something. Is about to. Happen.

Carefully, one step at a time, he made his way across Döbelnsgatan; reached the shadow of the chestnut trees in the Johannes cemetery, but there he collapsed. Couldn't go on. Everything was buzzing now; it sounded like a swarm of bees in the crown of the tree above his head. The field was stronger, his head was compressed as if far under water and through the open windows he could hear people scream.

This is it. I'm dying.

The pain in his head was beyond reason. Hard to believe such a little cavity could pack so much pain. Any second now his head was going to cave in. The light from the windows was stronger, the shadows of the leaves cast a psychedelic pattern over his body. Henning turned his face to the sky, opened his eyes wide and waited for the bang, the explosion.

Ping.

It was gone.

Like throwing a switch. Gone.

The headache vanished; the bee swarm stopped abruptly.

3

Everything went back to normal. Henning tried to open his mouth to let out a sound, an expression of gratitude perhaps, but his jaws were locked, cramped shut. His muscles ached from having been tensed for so long.

Silence. Darkness. And something fell from the sky. Henning saw it the moment before it landed next to his head, something small, an insect. Henning breathed in and out through his nose, savouring the dry smell of earth. The back of his head was resting on something hard and cool. He turned his head in order to cool his cheek as well.

He was lying on a block of marble. He felt something irregular under his cheek. Letters. He lifted his head and read what was written there.

CARL
4 December 1918 – 18 July 1987
GRETA
16 September 1925 – 16 June 2002

There were more names further up. A family grave. Greta had been married to Carl, but she'd been widowed these past fifteen years. Well, well. Henning imagined her as a small grey-haired woman, wrestling her walking frame through the door of a grand apartment. Pictured the inheritance wrangle that would have broken out a few weeks ago.

Something was moving on the face of the marble and Henning squinted at it. A caterpillar. A spotless white grub, about as big as a cigarette filter. It looked troubled, writhing on the black marble and Henning felt sorry for it, poked it with his finger to flick it onto the grass. But the caterpillar didn't budge.

What the hell...

Henning brought his face up close next to the caterpillar, poked it again. It might as well have been cemented to the stone. Henning extracted a lighter from his pocket, and flicked it on for a better look.

The caterpillar was shrinking. Henning moved so close that his nose almost brushed the caterpillar; the lighter singed a few hairs. No. The caterpillar was not shrinking. It was just that less and less of it was visible, because it was drilling down into the stone.

Naaah...

Henning rapped his knuckles against the stone. It was definitely stone all right. Smooth, expensive marble. He laughed and spoke out loud, 'No, come on. Come on, caterpillar...'

It was almost completely gone now. Only one last little white knob. It waved at Henning, sank down into the stone as he watched and was gone. Henning felt with his finger where it had been. There was no hole, no loose fragments where the caterpillar had dug through. It had sunk down and now it was gone.

Henning patted the stone with the flat of his hand, said, 'Well done, little feller. Good work.' Then he took his wine and moved up toward the chapel in order to sit on the steps and drink.

He was the only one who saw it.

13 August

What have I done to deserve this?

Svarvargatan 16.03

Death...

David lifted his eyes from the desk, looking at the framed photograph of Duane Hanson's plastic sculpture 'Supermarket Lady'.

A woman, obese, in a pink top and turquoise skirt, pushing a loaded shopping trolley. She has curlers in her hair, a fag dangling from the corner of her mouth. Her shoes are worn down, barely covering the swollen, aching feet. Her gaze is empty. On the bare skin of her upper arms you can just make out a violet mark, bruising. Perhaps her husband beats her.

But the trolley is full. Filled to bursting.

Cans, cartons, bags. Food. Microwave meals. Her body is a lump of flesh forced inside her skin, which in turn has been crammed into the tight skirt, the tight top. The gaze is empty, the lips hard around the cigarette, a glimpse of teeth. The hands grip the trolley handle.

And the trolley is full. Filled to bursting.

David drew in air through his nostrils, could almost smell the mixture of cheap perfume and supermarket sweat.

Death...

Every time his ideas dried up, when he felt hesitant, he looked at this picture. It was Death; the thing you struggle against. All the tendencies in society that point towards this picture are evil, everything that points away from it is…better.

The door to Magnus' room opened and Magnus emerged with a Pokémon card in his hand. From inside the room you could hear the agitated voice of the cartoon frog, Grodan Boll, 'Noooo, come ooooon!'

Magnus held out the card.

'Daddy, is Dark Golduck an eye or a kind of water?'

'Water. Sweetheart, we'll have to talk about this later…'

'But he has eye attack.'

'Yes, but…Magnus. Not now. I'll come when I'm ready. OK?'

Magnus caught sight of the newspaper in front of David.

'What are they *doing*?'

'Please, Magnus. I'm working. I'll come in a minute.'

'Ab…so…lut filth. What does that mean?'

David closed the newspaper and took hold of Magnus' shoulders. Magnus struggled, trying to open the paper.

'Magnus! I'm serious. If you don't let me work now I won't have any time for you later. Go into your room, close the door. I'll be there soon.'

'Why do you have to work *all* the *time!*'

David sighed. 'If you only knew how little I work compared to other parents. But please, leave me alone for a little while.'

'Yes, yes, *yes*.'

Magnus wriggled out of his grasp and went back to his room. The door slammed shut. David walked once around the room, wiped his underarms with a towel and sat back down at the desk. The window to the Kungsholmen shoreline was wide open but there was almost no breeze, and David was sweating even though his upper body was bare.

He opened the newspaper again. Something funny had to come of this.

Absolut filth!

A giveaway promotion featuring adult magazines and liquor; two women from the Swedish Centre Party pouring vodka over an issue of *Hustler* as a protest. *Distressed*, read the caption. David studied their faces. Mostly, they looked belligerent, as if they wanted to pulverise the photographer with their eyes. The spirits ran down over the naked woman on the cover.

It was so grotesque it was hard to make something funny out of it. David's gaze scoured the image, tried to find a point of entry.

Photograph: Putte Merkert

There it was.

The photographer. David leaned back in the chair, looked up at the ceiling and started to formulate something. After several minutes he had the bare outline of a script written in longhand. He looked at the women again. Now their accusing gazes were directed at him.

'So; planning to make fun of us and our beliefs are you?' they said. 'What about you?'

'Yes, OK,' David said out loud to the newspaper. 'But at least I know I'm a clown, unlike the two of you.'

He kept writing, with a buzzing headache that he put down to a nagging conscience. After twenty minutes he had a passable routine that might even be amusing if he milked it for all it was worth. He glanced up at Supermarket Lady but received no guidance. Possibly he was walking in her footsteps, sitting in her basket.

It was half past four. Four and a half hours until he was due on stage, and there were already butterflies in his stomach.

He made a cup of coffee, smoked a cigarette and went in to see Magnus, spent half an hour talking about Pokémon, helped Magnus to sort the cards and interpret what they said.

'Dad,' Magnus asked, 'what exactly is your job?'

'You already know that. You were there at Norra Brunn once. I tell stories and people laugh and…Then I get paid for it.'

'Why do they laugh?'

David looked into Magnus' serious eight-year-old's eyes and burst into laughter himself. He stroked Magnus' head and answered, 'I don't know. I really don't know. Now I'm going to have some coffee.'

'Oh, you're *always* drinking coffee.'

David got up from the floor where the cards lay spread out. When he reached the door, he turned around to look at his son, whose lips moved as he read one of his cards.

'I think,' David said, 'that people laugh because they want to laugh. They have paid to come and laugh, and so they laugh.'

Magnus shook his head. 'I don't get it.'

'No,' David said, 'I don't either.'

Eva came back from work at half past five and David greeted her in the hall.

'Hi sweetheart,' she said. 'What's up?'

'Death, death, death,' David replied, holding his hands over his stomach. He kissed her. Her upper lip was salt with sweat. 'And you?'

'Fine. A little bit of a headache. Otherwise I'm fine. Have you been able to write?'

'No, it...' David gestured vaguely at the desk. 'Yes, but it isn't that good.'

Eva nodded. 'No, I know. Will I get to hear it later?'

'If you like.'

Eva left to find Magnus, and David went to the bathroom, let some of the nervousness drain out of him. He remained on the toilet seat for a while, studying the pattern of white fishes on the shower curtain. He wanted to read his script to Eva; in fact, he needed to read it to her. It was funny, but he was ashamed of it and was afraid that Eva would say something about...the ideas behind it. Of which there were none. He flushed, then rinsed his face with cold water.

I'm an entertainer. Plain and simple.

Yes. Of course.

He made a light dinner—a mushroom omelette—while Magnus and Eva laid out the Monopoly board in the living room. David's underarms ran with sweat as he stood at the stove sautéing the mushrooms.

This weather. It isn't natural.

An image suddenly loomed in his mind: the greenhouse effect. Yes. The Earth as a gigantic greenhouse. With us planted here millions of years ago by aliens. Soon they'll be back for the harvest.

He scooped the omelette onto plates and called out that dinner was served. Good image, but was it funny? No. But if you added someone fairly well known, like...a newspaper columnist, say—Staffan Heimersson—and said he was the leader of the aliens in disguise. So therefore Staffan Heimersson's solely responsible for the greenhouse effect...

'What are you thinking about?'

'Oh, nothing. That it's Staffan Heimersson's fault it's so warm.'

'OK...'

Eva waited. David shrugged. 'No, that was it. Basically.'

'Mum?' Magnus was done picking the tomato slices out of his salad. 'Robin said that if the Earth gets warmer the dinosaurs will come back, is that true?'

His headache got worse during the game of Monopoly, and everyone became unnecessarily grumpy when they lost money. After half an hour they took a break for *Bolibompa*, the children's program, and Eva went to the kitchen and made some espresso. David sat in the sofa and yawned. As always when he was nervous he became drowsy, just wanted to sleep.

Magnus curled up next to him and they watched a documentary about the circus. When the coffee was ready, David got up despite Magnus' protests. Eva was at the stove, fiddling with one of the knobs.

'Strange,' she remarked, 'I can't turn it off.'

The power light wouldn't go off. David turned some knobs at random, but nothing happened. The burner on which the coffee pot sat gurgling was red-hot. They couldn't be bothered doing anything to it for the moment, so David read his piece out while they drank the heavily sugared espresso and smoked. Eva thought it was funny.

'Can I do it?'

'Absolutely.'

'You don't think that it's...'

'What?'

'Well, going too far. They're right, of course.'

'Well? What does that have to do with it?'

'No, of course. Thanks.'

Ten years they had been married, and hardly a day went by that David did not look at Eva and think, 'How bloody lucky I am.' Naturally there were black days. Weeks, even, without joy or the possibility of it, but even then, at the bottom of all the murk, he knew there was a placard that read *bloody good luck*. Maybe he couldn't see it at that moment, but it always resurfaced.

She worked as an editor and illustrator of non-fiction books for children at a small publishing company called Hippogriff, and she had written and illustrated two books herself featuring Bruno, a philosophically inclined beaver who liked to build things. No huge successes, but as Eva once said with a grimace, 'The upper middle classes seem to like them. Architects. Whether their children do is less certain.' David thought the books were significantly funnier than his monologues.

'Mum! Dad! I can't turn it off!'

Magnus was standing in front of the television, waving the remote control. David hit the off button on the set but the screen did not go black. It was the same as the stove, but here at least the plug was easy to get at, so he pulled on it just as the newscaster announced the start of the evening current affairs show. For a moment it felt like pulling a piece of metal off a magnet, the wall socket sucking at the plug. There was a crackling sound and a tickle in his fingers, then the newscaster disappeared into the dark.

David held out the plug. 'Did you see that? It was some kind of...short circuit. Now all the fuses have gone.' He flicked the light switch. The ceiling lamp went on, but he could not switch it off again.

Magnus jumped up in his seat.

'Come on! Let's keep playing.'

They let Magnus win Monopoly, and while he was counting his money. David packed his stage shoes and shirt, along with the newspaper. When he came out into the kitchen, Eva was pulling the stove out from the wall.

'No,' David said. 'Don't do that.'

Eva pinched a finger and swore. 'Damn...we can't leave it like this. I'm going over to my dad's. Fuck...' Eva tugged on the stove but it had become wedged between the cabinets.

'Eva,' David said. 'How many times have we forgotten to turn it off and gone to bed without anything happening?'

'Yeah, I know, but to leave the apartment...' She kicked the oven door. 'We haven't cleaned back there for years. Bloody thing. Damn, my head hurts.'

'Is that what you want to do right now? Clean behind the stove?'

She let her hands fall, shook her head and chuckled.

'No. I got it in my head. It'll have to wait.'

She made a final desperate lunge at the stove and threw up her hands, defeated. Magnus came out into the kitchen with his money.

'Ninety-seven thousand four hundred.' He scrunched up his eyes. 'My head hurts a whole lot. It's stupid.'

They each took an aspirin and a glass of water, said cheers and swallowed. A farewell toast.

Magnus was going to spend the night at David's mother's place, Eva was going to visit her father in Järfälla, but come back in the middle of the night. They picked up Magnus between them, and all three kissed.

'Not too much Cartoon Network at Grandma's,' David said.

'Nah,' Magnus said. 'I don't watch that anymore.'

'That's good,' Eva said. 'It'll be...'

'I watch the Disney channel. It's much better.'

David and Eva kissed again, their eyes telegraphing something about how it would be later that night when they were alone. Then Eva took Magnus' hand and they walked off, waving one last time. David remained on the sidewalk, watching them.

What if I never saw them again...

The usual fear gripped him. God had been too good to him, there'd been a mistake, he had got more than he deserved. Now it would all be taken away. Eva and Magnus disappeared around the corner and an impulse told him to run after them, stop them. Say, 'Come on. Let's go home. We'll watch *Shrek*, we'll play Monopoly, we...can't let ourselves be separated.'

The usual fears, but worse than usual. He got a grip on himself, turned and walked toward St Eriksgatan while he quietly recited his new routine in order to fix it in his mind:

How does this kind of picture come to be? The two women are upset, so what do they do? They go to the store and buy a case of vodka and then a stack of porn magazines. When they've been standing there, pouring and pouring for two hours, Putte Merkert, photographer at Aftonbladet, *just happens to catch sight of them.*

'Hi there!' Putte Merkert says. 'What are you doing?'

'We're pouring alcohol on porn magazines,' the women answer.

'Aha,' the photographer thinks. A chance for a scoop.

No, not 'the photographer'. Putte Merkert. All the way through.

Aha, thinks Putte Merkert. A chance for a scoop...

Halfway across the bridge, David caught sight of something strange and stopped.

Recently he had read in the newspaper that there were millions of rats in Stockholm. He had never seen a single one, but here there were three, right in the middle of St Erik's bridge. A big one and two smaller ones. They were running in circles on the footpath, chasing each other.

The rats hissed, showing their teeth, and one of the smaller ones bit the bigger one on the back. David backed up a step, looked up. An elderly gentleman was standing a few steps away on the other side of the rats, watching their battle open-mouthed.

The small ones were as big as kittens, the bigger one about the size of a dwarf rabbit. The bare tails whisked over the asphalt and the big rat shrieked as the second small one grabbed hold of its back and a damp, black stain of blood appeared on its fur.

Are they...its children, its little ones?

David held a hand up to his mouth, suddenly nauseated. The big rat threw itself from side to side spasmodically, trying to shake off the smaller ones. David had never heard rats shriek, had not known they could. But the sound that issued from the big one was horrible, as if from a dying bird.

A couple of people had stopped on the other side. Everyone was following the rat fight and for a moment David had a vision of people gathered to watch some kind of organised event. Rat fighting. He wanted to walk away, but couldn't. In part because the traffic across the bridge was steady, in part because he could not tear his gaze from the rats. He felt compelled to stay and watch, and see what happened.

Suddenly the big one stiffened, its tail pointing straight out from its body. The small ones writhed, scrabbling their claws over its belly and their heads moved jerkily back and forth as they tore at the skin. The big one shuffled forward until it reached the edge of the bridge, crept under the railing with its burden and toppled over.

David had time to peer over the railing in time to see it land. The noise from the traffic masked the splash when the rats landed in the dark water and a plume of drops glittered for an instant in the street lamps. Then it was over.

People continued on their way, talking about it.

'Never seen anything like it…it's this heat…my dad once told me that he…headache…'

David massaged his temples and kept walking across the bridge. People from the other direction met his gaze and everyone smiled bashfully, as if they had all taken part in something illicit. When the older gentleman who had been standing there from the beginning walked past, David asked, 'Excuse me, but…have you got a headache too?'

'Yes,' the man answered, and pressed his fist against his head. 'It's terrible.'

'I was just wondering.'

The man pointed at the dirty grey asphalt spotted with rat blood and said, 'Maybe they had one too. Maybe that was why…' He interrupted himself and looked at David. 'You've been on television, haven't you?'

He continued on his way. A muted panic hovered in the air. Dogs were barking and pedestrians walked more quickly than usual, as if trying to escape whatever was approaching. He hurried down Odengatan, took out his cell phone and dialled Eva's number. When he was level with the subway station, she answered.

'Hi,' David said. 'Where are you?'

'I've just got in the car. David? It was the same thing at your mum's place. She was going to turn the television off when we arrived, but she couldn't.'

'That'll make Magnus happy. Eva? I…I don't know, but…do you have to go see your father?'

'Why do you ask?'

'Well...do you still have a headache?'

'Yes, but not so I can't drive. Don't worry.'

'No. It's just that I have a feeling that...it's something horrible. Don't you feel it too?'

'No. Not like that.'

A man was standing inside the phone booth at the intersection of Odengatan and Sveavägen, jiggling the hook. David was about to tell Eva about the rats when the line went dead.

'Hello? Hello?'

He stopped and redialled the number, but couldn't get through. Just the crackle of static. The man in the phone booth hung up, cursed and walked out of the booth. David turned off the cell phone in order to try again but the phone refused to turn off. A drop of sweat fell from his brow onto the keypad. The phone felt unusually warm, as if the battery was heating up. He pressed the off button, but nothing happened. The display continued to glow and the battery indicator actually increased by one bar. The time was 21.05, and he half-ran down to Norra Brunn.

Even from outside the club, he could hear that the show had started. Benny Lundin's voice was thundering out onto the street, he was doing his thing about the difference between guys' and girls' bathroom habits and David pulled a face. Was pleased not to hear any laughter at the punchline. Then there was silence for a moment just as David reached the entrance, and Benny started on his next thread: about condom dispensers that stop working when you need them the most. David paused in the entrance, blinked.

The whole room was fully lit. The house lights, normally turned off to isolate the spotlight on stage, were up full bore. The people seated at the tables and at the bar looked pained, staring down at the floor and the tablecloths.

'Do you take American Express?'

That was the punchline. People usually laughed until they cried at Benny's story about how he had tried to buy black-market condoms from the Yugoslavian mafia. Not this time. Everyone just suffered.

'Shut your face, asshole!' a drunk man at the bar yelled, grabbing at his head. David sympathised. The microphone volume was on way too high and was distorting. With the ubiquitous headache, it amounted to mass torture.

Benny grinned nervously, said, 'They let you out of the asylum for this?'

When no one laughed at that either, Benny put the microphone back in the stand, said, 'Thanks everyone. You've been a fantastic audience,' and walked offstage toward the kitchen. There was a general moment of paralysis since everything had been cut off so abruptly. Then the microphone started feeding back and an atrocious ear-splitting squeal cut through the dense air.

Everyone in the room put their hands over their ears and some started to scream along with the feedback. David clenched his teeth, ran up to the mike and tried to disconnect the cord. The weak current shot trails of ants through his skin, but the plug stayed put. After a couple of seconds, the feedback was a butcher's saw hacking through the flesh of his brain and he was forced to give up, press his hands to his ears.

He turned in order to make his way to the kitchen, but was obstructed from doing so by people who had stood up from their tables to throng towards the exit. A woman without much respect for the club's property pushed him aside, wound the microphone cord once around her wrist and yanked. She only managed to knock the stand over. The feedback continued.

David looked up at the mixing booth, where Leo was pushing every button in sight, to no effect. David was about to shout at him to cut the power when he felt a shove and fell on the low stage. He lay there, hands still clapped over his ears, and watched as the woman swung the microphone over her head and dashed it into the concrete floor.

There was silence. The audience stopped, looked around. A

collective sigh of relief went through the room. David clawed himself up to standing and saw Leo waving his hands, pulling his index finger across his throat. David nodded, cleared his throat and said loudly, 'Hello!'

Faces turned toward him.

'Unfortunately we have to interrupt tonight's show due to... technical difficulties.'

A few laughs in the audience. Jeering.

'We would like to thank our major sponsor, the Vattenfall Power Company, and...welcome you back another time.'

Boos from around the room. David held out his hands in a gesture that was supposed to mean, *So fucking sorry for something that's not remotely my fault*, but people had already lost interest in him. Everyone was moving toward the exit. The place was empty in a matter of minutes.

When David reached the kitchen, Leo looked grumpy.

'What was that thing about Vattenfall?'

'A joke.'

'I see. Funny.'

David was about to say something about captains and sinking ships since Leo was the boss of the place—and OK, next time he *would* make sure he had a routine prepared for a reverse power cut—but he held back. In part because he couldn't afford to get Leo's back up, and in part because he had other things to think about.

He went into the office and dialled Eva's cell phone number from the landline. This time he got through, but only to her voicemail. He left a message asking her to call him at the club as soon as possible.

Someone brought some beers in and the comedians drank them in the kitchen, amid the roar of the kitchen fans. The chefs had turned them on to mitigate the heat from the cooking ranges that couldn't be turned off, and now they had the same problem with the fans. They could barely talk but at least it was cooler.

Most of them left, but David decided to stay put in case Eva called. On the ten o'clock radio news they heard that the electrical phenomenon appeared to be confined to the Stockholm region, that the current in some areas could be compared to an incipient lightning strike. David felt the hairs on his arms stand up. Maybe a shiver, maybe static electricity.

When he felt a vibration against his hip he thought at first it was to do with the electrical charge in the air as well, but then realised it was coming from his cell phone. He didn't recognise the number that came up.

'Hello, this is David.'

'Am I speaking with David Zetterberg?'

'Yes?'

Something in the man's voice generated a clump of anxiety in David's stomach and set it wobbling. He stood up from the table and took a couple of steps into the hall toward the dressing room in order to hear better.

'My name is Göran Dahlman and I am a physician at Danderyd Hospital...'

As the man said what he had to say, David's body was swept into a cold fog and his legs disappeared. He slithered down the wall to the concrete floor. He stared at the phone in his hand; threw it away from him like a venomous snake. It slid along the floor and struck Leo's foot. Leo looked up.

'David! What's wrong?'

Afterwards David would have no real memory of the half hour that followed. The world had congealed, all sense and meaning sucked out of it. Leo made his way with difficulty through the traffic; it was following the most rudimentary road rules now that all the electronics had been knocked out. David sat curled up in the passenger seat and looked with unseeing eyes at the yellow-flashing traffic lights.

It was only in the entrance of Danderyd Hospital that he was able to pull himself together and refuse Leo's offer to come up with him. He couldn't remember what Leo said, or how he found the right ward. Suddenly he was just there, and time started making its slow rounds again.

Actually, there was one thing he remembered. As he walked through the corridors to Eva's room, all the lamps above the doors were blinking and an alarm sounded continuously. This felt entirely appropriate: catastrophe eclipses everything.

She had collided with an elk and died during the time it took David to reach the hospital. The doctor on the phone had said that there was no hope for her, but that her heart was still beating. Not anymore. It had stopped at 22.36. At twenty-four minutes to eleven her heart had stopped pumping the blood around her body.

One single muscle in a single person's body. A speck of dust in time. And the world was dead. David stood next to her bed with his arms by his sides, the headache burning behind his forehead.

Here lay his whole future, everything good that he could even imagine would come from life. Here lay the last twelve years of his past. Everything gone; and time shrank to a single unbearable now.

He fell to his knees by her side, took her hand.

'Eva,' he whispered, 'this won't work. It can't be like this. I love you. Don't you understand? I can't live without you. Come on, you have to wake up now. It doesn't make sense without you, none of it. I love you so much and it just can't be like this.'

He talked and talked, a monologue of repeated sentences which, the more times he repeated them, felt more and more true and right until a conviction took root in him that they would start to take effect. Yes. The more times he said it was impossible, the more absurd it all seemed. He had just managed to convince himself of the feeling that if he simply kept babbling the miracle would happen, when the door opened.

A woman's voice said, 'How's it going?'

'Fine. Fine,' David said. 'Please go away.'

He pressed Eva's cooling hand against his brow, heard the rustling of cloth as the nurse crouched down. He felt a hand at his back.

'Can I do anything?'

David slowly turned his head to the nurse and drew back, Eva's hand still held in his own. The nurse looked like Death in human form. Prominent cheekbones, protruding eyes, pained expression.

'Who are you?' he whispered.

'I'm Marianne,' she said, almost without moving her lips.

They stared at each other wide-eyed. David took a firmer hold of Eva's hand; he had to protect her from this person who was coming to get her. But the nurse made no move towards him. Instead she sobbed, said, 'Forgive me...' and shut her eyes, pressing her hands against her head.

David understood. The pain in his head, the ragged pulsating heartbeat was not only his. The nurse slowly straightened up, momentarily lost her balance, then walked out of the room. For a moment, the outside world penetrated his consciousness and David heard a cacophony of signals, alarms and sirens both inside and outside the hospital. Everything was in turmoil.

'Come back,' he whispered. 'Magnus. How am I supposed to tell Magnus? He's turning nine next week, you know. He wants pancake cake. How do you make pancake cake, Eva? You were the one who was going to make it, you bought the raspberries and everything. They're already at home in the freezer, how am I supposed to go home and open the freezer and there are the raspberries that you bought to make pancake cake and how am I supposed to...'

David screamed. One long sound until all the air was gone from his lungs. He pressed his lips against her knuckles, mumbled, 'Everything's over. You don't exist any more. I don't exist. Nothing exists.'

The pain in his head reached an intensity that he was forced to acknowledge. A bolt of hope shot through him: he was dying. Yes. He was going to die too. There was crackling, something breaking in his brain as the pain swelled and swelled and he had just managed to think, with complete certainty—I'm dying. I am dying now. Thank you—when it stopped. Everything stopped. Alarms and sirens stopped. The lighting in the room dimmed. He could hear his own rapid breathing. Eva's hand was moist with his own sweat, it slid across his forehead. The headache was gone. Absently, he rubbed her hand up and down across his skin, drawing her wedding band across it, wanting the pain back. Now that it was gone, the ache in his chest welled up in its place.

He stared down at the floor. He did not see the white caterpillar that came in through the ceiling, fell, and landed on the yellow institutional blanket draped over Eva, digging its way in.

'My darling,' he whispered and squeezed her hand. 'Nothing was going to come between us, don't you remember?'

Her hand jerked, squeezed back.

David did not scream, did not make a move. He simply stared at her hand, pressed it. Her hand pressed back. His chin fell, his tongue moved to lick his lips. Joy was not the word for what he felt, it was more like the disorientation in the seconds after you wake from a nightmare, and at first his legs did not want to obey him when he pulled himself up so he could look at her.

They had cleaned and prepped her as best they could, but half of her face was a gaping wound. The elk, he supposed. It must have had time to turn its head, or make a final desperate attempt to attack the car. Its head, its antlers had been the first thing through the windshield and one of the points had struck her face before she was crushed under the weight of the beast.

'Eva! Can you hear me?'

No reaction. David pulled his hands across his face, his heart was beating wildly.

It was a spasm…She can't be alive. Look at her.

23

A large bandage covered the right half of her face, but it was clear that it was...too small. That bones, skin and flesh were missing underneath. They had said that she was in bad shape, but only now did he realise the extent of it.

'Eva? It's me.'

This time there was no spasm. Her arm jerked, hitting against his legs. She sat up without warning. David instinctively backed up. The blanket slid off her, there was a quiet clinking and...no, he had not realised the full extent of it at all.

Her upper body was naked, the clothes had been cut away. The right side of her chest was a gaping hole bordered by ragged skin and clotted blood. From it came a metallic clanking. For a moment, David could not see Eva, he only saw a monster and wanted to run away. But his legs would not carry him and after several seconds he came to his senses. He stepped up next to the bed again.

Now he saw what was making the sound. Clamps. A number of metal clamps suspended from broken veins inside her chest cavity. They swayed and hit against each other as she moved. He swallowed dryly. 'Eva?'

She turned her head toward the sound of his voice and opened her one eye.

Then he screamed.

Vällingby 17.32

Mahler made his way slowly across the square, his shirt sticky with sweat. He had a bag of groceries for his daughter in one hand. Soot-grey pigeons waddled under his feet with centimetres to spare.

He looked like a large, grey dove himself. He'd bought the worn suit jacket fifteen years earlier, when he became fat and could no longer use his old clothes. Same thing with the pants. Of his hair, only a wreath above the ears was left and the bald spot on top had become red and freckled from the sun. It was easy to imagine that Mahler was carrying empty bottles in the bag, that he was rooting around in garbage bins—a big pigeon plucking goodies from discarded takeaways.

This was not the case. But it was the impression he gave: a loser.

In the shadow of Åhléns Emporium, on his way down to Ångermannagatan, Mahler dug under his double chins with his free hand and took hold of the necklace. A present from Elias. Sixty-seven colourful plastic beads threaded on a fishing line, now tied around his neck for all eternity.

While he continued to walk he rubbed the beads one by one like a rosary, like prayers.

It was three flights up to his daughter's apartment; he had to stop and catch his breath for a while. Then he unlocked the door with his own key. Inside it was dark, stuffy and stale from unaired heat.

'Hi sweetheart. It's just me.'

No answer. As usual he feared the worst.

But Anna was there, and still alive. She lay curled up on Elias' bed, on the designer sheets that Mahler had bought, her face turned to the wall. Mahler put down the shopping bag, stepped over the dusty Lego pieces and perched himself gingerly on one corner of the bed.

'How's it going, little one?'

Anna drew in air through her nose. Her voice was weak.

'Daddy...I can feel his smell. It's still there in the sheets. His smell is still here.'

Mahler would have liked to lie down on the bed, against her back. Put his arms around her and been Daddy, and made everything hurtful go away. But he didn't dare to. The bed slats would crack under his weight. So he simply sat there, looking at the Lego pieces that no one had built anything with for two months.

When he had been looking for an apartment for Anna, there was one on the ground floor of this same building. He hadn't taken that one, out of fear of burglars.

'Come and have something to eat.'

Mahler put out two servings of roast beef and potato salad from plastic containers, cut up a tomato and placed the slices on the edge of the plates. Anna did not answer.

The blinds in the kitchen were drawn, but the sun pressed in through the cracks, drawing glowing lines across the kitchen table and illuminating the whirling motes. He should clean. Lacked the energy.

Two months ago, the table had been full of things: fruit, mail, a toy, a flower picked during a walk, something Elias had made at daycare. The stuff of life.

Now there was just the two plates of supermarket food. The heat and the smell of dust. The bright red tomatoes; a pathetic attempt.

He went to Elias' room, stopped in the doorway.

'Anna...you need to eat a little. Come on. It's ready.'

Anna shook her head, said into the wall, 'I'll eat it later. Thanks.'

'Can't you get up for a while?'

When she didn't answer, he went out into the kitchen again and sat down at the table. Started loading the food into his mouth automatically. Thought the sound of his chewing echoed between the quiet walls. Finally he ate the tomato slices. One by one.

A ladybug had landed on the balcony railing.

Anna had been busy packing. They were going to Mahler's summer house in Roslagen, staying a couple of weeks.

'Mummy, a ladybug...look.'

She had come out into the living room in time to see Elias standing on the outdoor table, reaching out for the ladybug as it flew away. One of the legs of the table gave way. She didn't get there in time.

Below the balcony was the parking lot. Black asphalt.

'Here, pumpkin.'

Mahler held out the fork with a serving of food for Anna. She sat up in bed, took the fork and put it into her mouth. Mahler handed her the plate.

Her face was red and swollen and there were grey streaks in her brown hair. She ate four bites, then handed back the plate.

'Thank you. That was delicious.'

Mahler put the plate down on Elias' desk, put his hands in his lap.

'Have you been out today?'

'I've been with him.'

Mahler nodded. Couldn't think of anything else to say. When he stood up he banged his head into the wooden duck suspended over the bed. It flapped its wings a few times, swishing air across Anna's face. Stopped.

Back in his own apartment on the other side of the courtyard, he removed his sweat-drenched clothes, showered, pulled on his robe and took a couple of painkillers for the headache. He sat down at the computer and logged into Reuters. Spent an hour searching for and translating three items.

A Japanese gadget that could translate the meaning of dogs' barks. Siamese twins separated. A man who had built a house of tin cans in Lübeck. There was no photograph of the Japanese machine, so he searched for a picture of a Labrador and attached that. Sent it to the paper.

Then he read an email from one of his old sources in the police who wondered how things were going for him these days, it had been a long time. He replied that things were hell, that his grandson had died two months ago and that he considered suicide daily. Deleted it without sending.

The shadows on the floor had grown longer, it was past seven. He stood up out of the chair, massaging his temples. Went out into the kitchen and fetched a beer from the fridge, drank half of it standing up, wandered back to the living room. Ended up next to the couch.

On the floor below the arm of the couch there was the Fortress.

It had been a present to Elias on his sixth birthday four months earlier. The biggest Lego fortress. They had built it together and afterwards they had played with it in the afternoons, arranging knights in different places, making up stories, rebuilding and extending. Now it stood there just as they had left it.

Every time Mahler saw it, it hurt. Each time he thought he should throw it away or at the very least take it to pieces, but he couldn't.

Most likely it would stay there as long as he lived, just as he would take the necklace to the grave.

Elias, Elias…

The abyss opened inside him. Panic came, the pressure on his chest. He hurried to the computer, logged into one of his porn sites. Sat and clicked for an hour, without so much as a movement in his groin. Only indifference, revulsion.

Shortly after nine he logged out and shut down the computer. The screen wouldn't turn off. He couldn't be bothered with it. The headache had started to press on the insides of his eyes, making him agitated. He walked around the apartment a few times, drank another beer; finally stopped and crouched in front of the fortress.

One of the Lego knights had leaned over the edge of the tower, exactly like he was shouting something to the enemy trying to break the door down.

'Watch out or I'll pour out the contents of our toilet on you!' Mahler had said in a creaky voice and Elias had laughed until he lost his breath, shouting, 'More! More!' and Mahler had gone through all the terrible things that a knight could conceivably pour on someone else. Rotten yogurt.

Mahler picked up the piece, turned it in his fingers. The knight had a silver helmet that partially concealed his resolute facial expression. The little sword he held in his hands was still shiny. The colour had flaked off the ones Elias had at home. Mahler looked at the shiny sword and two realisations dropped down through him like black stones.

This sword will always remain shiny.

I will never play, ever again.

He replaced the knight, stared at the wall.

I will never play, ever again.

In the grief after Elias he had gone over all the things that he would never get to do again: walks in the forest, the playground, juice and sweet rolls at the cafe, the zoo park and more and more and more. But there it was, in all its simplicity: he would never play again, and that was not restricted to Legos and hide-the-key. With Elias' death, he had lost not only his playmate but also his desire to play.

That was why he couldn't write, that was why pornography no longer stirred him and why the minutes went by so slowly. He couldn't fantasise any longer, make things up. It should have been a blessed state, to live only in what is, what exists before one's eyes, not to refashion the world. Should have been. But it wasn't.

Mahler fingered the scar from the operation on his chest.

Life is what we choose to make it.

He had lost his vigour, was chained to an overweight body that he would have to drag around joylessly in the days and years to come. He saw this, in a sudden realisation, and was overcome with the desire to smash something. The clenched fist trembled above the fortress, but he controlled himself, stood up and went out to the balcony where he grabbed the railing, shaking it.

A dog was running around in circles down there, barking. Mahler would have liked to be doing the same thing.

When in trouble, when in doubt
Run in circles, scream and shout.

He looked out over the railing, saw himself fall, split open against the ground like an overripe melon. The dog would maybe come over and start to gnaw at him. This thought made the act more tempting. To end his days as dog food. But the dog would probably not even notice, it seemed hysterical. Someone was probably coming to shoot it soon.

He pressed his hands to the sides of his head. It would probably split open anyway if the pain continued to escalate like this.

It was a little after half past ten when Mahler realised he probably did want to live after all.

30

He had suffered his first attack eight years ago, when he was out interviewing a fisherman who had caught a corpse in his net. When they stepped ashore from the trawler, the light had all of a sudden dimmed, shrinking to a point, and then Mahler couldn't remember anything more until he woke up lying on a pile of nets. If the fisherman had not been proficient in CPR, Mahler's troubles would have been over.

A doctor had told him that he had chronic myocarditis and needed a pacemaker to stabilise his heart. During that time Mahler had been so depressed that he'd considered taking his chances with death, but he had had the operation in the end.

Then Elias came along and Mahler finally found a reason for even having a heart after all these years. The pacemaker had ticked along faithfully and allowed him to play grandpa as much as he wanted.

But now...

Beads of sweat broke out along his hairline and Mahler pressed his hand over his heart; it was beating twice as fast as normal. Somehow his heart was managing to duck out from under the steady beat of the pacemaker and race off on its own. Under his hand, Mahler felt his pulse increase even more.

He put his fingers on his wrist, looked at the alarm clock and counted the seconds. He timed himself at 120 beats per minute, but he wasn't sure that was correct. Even the second hand on the clock appeared to be moving faster than usual.

Calm down...calm...it will pass.

He knew that this kind of heart spasm was not dangerous in itself as long as it did not become too extreme. It was the worry, the anxiety that did the damage. Mahler tried to breathe calmly while his heart raced faster and faster.

Then he had a thought. He placed his fingers over the pacemaker, the metal box just under his skin that was guarding his life. He couldn't tell if it was going faster than normal, but he suspected that's what was happening: the same thing that was happening to the clock.

He curled up in a foetal position on the couch. The pain was going to split his head open, his heart was racing insanely and to his own surprise he saw that he did not want to die. No. At least, he did not want to be killed by a machine whipping up his heart until it burst. He looked up and squinted at the computer screen. Even that had become more intense, and all the icons were engulfed in shining white light.

What should I do?

Nothing. He should do nothing that would strain his heart any more. He sank back again, resting his hand over the muscle of life. His heart was beating so quickly now that he could not make out the different pulses, it was a drum roll from the land of the dead increasing in tempo, and Mahler closed his eyes and waited for the climax.

Just as he thought the drum skin was going to burst and vision close in, like that other time, it was over.

The heart palpitations eased back to the old, deliberate rhythm. He lay completely still with his eyes closed, then breathed in deeply and felt his face as if checking that he was still there. His face was there; it was covered in sweat, warm drops trickling down through the folds on his belly, tickling.

He opened his eyes. The icons on his computer were back, set against their usual cerulean background. Then the screen went dark. The dog in the yard stopped barking.

What is happening?

The clock was marking the seconds at a normal pace, and an enormous silence had fallen over the world. For the first time, now that they had stopped, he became aware of the cacophony of sounds and screams that had preceded this lull. He licked his salty lips, crouched down and stared at the clock.

Seconds, minutes...one second we are born, one second we die.

32

He had been lying there for twenty minutes or so when the telephone rang. He slid off the couch and crawled over to the desk. His legs would probably have carried him, but he felt that he should crawl. He pulled himself up onto the desk chair and lifted the receiver.

'This is Mahler.'

'Hi, Ludde here. At Danderyd.'

'Oh...hi.'

'I've got something for you.'

Ludde had been one of his innumerable sources when he was working at the paper. As a custodian at Danderyd Hospital, he would sometimes hear or see things that could be 'of public interest', as Ludde put it.

Mahler said, 'I'm not working anymore, you'll have to call Benke...Bengt Jansson, evening editor at...'

'Listen, the stiffs have come back to life.'

'What are you saying?'

'The stiffs. The corpses. In the morgue. They've come back to life.'

'No.'

'Yes, listen to me. The pathology department just called here completely hysterical, wanting more personnel to go down and help out.'

Mahler watched his hand reach automatically over the desk for his notebook, but pulled it back, shaking his head.

'Ludde, calm down. Do you hear what you...'

'Yes, I know. I know. But it's true. People are running around here like...it's complete chaos. They've come back. All of them.'

Mahler could actually hear voices in the background, speaking agitatedly, but could not make out what they were saying. Something was clearly up, but...

'Ludde, let's take this one more time. From the top.'

Ludde sighed. In the background someone cried out, 'Check

with Emergency!' and when Ludde spoke again, he had his mouth closer to the mouthpiece, his voice almost erotic.

'First everything was haywire here because of the electrical stuff. Everything was on and nothing worked. You know? The electricity?'

'Yes…yes, I know.'

'OK. Then five minutes ago…the body butchers called the reception desk, said to send down a couple of guys from Security because there was a bunch of stiffs that were…escaping. OK. The security guys have a laugh, great joke, but they go down there. OK. A couple of minutes later *the security guys* call, say they need reinforcements because now everyone has woken up. An even funnier joke. A couple more go down, maybe there's a party on down there. OK. Then a *doctor* calls and says the same thing…and now there are even emergency surgeons heading down there.'

'How many corpses do you have there?'

'No idea. A hundred, at least. Are you coming, or what?'

Mahler checked the time. Twenty-five minutes past eleven.

'Yes. Yes, I'm coming.'

'Great. Will you bring…?'

'Yes, yes.'

He put on his clothes, packed his tape recorder, his cell phone and the digital camera he had never got around to returning to the paper, took some money for Ludde, two thousand kronor, to be on the safe side, and ran down the stairs as fast as he dared.

His heart was still with him as he wedged himself into his Ford Fiesta, started the engine and drove east. When he was out on the Blackeberg roundabout he called Benke, told him, yes, he had quit but he'd just got a tip-off about a thing at Danderyd and was checking up on it. Benke said welcome back.

The roads were empty and Mahler accelerated to 120 when he was through Islands Square. The western suburbs rushed by

34

and somewhere in the vicinity of the Tranebergs Bridge he caught sight of himself. He was more alive than he had been in a month. Almost happy.

Täby Municipality 21.05

'Darling, you'll have to turn that off now.' Elvy wagged her finger at the television screen. 'That groaning is too much for my head.'

Flora nodded without taking her eyes off the screen, said, 'OK. I'll just save this.'

Elvy laid Grimberg aside—she had not been able to concentrate on her reading anyway since this headache began—and watched as Jill Valentine made her way back to her safe room. Flora had explained how the video game worked and Elvy understood the basics.

There were two things she didn't understand: how such worlds could be created in *computers*, and how Flora could remember everything. Her fingers flew over the buttons, and text, maps, indexes flickered past and were replaced so rapidly that Elvy could never take in what was happening.

Jill moved down a dark corridor with her pistol raised, her body tense. Flora's lips were compressed, her heavily made-up eyes narrowed. Elvy's gaze caressed the thin, pale inner arms marked with scratches and scabs from old cuts. The head with its red, straggling hair looked too large for her small body. For a while she had coloured it black, but had been letting it grow out for a year or so.

'Is it going all right?' Elvy asked.

'Mmm. I just got a thing I needed. Just have to…save.'

The map came up, then disappeared. A door opened to a dark background and Jill was standing at the top of some stairs. Flora moistened her lips and steered her toward the steps.

Margareta, who was Flora's mother and Elvy's daughter, would have objected if she had known what kind of game Flora was playing: deemed it unsuitable for both of them, for different reasons.

The Gamecube had ended up at Elvy's three months ago, as a compromise. Flora had been glued to the machine three, four, five hours a day for the past six months, her parents had issued an ultimatum: either sell the machine or keep it at her grandmother's, if Elvy agreed.

And Elvy agreed. She was very fond of her grandchild and vice versa. Flora dropped by two or three evenings a week to play and didn't usually spend more than a couple of hours at the console. They had tea, talked, played cards and sometimes Flora spent the night.

'Ooooohh…'

'Damndamndamn!'

Elvy looked up. Flora's body was curled, tense.

A zombie had staggered out from around a corner and Jill raised her gun, managed to fire a shot before it was upon her. The control in Flora's hand creaked as she tried to turn away but the blood spewed out in red spouts and soon Jill lay at the zombie's feet.

You are dead.

'Idiot!' Flora slapped her forehead. 'Ow. I forgot to burn him. Ow.'

Elvy leaned forward in the armchair. 'Is it…over now?'

'No…I know where it is now.'

'Uh-huh.'

Flora had self-destructive tendencies, according to her school counsellor. Elvy didn't know if that was better or worse than the diagnosis she'd received herself at the same age: hysterical. In the fifties, as the welfare state flowered and the final victory of rationality seemed imminent, it was not a nice thing to be hysterical. Even Elvy had cut her arms and legs then—inner pain, outer pressures. This problem hadn't even existed back then. No one had the right to be unhappy.

Ever since Flora was very little, Elvy had felt a strong connection to the serious, imaginative child, had sensed that she might have troubles. The sensitivity they were cursed with had skipped a generation. Maybe in reaction to her emotional mother, Margareta had studied law and become neat, polished and successful. Had married Göran, another law student who might have come from the same pod.

'Do you have a headache too?' Elvy asked, watching Flora push the hair off her forehead as she leaned forward and turned off the game.

'Yes, it's...' Flora pushed the button. 'Oh. It won't turn off.'

'Then turn off the television.'

But the television could not be turned off either. The game started to display self-generated scenes. Jill shocked two zombies, another was shot in a corridor. The shots echoed in Elvy's head and she grimaced. The volume couldn't be cut either.

When Flora tried to pull the cord out of the socket it crackled and she jumped back with a scream. Elvy stood up from the armchair, 'What happened?'

Flora stared at the hand that had grabbed the cord.

'I got a shock. Not that strong, but...' She shook her hand as if to cool it down and pointed at the screen where Jill was again electrocuting the undead, chuckled and said, 'No, not like that.'

Elvy held out her hand, helped her up on her feet.

'Let's go out in the kitchen.'

Everything electrical and mechanical had been Tore's domain. After he fell ill with Alzheimer's, Elvy had been forced to call an electrician the first time a fuse blew. She'd never been entrusted with that kind of information because she was considered delicate. But the electrician, who didn't know about her limitations, showed her what to do and now she could do it. A malfunctioning television, however, exceeded her abilities. That would have to wait until tomorrow.

They played a hand of canasta in the kitchen, but they both had trouble concentrating on the cards. Beyond the headache there was something else in the air, something they both sensed. At a quarter past ten, Elvy gathered up all the cards, asked, 'Flora? Do you feel...'

'Yes.'

'What is it?'

'I don't know.'

Both stared down at the table top, tried to...sniff it out. Elvy had occasionally encountered other people who had this ability: in Flora's experience Elvy was the only other one. It had been a relief to her when they had first spoken of it a couple of years ago. There was someone else as crazy as her, who had the Sense.

In another society, in another time, they might have been shamans. Or burned at the stake, for that matter. In Sweden in the twenty-first century they were hysterical and self-destructive. Overly sensitive.

The Sense was as difficult to describe, to put one's finger on, as a scent-impression. But just as the fox knows that there is a hare somewhere out there in the dark and even knows, from the smell of the hare's fear, that the hare is aware of the fox's presence, both women could discern something that lingered in the air around places and people.

They had started talking about it last summer when they had been walking along Norr Mälarstrand. Just short of the City Hall they had both, as if on cue, turned away from the wharf and gone up onto the bike path. Elvy had stopped and asked, 'Didn't you want to walk there?'

39

'No.'

'Why not?'

'Because...' Flora had shrugged, looked down at the ground as if she was ashamed. 'It just didn't feel good.'

'You know...' Elvy had taken Flora's chin in her hand, lifted her face, 'I felt the same thing.'

Flora had looked searchingly into her eyes. 'Seriously?'

'Yes,' Elvy said. 'Something has happened there. Something bad. I think...someone drowned.'

'Mm, yeah,' Flora said. 'He was going to jump from the boat...'

'...and then he hit his head on the edge of the wharf,' Elvy filled in.

'Yes.'

They had not checked if they were right. They knew. They spent the rest of the afternoon swapping stories. The Sense had come to both of them in their early teens and Flora's pain stemmed from the same source as Elvy's at that age: she knew people too well. The Sense told her the exact state of mind of the people around her, and she could not accept their lies.

'My dear,' Elvy had said, 'all of us lie in some way. It is a precondition for society to function, that we lie a little bit. You can view it as a form of consideration. The truth is, in a way, very self-centred.'

'I know, Grandma, I do know that. But it's so...revolting. The air sort of stinks around people who...you know?'

'Yes,' Elvy sighed. 'Yes, I do.'

'You don't have to be out in it. You interact with, like, Grandpa and the old ladies at church. But at school, there are like a thousand people and *all*, almost all of them, are unhappy. Some of them don't know it themselves, but I know and it hurts. It hurts. All the time. When some teacher calls me over and wants to have a serious discussion and tell me everything that's wrong with me...I just want to throw up because while he's talking he just reeks of different stuff.

Anxiety and worry and he's afraid of me and has a lousy life and *he's* the one who is telling me how *I* should act?'

'Flora,' Elvy said. 'I know it's no comfort now, but you will get used to it. When you've been sitting in the outhouse for a while, you don't notice the smell anymore.' Flora laughed at this, and Elvy went on. 'And as far as the ladies in the church are concerned, I can tell you I wish I had a clothes peg sometimes.'

'A clothes peg?'

'To put on my nose. And Grandpa...we'll get to that another time. But there is no way to turn it off. You should know that. If you are like me, then there is no clothes peg. You have to get used to it. It's purgatory, I know. But you have to get used to it if you want to live.'

The positive result of the conversation was that Flora stopped cutting herself. And she started visiting Elvy more often. Even in the middle of the week, she would take the bus to Täby Church, going back to school the next morning. She volunteered to help care for Grandpa, but there wasn't much to do. Elvy let her feed him his porridge a couple of times so that she could feel involved when she wanted.

Elvy started hesitant conversations about God a couple of times; but Flora was an atheist. Flora tried to play Marilyn Manson for Elvy, with the same unsatisfactory result. There were limits to their friendship. But Elvy could tolerate the horror films, in modest amounts.

When they returned to the living room the television had got louder. Flora tried turning it off again, but nothing happened.

She had received the Gamecube from Elvy on her fifteenth birthday. There had been heated discussions with Margareta, who claimed that videogames made teenagers switch off from the real world. Elvy thought she was right, which was the precise reason she had bought the game. She herself had been fifteen when she started to drink: to switch off, to dull the emotional antennae. From that perspective, she felt that the game was a better option.

'Let's go out for a bit,' Elvy said.

They couldn't hear the television from the garden, but the air was still and the heat oppressive. All the surrounding houses were lit up, dogs were barking and an aura of foreboding hung over them.

They walked to the guardian tree: the apple tree planted when the house was built, to stand beside it and keep the household from harm. Hundreds of green fruit peeked through the dark leaves, and shoots that had not been pruned back during Tore's years of illness splayed up toward the sky.

I'll get the shotgun, walk up the stairs and shoot the dogs.

'Did you say something?' Elvy asked.

'No.'

Elvy searched the sky. The stars were pinpricks of light against the dark blue, unimaginably distant. She saw them loosen, become needles that flew down and pierced her brain, throbbing and aching.

'Like an iron maiden,' Flora said.

Elvy looked at her. Flora was also staring up at the sky.

'Flora,' she said, 'Were you thinking about a shotgun just now and...dogs?'

Flora raised her eyebrows, let out a laugh.

'Yes,' she said. 'I was planning what I was going to do in the game. How...?'

They looked at each other. This was something new. The headache was increasing in intensity, the needles pressing deeper; and then, in a sudden gust, it was over them.

Not a leaf moved, not a blade of grass bent, but they both staggered as a great force blew through the garden and for a second was over, around, inside them.

sa...rack...me...j...i...tess...st...kla...rm...kss

It was as if a radio had spun through hundreds of frequencies, filling their heads with voices; only staccato half-sounds, but nonetheless they could hear that the voices belonged to people in a state of panic. The strength drained from Elvy's legs, she fell on her knees on the lawn and mumbled, 'Our Father who art in Heaven hallowed be Thy name Thy Kingdom come Thy will be done on Earth as it is in Heaven give us this day our daily bread and forgive us our trespasses as we...'

'Grandma?'

'...forgive those who trespass against us and lead us not into temptation but deliver us from evil...'

'Grandma!'

Flora's voice trembled, and with an effort Elvy pulled herself away from her faith, looked around. Flora was sitting wide-eyed on the lawn, staring at her. A beam of pain pierced Elvy's mind, so sharp that she feared she might be having a stroke and she whispered, '...yes?'

'What was that?'

Elvy grimaced. Everything hurt. It hurt to move her head, it hurt to open her mouth. She tried, and failed, to form the words inside her head and then...it was gone. She closed her eyes, breathed. The ache simply switched off, the world fell back into place, took on its normal colours. She could read her own relief in Flora's face.

A deep breath. Yes. It was gone. Over. She reached out her hand, took hold of Flora's.

'I'm so glad,' she said. 'That you are here. That I was not the only one who...experienced this.'

Flora rubbed her eyes. 'But what was it?'

'Don't you know?'

'Yes. No.'

Elvy nodded. Of course. In a way it was a matter of faith.

'It was the spirits,' she said. 'The souls of the dead. They have been let out.'

43

Danderyd Hospital 23.07

She was his wife, how could he be afraid of her? David took a step closer to the bed. It was that eye, the one eye, and how it looked.

It's impossible to describe a human eye; all expectations end up ghost-like, paintings and photographs acceptable only because we know they are frozen moments of time. A living eye cannot be described or recreated. But we know all too well when it is not there.

Her eye was dead. It was covered by a microscopically thin grey membrane, and it might as well have been a stone wall. She was not switched on, not…present. David leaned over, whispered, 'Eva?'

He had to hold onto the steel bed rail in order to keep himself from recoiling when she looked straight at him—

there are diseases that do that to the eye

—and opened her mouth, but there was no sound. Only a dry clicking. David ran over to the sink and filled a plastic cup of water, held it up to her. She looked at it but made no attempt to take it.

'Here, my love,' David said. 'A little water.'

Her hand swung up and knocked the cup out of his hand. Water splashed over her face and the cup landed on her stomach. She looked at it, put her hand over it and scrunched it up with a crackle.

David stared at the hole in her chest, the clamps dangling inside like Christmas decorations from hell, and finally came out of his paralysis. He pressed the button at her bedside and when no one had turned up after five seconds he rushed out into the corridor and shouted, 'Hello! Help!'

A nurse responded quickly from a room further down the corridor. Before she had reached him David was screaming, 'She's woken up, she is alive she...I don't know what I should...'

The nurse gave him a look of bewilderment before she squeezed past him, into the room and stopped at her first step inside the room. Eva was sitting in the bed and stiffly picking at pieces of the plastic cup. The nurse clapped her hand over her mouth and turned to David, shaking her head, said, '...it...it...'

David grabbed her by the shoulders. 'What? What is it?'

The nurse turned half-way into the room again, gestured with her hand and said, 'It...isn't possible...'

'Do something, then!'

The nurse shook her head again and ran without another word back toward the nurses' station. When she reached the door, she turned to David and said, 'I'll call someone who...' and disappeared inside.

David remained in the corridor for a moment. He realised he was hyperventilating and tried to calm his breathing before he went back inside to Eva. The thoughts were racing through his head...A miracle...her eye...Magnus. He closed his eyes, and conjured up an image of Eva's gaze when she was looking at him with her utmost love. The glimmer, the play of living light. He breathed deeply, held onto this image and went in.

Eva had lost interest in the cup, which lay on the floor below the bed. David moved closer trying not to look at her chest.

'Eva. I'm here.'

The head turned toward him. He looked just below the eye; toward the smooth, undamaged cheek. He stretched out his hand, stroking her cheek with the back of his fingers.

'Everything will be fine...everything will be fine...'

Her hand came up so fast that he instinctively pulled back, but then steeled himself and held it out to her again. Her hand gripped his. Hard. A stiff, mechanical grip, painful. Her nails dug into the back of his hand. He clenched his teeth and nodded.

'It's me. David.'

He looked into her eye. There was nothing there. Her mouth opened and a hissing sound emerged, '...aavi...'

The tears welled up in his eyes. He nodded.

'That's right. David. I'm here.'

The grip on his hand grew tighter; a shaft of pain as a nail pierced his skin.

'...Daavi...hee...heeere...'

'Yes. Yes. I'm here. With you.'

He eased his hand out of her grip, replacing it with the other, but angled so that she was squeezing the fingers instead. A trickle of blood ran from the hand she had been holding. He wiped it on the sheet, sat down on the bed.

'Eva?'

'Eeva...'

'Yes. Do you know who I am?'

A moment's silence. The hold on his fingers loosened a little. She said, 'aa...aam...davi...d.'

It's getting better. It must be getting better. She understands.

He nodded, pointing to his chest like Tarzan, said, 'I David. You Eva.'

'Youu...Eva.'

They got no further. A doctor burst into the room, stopping short when she caught sight of Eva. She too seemed on the verge of some exclamation of protest but instead, diverted by a professional reflex, she took a stethoscope out of her pocket and approached the bed without looking at David.

David drew back to let her pass, and saw the nurse again standing in the doorway with another nurse who had no apparent function except curious bystander.

The doctor placed the bell of the stethoscope on the uninjured side of Eva's chest. Listened. Moved the stethoscope, listened again. Eva's hand flew up, grasped the tube—

'Eva!' David yelled, 'No!'

—and yanked on it. The physician screamed, her head yanked forward before the earpieces came free. David grimaced in sympathetic pain.

'Eva, you can't...do that.'

A shiver ran through him. He was acting to shield her from authority, as if he feared that they would punish her in some way if she did not behave herself.

The doctor let out a whimper, holding her hands up to her ears for a couple of seconds, but then with an effort she restored her face to a professional calm and turned to the nurses.

'Call Lasse in Neurology,' she said. 'Otherwise, Göran.'

The nurse took half a step into the room and echoed, 'Otherwise?'

'If Lasse isn't there,' the doctor said with irritation, 'then ask Göran to come.'

The nurse nodded and said something in a low voice to the other one, and both of them ducked out into the corridor.

Eva plucked the head of the stethoscope free of the tubes and it clattered to the floor. The doctor, who was simply sitting there staring at Eva, made no movement to pick it up, so David retrieved it instead. When he placed it in her hand she appeared to become aware for the first time that there was another person in the room.

'How is she?' David asked.

The doctor looked at him with a half-open mouth as if he had just asked a question so stupid there was no answer.

'The heart isn't beating,' the doctor said. 'There. Are. No beats.'

47

David felt a pain in his chest.

'But don't you have to...' he said, 'aren't you going...get it going?'

The doctor looked at Eva pulling on the rubber tubing and said, 'She doesn't seem to...require it.'

They had to wait quite a long time for Lasse. When he finally arrived, Eva's awakening no longer appeared to be a sensation.

Danderyd Hospital 23.46

Mahler parked the Fiesta in the short-term lot closest to the hospital and made an ungainly exit. The car was not designed for his 190 centimetres—nor his 140 kilos. Legs first, then the rest. He stood up next to the car, fanning his shirt against his chest. Dark stains had already started forming under his arms.

The hospital building loomed in front of him, enormous and expectant. No sign of activity. Only the quiet breath of the air conditioning, the building's respirator, its way of saying, 'I am a living being, even if it doesn't look like it.'

He slung his bag over his shoulder, walked to the entrance. Checked his watch. A quarter to twelve.

The shallow pool of water next to the revolving doors reflected the night sky, became a star map; standing next to it like a sentry was Ludde, smoking. When he caught sight of Mahler, he raised a hand in greeting and tossed the butt into the water with a sharp hiss.

'Hi Gustav, how you going?'

'Fine. Sweaty.'

Ludde was in his forties but looked younger, in a sickly way. If it hadn't been for the blue shirt with the nametag ('Ludvig') you could have taken him for a patient. Thin lips and pale, almost unnaturally taut skin, as if he had had a facelift, or was standing in a wind tunnel. Nervous eyes.

They walked in through the regular door since the revolving door was closed for the night. Ludde kept looking around him the whole time, but his watchfulness was redundant. The hospital seemed to be deserted.

When they left the entrance area and reached the corridors, Ludde relaxed, asked, 'Did you bring...?'

Mahler pushed his hand down into his pocket, but kept it there.

'Ludde, don't take this the wrong way, but all this seems...'

Ludde stopped and stared at him with reproach.

'Have I ever tried to con you? Huh? Have I said there was something and then there wasn't anything? Have I?'

'Yes.'

'You're thinking about that thing with Björn Borg. Yeah, yeah. But it was a damn close resemblance, you have to admit it. OK, OK. But this...well anyway. Hold onto your cash then, you bloody miser.'

Ludde took off down the corridor with angry strides, and Mahler had trouble keeping up. They took the elevator down in silence and then walked along a long, slightly inclined corridor with an iron door at the far end. Ludde pointedly hid the touch pad as he ran his card through and punched in his code. The lock clicked.

Mahler took out his handkerchief and wiped his brow. It was cooler down here but the hike had taken its toll. He leaned against the green concrete wall, pleasantly cool against his hand.

Ludde opened the iron door. In the distance, through one or more walls Mahler could hear cries, clanking metal. The first and only time he had ever been here it had been as quiet as...the grave. Ludde looked at him with a *what did I tell* you grin. Mahler nodded, held out the wrinkled bills and Ludde softened, made a generous gesture toward the open door.

'Be my guest. Your scoop awaits you.' He glanced swiftly down the corridor. 'The rest of them use the other entrance so you don't have to worry.'

Mahler tucked his handkerchief in his pocket, adjusted his bag. 'Aren't you coming?'

Ludde snorted. 'How long do you think I'd keep my job after that?' He pointed around the corner inside the door. 'Take the elevator down one floor—that's it.'

As the door banged shut behind him Mahler started to feel uncomfortable. He walked up to the elevator and hesitated before he pressed the call button. He was starting to get twitchy in his old age. The cries and clatter could still be heard below and he stood still, willing his heart to calm down.

It was not the thought of seeing dead people wandering around that unsettled him as much as the fact that he had no right to be here. When he was younger, he couldn't have cared less about all that. 'The truth must be told,' he would think, and plunge into the fray.

But now…

Who are you, what are you doing here?

He was rusty, and much too uncertain to be able to fake the authority you needed in such situations like that. He pressed the button anyway.

Have to see what's going on.

The elevator rumbled into action and he bit his lip, backing away from the door. He was a little afraid after all, had seen too many movies. Elevators that arrived and someone…something is inside. But the elevator arrived and through the narrow window in the door he could see it was empty. He stepped in and pressed the button for the level below. As the elevator descended he tried to empty his mind, switch modes to become simply descriptive, a camera whose images develop words.

The elevator starts with a jerk. Through thick concrete walls, I can hear screams. The morgue level comes into view through the window and through it I can see...

Nothing.

A bit of a corridor, a wall and nothing more. He pushed open the elevator door.

The chill came at him. The corridor he was standing in was several degrees colder than the rest of the hospital. The sweat on his body congealed into a cold film, made him shiver. The elevator door shut behind him.

To his right, an open door gave onto a cold storage room. Outside two people were sitting on the floor, embracing with bowed heads.

What are they doing?

The clatter of metal from the autopsy room to the left made one of them raise her head and Mahler now saw that it was a young nurse. Her face was panic-stricken.

She was holding a very old woman in her arms; white hair like a halo around her head, delicate body and spindly legs that moved over the floor, trying to gain a foothold in order to stand up. She was naked apart from a white sheet that hung around her neck and down one side of the body. Someone's mother and grandmother; perhaps a great-grandmother.

Her face was nothing but hard bones under a pale yellow skin and her eyes...her eyes. Two windows opening onto the great Nothing. They were a translucent blue and seemed to be covered in a film of white slime, gelatinous, expressing absolutely no emotion.

From the sunken lips—a mouth robbed of dentures—there came only a single mournful note, 'Oooooommmm...ooommm...'

And Mahler knew, with immediate comprehension, what it was she wanted. The same as everyone wants.

To go home.

The nurse caught sight of Mahler. She looked at him in entreaty as she said, 'Can you take over?' and inclined her head toward the old woman. When Mahler made no reply she added, 'I'm freezing to death...'

Mahler crouched down, put his hand on the old woman's foot. It was ice cold, stiff; it was like putting your hand on an orange that has been in the freezer. At his touch, the woman's lament began to rise—

'OOOOOOMMM!'

—but Mahler stood up with a groan while the nurse screamed at him, 'You've got to help me! Please!'

He couldn't. Not right now. Had to see what was going on. Shamed, he staggered away to the autopsy room; the photographer who takes pictures of the famine victims, goes back the hotel room and drinks to assuage his guilt.

Photographs…the camera…

As he walked toward the large brightly lit room, he opened the bag. White sheets lay spread along the corridor.

Later he would have trouble sorting out the scene that was laid out in front of his eyes. It was as if it should have been staged in half-darkness, a battle between the living and the dead pitched in the Goya-esque lighting of some cave.

But everything was clinically precise and illuminated. The large neon tubes in the ceiling spewed light across the stainless steel counters and over the people who moved around in the room.

Bare skin everywhere. Almost all of the dead had managed to rid themselves of their shrouds, and the sheets lay strewn across benches and floor. A toga party that had spiralled out of control into an orgy.

There were around thirty people there, living and dead. Doctors and nurses and morgue staff in white, green and blue coats who struggled to hold onto the bare bodies. All of the dead were very old, many had large, roughly stitched autopsy scars that stretched from the lower abdomen to the throat.

The dead were not violent. But they were striving, wanted to get away. Lined faces, bodies with the proportions of ill-health. The waving bird-fingers of old ladies, old men who slung their club-fists in the empty air. And the bodies pulled, strained but were embraced, held in check.

And the din, the din.

A whimpering and howling as if a football team of newborns had been thrown into the same room and told to express their terror and astonishment at the world they'd come to. Come back to.

The doctors and nurses talked continuously, soothing—

'Take it easy it will be all right everything is fine take it easy'

—but their eyes were wild. Some of them had cracked. A nurse was huddled into a corner, her face in her hands, her body shaking. A doctor was standing at a sink, washing his hands calmly and methodically as if he was at home in his bathroom. When he was done he took a comb out of his breast pocket, started to comb his hair.

Where is everyone?

Why weren't there more…living people here? Where were the reinforcements, the agencies—the things that despite everything worked so well in Sweden in the year 2002?

And Mahler had been here once before. Therefore he knew that the majority of the bodies were stored in refrigerated boxes one floor down. This was only a small proportion. He took a step into the room and fumbled for his camera.

Just then a man broke free. One of the few whom the process of decomposition had not had time to work on. He was big and strong, with hands that looked like they were used to heaving rocks. Maybe a retired and prematurely deceased construction worker. He moved toward the exit on mottled white legs, jerkily as if on stilts of rough-cut birch trunks.

The doctor who had lost it shouted, 'Take him!' and Mahler didn't think, simply obeyed the command and barricaded the doorway with his body. The man moved toward him and their eyes met. His were watery brown; it was like staring into a muddy pool where nothing was stirring. No response.

Mahler's gaze slid down to the throat, to the small scar above the collar bone where the formaldehyde had been injected and for the first time in this room of horrors Mahler became...afraid. Afraid of touch, of infection, fingers that groped. Wished that he could pull out his press card and shout, 'I'm a reporter! I have nothing to do with this!'

He clenched his teeth. He couldn't very well run away.

But when the man came at him he couldn't bear to take hold of him. Instead he simply pushed him away—

get this away from me!

—and the man lost his balance, tumbled to the side and fell on the doctor who had started washing his hands again. The doctor looked up indignantly, like someone interrupted in the middle of an important task, said, 'One at a time!' and pushed the man away toward the wall.

Some kind of alarm started nearby. Mahler thought he recognised the melody of the signal, but had no time to think about it, because at that moment the reinforcements arrived. Three doctors and four green-clad guards forced their way past him. Stopped short for an instant, exclaimed, 'Jesus Christ, what the...' and various other expressions of amazement, then overcame their fear and ran into the room to intervene where they were needed.

Mahler touched one of the doctors on the shoulder and the man turned to him with the expression of someone who was planning to punch him.

'What are you doing with them?' Mahler asked. 'Where are you taking them?'

'Who the hell are you?' the doctor asked and the wallop appeared to came an inch closer to reality. 'What are you doing here?'

'My name is Gustav Mahler and I'm from...'

The doctor let out a high-pitched hysterical laugh, and shouted, 'If you've brought Beethoven and Schubert with you, can you get them to pitch in?' Whereupon he took hold of the man Mahler had pushed, restrained him and shouted out into the room, 'Everyone to the elevators, two at a time! We're taking them to Infectious Diseases!'

Mahler backed out. The alarm continued stubbornly.

When he turned around he saw that the nurse on the floor had also received help. She rose on shaky legs and transferred the woman she had been holding to a guard. She spotted Mahler and her face was distorted into a grimace.

'Bastard,' she spat and sank to the floor again, a couple of metres from the corpse. Mahler took a step toward her, but decided that it was best to let it go. He didn't need to hear more about what a coward he was.

The alarm, the alarm.

The melody was 'Eine kleine Nachtmusik' and Mahler started to hum along. A nice little tune for this chaos. The same one he had on his mobile phone. And the same one that he had...

He dug the phone out of his bag, staring at the ridiculous thing while it continued to play its cheerful little song. He started to laugh. With the phone in his hand he took a few steps away toward the corridor and leaned against the wall next to a sign that said 'Turn off all mobile phones.' He was still sniggering as he answered.

'This is Mahler.'

'Benke here. Hey, how are things out there?'

Mahler looked back at the autopsy room, at the bodies that were moving in there. Green, blue, white.

'Yes. It's true. They're alive.'

Benke breathed into the phone. Mahler thought he was going to say something funny, thought he should hold the phone up to the room so Benke could hear. But Benke didn't say anything funny. He said slowly, 'Apparently it's happening...at a number of places. All over Stockholm.'

'They're coming back?'

'Yes.'

They were quiet for a couple of breaths. Mahler imagined how the same scene was unfolding in other locations. How many dead people could be affected? Two hundred? Five hundred? Suddenly he went cold, stiff, asked, 'The cemeteries?'

'What?'

'The cemeteries. The ones who are buried.'

Almost inaudibly, Benke whispered, 'Oh my God...' and added, 'I don't know...I don't know...we haven't had any...' He broke off.

'Gustav?'

'Yes?'

'This is a joke. Isn't it? You are joking with me. You're the one who...'

Mahler held up the receiver toward the autopsy room, stared vacantly into space for a couple of seconds, then brought the receiver back to his ear. Benke was in the middle of a monologue, '...makes no sense whatsoever, how can it...here in Sweden...'

He interrupted. 'Benke. I have to go.'

The night editor in Benke won out over the sceptic. He said, 'You'll get me some shots, right?'

'Yes, yes.'

Mahler put away the phone. His heart was beating wildly.

Elias wasn't cremated. Elias was buried in the ground, Elias was buried in the ground, Elias is at Råcksta cemetery, Elias...

He got the camera out of the bag and snapped a couple of quick shots. The situation had been stabilised, everything was under control. Here, anyway. For the moment. One of the guards, holding onto an old gentleman whose head was bobbing up and down and up and down as if he wanted to say, 'Yes, yes, I am alive!' saw him and yelled, 'Hey you! What are you doing?'

Mahler made a sweeping gesture—*don't have time*—and backed out of the room again. He turned and jogged toward the staircase.

Outside the staff room there was an ancient stick-thin man, fingering the ruffles on his burial shirt. One of the sleeves had come off and the man's mouth was hanging open as if he was wondering how he had ended up in this magnificent piece of clothing and what he should do now that he had destroyed it.

There were several patrol cars parked outside the entrance and Mahler muttered, 'Police? What are the police going to do? Arrest them?'

Sweat was pouring down his whole body by the time he reached his car. The lock on the driver's side was broken and he had to use the full weight of his body against the door to open it. As he did so, the lock ripped out of his hands and the asphalt under his feet rotated ninety degrees, hitting him over the shoulders and the back of his head.

He was lying next to his car, staring up at the stars. His belly moved up and down: deep breaths, like bellows. He heard sirens in the distance, fine music for a newspaperman, normal. But he couldn't go on.

The stars twinkled at him, his breathing steadied.

He focused on a point far beyond the stars, whispered, 'Where are you, my darling boy? Are you there? Or...here?'

After several minutes, feeling capable of action again, he crawled up, got into the car, started the engine and drove out of the hospital parking lot, toward Råcksta. His hands trembled with exhaustion. Or anticipation.

Täby Municipality 23.20

Elvy made up the bed in Tore's room for Flora. The stubborn antiseptic hospital smell had been softened three weeks back by almond-oil soap and detergent. Of Tore there was nothing left. Only the day after he died Elvy had thrown out the mattress, pillows and all the bed linen and bought new ones.

When Flora visited her the next day, Elvy had been surprised that she'd no objection to sleeping in the room where her grandfather had died so recently, especially in light of her sensitivity. But Flora simply said, 'I knew him. He doesn't frighten me,' and that was that.

Now Flora came in and sat down on the edge of the bed. Elvy looked at the Marilyn Manson shirt that hung to her knees and asked, 'Do you have any other clothes for the day after tomorrow?'

Flora smiled. 'Yes. Even I have limits.'

Elvy fluffed up the pillows, said, 'Not that it matters to me or anything, but...'

'The ladies,' Flora filled in.

'Yes. The ladies.' Elvy frowned. 'Or rather, I agree that one should...'

Flora laid a hand over hers, interrupting. 'Nana. Like I told you. I think it's right to dress nicely for a funeral.' She made a face.

'*Weddings*, however...'

Elvy laughed. 'One day you'll be standing there yourself,' she said, and added, 'Maybe. Or maybe not.'

Flora said, 'Probably not,' and let herself fall back onto the bed, arms outstretched. She stared up at the ceiling, opened and closed her hands as if she were catching invisible, falling balls. When she had caught ten of them, she asked straight out into the air, 'What happens when you die? What happens when you die?'

Elvy didn't know if the question was directed at her, but answered it anyway. 'You go somewhere.'

'Somewhere where? Heaven?'

Elvy sat down on the bed next to Flora, smoothing out the already-smooth sheet.

'I don't know,' she said. 'Heaven is probably a name we've given to something completely unknown to us. It's simply...somewhere else.'

Flora didn't answer, catching a few more balls. Suddenly she sat up, close to Elvy, and asked, 'What was that before? What happened in the garden?'

Elvy sat quietly for a moment. When she spoke, her voice was low, tentative.

'I know that you don't share my faith,' she said, 'but maybe you could look at it like this. Put aside God and the Bible and all of that, and think about the soul: a human being has a soul. Do you think that's reasonable?'

'No,' Flora said. 'I think we die and get burned up and then that's it.'

Elvy nodded.

'Yes. Of course. But this is what I think. A person lives a life. Accumulates thoughts, experiences, love, and when she is eighty years old and still has a razor-sharp mind the body slowly begins to falter. Inside that human being is still the same person, just as fully alive and thinking, but the body is worn down, is worn away and at last the person sits there inside crying: No, no, no...and then it's over.'

'Yes,' Flora said. 'It is.'

Elvy became excited, grabbed Flora's hand and raised it to her lips, kissing it lightly.

'But for me,' she said, 'for me that's completely absurd. Always has been. For me...' Elvy stood up from the bed, waved her hands, 'it is completely obvious that a person has a soul. We must have one. To think that we are all—that a consciousness which can embrace the whole universe in an instant should be dependent on this kind of...' Elvy swept her hand across her body 'this kind of...sack of meat in order to exist...No, no, no. I can't accept that.'

'Nana? Nana?'

Elvy's eyes, which for a moment had been fixed far away, returned to her granddaughter. Elvy sat down on the bed again, clasped her hands in her lap.

'Forgive me,' she said. 'But tonight I was shown proof that the things I believe are true.' She glanced at Flora and added, almost sheepishly, 'I think.'

After she had said goodnight and closed the door on Flora, Elvy began to pace. She tried to sit down in the armchair, picked up Grimberg, read several sentences and then put it away.

That had been one of her projects that she had promised herself she'd take on when Tore was gone: to read *The Wonderful Adventures of the Swedish People* before she died herself. She was well underway, was already half-way into the second volume, but tonight she would get no further. She was too restless.

It was past midnight. She should go to bed. Admittedly, she didn't need so much sleep these days, but frequently she'd wake up at around four in the morning and have to sit on the toilet for a couple of hours while the urine trickled out of her.

Tore, Tore, Tore...

Earlier in the day she had been down to the funeral parlour with his best suit, for the service scheduled two days later. Was he lying in the cold storage box at the church now, ready and dressed for his last big day? They had asked her if she wanted to dress him herself, but she had been more than happy to hand the matter over to them. She'd done her bit.

It was ten years since she'd started to make his sandwiches; seven since she'd begun feeding them to him. For the last three years, he hadn't been able to take anything by mouth except porridge and purées, needed supplements through a feeding tube just to stay...yes, alive. Or whatever you would call it.

Confined to a wheelchair, unable to speak or, probably, think. Just occasionally when she said something to him a glint of understanding flickered in his eyes, only to disappear just as quickly.

She had fixed his food, changed his nappy and his bag, washed him. The only help she received was in putting him to bed at night and getting him up in the morning—for yet another day sitting in his wheelchair unable to move.

For better or worse, until death us do part. She had kept her promise without joy or love; but also without complaint or hesitation, for that was how it went.

In the bathroom she removed her dentures, brushed them thoroughly and put them in a glass that she kept in the bathroom. Did not understand people who kept them next to the bed like a grinning reminder of time passing. Glasses, yes. The security of having one's eyesight close at hand if anything should happen, but the teeth? As if something you had to chew was suddenly going to appear.

She went into her bedroom, took off her clothes and put on her nightgown. She folded the clothes carefully and placed them on the rolltop desk. She paused, looked at the photograph on the desk. Their wedding picture, her and Tore.

What a pair of lovebirds.

The photograph was originally black and white, but had later been hand coloured in still-vivid hues. She and Tore looked like an illustration in a book of fairytales. The King and Queen—shortly after 'and then they lived happily ever after'. Tore in tails, she in a white dress with a colourful bouquet of flowers at her breast. Both staring into the future with spookily blue eyes. (Tore had not even had blue eyes; the retoucher had made a mistake, but they'd never got around to having it corrected.)

Elvy sighed, stroking the photograph with her finger.

'That's how things can end up,' she said, not thinking of anything in particular.

She turned on the bedside lamp, wondering if she should try another session with Grimberg before she fell asleep, but before she had made up her mind there was something at the front door. She listened. The sound came again. A...scratching.

What in the name of heaven...?

The clock on her bedside table said it was twenty past twelve. The scratching came again. Probably some animal, perhaps a dog, but what would it be doing at her house? She waited a while, but the scratching continued. Stray dogs were unusual round here. In the winter you might get a deer, wandering into the suburbs, but they never came to the door to pay a visit.

She pulled on her robe and walked to the front door, listening. Not a cat, she thought. Partly because the scraping was too strong, and partly because it appeared to be coming from chest height. Elvy leaned against the door post and whispered loudly, 'Who is it?'

The scraping stopped. Now there was a low whimpering instead.

It must be someone who's been injured in some way.

She stopped thinking about it and opened the door.

He was dressed in his best suit, but it did not hang well on him. During his final years of illness he had lost about twenty kilos and the gabardine now drooped from his shoulders where he stood on the front steps, his arms dangling. Elvy backed up a couple of steps until her feet bumped the doorstop and she almost lost her balance, but grabbed the coat rack and straightened again.

Tore was standing still, staring at his feet. Elvy looked down. His feet were bare and white, his toenails untrimmed.

She stared at his feet and thought:

They cheated. They haven't trimmed his toenails.

For it was not terror or horror that she felt when she looked at her husband, dead three years after their fiftieth anniversary, now returned. No. Only surprise and…a kind of exhaustion. Then she took a step towards him and said, 'What are you doing here?'

Tore did not answer. But he lifted his head. There were eyes, but no gaze. Elvy was used to this, she'd had the non-gaze turned on her for three years. It was just that now it was even more frozen, lifeless.

This is not Tore. This is a doll.

The doll took a couple of steps forward and entered the house. Elvy could not bring herself to do anything to stop it. She wasn't afraid, but she had no idea what she should do.

It was Tore, there was no sense in pretending anything else. But how was this possible? She had felt for his absent pulse; had held the little hand mirror to his mouth and seen that he was no longer breathing. She had heard the ambulance driver say it, she'd been given certificates confirming the fact that Tore was dead, deceased, gone.

The resurrection of the flesh…

He brushed past her and went on into the house. A cloud of chilled hospital smell reached her nostrils; disinfectant, starch… and something sweeter, more fruity underneath. She quickly pulled herself together, grabbed hold of his shoulder and whispered, 'What are you doing?'

He paid her no attention, and continued his steps—jerkily, as if each one was an effort—in the direction of the other bedroom. *His* room.

It struck her suddenly that for the first time in seven years she was seeing him *walk*. Stiffly, as if unused to his new-found body, but walking nonetheless. Straight to the room where Flora was sleeping.

Elvy turned around, grabbed hold of both his shoulders from behind and whisper-shouted, 'Flora is sleeping in there! Let her be!'

Tore stopped, the cold from his body seeping through the cloth into her hands. After they had stood like this for several seconds, a memory rose up: those times when Margareta was little and Tore had come home drunk. The daughter sleeping in her bed, Elvy playing sentry in the hallway to prevent Tore from stumbling into Margareta's room and dribbling endearments over the terrified child.

She's sleeping! Let her be!

Often it had worked. But not always.

Tore turned around. Elvy tried to fix him with her gaze, nail him to the wall as she had done forty years ago. Make him stop moving, start talking. But it was like trying to pin a tack to a bowling ball; her gaze slipped, could not pierce his and for the first time she began to be afraid.

Despite the shadows on his hollow cheeks, the sunken lips and the missing twenty kilos, he was still significantly stronger than she. And in his eyes there was no emotion, no recognition. She could not bear to look any longer and backed away, defeated.

Tore turned and continued towards the room. Elvy tried to grab hold of him again, but just as his shoulders slipped from her grasp, the bedroom door opened and Flora came out.

'Nana, what...'

She caught sight of Tore. A whimper escaped her and she threw herself aside, out of the way of his cold determination. Tore appeared not to notice her and entered the bedroom as Flora stumbled and fell over the armchair and crawled toward the balcony door. She sat down on the floor, wide eyed and screaming at the top of her lungs.

Elvy hurried over to her, took her in her arms and stroked her hair, her cheeks.

'Shushh...shushhh...it isn't dangerous...shushhhh.'

The screaming stopped. Elvy felt Flora's jaw muscles tense under her hand. Her body started to tremble and she leaned towards Elvy, still tensed, her gaze directed at the bedroom. Tore had walked over to his desk and sat down, as if he had just come home from work and had a little paperwork to get through before going to bed.

They saw his arms moving, heard the quiet rustle as the papers moved over each other. They huddled there for a long time unable to move, until Flora freed herself from Elvy's arms and sat up straight on the floor.

Elvy whispered, 'How are you going there?' Quietly, so Tore wouldn't hear.

Flora opened and closed her mouth, made a half-hearted gesture at the coffee table, at the bedroom. Elvy looked over and saw what she meant. The cover of Flora's video game, Resident Evil, was on the coffee table. Flora mumbled something and Elvy leaned forward.

'What did you say?'

Flora's voice, less than a whisper, was quite clear, 'This is... ridiculous.'

Elvy nodded. Yes. Ridiculous. Laughable, except that neither of them was laughing—and the facts remained. She stood up. Flora fumbled at the hem of her robe.

'Shh...' Elvy whispered. 'I'm just going to see what he's doing.'

She crept up to the bedroom. Why were they whispering, why was she creeping if all of this was so ridiculous? Because the ludicrous, the impossible, is located at the outermost limits of existence. One wrong move, the least little disturbance, and it falls. Or rises, roaring. You never know which. And you have to be careful; take precautions.

Elvy leaned against the doorpost, but only Tore's back and one elbow, pulled in, were within her line of vision. She took a step into the room, sliding along the wall to get another angle.

Is he looking for something?

Ghosts coming back to put something right. The fruity smell had grown stronger. She rested the tips of her fingers against the wall as if to maintain contact with reality.

Tore's white, stiff hands moved across the desk, over the photocopied texts of psalms they'd sung at the funeral, blank stationery, the copy of today's newspaper that Flora had brought. He lifted a piece of paper to his eyes, moving his head back and forth as if he were reading—

Only a day, one moment at a time

—whereupon he put the paper down, and picked up a new piece with the same text and read it with equal care.

'Tore?'

Elvy started at the sound of her own voice. She had not been planning to say anything, it just slipped out. But there was no reaction from Tore. Elvy relaxed. She did not want him to turn around, do anything or—

God help me

—say anything.

She shuffled out of the room along the wall and closed the door gently behind her, listening. The paper sounds continued. She pulled the armchair up to the door, jammed the chair back under the door handle and wedged in a couple of books so that the handle wouldn't turn.

Flora was still sitting on the floor in the same position as before. Tore's return was inconceivable, quite beyond Elvy's comprehension, but she was afraid for Flora's sake. This was too much for her sensitive girl.

Elvy sat down next to her, and it was a relief when Flora asked, 'What's he doing?' since it meant she had not completely dissociated; she was interested. And Elvy had an answer for her.

'I think,' she said, 'that he is pretending to be alive.'

Flora gave a little nod, as if this was just the answer she had been expecting. Elvy didn't know what to do. Flora shouldn't be anywhere near this, but Elvy couldn't see how she could get her away. The buses had stopped running and Margareta and Göran were in London.

She couldn't have called her daughter anyway. Margareta might be generally better socially adapted than Flora and Elvy, but her capacity for hysteria, on the few occasions when it did break out, was enormous. Margareta would come over, and she would take care of everything. Margareta would be speaking very rapidly in a high-pitched voice, and if the smallest detail went wrong she would start to claw at her face.

Damn Tore.

Yes. As Elvy sat wrestling with the problem, she began to feel increasingly hostile toward Tore, whose fault this all was. Hadn't she already done enough? Hadn't she done everything that could possibly be done?

Wait a minute.

Something occurred to her and she smiled, in spite of everything. Of course it was only theological hairsplitting; but didn't it say, 'For better or for worse, until death us do part?' She looked over at the closed door. Tore was dead. Therefore this was no longer her responsibility. She'd made no promise to the priest, forty-three years earlier, to have, hold or cherish anyone *after* death.

A sound from Flora. Elvy asked, 'Sorry? What did you say?'

Flora looked her straight in the eyes and said, 'Aaaaah.'

A jolt of terror ran through Elvy. This was it. She'd failed to protect the girl, and now…Her hands went up to Flora's face, stroking her cheeks. She said, 'I'm sorry, I'm sorry. I should call a taxi. Does that sound good? I'll call a taxi and then…you and I can get out of here. Yes?'

Flora shook her head slowly, grabbed Elvy's hands and held them. 'Aaaaahhh,' she said again, with the shadow of a smile this time. Elvy gave a short, sharp laugh, almost a bark, of relief. Flora was joking. She was making the sound the undead made in her computer game.

'Oh, Flora, you scared me. I thought...'

'Sorry, Nana.' Flora looked around the room with her normal eyes. The emptiness in them had vanished. 'What should we do?'

'Flora, I don't know.'

Her granddaughter frowned.

'Let's think this through,' she said. 'The first thing is: is there a chance that he never really died? That he's sort of been gone, and now he's come back?'

Elvy shook her head. 'No. Unless we've all simply been duped somehow. I looked at him when I went down with his suit the day before yesterday and...Flora, are you all right?'

'I'm fine. I'm just trying...to work this out.'

Elvy was amazed. She was speaking in a completely normal voice, holding her fingers up in front of her and checking off the possibilities. It was as if she had gone through a few minutes of shock and doubt, and was now done with that. In its place, the side of her had emerged that she usually tried to suppress: the lawyer's daughter.

'Secondly,' Flora checked off on her middle finger, 'if he really is dead, what is it that brought him back to life? Does it have anything to do with what happened in the garden?'

'Ye-e-e-s...I think that's likely.'

'Thirdly...'

Elvy began to understand. This change in Flora, she thought, was not as straightforwardly positive as she'd believed at first. The rational way of talking had taken over beause she'd started to look at the whole situation as a video game; not as an impossible event, but as a series of problems, there to be cracked.

Well, Elvy thought, *it could be worse.*

'...thirdly: is this something that only we can see or is it like real...well, you know what I mean.'

Elvy thought of the feeling of Tore's sloped shoulders under her hands, the chill that had radiated from them.

'It is real, and I think we should...call an ambulance.'

Flora stood up. 'Can I?'

'Don't you think it's better if I...'

'Yes. But can I do it?'

Flora had actually clasped her hands in front of her, entreating, and Elvy shrugged. She did not understand the child's enthusiasm but thought this was a good enough way to be. Flora went to make the call while Elvy sat on the floor, thinking.

It means something.

All of this...means something.

Overview

23.10–23.20: The dead come back to life at every morgue in the greater Stockholm area.

23.18: An old man is observed on the street, completely naked, outside the aged care facility in Solkatten. Does not respond to speech. The police are called to the scene in order to return the individual to his home.

23.20: A young man is run over by a van about a hundred metres from the Medical Examiner's office in Solna. When the police arrive at the scene, the victim has walked away. The driver of the van is in a state of shock, claiming that the victim had a big scar on his abdomen. The man was thrown some ten metres in the collision, and his stomach split open, but he stood up and walked away.

23.24: The first call to the emergency line. An elderly woman has received a visit from the sister she's lived with for the past five years, who died two weeks ago.

23.25: The staff of Danderyd Hospital start calling around to those aged care facilities and churches that have mortuaries, to inform them of the situation.

23.25–23.45: Twenty-odd reports of old people wandering around on the street.

23.26: Nils Lundström, retired nature photographer, takes the picture that will dominate the front page of the tabloid *Expressen* the next day. At the cemetery by Täby Church, seven old people in shrouds come staggering out of the mortuary, heading for the exit. The photograph captures them among the gravestones.

23.30–23.50: Radio communications from patrol cars dispatched to take care of disoriented old people reveal that all of the individuals concerned died over the course of the past few weeks. The Ministry of Health and Social Affairs is informed.

23.30 and on: The emergency call centre in inundated by callers in a state of shock, sometimes hysterical, reporting the return of dead relatives. Paramedics, counsellors and religious ministers are quickly rounded up to be assigned to the families concerned.

23.40: The infectious diseases ward at Danderyd Hospital is designated as a temporary gathering place. Extra staff are summoned urgently.

23.50: There is a report from Danderyd that two bodies have not come back to life. Their medical records show that one has been dead for ten weeks, the other for twelve. Both corpses had been treated repeatedly with formaldehyde while the formalities regarding their funeral arrangements were cleared up.

More reports of non-awakenings follow. It appears that only those who have been dead two months or less have come back.

23.55: Databases are correlated: numbers of deceased unburied in the greater Stockholm area going back two months, yields a total of exactly 1042 people.

23.57: It is decided that the unthinkable must be investigated. A delegation with sound amplification and digging equipment is dispatched to the Stockholm Woodland Cemetery in order to listen to the graves, possibly with a view to opening them.

23.59 and on: Emergency psychiatric units begin to receive relatives who have had breakdowns upon being reunited with their dead.

14 August

Where is my love?

Råcksta 00.12

Ängbyplan, Islandstorget, Blackeberg...

Mahler's sweating hands slipped on the steering wheel as he turned out of the space-age roundabout and took a right at the Råcksta Crematorium and Cemetery.

His mobile rang. He slowed down, managed to extract it from his bag and checked the number. Editorial. Benke probably wanted to know how he was doing with the pictures, where his story was. No time. He put the phone back and let it ring as he turned into the small parking lot, turned off the engine. He opened the door, reflexively grabbing the bag, heaved himself out of the car and...

Stop.

He stood by the car, leaning against the door. Hiked up his pants.

There was no one here.

There was utter silence inside the high brick walls. A yellow early-summer moon spilled soft light onto the angular outline of the crematorium. Nothing moved.

What had he expected? To see them standing here, shaking the bars and...?

Yes. Something like that.

He walked up to the gate, looked in. The large open area in front of the chapel where he had stood only a month ago, sweating in his dark suit with his heart in shreds, had been given over to the night. The moon spread its blanket over the headstones, lit the occasional star in the gravel.

He looked up toward the memorial grove. Weak dots of light illuminated the pines from below. Memorial candles, placed there by grieving loved ones. He felt the gates. Locked. He stared up at the spikes on top. Impossible.

But he knew the cemetery by now; it was easy to get in. More difficult to see why they locked it in the first place. He walked along the wall until it gave way to a sharply inclined grass embankment where some artificially watered annuals bloomed when everything else in sight had withered.

Easy?

Sometimes his brain still believed that it inhabited his thirty-year-old body. Back then it would have been easy. Not now. He looked around. A couple of windows in the tenements on Silversmedsgränd flickered TV-blue. There were no people outside. He licked his lips and peered up at the top of the ridge.

Three metres; maybe a forty-five degree angle.

He leaned over, gripped a couple of tufts of grass and started to heave himself up. The weakened roots of the grass gave way and he was forced to dig his toes into the earth so as not to fall back. He lay with his face pressed into the ground. His belly was in the way, braking him as he dragged himself, sloth-like, foot by foot up the slope and in the midst of his misery he started to laugh, then stopped abruptly as the movement threatened to throw him off balance.

What I must look like.

At the top, he collapsed panting for a while, staring out over the cemetery. Gravestones and crosses stood in neat rows, raised out of their moon-shadows.

Most of those at rest here were cremated, but Anna had wanted

Elias to be buried. Where Mahler had felt terror at the image of his little body in the cold earth, Anna had found comfort. She had not wanted to let him go from her at all, and this was as close as she had been able to get.

Mahler had thought then that it sounded like a bad reason, something that would lead to regrets later on, but perhaps he'd been wrong. Anna went to the grave every day and said that it felt good to know that Elias was actually down there. Not just ashes, but hands, feet, head. Mahler had still not grown accustomed to it and, beyond his grief, he felt a kind of unease every time he visited the grave.

The worms. Decomposition.

Yes. Now it struck him that this was a serious question, and he hesitated before making his way down the slope.

If...if this really was happening...what would Elias look like?

Mahler had attended countless crime scenes. He'd seen body parts dug out of plastic bags, corpses removed from apartments where they'd spent a couple of weeks alone with the dog, bodies mangled in canal locks, in trawler machinery. It was never pretty.

Elias' white coffin was burned on his retina. The final goodbye, an hour before the ceremony. Mahler had bought a box of Lego that morning and he and Anna had stood together next to the open casket, looking at Elias. He was dressed in his favourite pyjamas, the ones with penguins, his teddy bear was tucked under his arm and everything was so terribly *unnecessary.*

Anna had gone up to the coffin and said, 'Wake up, Elias. Come on, little one, that's enough,' and stroked his cheek. 'Wake up, honey. It's morning now, time to go to daycare...'

Mahler had held his daughter and there were no words to be said, for he felt the same thing. He put the box of Harry Potter Legos that Elias had been wanting next to the teddy bear, thought for a moment it would bring him round, make him stop lying there when he was so nice and whole and only had to get up in order for this nightmare to be over.

Mahler slip-slid down the slope, entering the cemetery warily, afraid of disturbing the peace. Elias' grave lay quite a distance away and en route he passed a gravestone at the head of a relatively fresh grave:

DAGNY BOMAN

14 September 1918 – 20 May 2002

He stopped. Listened. Heard nothing. Continued.

Elias' marker came into view, the very last on the right. The vase of white lilies that Anna had placed there gleamed faintly in the moonlight. A graveyard could be so densely populated and yet it was the loneliest place on earth.

Mahler's hands trembled and his mouth was dry as he sank to his knees at the grave. The turf squares laid on top of the exposed soil had not yet had time to grow in. The seams stood out like black shadows.

ELIAS MAHLER

19 April 1996 – 25 June 2002

In Our Hearts

Always

Nothing could be heard. There was nothing to be seen. Everything was normal. No bulging ground, no—

Yes, he had thought as much

—hand that reached up, seeking.

Mahler stretched out on the ground, embracing the earth where the coffin lay buried. Pressed his ear against the grass. This was insanity. He listened down, pressing his hand against the ear that was not on the ground.

And heard it.

Scraping.

He bit his lip hard enough to draw blood, pressed his head down harder, felt the grass give way.

Yes, there was scraping down there.

Elias was moving, trying to…get out.

Mahler flinched, got to his feet. He stood at the foot of the grave and hugged himself, trying to keep from going to pieces. His mind was blank. Even though this was precisely why he'd come, he'd been unable, right till the last minute, to believe it could really be true. He had absolutely no plan of action, no tools, no way of…

'Elias!'

He dropped to his knees, ripping out the clumps of grass and started to scratch away at the ground with his bare hands. He dug like a man possessed, nails breaking, dirt in his mouth, dirt in his eyes. From time to time he laid his ear against the ground, hearing the scraping more and more clearly.

The soil was dry and porous, not yet reinforced by a net of roots. The sweat that fell from Mahler's brow was the first moisture it had tasted in weeks. After twenty minutes he had gone so deep that his arms could no longer touch the bottom, and still there was no sign of the coffin.

He worked for a long time with his head lowered over the edge and his blood surging against his skull like the clapper of a bell. Everything went dark. He was forced to pause so he would not faint.

His back screamed as he heaved himself back, landing softly in the piled earth. The scraping continued, amplified in the open hole. He thought he heard a thin wail, almost a whistle, and held his breath. The whistling stopped. He took a breath. That wail again. He snorted: dirt and mucus flying from his nose. It was his airways that were wailing. He let them wheeze on.

Dry earth.

Thank you God: dry earth.

Mummifying. Not decomposing.

He lay for a while and breathed, trying not to think. His mouth was dry, his tongue sticking to the roof of his mouth. This could not be happening. And yet it was. What do you do in this situation?

Either you lie down and attempt not to exist. Or else you accept, and go on.

Mahler stood up. Tried to stand up, but his back said no. He lay like a beetle, arms flailing, trying to bend unbendable joints. It didn't work. Instead he rolled over on his stomach and dragged himself up to the opening in the ground.

He shouted, 'Elias!' and pain shot down his spine toward his tailbone.

No answer. Only scraping.

How much farther to reach the coffin? He did not know, and he couldn't move any more dirt without tools. His fingers closed around the beaded necklace and he lowered his head like a penitent, praying for forgiveness. He spoke down into the hole, 'I can't. I'm sorry, buddy. I can't. You're too far down. I have to get someone, I have to...'

Scrape, scrape.

Mahler shook his head. Started to weep quietly.

'Stop it, little buddy. Grandpa is on his way. I'm just going to... get someone...'

Scraping.

Mahler clenched his teeth to hold the tears and the back pain, forced himself to his knees. Turned, sobbing, and coaxed himself down backwards into the hole.

'I'm coming, buddy. Grandpa's coming.'

He barely fit. The walls of the hole rubbed against his belly, crumbling dirt fell as he ignored the howl from his back and bent down and resumed his digging.

After only a couple of minutes his fingers reached the smooth surface of the lid.

If it breaks...

There was no noise from inside the coffin while Mahler brushed it clean, revealing the white lid that shone like a pale moon under his feet. He had one foot on the bottom end and the other at the top.

Manoeuvring for better access, he put one foot in the middle, heard the wood crack, moved the foot to the side with alarm.

His sweat-soaked shirt lay glued to his body, straining. The pressure had built up inside his skull while he'd been bent over and it felt as if the next time he lowered his head it would blow up like an overheated boiler.

His bottom rib was at ground level. He started seeing stars again as he leaned over the edge, panting, resting his head on the grass. He closed his eyes, heard the scarlet coursing of blood through his body.

God, this is hard.

When he'd started to dig, he'd imagined that although it would surely take a superhuman feat of strength to reach the coffin, all he would have to do after that would be to pull it up, open it and...be reunited.

But only the dirt they'd taken out to lower the casket had been loose. That was the earth he had managed to remove. To bring *up* the casket from this same hole was another matter. They didn't dig graves with that in mind.

He slipped his hands behind his head, resting on his feet. A mild breeze drifted over the cemetery, rustling in the aspen leaves and cooling his overheated body. In the stillness it suddenly occurred to him that perhaps he had imagined the whole thing. His desire so intense that he had willed the sound into being. Or perhaps an animal, perhaps a...

rat.

He screwed up his eyes. A new breeze caressed his brow. He was absolutely exhausted, could feel the over-exerted muscles in his arms and legs contracting, tensing up as he stood. He did not think he would even be able to get himself up out of the grave without help.

Things are as they are.

The furrows in his brows smoothed, and he felt a strange kind of peace. Images danced faintly before his eyes. He was moving through a field of reeds. Green, rustling stalks surrounded him, breaking under his advance. Through the curtain of reeds he glimpsed naked bodies; women playing peekaboo like Bollywood sirens.

He too was naked and the reeds scraped his body, cutting deep into his skin. It stung everywhere and a film of blood covered his body as he moved on, dizzy and goaded by the mild pain, the desire for the teasing bodies. An arm here, a breast there, a fluttering strand of brown hair. He stretched out his arms, grabbed only reeds, and more reeds.

There was a crackling and crunching under his feet, the women's laughter rose above the rustling of the reeds and he was a bull, a lumbering fleshly beast trampling the delicate vegetation to satisfy his lust...

He opened his eyes, suddenly alert.

That scraping again.

And he didn't just hear it. He *felt* it. The vibrations, under his feet, of nails scraping against wood. He raised his head, looked down at the coffin.

Krrrr...

Half a centimetre of wood between the fingers and his foot.

'Elias?'

No reply.

He made his way up, one vertebra at a time.

Among the trees in the memorial grove, he found a long, thick stick that he carried back to the grave. When he surveyed all the dirt that lay scattered around the gaping hole, it didn't seem possible that he could have summoned the strength.

But he kept going.

He pushed the stick down between the head of the coffin and the packed wall of earth, pressed down. The coffin tipped slightly and it felt as if his tongue was swelling in his mouth as he heard something glide, changing position inside.

How does he look, how does he look...

But not just that. There was a clatter as well. As if there were pebbles in there.

Finally he managed to raise the coffin enough so that he could get down on his stomach, grip it with both hands and pull it up.

It did not weigh much. Not much at all.

He stood there with the little box in front of his feet. It was not disfigured by rot, it looked the same as it had done in the chapel. But Mahler knew that what altered a corpse did not come from the outside, but from within.

He rubbed a hand over his face. He was scared.

Sure, he had heard fantastical stories about dead bodies, especially of dead children, exhumed *many years* after the funeral, which had not changed at all. Simply looked as if they were sleeping. But that was fairy tales, legends of the saints; extraordinary circumstances. He had to be prepared for the worst.

The coffin was rocked by a soft blow from inside, there was a rustling sound, and for the first time since he arrived, Mahler felt a strong urge to run away. The Beckomberga mental hospital was only a kilometre away. Run there. With his hands over his ears, screaming. But...

The Lego fort.

The Lego fort was still in his apartment. The tiny figures left in the same place as the last time they had played. Mahler could see Elias' hands manipulate the knights, the swords.

'Were there really dragons back then, Grandad?'

He bent over the coffin.

The lid was only fastened with two screws, one at the top and one at the bottom end. He managed to remove the top one with his apartment key, took a deep breath and twisted the lid to the side.

Held his breath.

That isn't Elias.

He took a step back from the body that lay nestled in the plush upholstery. It was a dwarf. An ancient dwarf-man who had been buried in Elias' place.

He involuntarily gulped for air through his mouth, his nose, and the pungent smell of over-aged cheese prompted a retching that he was able—with some difficulty—to prevent from becoming full-blown vomiting.

That isn't Elias.

The moonlight was strong enough so he could see what had happened to the body. The tiny hands that were now fumbling in the air were desiccated, blackened, and the face...the face. Mahler closed his eyes, clapped his hands over them, whimpered.

He realised now how much he had still believed, against all odds, that Elias would look the same as in life. Why not, given that all of this was impossible anyway?

But he didn't.

Mahler clenched his lips, sucked them into his mouth, and removed his hands from his eyes. He had seen so many terrible things in his work, he knew the trick of making himself blank, empty, not present. He did this now as he went up to the casket and lifted Elias in his arms.

The penguin pyjamas were silky to the touch. Underneath he could feel hardened skin, stiff as dried leather. The entire abdomen was swollen from gases that had formed in the intestines and the smell of rotting protein was worse than he could have imagined.

But Mahler was not here. The person here was a man carrying a child. A very light child. He cast a last glance into the coffin to see if he forgotten anything. Yes, he had. The Legos.

That was what had made the clattering sound. Elias had opened the box of Legos that had been placed with him, and the plastic pieces were now lying in a pile at one end, together with the ripped cardboard.

Mahler stopped short, seeing it in his mind. Elias had lain there and...

He screwed his eyes shut. Erased. Stood there one crazy moment and hesitated, wondered if he should put Elias down and put the Lego pieces in his pocket.

No, no, I'll buy new ones, I'll buy the whole store...I...

With short strides and ragged breaths that did not seem to be enough to oxygenate his blood, he started to walk towards the exit, whispering, 'Elias...Elias...everything will be fine. We're going home...to the Lego fort. All this is over. Now we're...going home...'

Elias twisted slowly in his arms, as if sleepy, and Mahler saw all the times he had carried the sleeping little body from the car or from the couch to the bed. In the same pyjamas.

But this body was not soft, nor warm. It was cold and unyielding, stiff like a reptile. Half-way to the exit he dared to peek at the face again.

The skin was orange-brown, drawn taut so the cheekbones were sharply outlined. The eyes were just a couple of slits and the whole face looked vaguely...Egyptian. The nose and lips were black, shrunken. There wasn't much that resembled Elias except for the brown curly hair tumbling down over the wide forehead.

And yet, it was a stroke of luck.

Elias had started to mummify. If it had been damp in that earth he would most likely have rotted away.

'You were lucky, my boy. That it's been such a warm summer. Yes, you wouldn't know, but it has been...lovely and warm every day. Like the time we went fishing for perch...do you remember? When you felt so sorry for the worm and we fished with gummy worms instead...'

Mahler kept on talking the whole way until he was back at the gates again. They were still locked. He had forgotten about that.

Exhausted, unable to take another step, he sank into a heap next to the wall by the gates with Elias in his arms. He couldn't smell him anymore. The world smelled like this.

He held Elias pressed against his chest, looked up at the moon. It looked back down at him, kind and yellow, approving. Mahler nodded, allowed his eyes to shut, stroked Elias' hair.

His soft hair.

Danderyd Hospital 00.34

'How are you feeling now?'

A microphone was stretched in toward his chin and David almost grabbed hold of it out of habit.

'How I...feel?'

'Yes. How do you feel right now?'

He did not understand how the Channel-4 reporter had tracked him down. After having been turned out of Eva's room he had gone and sat down in the waiting room and fifteen minutes later this reporter had turned up, wondering if he could ask some questions. The man, who was close to his own age, had a shiny look about his eyes that was either due to sleep-deprivation or makeup. Or excitement.

David pulled up the corners of his mouth into a grin that looked horrible on camera, answered, 'It feels good. I'm already looking forward to the semis.'

'Pardon?'

'The semi-finals. Against Brazil.'

The reporter glanced at the cameraman and they exchanged a silent code: re-take. The reporter changed his tone, as if he was saying his line for the first time.

'David, you are the only person who was actually present at an awakening. Can you describe what happened?'

'Yes,' David said. 'After we nailed that first penalty I just felt the game swung our way…'

The reporter frowned and put the microphone down, waved the cameraman over and leaned close to David.

'Forgive me, I know this must be hard for you, but you have been through something that the public…I mean, you must understand. Lots of people are interested in hearing this.'

'Go away.'

The reporter threw his arms out wide. 'I get it. Sure. Here I am attaching myself to your pain like a kind of parasite, in order to make entertainment out of it, I know it feels that way to you, but…'

David looked the reporter straight in the eye and babbled mechanically, 'I think a lot of it's due to the fact that we've shaken loose a bunch of people who don't ordinarily come home to Sweden for these events I'm not saying we don't normally have a strong team but it's true that when you've got Mjällby covering you from behind and Zlatan in the kind of form he showed today…'

He grabbed his head in his hands, fell and curled up on the couch, closing his eyes as he went on, '…well you know it's almost impossible to win no sorry I mean not to win of course I felt it from the moment we ran onto the pitch…'

The reporter stood up, signalling to the cameraman to film David as the latter continued his recitation in the empty room, curled up in a ball.

'…and I said to Kimpa Now let's take them and he just nodded like this and I thought about that how he'd nodded when he passed me that long ball and I sent it on to Henke…'

They drew back, zooming out. It was a good shot.

David stopped at the moment he heard the door glide shut, but remained in the same position. He was never going to be human again. This is what the darkness looked like from the inside. The famines, torture victims, massacres. The other half of the world, the one the comfortable people sighed over, racked their conscience over and had no way into. The darkness that he flirted with in his routines sometimes. Hypothetically, with no knowledge.

The reporter was living in the sunlit world, and speech with him was meaningless. There were no words. David pressed his palms against his eyes until red flowers bloomed. The worst thing was that Magnus was still there. He was sleeping at his grandmother's and knew nothing. In a couple of hours David would have to go there and let in the darkness.

Eva, what should I do?

If he could only ask her advice about this one thing: how he should tell Magnus.

But there were other people asking her questions right now. About other things.

After the initial burst of chaos waned, the doctors had become extremely interested in the fact that Eva could *talk*. Apparently she was one of the few who could. Perhaps it was due to the fact that she had died so close to the awakening, perhaps it was something else. No one knew.

David had not been particularly surprised to hear about what was happening in the morgue. It seemed to him as abhorrent, implausible—and as logical—as everything else. The world had been thrown into darkness tonight: why shouldn't the dead come back to life as well?

He got up after an immeasurable length of time, walked out into the corridor and turned the corner on his way to Eva's room. He stopped. A throng of people had gathered outside the closed door, he spotted a couple of television cameras, microphones.

My only love...

Each time he saw a shooting star, every time he played a game where he got a silent wish, he had wished this:

Let me always love Eva, let my love for her never fade.

For him, she was the one who dominated the heavens and made the world a place it was possible to live in. For the people in the corridor she was an object, a novelty, a source of information. But they were the ones who owned her now. If he approached them, they would throw themselves upon him.

He found a waiting room further down the corridor where he sat down and stared at a Miró poster until the figures in the artwork started to crawl, move along the edges of the frame. At that point he approached a doctor who knew nothing, could give no news but the word itself: no. No visitors allowed.

He walked back to Miró. The longer he stared at the figures, the more evil they looked. He stared at the wall instead.

Täby Municipality 00.52

When Flora got off the telephone she looked, for the second time this night, as if she had seen a ghost. She walked over to the bedroom door, listening for something from inside.

'How did it go?' Elvy asked. 'Did they believe you?'

'Yes,' Flora said. 'They did.'

'Are they sending an ambulance?'

'Yes, but...' Flora sat down next to Elvy on the couch, knocking her teaspoon against her cup, 'it may take a while. They have a lot to do...right now.'

Elvy gently took hold of her hand to make her stop clinking.

'Why is that? What did they say?'

Flora shook her head, turning the spoon in her fingers.

'It's happening all over. There's several hundred that have woken up. Maybe thousands.'

'No.'

'Yes. She said that every ambulance is out at the moment... picking them up. And that we shouldn't try to do anything, that we shouldn't...touch him or anything.'

'Why not?'

'Because there could be a danger of contagion or something.

They don't know.'

'What kind of contagion?'

'I haven't the faintest. That's just what she said.'

Elvy sank back on the couch, staring at the crystal vase on the coffee table that she and Tore had been given by Margareta and Göran on their fortieth wedding anniversary. Orrefors. Heinous; probably very expensive. A couple of withered condolence-roses hanging from it doubled-over.

It started with a twitch at the corners of her mouth, a trembling in the lips. Then she felt her mouth tugged back, irresistibly back and up, until a grin wide enough to strain her cheeks covered Elvy's face.

'Nana? What is it?'

Elvy wanted to laugh. No. More than that. She wanted to jump out of her seat, do a few dance steps and laugh. But Flora's head drew back ten centimetres, as you might draw away from an uncertain phenomenon, and Elvy used her right hand to wipe the smile mechanically from her face. The corners of her mouth wanted to turn up again, but she kept them in place by sheer force of will. She didn't want to cause alarm.

'It's the Resurrection,' she said with suppressed glee. 'Don't you see? It is the Resurrection. The raising of the dead. What else could it be?'

Flora tilted her head. 'You think?'

There weren't words for it. Elvy could not explain. Her joy and anticipation were too great to be contained in mere language, so she said, 'Flora, I don't want to talk about this right now. I don't want to discuss it. I just want to sit undisturbed for a little while.'

'Why? What for?'

'I just want to be alone. A little while. Can you do that for me?'

'Yes. Sure.'

Flora walked to the window, stood looking out either at the faint outline of the fruit trees outside, or at Elvy's reflection in the glass.

Elvy savoured her bliss in silence. After a while Flora smacked the metal wind chimes hanging in the window, opened the french doors and walked out. The sound of her steps mingled with the clanging of the chimes, but after several seconds both had died away.

The heavenly kingdom. And on the last day ye shall all...

Euphoria. There was no other word to describe what was bubbling in Elvy's breast.

As if it were the last evening before a long, long trip. You've got a ticket in your pocket and at last everything is packed. And you can simply sit and feel the nearness of distant lands...

Yes. Like that. Elvy tried to visualise the distant land she would soon be travelling to, that everyone would soon be travelling to, but here there were no travel brochures to pore over, everything was up to her and she couldn't see. It slipped away, defied description.

But she sat there and felt that...*soon...soon...*

A couple of minutes went by in this way, and then some drops of guilt began to drip into her goblet of joy. Flora was with her. Here. Now. Where had the girl got to? As she stood up out of the couch in order to go and look, she caught sight of the armchair pushed up against the bedroom door and had time to think *why is that there?* before she remembered why. Because Tore was sitting in there. At his desk. Shuffling papers. As in life. Elvy stopped in the middle of the floor and a dark suspicion trickled in.

If this is the way it is.

When Flora had returned from the telephone and told her what she wanted to know, Elvy had imagined that silent army of the resurrected, hundreds, thousands striding in dignity down the streets, a beautiful sign of what was to come. Even though she'd known better. She walked over to the bedroom door. Paper sliding, being turned. Unclipped toenails on bare feet, the icy hands, the smell. No exalted host of angels, but flesh and blood bodies forcing their way all over the place, creating problems.

But the ways of the Lord...

...are mysterious, yes. We know nothing. Elvy shook her head, said it out loud, 'We know nothing', and that would have to suffice. She walked out on the verandah to look for Flora.

The August night was dark and not a breeze was moving the leaves. *It is night but so still that the light burns without flickering.* When Elvy's eyes had grown accustomed to the dark, she picked out Flora's dark silhouette leaning against the trunk of the apple tree. She walked down the stairs and over to her.

'You're sitting out here?' she said.

It wasn't really a question; Flora didn't reply. 'I've been thinking,' she said and got to her feet, picking a half-ripe apple from the tree and tossing it back and forth between her hands.

'What have you been thinking?'

The apple went up into the air, hung for a moment in the light from the living room and then fell back into Flora's hand with a slap.

'What the hell will they do?' Flora said, and laughed. 'Everything is different now. Nothing makes sense. You know? Everything they've based all their shit on...pfff! Gone! Death, life. Nothing makes sense.'

'No,' said Elvy. 'That's true.'

Flora's bare legs took a few prancing steps across the lawn. Suddenly she sent the apple high and far into the air. Elvy watched it fly in a wide arc across the hedge and heard it thud onto the neighbour's roof, roll across the brick tiles.

'Don't do that,' she said.

'Or what? Or *what*?' Flora threw her arms wide as if she wanted to embrace the night, the world. 'What will they do? Call in the National Guard, arrest someone? Call the Pentagon and ask them to bomb the place? I want to see...I really want to see how they fix *this* one.'

Flora picked a new apple, threw it in the other direction. This time it didn't hit a roof.

'Flora...'

Elvy tried to lay her hand on Flora's arm, but the girl pulled away.

'I don't get it,' she said. 'You think this is Armageddon, don't you? I don't know the story, but the dead come to life, the seals are broken and the whole deal and then it's all over—that it?'

Elvy felt a strong resistance to this description of her beliefs, but said, 'Well...yes.'

'OK. I don't believe it. But say you did believe it, then what the hell does it matter if an apple gets on a neighbour's roof?'

'Show some common courtesy. Please Flora, pull yourself together.'

Flora roared with laughter, but not meanly. She hugged Elvy, rocking her side to side as if she were a foolish child. Elvy could take that. She allowed herself to be rocked.

'Nana, Nana,' Flora whispered. 'You think the whole world is about to end and you're telling *me* to pull myself together.'

Elvy snorted. It actually was quite funny. Flora let go of her, took a step back and held her palms pressed together in front of her, bobbing in an Indian greeting.

'Like you said before, I don't share your beliefs. But what I believe, Nana, is that there is going to be a fucking incredible amount of mayhem. You should have heard the woman's voice, at the call centre. It was as if the zombies were panting down her neck. It is going to be chaos, it is going to be something else, and damn if I don't think that's good.'

The ambulance arrived like a thief in the night. No sirens; not even the emergency lights. It glided up the street in front of the house, the front doors opened and two paramedics in light blue shirts stepped out. Elvy and Flora walked out to meet them.

It was half past one and the men looked bleary. They had prob-ably been called in from their beds to take care of the handling.

93

The one who had come out of the driver's side nodded to Elvy and pointed at the house.

'Is he in there?'

'Yes,' Elvy said. 'I...I locked him in the bedroom.'

'You're not the only one, believe me.'

They pulled on rubber gloves and continued up the stairs. Elvy didn't know what to do. Should she follow them in and help or would she be in the way?

She stood there, rocking on her feet, when the back doors of the ambulance opened and yet another man stepped out. He was quite unlike the paramedics; older, rounder. His shirt was black. He stood for a moment outside the ambulance and took stock of his surroundings. Or rather, *enjoyed* them. Perhaps he had been shut in too long.

As he turned to the house, Elvy saw the white rectangle in his collar, and she wiped her hands on her robe, preparing herself to greet him. Flora whistled, but Elvy paid her no attention. This was serious.

The man arrived swiftly at the house—his gait was surprisingly energetic for someone so rotund—and stretched out his hand.

'Good evening. Or good morning, perhaps. Bernt Janson.'

Elvy took his hand, which was warm and firm, curtsied and said, 'Elvy Lundberg.'

Bernt shook hands with Flora as well, and went on, 'Yes, I'm a hospital chaplain at Huddinge normally, but tonight I'm out riding around in an ambulance.' His expression became more grave. 'How are you coping with this, then?'

'Fine,' Elvy said. 'We're doing fine.'

Bernt nodded and kept silent to let Elvy continue. When she didn't, he said, 'Yes, it's an extraordinary situation, this. Many people are finding it extremely disturbing.'

Elvy had nothing to add. She really only had one question, which she now posed.

'How can this be happening?'

'Well,' Bernt said, 'that's something everyone's wondering, naturally. And unfortunately I can only say: we don't know.'

'But surely you must know!'

Elvy's voice took on a more forceful note and Bernt looked surprised. 'How...do you mean?'

Elvy glanced at Flora, forgetting that her grandchild was not the person from whom to seek support. Even more irritated, she stamped her foot into the paving and said loudly, 'Are you standing here in front of me, a minister of the Church of Sweden, and telling me that you do not know what this means? Do you have a Bible on you, shall I look it up for you?'

Bernt raised his arm to placate her. 'I see, you mean...'

Flora left them and walked into the house. Elvy didn't notice.

'Yes, I do. You can't seriously mean that this is just an unusual occurrence, like...snow in June. Can you? "On the last day the dead shall rise from their graves"...'

Bernt made a calming gesture. 'Yes, well, perhaps it's a little early to comment on...these matters.' He looked up and down the street, scratched the back of his neck and lowered his voice, 'But of course these things may turn out to have a greater significance.'

Elvy did not give up. 'Don't you believe it?' she asked.

'Yes...' Bernt looked at the ambulance, took half a step closer to Elvy and said, right next to her ear, 'Yes. Yes, I do.'

'Well then, say so.'

Bernt resumed his earlier posture. He looked somewhat more relaxed now, but still spoke in a low voice. 'Yes, that opinion is not completely *comme il faut*, so to speak. That is not why I am here. It wouldn't be acceptable for me to go around in this kind of situation and...preach.'

Elvy understood. She may have felt it was cowardly, but of course most people would not want a doomsday preacher on a night like this.

'So you do believe,' she said, 'that this is the Second Coming. All of that. That it will be as it's written?'

Now Bernt could no longer retain his composure. His face broke out in a wide, joyous grin and he whispered, 'Yes! Yes, I believe it will!'

Elvy smiled back. At least now there were two of them.

The paramedics returned with Tore between them. Both wore expressions of controlled revulsion. As they came closer, Elvy understood why. The front of Tore's shirt was damp, spotted with a yellowish fluid, and a stench of rotting organic matter enveloped him. He had started to defrost.

'Well, now,' Bernt said. 'Here we have…'

'Tore,' Elvy said.

'Tore, I see.'

Flora came after him. She had been in the bedroom and collected her clothes, her bag. She walked up to Bernt, looking him up and down. Bernt did the same; his eyes locked for one second with Marilyn Manson's, and Elvy clasped her hands in front of her chest, tried to send Flora a telepathic signal that this was not the right moment for a theological discussion. But Flora's question was of a more practical nature.

'What are you doing with them?' she asked.

'We…For now we're taking them to Danderyd.'

'And then? What will they do?'

Tore had been led into the ambulance and Elvy said, 'Flora, they are very busy…'

Flora turned to Elvy. 'Aren't you interested? Don't you want to know what they'll do with Grandpa?'

'It is, of course…' Bernt cleared his throat, 'a very natural question. And the fact is that we do not know. But I can assure you that no one will do anything with them, so to speak.'

'What do you mean?' Flora asked.

'Well…' Bernt frowned. 'I didn't know what you meant, but I

assumed…'

'How can you be so sure, then?'

Bernt shot Elvy a look, *these young people*, which Elvy returned half-heartedly. One of the paramedics had stayed with Tore, but the other came over to them and said, 'Loaded and ready to go.' Bernt made a faint grimace and the man grinned and said, 'You done?'

'Yes,' Bernt turned to Elvy, 'Perhaps you'd like to accompany us?' When Elvy shook her head, he said, 'No, no. But someone will be in touch as soon…as soon as we know something.'

He shook Elvy's hand goodbye. When he stretched his hand out to Flora, she took it and said, 'I'll come with you.'

'Well,' Bernt said, looking at Elvy, 'I'm not sure that's appropriate.'

'Just into town,' Flora said. 'A lift. I've already asked.'

Bernt turned toward the ambulance driver who confirmed this with a nod. Bernt sighed, turned to Elvy. 'If that's all right with you.'

'The girl can do as she likes,' Elvy said.

'I bet she can,' Bernt said.

Flora walked over and hugged Elvy. 'I have to go talk to a friend.'

'*Now?*'

'Yes. As long as you're going to be OK, that is.'

'I'll be fine.'

Elvy stayed at the gate and watched Flora climb into the back of the ambulance with Bernt. She waved, and thought about the smell. The doors were closed. The ambulance engine started, the flashing lights were turned on for an instant, then immediately switched off. Slowly, the ambulance backed up into the driveway of the house opposite, turned and—

Elvy's fingers splayed, her eyes widened and an ever-intensifying feeling drove through her body like a stake: Tore. She staggered slightly, bracing herself against the fencepost. Tore was here. The same trace impression that had lingered in his room, slowly receding, was in her head at full force. He filled her and in her head she heard his voice:

Mum, help me! I'm stuck...I don't want to go away...I want to stay home, Mummy...

The ambulance turned out of the driveway.

Mum...she's coming, she...

And Tore's voice was on its way out of her, shedding her like a skin. But if his voice had been strong, as if amplified, she could now discern Flora's weaker voice through the din.

Nana...can you hear it? Are you the one he...

Elvy perceived physically how the field dissolved and her body became her own again, and only had time to send—

I hear

—before it was gone and she was just Elvy, leaning up against the fencepost. The ambulance accelerated down the street and she only glimpsed it as a white blotch before her head fell down, forced down by the whining of a thousand mosquitoes pressing in through her ears and the headache flaring up like red suns on the inside of her eyelids.

But she had seen it.

She squeezed the post to stop herself from falling to the asphalt. Her head pressed down, she was unable to open her eyes in order to get a better view. She was not allowed to. It was forbidden.

The pain only lasted a few seconds, then disappeared immediately. She lifted her head, looking at the point where the ambulance had been a moment before.

The woman was gone.

But Elvy had seen her. The second before the ambulance had disappeared from her field of vision, she had seen—out of the corner of her eye—a tall slender woman with dark hair, emerge from behind the vehicle and stretch her arms toward it. Then the pain had forced Elvy to look away.

She gazed up the street. The ambulance was just up at the bend by the big road. The woman was gone.

Is she...inside the ambulance now?

Elvy put her hand against her forehead and thought as hard as she could:

Flora? Flora?

No answer. No contact.

What had the woman actually looked like? How had she been dressed? Elvy was unable to visualise her. When she tried to conjure up the face, the body that she had seen for a split second, her mind could gain no purchase on the image. It was like trying to recapture a memory from early childhood; you could snare a certain detail, something you had latched onto. Everything else lay in shadow.

She could not see the face, the clothes. They were gone. She could only say one thing with any certainty: something had been sticking out between the woman's fingers. Something that gave off a faint reflection in the streetlamp. Something thin, something metallic.

Elvy ran into the house in order to try to reach Flora by conventional means. She dialled her mobile.

'The person you are trying to reach is unavailable...'

Råcksta 02.35

Mahler was awakened by voices, the clatter of metal.

For a moment he was disoriented. He sat up. There was something in his lap. His body ached. Where, and why?

And then he remembered.

Elias was still lying across his knees, unmoving. The moon had wandered as Mahler sat there, was now more or less obscured by the tops of the spruce trees.

How long? One hour? Two?

There was a squeaking sound as the gates opened and a number of shadows slipped into the open area in front of the chapel. Flashlights were turned on and beams of light danced over the flagstones. Voices.

'…too early to answer at this stage.'

'But what will you do if that turns out to be the case?'

'First we'll listen and try to determine how…widespread it is, then…'

'Are you planning to open the graves now?'

Mahler thought he recognised the voice of the person asking the questions. Karl-Erik Ljunghed, one of his colleagues from the paper. He didn't hear the reply. Elias lay still in his arms, as if dead.

As long as they didn't shine their lights toward the wall they wouldn't spot him. He was sitting in almost total darkness. He shook Elias gently. Nothing happened. Terror blossomed in his chest.

All this, and then...

He found Elias' dry, hard hand, put his index and middle finger in it, and pressed. The hand closed, squeezing his fingers. Five flashlights moved in toward the cemetery, with the shadows in a line.

His body was stiff as a board after this period of sitting, and while he had been unconscious his spine had been replaced with a red-hot iron rod. Why didn't he let his presence be known? Karl-Erik could have helped him. Why didn't he call out to them?

Because...

Because he shouldn't. Because it was them. The others.

'Elias...I have to put you down.'

Elias didn't answer. With a feeling of loss, Mahler drew his fingers out of his grip and softly coaxed him onto the ground. By tensing his back against the wall and only using his thigh muscles, Mahler was able to get to his feet.

The lights were dancing along toward the grave area like excited spirits, and Mahler listened for sounds from new visitors. The only thing he heard was the distant voices of the recent arrivals, and very faintly the sound of 'Eine kleine Nachtmusik' from the phone in his car. The hint of a morning blush coloured the sky.

'Elias?'

No reply. The little body lay stretched out on the stonework, a child-shaped condensation of darkness.

Can he hear me? Does he see me? Does he know that it's me?

He crouched down, got his hands in under Elias' knees and neck, stood up and walked toward the car.

'We're going home now, buddy.'

There were now three more cars in the parking lot. An ambulance, an Audi with the newspaper's logo on it as well as a Volvo with a strange licence plate. Yellow numbers on a black background. It took a moment before Mahler made the connection: a military vehicle.

The military? Is it that widespread?

The presence of the military car strengthened him in his belief that he had done the right thing not to reveal himself. When the military comes into the picture, something else goes out the window.

Elias was light, light in his arms. Unnaturally light in view of how...large he had become. His stomach protruded so far that the bottom buttons of his pyjamas had been torn off. But Mahler knew that inside there was only gas, created by the decomposition of the intestinal bacteria. Nothing that weighed anything.

He laid Elias carefully in the back seat and laid back the driver's seat as far as it would go so that he could sit with his back outstretched, almost lying down himself, as he drove out from the parking lot. He wound the windows down on both sides.

His apartment was only a couple of kilometres away. He talked to Elias the whole way, but got no answers.

He placed Elias on the couch in the dark living room, leaning over and planting a kiss on his forehead.

'I'll be right back, love. I just have to...'

He found three painkillers in the medicine drawer in the kitchen, swallowing them with a gulp of water.

And now...and now...

The touch of Elias' forehead was still on his lips. Cool, hard unyielding skin. Like kissing a stone.

He didn't dare turn on the lamps in the living room. Elias was lying absolutely still. The satin material of his pyjamas shimmered in the first light of dawn. Mahler rubbed his hands over his face and thought:

What am I doing?

Yes, what the hell was he doing? Elias was gravely ill. What do you do with an acutely sick child? Carry it home to your apartment?

Wrong. You call an ambulance, you see to it that the child goes to hospital—

morgue

—that it is looked after.

But that was the thing about the morgue. What he had seen there. The dead, held fast, struggling. He didn't want to see Elias in that picture. But what could he do? There was no way for him to care for Elias, to do…whatever it was that was required.

You think the hospitals can do it?

The pain in his back was starting to let up a little. Reason returned. Of course he would call an ambulance. There was nothing else to do.

The little darling. My darling little boy.

If only the accident had occurred a month later. Yesterday. The day before yesterday. If Elias hadn't had to lie in the earth so long, had escaped what death had changed him into: a desiccated, lizard-like creature with blackened extremities. However much Mahler loved him, his eyes saw that Elias no longer resembled anything human. He looked like something you kept behind glass.

'Buddy, I'm going to call a doctor. Someone who can help you.'

His mobile rang.

The display showed the newspaper office number. This time he took the call.

'This is…'

Benke sounded close to tears when he interrupted, 'Where have you been? First you get all this shit started and then you go up in a puff of smoke!'

Mahler couldn't help smiling.

'Benke, it wasn't me who "got all this started". I'm completely innocent.'

Benke fell silent. Mahler could hear people speaking in the background, but could not identify their voices.

'Gustav,' Benke said. 'Elias. Is he…?'

What clinched it for him was not the fact that he trusted Benke—which in fact he did—but the realisation that he needed some form of connection to the outer world. Mahler drew a deep breath and said, 'Yes. He's here. With me.'

The background noises changed and Mahler knew that Benke had taken the phone and gone somewhere no one else could hear him.

'Is he...in bad shape?'

'Yes.'

Now everything was quiet on Benke's end. He had probably slipped into an empty office.

'OK, Gustav. I don't know what to say.'

'You don't have to say anything. But I want to know what they are doing. If I'm doing the right thing.'

'They're collecting them, taking them all to Danderyd. They've started opening graves all over. The armed forces have been called in. They're citing some regulation about mass epidemics. No one knows anything, really. I think...' Benke paused. 'I don't know. But I have grandkids too, as you know. Maybe you are doing the right thing. There's a general feeling...of panic.'

'Does anyone know why this is happening?'

'No. And now, Gustav...to my other point.'

'Benke, I can't. I'm completely done in.'

Benke breathed into the receiver; Mahler sensed the effort it cost him to remain calm, not to start haranguing him.

'Do you have the photos?' he asked.

'Yes, but...'

'In that case,' Benke said, 'they're the only independent photos available from the inside. And you are the only journalist who managed to get in before they closed. Gustav...with all due respect for your situation—which I cannot even imagine—I am trying to put together a newspaper. Right now I'm talking to my best writer who is sitting on incomparably the best material. You, on the other hand, can probably imagine *my* situation.'

'Benke, you have to understand that…'

'I understand. But please, please, please Gustav, can't you just… anything? The pictures, a little text in the present tense, straight on? Please? And, if nothing else, then the pics? Just that?'

If Mahler had been able to laugh, he would have. Now all that came out of him was a groan. During the fifteen years that they had worked together he could not recall a single instance when Benke had actually begged for something. The word 'please' with a question mark after it had not been in his vocabulary.

'I'll try,' he said.

As if this was what he had expected the whole time, Benke said, 'I'll hold the centre spot. Forty-five minutes.'

'Jesus Christ, Benke…'

'Yes. And thanks, Gustav. Thanks. Get cracking now.'

They ended the call. Mahler glanced at Elias who had not moved. Walked over and placed a finger in his hand, which closed. He wanted to sit down next to him, fall asleep with his finger in his hand.

Forty-five minutes…

Insanity. Why had he agreed?

Because he couldn't help himself: he had been a reporter his whole adult life, and he knew what Benke had said was true. He was in possession of potentially the best material anyone had, of the biggest story…ever. He couldn't not do it. In spite of everything.

He sat down at the computer, took the film out from inside his head, and his fingers started to move across the keyboard.

The elevator starts with a jerk. I can hear screams through the thick concrete. The morgue level comes into view through the door glass…

Overview

00.22: The Minister of Health and Social Affairs arrives at the department. Under his supervision, a provisional command unit is formed consisting of representatives of various departments and the police, as well as eminent physicians from a number of disciplines.

A conference room at the department has been set up as a temporary command centre. It will quickly come to be known as the Dead Room.

00.25: The Prime Minister is informed of the situation, in Cape Town. The situation is deemed to be so extraordinary that a planned meeting with Nelson Mandela the next day is cancelled and the state plane is made ready for take-off. The flight takes eleven hours.

00.42: The first reliable report about awakenings at cemeteries reaches the Dead Room. The calculations have already been made. It is a matter of around 980 people. The police report that they do not have the resources to manage the exhumations.

00.45: Public pressure for a press statement from the Dead Room increases. A certain confusion about terminology abounds. After a brief meeting the term 'reliving' is unanimously adopted to refer to the awakened dead.

00.50: The task of exhumation is transferred to the military. As collaboration between the police and the armed forces is forbidden by law, no military representatives can be included in the command unit. The military is given the same authority as in a state of emergency and has to address the matter as best they can.

01.00: Danderyd reports that 430 reliving have now been admitted to the Clinic for Infectious Diseases and work is underway to clear the wards in order to make more room. Only two ambulances at each hospital have been set aside for emergency dispatches, the rest are being used for transportation. Additional assistance is requested.

01.03: There is a discussion in the Dead Room about allowing funeral homes to help transport their former clients. It is decided, however, that this may be perceived as inappropriate, and instead all available taxi cabs are called in to transport patients from Danderyd to other hospitals.

01.05: A statement issued to the press by General Johan Stenberg—who has been appointed head of the military emergency action—reaches the Dead Room. 'At present we view the corpses largely as a logistical problem,' the general has apparently said. A press secretary from the department agrees to take on the task of informing the general of the correct terminology.

01.08: Two emergency technicians and a chaplain are threatened with a rifle when they try to pick up a reliving woman in Tyresö. Police are dispatched to the scene.

01.10: CNN becomes the first foreign television station to carry reports on the events in Stockholm. Their images are limited to the chaos outside Danderyd and in the report, those patients who are being moved to other hospitals are erroneously referred to as 'the living dead'.

01.14: Pressure on the Dead Room from foreign media increases after the CNN report. A media spokesperson from the Foreign Ministry is given the task of fielding the telephone calls.

01.17: The first military exhumation division sets off, comprising mine-clearing experts as well as personnel with UN experience opening mass graves in Bosnia. While waiting for further similar groups to be dispatched, they set off to the Stockholm Forest Cemetery in order to start there.

01.21: The man in Tyresö who had refused to hand over his reliving wife opens fire at the police. No one is injured.

01.23: The Minister of Health and Social Affairs decides in consultation with judicial experts to apply to this situation those laws relating to mass epidemics, which affords the police corresponding interim authority before the results of the medical analysis. A plea is dispatched to the Medical Examiner to hurry up the work.

01.24: The police in Tyresö are given permission to use teargas, but decide not to since the armed man is elderly and may be seriously injured. A police negotiator establishes telephone contact with the man as he is making his way to the scene.

01.27: An initial medical report indicates that the reliving apparently do not employ respiratory or circulatory organs. Hasty cell tests indicate, however, that some kind of metabolic function may be present. According to the specialist in internal medicine who is spear-heading the investigation, 'Everything is completely impossible, but we are doing what we can.'

01.30: At Danderyd they have now admitted 640 reliving and ask for additional reinforcements from other hospitals. For unknown reasons, conflicts constantly erupt among members of the staff, which makes cooperation more difficult.

01.32: After significant pressure from the national and international media, the Dead Room's press secretary now announces a planned press conference in City Hall at 06.00.

01.33: Psychiatric clinics and emergency rooms are overwhelmed with family members in various states of hysteria. The internal psychiatric unit of the police force starts to see psychologically burnt out officers.

01.35: The search for those reliving who are at large is more or less ended. Reinforcements are, however, called out to the shelter of the City Mission, where clients have resisted police attempts to remove a homeless man—dead for two weeks—who has returned.

01.40: The first reliving at the Forest Cemetery is freed. The man is reported to be in the 'most miserable state imaginable' as he has been lifted out of a deep-lying area where the ground is water-logged.

01.41: The facilitator arrives in Tyresö. The last thing the armed man says on the phone is, 'I'm going to her now' whereupon he shoots himself. The emergency technicians fetch his wife while police cordon off the area. The man shows no signs of awakening.

01.41: There is a request to the general public from the Forest Cemetery for 'people with strong stomachs'. The exhumed man makes an attempt to get away.

01.45: Danderyd starts to lose control. 715 reliving have now been admitted and a number of disputes and several cases of fistfights have erupted among staff members in direct contact with the reliving.

01.50: The military calls in members of the Army Corps—without consultation with the Dead Room—in order to erect a temporary holding facility for the reliving until they can be transported.

01.55: Questioning of Danderyd staff members reveals that their conflicts have arisen due to a claimed ability to read one another's thoughts.

02.30: Reliving of particular significance to gaining a greater understanding of the phenomenon are moved to the Medical Examiner's office at Karolinska Medical Institute in Solna. Among these is Eva Zetterberg, who has the power of speech, as well as

Rudolf Albin—the one who has been dead the longest before awakening.

02.56: Tomas Berggren, professor of Neurology, conducts an initial interview with Eva Zetterberg.

Interview 1

The following is a transcript of my first interview with patient Eva Zetterberg. The patient is of particular interest as a very short period of time elapsed between the cessation of her life-sustaining functions and her subsequent awakening without the support of said functions.

The patient's ability to speak has shown continuous improvement since the awakening.

This interview was conducted in Solna, Wednesday the 14th of August 2002 at 02.56-03.07.

TB: My name is Tomas. What is your name?

EZ: Eva.

TB: Can you tell me your whole name?

EZ: No.

TB: Can you tell me your last name?

EZ: No.

[*Pause*]

TB: Can you tell me your first name?

EZ: No.

TB: What is your name?

EZ: Eva.

TB: Eva is your first name.

EZ: Eva is my first name.

TB: Can you tell me your first name?

EZ: Eva.

[*Pause*]

TB: Do you know where you are right now?

EZ: No.

TB: What does it look like around here?

EZ: Where is here.

TB: Here is the place where Eva is.

EZ: No.

TB: Where is Eva?

EZ: Eva is not here.

TB: You are Eva.

EZ: I am Eva.

TB: Where are you?

[*Pause*]

EZ: Hospital. A white man. His name is Tomas.

TB: Yes. Where is Eva?

EZ: Eva is not here.

[*TB touches EZ's hand*]

TB: Whose hand is this?

EZ: Hand. I's hand.

TB: Who is I?

EZ: Tomas.

[*Pause*]

TB: Who are you?

EZ: I am Eva.

[*TB touches EZ's hand*]

TB: Whose hand is this?

EZ: Eva...'s hand.

TB: Where is Eva?

EZ: Eva is here.

[*Pause*] No.

TB: What does it look like where Eva is?

EZ: No.

[*Pause*]

TB: Can I speak with Eva?

EZ: No.

TB: What do your eyes see?

EZ: A wall. A room. A man. His name is Tomas.

TB: What do Eva's eyes see?

EZ: Eva has no eyes.

TB: Eva has no eyes?

EZ: Eva cannot see.

[*Pause*]

TB: What can Eva hear?

EZ: Eva cannot hear.

TB: Does Eva understand what I say?

[*Pause*]

EZ: Yes.

TB: Can I speak with Eva?

EZ: No.

TB: Why can't I talk to Eva?

EZ: Eva has no...mouth. Eva afraid.

[*Pause*]

TB: Why is Eva afraid? [*Pause*]

Can you tell me why Eva is afraid?

EZ: Eva stay.

TB: Does Eva want to stay where she is?

EZ: Yes.

TB: What is Eva afraid of?

EZ: No.

[*EZ shakes her head violently.*]

After this EZ refuses to answer any further questions.

The Heath 03.48

On the night bus to Tensta, Flora checked her voicemail and saw that Elvy had called five times. She immediately dialled her number.

'Hi, it's me...'

A strong exhalation on the other end hissed in Flora's ear.

'My dear child! Is everything all right?'

'Yes. Why?'

'I don't know, I just thought...I've been trying to call.'

'I wasn't allowed to have my mobile on in the ambulance.'

'No, of course...' Flora could imagine Elvy slapping her forehead lightly, 'of course not. How silly of me.'

There was silence for a couple of seconds. The dark floors of Rissnes apartment buildings glided by outside the window.

'Nana? You heard him too, didn't you?'

'Yes.'

'The minister didn't notice anything. And you couldn't see it on Gramps. He was just lying there.'

Silence again. Flora took her walkman out of her bag. It was such an ancient model that you had to take the cassette out and turn it to switch sides. She flipped the tape over from *Holy Wood* to *Antichrist Superstar*. Then she waited.

'I...thought I saw something,' Elvy said finally.

'What?'

Elvy hesitated for two seconds and then said, 'I just wanted to hear that everything was all right with you. Are you on a bus?'

'Yes.'

Flora didn't add anything, and Elvy had run out of questions. They ended the conversation with a promise to be in touch the next day. Flora curled up in the corner of one of the seats, put the earpieces in and pushed play, leaned her head against the window and closed her eyes.

We hate love...we love hate...we hate love...

After the bus let her off at Tensta centrum she had to walk a kilometre. The Akalla path brought her almost the whole way, but on the last bit across the Järva field there were no trails other than those that the construction machines had left behind ten years earlier, and even they were returning to nature now.

She came up on a hill and looked out across the Heath. A hint of dawn brought the grey buildings out in sharp relief. She had been here at night once before, this spring. In the full dark she hadn't been able to make out the city at all from this vantage point. It had been present only as suggestion, a change in the soundscape.

There were no street lights, no lamps on in any windows, neither power, water nor drains had been laid all the way. They had never gotten that far.

As Flora walked down the slope with 'Tourniquet' winding through her ears, dawn slowly turned up its light and glinted in the few windows that remained unbroken. Until a few years ago the area—in theory still a construction site—had been enclosed by a fence but since the residents of the Heath created new entrances for the umpteenth time it had finally been left as it was. Large parts of the fence had had other uses found for them, and what was left lay fallen, scattered in the grass.

The graffiti clean-up crews had given up long since and the lower portions of the buildings were a profusion of spikes and real art. The court case to determine the party responsible for the demolition of the Heath had been underway for five years. Until it was resolved no one was going to do a thing. The Heath was a blot of shame on the city; a failed and slightly dodgy construction project, now a gathering place for those displaced from the rest of the city. From time to time the police went in and cleaned the place out, but since there were no resources for dealing with the results, they really didn't want to know.

Flora stepped from grass to asphalt. The sign on the building next to her indicated that she was now on Ekvatorvägen. A graffiti design around the sign made it look like a naked, laughing devil with dreadlocks holding an enormous erection in his hand.

Flora turned off her walkman in the pause between 'Tourniquet' and 'Angel with Scabbed Wings'. In order to have room for the album on the tape she had been forced to weed out some tracks and the choice had been simple. She took the earpieces out and turned her deafened eardrums toward the silence, chiding herself for the fear that whimpered in her stomach—

middle-class loser

—because the only thing you could hear in the area were the sounds of people. They had never got as far as planting trees and bushes, and therefore there were no birds, no rustling leaves. Only people; voices, cries. She turned with rapid steps from Ekvatorvägen onto Latitudvägen and came to Peter's courtyard.

Broken glass crunched underfoot and the sound was magnified, bouncing back and forth between the bare concrete walls. All of the buildings around were three storeys high and the courtyard was dominated by the large structure in the centre. According to Peter it had been planned as a combined laundry, social space and refuse centre. However, there was no water to wash with, no garbage collection, and no desire for social gatherings.

Flora gingerly made her way across plastic bags and strips of cardboard, but could not help stepping on the glass. She was noticed. Someone who had been slumped against the iron door to the laundry room stood up and started to approach her. Flora kept moving, a little faster now.

'Hey there…babe…'

The man placed himself directly in front of her on the narrow path. Flora's eyes scanned the surroundings. There was no one else around. The man, who was a head taller than she, had a Finnish accent. A smell she could not identify wafted from him. When the man raised his hand and she saw the bottle, she recognised the smell: T-röd. He held it out to her; a juice bottle with something, maybe bread, stuffed down the neck like a filter.

'Hey Pippi Longstocking, do you want a drink?'

Flora shook her head. 'No, I'm good.'

Her voice appeared to spark some thought in the man. He leaned over, studied her face. Flora stood still.

'Jesus…' the man said. 'You're just…a kid. What are you doing here?'

'I'm here to see a friend.'

'Ah.'

The man stood swaying, thinking this over. He placed the bottle carefully on the ground next to him. Flora watched him closely, prepared to jerk into action if necessary. The man spread out his arms.

'Can I get a hug?'

Flora didn't move. Admittedly, the man did not look mean, just pathetic. But the bad guys only look bad in children's movies. The lowest buttons on his shirt were either unbuttoned or missing, revealing a white belly. His face looked too small for the swollen body and even in the weak light you could see the veins on his cheeks and nose. The man let his arms sink down.

'I have a daughter…had a daughter…she is alive, but…she is your age now, I think.' He reflected. 'Thirteen. Haven't seen her for eight years. Kajsa. That's her name.' He motioned to his pants' pocket, then let the motion die in a *not-there* gesture. 'Had a picture, but...'

He hunched his shoulders and Flora thought he was going to start crying. When she walked past him he stayed put, muttering something to himself.

Peter's window was at ground level and the glass was intact. Since his rooms were originally intended to serve as bicycle storage—and did actually function as such—the window was made of reinforced glass and it would take some determination to smash it. Flora crouched down and knocked.

She heard dragging steps behind her, turned and saw the Finn towering up above her. His arms were outstretched again and an image worthy of Manson flashed through Flora's mind—

crucified broiler

—then the Finn pouted and said in a baby-voice, 'Can I get a wittle hug?'

Flora stood up and moved out of reach. The Finn stayed where he was, arms spread, dog-eyed. Flora narrowed her eyes and tilted her head. 'Don't you get how disgusting you are?'

A flashlight went on behind the glass and she heard Peter's voice, 'Who is it?'

Without taking her eyes off the Finn, Flora said, 'It's me.'

She walked down the small stairs in the bike ramp and came to a locked metal door, decorated with a spray-painting of a summer landscape. It was one of the few doors in the area that had a lock, since Peter had put it in himself. The lock rattled and the door opened. Peter was holding a thin sleeping bag around himself with one hand; in the other he had a flashlight.

'Come in.'

Flora cast a final glance at the Finn who was still standing there, swaying, still with his arms outspread to the night and the memories. Once Peter had closed the door behind them and his flashlight swept across the room she could have been in any residential area. The bicycles were neatly lined up along one side of the room while another wall was reserved for Peter's delivery moped.

Peter continued down toward the far end of the room, the divided section he had built himself, and opened the door hidden in the wall mural. He had managed to avoid eviction every time the police came in; they never noticed his hideaway in their cursory searches.

The room behind the wall was only six metres square. There was room for the bed that Peter had found in a skip and driven home on his moped, a chair, and a table where food items were arranged, a kerosene stove and a container of water—nothing more. On the floor next to the bed he had a boombox connected to a car battery. As if he was playing with the constraints of his environment, Peter used an electric toothbrush and razor. He had a Gameboy and an alarm clock, a mobile phone. The flashlight was an exception, of course. Flora usually brought batteries as a gift.

Peter locked the door and jumped into bed, unzipping the sleeping bag so it became a blanket. Flora took off her shirt and pants, curling up next to him and leaning her head against his shoulder.

'Peter...'

'Mm?'

'Do you know what's happened? Tonight?'

'No.'

She told him the whole story. From the part where she woke up at Elvy's to where she rode into town in the ambulance. When she finished Peter said, 'Strange,' and nestled his arm around her head. After a couple of seconds she heard his breaths deepen, asleep.

Dawn had made a light grey rectangle of the only window by then and Flora lay staring at it for so long that it hovered on her retina for a long time after she closed her eyes.

She could tell by the pressure in her head that she had only been sleeping for a few hours when she was woken by noise in the next room. She sat up in bed and looked through the peep hole. A man of Arab appearance—unusually well-dressed by the area's standards—was coaxing a bike out. Flora wasn't certain, but she thought she recognised him: he had a regular gig holding up one end of a protest banner on Drottninggatan.

The man took his bike and left, locking the door behind him. Peter had only given out keys to those who rented space there. It cost twenty kronor a month to keep a bike in the locked and guarded space. Naturally, the deal came with no guarantee that the police wouldn't confiscate everything if they made a raid.

Flora lay down again but could not fall back to sleep. She alternated between staring at the ceiling, the golden-yellow rectangle and Peter's pimply face on the pillow. After an hour she got up and started to heat water for tea on the kerosene stove.

The hissing from the kitchen area woke Peter. He sat up, looking at the window to judge the time of day, rather than the clock, said, 'Early' and slumped back down on the bed.

When Flora had let the two tea bags sit long enough in the simmering water, she poured out two cups, heaped two teaspoons of sugar in each and took them with her into bed. When they had downed a few sips, Peter said, 'Those things you told me when you got here...'

'Yes?'

'Is it true?'

'Yes.'

He nodded, giving the tea cup a shake, then said, 'Good.' He got up and poured one more teaspoon of sugar in and came back to bed. There were periods when he lived exclusively on tea and sugar.

'You think it's good?' Flora asked.

'Of course.'

'Why?'

'I don't know. Is there more tea?'

'No. The water's finished.'

'We'll get more later.'

Peter got up to pee. His ribs jutted out sharply, as if he had much thinner skin than other people. He removed the wet rag from the pee bucket, got on his knees and tilted it in order to get the right angle. A faint rumble could be heard as the stream hit the metal side. Flora couldn't handle all that. When she was here she dealt with her needs in one of the portaloos outside the area. Even though the county did not want to acknowledge the existence of the Heath, they had brought in the portaloos several years ago and had them emptied regularly after the patch of forest around the corner had become a shit-smelling litter of toilet paper and urine-burned plants.

'It's good if the police have something else to do,' Peter said. 'And it's good if this kind of thing happens. It has to happen.'

'But don't you think it's strange?' Flora said.

'I think it's strange it hasn't happened before. Should we go get more water?'

They put their clothes on and Peter took out the moped. It had taken him half a year to restore and repair the pile of scrap that he had found abandoned and stripped in the woods. Basically, he had only been able to salvage the frame and the wheels. But with found and bartered parts he had managed to make it roadworthy, mounted a cargo tray, sprayed it metallic silver and written 'The Silver Arrow' on the tank in black letters. It was the only possession he cared about. If Flora pictured Peter as Snuffkin from the Moomin books, then the moped was his harmonica.

Flora brought the water container along, sat down on the flatbed. They made a round of the area, helping themselves to three containers that were outside the gates. This was Peter's entire business; he guarded bicycles and fetched and carried—water, among other things. He kept himself alive on food bought from the surplus store with the thousand or so kronor this brought in. Sometimes the market traders in Rinkeby let him have a box of left-over vegetables at the end of the day.

They drove, bumping across the field, onto Akallavägen, and Peter filled up the water containers at the Shell station. It was shortly before nine o'clock and the headline screamers were out.

The dead awaken.
2000 Swedes came back from the grave last night.
The dead awaken.
Exclusive pics of the Fright-Night.

The paper that promised the pictorial spread had a snapshot of what looked like a fistfight on the billboard screamer. People in white were fighting with naked old people between metal counters. The other one looked more like a classic horror film poster; a number of old people in shrouds among gravestones.

'Check that out,' Flora said.

'Yes,' Peter said. 'Can you help me with the containers?'

Together they loaded up the four ten-litre containers. Flora looked around and couldn't help being disappointed. Everything looked normal. The sun shining sleepily on people filling up their cars, walking along the footpath. She went into the station and bought both newspapers. The clerk took the money in silence. When she came back outside there was a guy crouched beside his car filling the tyres.

As if nothing...

Peter started the moped, and she squeezed on holding onto the containers as they drove back across the rutted field. There were no signs anywhere that the world had gone over the edge last night.

She had seen Romero's zombie trilogy and even if *that* wasn't what she had expected, then...something. Anything, other than the newspapers getting a new story to feast on. Peter didn't ask anything, was not getting worked up. That was why she had sought him out; to get away from it. But now as she sat on the shaking flatbed, hugging the containers, she almost longed to get back to the city, to her school, to the hysteria she assumed must be in full bloom there.

What if that's the end of it? Something to talk about for a week and then...gone.

She punched her fist into one of the containers and blinked as the rising tears stung her eyes. She boxed the container again. Peter did not ask why.

Industrigatan 07.41

'How are you, dear? Are you sick?'

'No, I'm just…I just slept badly.'

'How did things go at Norra Brunn?'

'That ended up being cancelled. That thing with the power. I think I have to get going now.'

David reached past his mother for Magnus, who smiled broadly and said, 'I watched TV until ten-thirty! Didn't I, Grandma?'

'Yes,' she said with a sheepish smile. 'It wouldn't turn off, and my head was hurting so much…'

'Mine was too, actually,' Magnus interrupted. 'But I watched anyway. It was Tarzan.'

David nodded mechanically. A lava flow was welling up inside his head, behind his eyes. If he stood here one more second he was going to erupt in some way. He had not slept at all. It wasn't until six o'clock in the morning that someone had told him Eva had been moved to the Medical Examiner's department. He had tried in vain to get more information, then gone home and splashed cold water in his face, listened to messages on the answering machine.

Nothing from the hospital. Only reporters, and Eva's father who was wondering what had happened to her. David couldn't bring himself to talk to either him or his mother. Luckily she had not heard anything.

When Magnus took his hand, he pulled him along somewhat too forcefully. His mother wrinkled her brow and asked, 'And how are things with Eva?'

'Fine. We have to go now.'

They said goodbye and David hurried Magnus down the stairs. On the way to school, Magnus told him about the episode of *Tarzan* he had seen and David nodded, grunting without listening. Half-way there, he guided Magnus to a park bench.

'What is it?' Magnus asked.

David let his hands rest on his knees, stared down into the pavement. He tried to will the glowing heat inside his head to cool off, to calm down. Magnus fussed with his backpack.

'Dad! I don't have any fruit!'

He displayed his empty backpack as evidence and David said, 'We'll buy an apple at the newsstand.'

The everyday words, the normal actions brought a stillness. A sliver of light opened and through it he saw his eight-year-old examine the bottom of his backpack; maybe there was an old apple hidden in there somewhere after all? The morning sun shone on the thin hair at the back of his head.

I'll never let you down, little man. Whatever happens.

The panic ebbed away, replaced by an enormous grief. If only it were this simple: it was a beautiful morning, the sun was pleasantly warm, throwing misty shadows on tree trunks and concrete. Here he was, sitting on a park bench with his son who was on his way to school and needed an apple for his snack. And he was the dad, who could walk into a store, fish out a couple of kronor and buy a large, red apple, and give it to his son, who would say 'nice one' and tuck it into his bag. If that was only the way it was.

'Magnus...' he said.

'Yeah? I'd rather have a pear.'

'OK. But Magnus...'

A great deal of the night had been passed thinking about this moment. What he should say, what he should do. Eva was the one who was good at this stuff. Eva handled the conversations about how Magnus should act if the big kids were mean, if he was scared, or anxious about something. David could be supportive, could follow Eva's guide, but he didn't know where to start. What was right.

'It's just that...Mum was in an accident last night. And she's in the hospital.'

'What accident?'

'She was in a car crash. With an elk.'

Magnus eyes grew wide.

'Did it die?'

'Yes. At least I think so. But it's...Mum will be gone for a few days so that they can...make her better again.'

'Can't I see her?'

A lump grew in David's throat, but before it had time to dissolve into tears he stood up, took Magnus by the hand and said, 'Not right now. But later. Soon. When she's better.'

They walked for a while in silence. When they were almost at the school Magnus asked, 'So when will she be better?'

'Soon. Do you want a pear?'

'Mm.'

David ducked into the newsagents and bought a pear. When he came out, Magnus was staring at the newspaper headlines.

The dead awaken.

2000 Swedes came back from the grave last night.

The dead awaken.

Exclusive pics of the Fright-Night.

He pointed, and asked, 'Is that *true*?'

David glanced at the black letters, screaming on a yellow background. He said, 'I don't know', and put the pear in the backpack. Magnus asked more during the last little bit before school, and David told some more lies.

They hugged at the school gates and David stayed crouched there for a while—saw Magnus walk in through the tall doors with his large bag thumping against his back.

He picked up snippets of a conversation between two parents standing next to him, '...like a horror film...zombies...you can only hope they manage to round them all up...think of what the children...'

He recognised them as parents of children in Magnus' class. He was gripped by a sudden rage. He wanted to throw himself at them, shake them and scream that this wasn't some movie, that Eva wasn't a zombie, that she had just died and then come back to life and soon everything was going to be fine.

As if she had felt his anger streaming toward her, the woman turned around and noticed David. Her hand flew up to her lips and immediate pity altered the expression in her eyes. She walked up to David with nervously fluttering fingers and said, 'I'm so sorry...I heard...how awful.'

David glared at her. 'What are you talking about?'

This was apparently not the reaction she had been expecting, and her hands swung up in front of her as if to ward off his animosity.

'Well,' she said, 'I understand...it was on the news this morning, you see...'

It took several seconds until David made the connection. He had completely forgotten the exchange with the reporters, had experienced it as something so meaningless that it couldn't possibly carry any meaning in the outer world. Even the man now came forward.

'Can we do anything?' he asked.

David shook his head and walked away. Outside the newsagents he stopped in front of the headlines.

Magnus...

Had any of the parents who had watched the morning news said anything to their children, so that Magnus would find out that way? Were people really so stupid? Should he go get Magnus?

He couldn't summon the energy to think. Instead he walked in and bought both papers, then sat down on a bench to read them. When he was done he was going to go out to the Medical Examiner's department and figure out what the hell they were up to.

He had trouble concentrating on the text. The words he had overheard from the other parents kept running through his head.

Horror film...zombies...

He never watched horror movies, but this much he knew: zombies were dangerous. Something that people had to protect themselves against. He rubbed his eyes firmly and focused on the photographs, the text.

The elevator starts with a jerk. I can hear screams through the thick concrete. The morgue level comes into view through the door glass...

The article's rigorous tone of reportage gave way to a plea at the end that made David sit up a little. The writer—Gustav Mahler, David read—had completely inappropriately inserted his own voice in closing.

...we must nonetheless ask ourselves: Is it not for the family members to say what should be done? Can the state authorities alone decide a matter that in the final analysis is about love? I do not think so, and I think others feel the same.

David lowered the paper.

Yes, he thought. Ultimately this is about love.

He folded the newspaper into his pocket like a silent support and hailed a taxi to take him to Solna, where they were keeping Eva prisoner.

Vällingby 08.00

Mahler thought he had just closed his eyes for a few seconds when the alarm went off, but he had slept for three hours, sitting up in the armchair. His body felt like part of the chair, hard to dislodge. Elias was lying on the couch with his head right next to him. He stretched out his arm and placed his finger in Elias' palm; it responded.

He had a memory of writing something for the paper, and it made him anxious. Had he mentioned Elias? In some way he had, but he couldn't recall what. Composing it had been a forty-five-minute rush of letters and cigarettes. Then he had retreated to the armchair, and switched off.

Enough. There were too many other things to consider. He heaved himself up out of the chair and went out on the balcony, lit a cigarette and leaned over the railing. It was a beautiful morning. A clear blue sky and not yet warm. A soft breeze set the cigarette glowing, caressed his chest. His whole body was sticky with dried sweat, and his shirt was stiff, oily. The smoke he was sucking into his lungs tasted of thick heat.

He looked across the courtyard at Anna's window.

I have to tell her.

At around ten o'clock she would visit the grave and see what had happened. He had to spare her that shock, but he was afraid; did not know how she would react. Since Elias' death, only a thin membrane had kept her from tumbling into the final darkness. Maybe it would break now. There was one thing that spoke against this: she had not chosen cremation. She had wanted to have Elias' skin, face, bones to think of, down in the earth. Had wanted to keep him present. Perhaps it even meant that she would get through this. Perhaps.

He put out the cigarette, drew a couple of deep breaths, as deep as he could with his wheezing pipes, and went back in.

Now, with the outside air as a point of comparison, he could tell how bad the room smelled. Stale cigarette smoke mixed with dust and behind this, penetratingly, a strong smell of—

what is it called

—Havarti. Aged cheese. That smell that stayed on your fingers, in scent-memory, hours after you opened the plastic packaging. While he stood still and drew in air through his nose it grew stronger. Elias' belly was swollen like a balloon, yet another button had come off during the night and now his pyjama top was fastened only by a button at the neck.

She can't see him like this.

He half-filled the bathtub, then carried Elias to the bathroom and undressed him. Soon he would be used to it. Soon there would be no more surprises.

Elias' skin was dark green, olive-coloured, and appeared thin—Mahler could clearly make out the blood vessels underneath. There were small fluid-filled blisters scattered across his chest as if he had chickenpox. If he could only eliminate the gas that was inflating his belly. It would make Elias appear less deformed, it would be possible to view him as...as if he had severe burns or something like that.

Elias' face was unmoving as his clothes were removed. Mahler did not know if he could see anything. The eyes were only visible as two drops of dried sap under the sunken eyelids.

Mahler gently lowered him into the bathtub. Elias did not protest. As the water closed around his body he let out a sigh of fetid air. Mahler filled his tooth-brushing glass with water and held it up to the blackened lips. Since Elias made no move to drink it, Mahler tilted the glass so that a little liquid ran into his mouth. It ran out again.

Then he remembered something. Something he had read about Haiti, about the risen dead.

He resisted the impulse to go to the bookshelf and check, he daren't leave Elias alone in the bathtub. He painstakingly sponged off every bit of his body. The worst was the fingers, toes, the penis that were all blue-black with some kind of gangrene and completely bereft of life.

He finished by shampooing Elias' hair. As he slowly rubbed his scalp, Mahler closed his eyes and was able to pretend for a moment. It was basically no different than when he had washed Elias' hair before. But when he opened his eyes and was going to rinse he saw that tufts of hair were hanging from his fingers.

No, no...

He scooped water over the hair, not daring to dry it for fear that more would fall out. The water in the bathtub was brown and Mahler pulled out the plug, then rinsed Elias off with warm water from the hand-held shower.

The belly...that belly...

He laid his hand on Elias' stomach and pressed lightly. When nothing happened, he pressed a little harder. It gave way with a farting sound. He pressed more. The farting continued, as when you let air out of a balloon; a light-brown fluid trickled out of the anus, ran down toward the drain and a smell rose up out of the tub that forced Mahler to turn away, open the lid to the toilet and vomit.

This will be fine...this will be fine...

Yes. Elias looked a little better now, he decided when he turned back. The body had lost its look of starvation, but his skin...

Mahler rinsed Elias off once more, then lifted him out of the tub, swept him up in a white bath towel and carried him to his bed. He fetched a tube of body lotion and rubbed it into every centimetre of his leathery skin. To his elation he saw that after one minute the skin looked as dry as before. That must mean it was absorbing it. He went over the body with lotion again and again until the tube was empty.

When he pinched the skin on Elias' armpit with his thumb and forefinger it was less hard than before. Less like leather, more like rubber. But just as dry. He would have to buy more lotion.

The work granted him a measure of relief. Softening his skin was the first thing he had been able to do for Elias, the only improvement he had been able to achieve.

Haiti...

He did not need to read; he remembered.

In the kitchen he half-filled a glass with water, then poured in a teaspoon of salt and mixed it until it was fully dissolved. He tasted it. Super salty. He filled the glass to the top, mixed it and tasted again. Poured out half and filled it up again. Yes. Now it tasted more or less like sea water.

He hesitated when he came back into the bedroom. The very sick were often given glucose, a sugar solution. He only had superstition to lean on in order to justify this.

But surely it can't actually be...dangerous. Can it?

Elias' life flame was so terribly weak. It felt as if it wouldn't take much to extinguish it completely. But surely a mouthful of salt water wouldn't...?

He sat on the edge of the bed with the glass in his hand.

Haiti was the only place in the world with a widespread belief in zombies. And what the dead need when they return to the world of the living is sea water. In all mythology there is some kernel of truth, otherwise it would not survive. So therefore...

He cupped his hand behind Elias' neck. Drops from the wet

hair ran down over the back of his hand as he lifted Elias into a sitting position and brought the glass to his lips, tilted it and let a small quantity pour in. Elias' throat moved up in a short spasm. And down. He swallowed.

Mahler had to put the glass down on the bedside table and scoop Elias into his arms. He was careful not to use too much force, and risk injuring something in the frail body.

'You can do it, bud, you can do it!'

Elias did not move, his body was as stiff as before, but he had *done* something. He had drunk something.

Maybe Mahler's happiness was not so much to do with the sign of life in Elias, as with the fact that he was able to do something for him. He did not have to stand there at a loss and simply look at him. He could apply lotion to his body, he could give him something to drink. Maybe there were more things he could do, time would tell. Now...

Heady with his success, he took the glass again and brought it to Elias' lips. But he poured it too fast and it ran out again. Elias' throat did not move.

'Wait...wait...'

Mahler ran out into the kitchen and found a small plastic syringe that had come with a bottle of medicine he had bought the last time Elias had a fever. He filled the syringe with salt water from the glass and slowly squeezed ten mils of liquid between Elias' lips. He swallowed. Mahler continued until the syringe was empty. Then he refilled it. After ten minutes Elias had drunk the whole glass and Mahler lowered his wet head against the pillows.

There was no visible difference, but whatever Elias was now, it had a will, or at least an impulse to take something in from the external world...

Mahler tucked Elias into bed, and lay down beside him.

Elias still stank, but the bath had removed the worst of it. The remaining smell was now mixed up with the scent of soap and shampoo. Mahler leaned his head against the pillow and narrowed his eyes, trying to see his grandchild, but it didn't work. The soft profile was competely altered by the jutting cheekbones, the sunken nose, the lips.

He isn't dead. He exists. It will be fine...

Mahler fell asleep.

The clock on the bedside table said half past ten when he was awakened by the telephone. His first thought was: Anna!

He hadn't spoken with her; maybe she had already had time to go to the graveside. He glanced quickly at Elias who was lying exactly as he had left him, then grabbed the phone on his side of the bed.

'Yes, this is Mahler.'

'It's me. Anna.'

Fucking hell. Idiot. How could he have slept? Anna's voice sounded shredded, trembling. She had been out to Råcksta. Mahler lowered his legs over the side of the bed, sat up.

'Yes...hi there. How are you?'

'Daddy. Elias is gone.' Mahler drew in air in order to tell her, but did not get a chance before Anna continued, 'Two men were just here and asked me if I...if I had...Daddy, there has...last night...there are dead people who have come back to life.'

'What kind of men?'

'Daddy, do you hear what I'm saying? *Do you hear what I'm saying!*' Her voice was hysterical, about to escalate into a scream. 'Dead people have come back to life and Elias...they said that his grave...'

'Anna, Anna. Calm down. He is here.' Mahler looked at Elias' head resting on the pillow, touched his forehead with his hand. 'He is here. With me.'

There was silence on the other end. 'Anna?'

'He...is alive? Elias? Are you saying that...'

'Yes. Or rather...' there was a rattling sound on the line. 'Anna?

Anna?' Through the receiver, in the distance, he heard a door open and close.

Damn it...

He got up, groggy. Anna was on her way over. He had to...
What did he have to do?

Lessen, soften...

The blinds in the bedroom were lowered, but that was not enough to conceal Elias' appearance. Quickly, Mahler took a blanket out of the closet and hung it over the curtain rod. Some light came in through the crack on the side, but it was significantly darker.

Should I light a candle? No, then it will be like a wake.

'Elias? Elias?'

No reply. With trembling hands, Mahler drew up the very last water from the glass into the syringe, brought it to Elias' lips. Perhaps his eyes were playing tricks on him now that it was so dark, but Elias did not only swallow, Mahler even thought he moved his lips a little in order to take in the syringe.

He had no time to reflect on this because the front door opened at the bottom of the stairs and he walked out into the hall in order to meet Anna. Ten seconds during which his thoughts whirled, then the doorbell rang. He breathed in and opened.

Anna was only dressed in a T-shirt and panties. No shoes.

'Where is he? Where is he?'

She forced her way into the apartment but he got hold of her, restrained her. 'Anna...listen to me for a moment...Anna...'

She squirmed in his grip, cried, 'Elias!' and tried to free herself. With all the strength he could muster he shouted:

'ANNA! HE IS DEAD!'

Anna stopped struggling, stared at him in confusion. Her eyelids twitched and her lips quivered.

'Dead? But...but...you said...they said...'

'Can you just listen to me for one second?'

Anna suddenly went limp, would have fallen down in a heap

on the floor if Mahler had not caught her and set her down in the chair next to the phone. Her head turned from side to side as if by an invisible power. Mahler placed himself in front of her, blocking the way between her and the bedroom, leaned down and took her hand in his.

'Anna. Listen to me. He lives…but he is dead.'

Anna shook her head, pressed her hands to her temples.

'I don't understand I don't understand what you are saying I don't…'

He took her head between his hands, twisting it with some force to meet his eyes.

'He has been in the ground for a month. He doesn't look like he did before. Not at all. He looks…pretty awful.'

'But how can he…he must…'

'Anna, I don't know. No one knows anything. He doesn't speak. He doesn't move. It is Elias, and he is alive. But he is very changed. He is…as if dead. Maybe there is something that can be done, but…'

'I want to see him.'

Mahler nodded. 'Yes, of course you do. But you have to prepare yourself for…try to prepare yourself for…'

For what? How can one prepare oneself for something like this?

Mahler took a step back. Anna remained seated.

'Where is he?'

'In the bedroom.'

Anna pressed her lips together, leaning forward a little so she could see the bedroom door. She had collected herself. Now she seemed afraid instead. Fumbling with her hand in the direction of the door, she asked, 'Is he…broken?' Her eyes looked at Mahler, pleading. He shook his head.

'No. But he has…dried up. He is…blackened.'

Anna clasped her hands tightly in her lap.

'Was it you who...'

'Yes.'

She nodded, said flatly, 'They were wondering,' and stood up, walking toward the bedroom. Mahler followed, half a step behind. In his thoughts he went through the contents of the medicine drawer, if he had anything tranquilising in case Anna...No. He had nothing like that. Only his words, his hands. Whatever help they might be.

She did not collapse. She did not scream. She quietly approached the bed and looked at what was lying there. Sat down on the bed. After sitting there for a minute looking without saying anything, she asked, 'Would you please go out for a while?'

Mahler backed out and shut the door on them. Stood outside, listening. After a while he heard something that sounded like an injured animal. A drawn-out, monotone whimper. He bit his knuckles, but did not open the door.

Anna came out after five minutes. Her eyes were red, but she was calm. She closed the door gently behind her. Now Mahler was the one getting nervous. He had not expected this. Anna walked out and sat down on the couch. Mahler followed, sitting down next to her and taking her hand.

'How is it?'

Anna stared at the dark television screen. Her gaze was without expression. She said, 'It isn't Elias.'

Mahler did not answer. A pain that started in his heart region radiated out along his shoulder, the arm. He leaned back against the cushions, trying to will his heart to be still, stop fluttering. His face was contorted in a grimace of pain when a hot hand gripped his heart, squeezed and...let go. His heart took up its usual rhythm. Anna had not noticed anything. She said, 'Elias doesn't exist any longer.'

'Anna...I,' Mahler panted.

Anna nodded at her own statement, adding, 'Elias is dead.'

'Anna, I'm...sure that it is...'

'You misunderstand me. I know that it is Elias' body. But Elias no longer exists.'

Mahler did not know what to say. The pain in his arm subsided, leaving behind a peace, the calm after a successful battle. He closed his eyes, said, 'What do you want to do?'

'Take care of him, of course. But Elias is gone. He lives in our memories. That's where he should be. Nowhere else.'

Mahler nodded, said, 'Yes...'

Meant nothing by it.

Solna 08.45

The taxi driver had spent the night transporting patients from Danderyd and was talking about how stupid people were. Scared of the dead in the way they'd be scared of ghosts, when that was not the problem. The problem was *bacteria*.

Take a dead dog in a well. After three days the water is so toxic that you'd be risking your life to drink it. Or take the war in Rwanda: tens of thousands dead, sure, but that in itself wasn't the great tragedy. It was water. Corpses had been tossed into the rivers and then even more had died from lack of drinking water, or from drinking what was there.

The bacteria the corpses brought with them. There was the real danger.

David noted that the driver had a box of tissues attached to the control panel under the meter. He did not know if what the man was saying was true, but the very fact that he believed it...

He stopped listening when the man started to talk about the meteorite from Mars that had landed four years ago. The guy was clearly obsessed, and David paid no attention to the rigmarole about secret test results that had been concealed from the public.

Were they planning to perform an autopsy on her? Had they

already done it?

When they arrived at the Karolina Institute campus the driver asked for a more specific address, and David said, 'The Medical Examiner's Department.'

The driver looked at him. 'Do you work there, or what?'

'No.'

'Lucky for you.'

'Why?'

The driver shook his head and said in the tone of one confiding a secret, 'Let me put it this way…they're a fairly cuckoo lot, some of them.' When David stepped out of the car outside a mundane-looking brick building, the driver looked at him and said, 'Good luck' before driving away.

David went up to the reception and explained his business. The receptionist, who did not appear to have the least idea what he was talking about, made various calls and eventually found the right person. She asked David to have a seat and wait.

The waiting room consisted of a couple of vinyl-covered chairs. These surroundings conjured up a feeling of anxiety in him and just as he was about to get up and wait in the parking lot, someone came through the glass doors that led to the inner region.

Without having thought about it, David had expected a giant of a man in a blood-spattered apron. But it was a woman who came toward him. A small woman in her fifties with short, greying hair, and blue eyes behind enormous glasses. No blood on the white coat. She stretched out her hand.

'Hello. Elisabeth Simonsson.'

David took her hand. Her grip was firm and dry.

'David. I…Eva Zetterberg is my wife.'

'Oh. I see. I am terribly…'

'Is she here?'

'Yes.'

Despite his determination, David grew nervous under the

scrutinising gaze she directed at him, as if searching his innards for the trace of a crime. He crossed his arms over his chest to shield himself.

'I want to see her.'

'I'm sorry. I understand how you must feel. But it's out of the question.'

'Why?'

'Because we are in the process of...examining her.'

David grimaced. He had caught the brief pause in front of the word 'examining'. She had been planning to say something else. He balled his hands into fists, said, 'You can't do that to her!'

The woman tilted her head. 'What do you mean?'

David waved his arms toward the doors the woman had come out of, towards the...wards. 'You can't bloody do an autopsy on someone who is still alive!'

The woman blinked and then did something that David had not been expecting. She burst into laughter. Her little face unfolded in a network of laugh lines that quickly disappeared again. The woman waved her hand, said, 'Excuse me,' pressed her glasses back onto the bridge of her nose and went on, 'I understand that you are...but you shouldn't be concerned.'

'Oh really, then what are you doing?'

'Exactly what I said. We are examining her.'

'But why are you doing it here?'

'Because...well, for example, I'm a toxicologist, that is, a specialist in detecting foreign substances in dead bodies. We are examining her under the assumption that something has, so to speak, been introduced. Something that should not be present. Exactly as we do in the case of suspected murder.'

'But you...cut people up here. Under normal circumstances.'

The woman wrinkled her nose at this description of her place of work, but nodded and said, 'Yes, we do. Because we have to. But in this case...we also have access to equipment that does not exist elsewhere. That can be used even when we are not…cutting people up.'

David sat down on the vinyl chair, cradled his head in his hands. Foreign substances…something that has been introduced. He did not understand what they were looking for. He only knew one thing.

'I want to see her.'

'In case it's any comfort to you,' her voice softened somewhat, 'you should know that all of the reliving have been isolated. Until we know more. You are not the only one.'

The corners of David's mouth twitched. 'The bacteria, right?'

'Among other things, yes.'

'And if I don't give a damn about the bacteria? If I say I want to see her anyway?'

'It doesn't matter. You will have to excuse me. I understand how you…'

'I don't think so.' David stood up and walked toward the door. Before he left, he turned back. 'I may be wrong, but I don't believe you have any right to do this. I'm going to…I'm going to do something.'

The woman did not reply. Just looked at David with a pitying, owl-like gaze that made him furious. The door banged mutely against the doorstop as he flung it open and stormed out into the parking lot.

Attachment 1

Newspapers
[From *Aftonbladet*, 14 August 2002]

Corpses dug up, try to flee
Military open graves

It is six weeks since the 87-year-old died, and his body is in an advanced state of decomposition. But he lives, and early this morning he tried to elude the military cadets who were opening his grave. Shocking scenes such as this were enacted as the military began their work of examining at least 200 graves at the Stockholm Forest Cemetery.

'It is abominable, the worst thing I have ever experienced,' said a young national serviceman.

At half past one this morning, their fears were realised: the buried were alive. *Aftonbladet* was on the scene when the military began their operation at the Stockholm Forest Cemetery. An 87-year-old man was the first to be uncovered. He lived, although six weeks have passed since his burial. His body was in an advanced state of decomposition. The man attempted to flee the scene, but was restrained. Sections of the man's flesh peeled away at the touch. With the aid of the burial shroud, soldiers were finally able to force the man to the ground. Two people were needed to restrain him.

Tried to flee

'There is no alternative, but it is only a temporary measure,' Colonel Johan Stenberg said about the fence that the cadets had just started to construct. In order to restrain the dead the army engineers erected an enclosure. Meanwhile others were digging up coffins without opening them.

'It isn't pleasant, but what can we do?' Colonel Stenberg said, shrugging. The enclosure was finished at two-thirty in the morning and the cemetery was filled with military personnel. No hospital transports were to be seen. The opening of the coffins was begun and a horrifying sight awaited.

The dead attempted to find their way out, fumbling, uncertain. Many tried to elude the military but were quickly brought back.

Psychological pressure
'This is hell on earth,' a cadet said, sitting apathetically next to the enclosure. Behind him stood fifteen of the dead, pressed up against the fence. They stared toward us with their empty eye sockets. The cadet threw himself headlong onto the ground, holding his hands over his ears.

'We assumed this would happen,' Johan Stenberg said. 'That is why we have so much personnel. I feel sorry for the kid. Psychological pressure.'

It was obvious that the colonel did not mean what he was saying.

The ambulances arrive
Three more corpses were dug up before the ambulances arrived. Quarrels erupted in several quarters. Commanding officers had to intervene in several fights. As we went to press, the situation at the Forest Cemetery had basically been reduced to chaos. A few of the dead may have escaped. Nearby residents are urged to keep their doors locked. Today the rest of the graves are scheduled to be opened and then the work will continue at the rest of the eighteen city cemeteries.

[Editorial, *Expressen*]
The impossible happened last night. Two thousand Swedes, either declared dead or buried, returned to life. How this is possible and what will happen remains to be seen, but even now a

fundamental question may be posed: after this, can we regard death as the end?

Probably not.

One of the definitions of man is that he is an animal who is conscious of the fact that he will die. Perhaps the only one. The events of last night will force us to reformulate the conditions of our own existence.

Death is another word for the cessation of metabolism. If we rule out religious or paranormal explanations, then only one alternative remains: the biological mechanism that is our body has the capacity to restart the process of metabolism. At this point there is no definitive research, but there are many indications.

None of the classic signs of death are valid now. We no longer have a way to declare someone dead. Everyone may come back.

During the 1980s a trend began called cryogenics. Wealthy individuals stipulated in their wills that their bodies should be frozen after death. In the USA, in particular, there are thousands of people resting in this state.

It would not be surprising if the much-maligned cryogenics now experiences an upswing. A solution that allows us to preserve our dead body must at least be discussed.

In all likelihood, researchers will be able to determine what has caused the dead to become reliving. Possibly they will be able to repeat the results. A serum against a certain disease can be produced from the blood of a patient who has overcome it. Tonight we have seen thousands of people overcome death. What will we be able to learn?

Our present method of handling the corpse of a human being is basically organised around destroying it. Either quickly, through cremation, or slowly by way of decomposition in the ground.

In the future it must be up to each individual to decide what is to be done. In a month, a year, or perhaps ten years—we may find ourselves with a cure for death.

Who will want to be cremated then?

Radio
[From *Morning Echo* 06.00]

According to military sources this morning, there are around one hundred and fifty graves left to be opened. All of Stockholm's cemeteries will, however, remain closed to the public for the rest of the day...

Twelve people are still missing. In three of the cases, the graves have been found dug up, and the deceased removed...

Press conference currently underway in the Stockholm parliamentary building...

[From *Morning Echo* 07.00]

Family members of the reliving have gathered outside Danderyd Hospital. Head physician Sten Bergwall tells an Echo reporter that at present they cannot allow visitors.

'We still don't know enough. The reliving have been isolated but are receiving the best possible care. As soon as the situation is considered safe we will let in visitors. That could be today, that could be in one week.'...

...from the press conference just ended:

Minister of Social Affairs: At the parliamentary meeting this evening we have decided to prohibit all burials and cremations for an indeterminate amount of time. The four people who have passed away in the Stockholm area during the night have admittedly not shown any signs of awakening, but…

Journalist: Is there room to store so many bodies?

Minister: Yes, for the moment at least. The morgues have never been this empty.

Journalist: But down the track?

Minister: Down the track…we will have to think of something. As you can imagine, there is quite a lot that must be…thought of in this kind of situation.

…the police have now found two of the reliving who were missing. In both cases, family members had concealed them in their homes…

[From *Morning Echo* 08.00]

Staff at Danderyd Hospital with whom Echo news teams have spoken say that the situation has been chaotic throughout the night. In certain wards cooperation has been impossible.

At a crisis meeting earlier this morning it was decided that staff from all wards would be shifted around in order to offset further conflicts…

Even military sources report certain phenomena breaking out in cases of direct contact with large gatherings of the reliving…

Sten Bergwall discusses the practical difficulties of caring for the reliving, particularly those who have been retrieved from the ground, 'Well, technically they are dead, with all the resulting consequences for the human organism. In order to put this more simply, we have had people here all night with equipment in order to change our ordinary rooms to cold storage…on ethical grounds we would rather not use the morgue, but…we are talking of close to two thousand people…'

The funeral home Fonus says that they will naturally comply

with the government's recommendations, but they request a swift notification on technical grounds...

Television
[TV4 morning news 08.30]
In the studio: STEN BERGWALL (SB), head physician at Danderyd. JOHAN STENBERG (JS), Colonel. RUNO SAHLIN (RS), PhD in Parapsychology.

Interviewer: If we could start with practical matters. How many reliving are currently at Danderyd?

SB: One thousand nine hundred and sixty-two. A few more may have been admitted as we are sitting here.

Int: From what I've heard there have been several reliving who have...died again during the night.

SB: That is correct.

Int: Do we know why?

SB: Not really, no. But primarily this involves a few reliving who were...in a very bad state to begin with.

Int: How do you know they've died?

SB: [*smiling*] I could say 'you just know' because that is the case, but more concretely there is a certain...electrical activity in the cerebral cortex that can be measured with an EEG, and when this ceases, there is death. According to current definitions. And the EEG that has been taken on the reliving shows that a certain rudimentary brain function has restarted.

Int: Johan Stenberg, there has been talk of telepathic phenomena?

JS: Yes.

Int: Is it true that those of you who have been in direct contact with the reliving have been able to read their thoughts?

JS: No, the phenomena that have been reported have exclusively involved the living.

Int: Can you tell me about the conflicts that have broken out?

[*JB looks at SB, passing the question over to him.*]

SB: Well, I don't know what has occurred at the cemeteries, but it is true that we have experienced some…differences of opinion at the hospital.

Int: Because you've been able to read each other's thoughts?

SB: There are conflicts in all staff teams and in a stressful situation they have a tendency to come to the fore. We have no reliable evidence that it really is…mind-reading that is the basis for this.

Int: Runo Sahlin…

RS: I think it's remarkable to see two grown people deny evident facts only because it happens not to fit their world view, and the facts are as follows: when a large group of the reliving assembles a kind of force field arises that makes it possible for people around them to read each other's thoughts. I have been to Danderyd myself and experienced this.

Int: Sten Bergwall. How do you explain this?

SB: [*sighing*] The electrical activity in their brains…the amplitude is at most half a microvolt and the frequency of the alpha waves alternates between one and two Hertz. The frequency can therefore be compared to that of a newborn and the amplitude, that is, the strength of the electric current, is so weak that…what would be the comparison? Someone who is going to die in a few seconds. That weak.

RS: You're trying to explain this field not by the fact that their electrical activity is so strong, but that it's so weak?

SB: What I'm saying is that we have never seen patterns like this in living, fully grown humans. It is not impossible that certain kinds of…side effects could arise. We are still waiting for the RMV's results in order to be able to say anything about how it is biologically possible that these bodies can live. [*Sarcastically, to RS*] But maybe you already have an explanation?

RS: Yes. I think their souls have returned. [*Laughing*] If I had been sitting here yesterday morning, telling you that 'tonight the dead will awaken in their graves' I think you would regard me as not simply ridiculous but completely off my rocker. The idea of the soul is ancient and is still cherished by many. There is evidence for the possibility of thought transmission…

SB: Evidence.

RS: Weak, I admit. But it is a possibility. It is not completely out of the question. As opposed to, say, the dead coming back to life. That *is* impossible. Well. And now they have come back to life. And yet you still regard telepathy and the existence of the soul as an absurdity.

Int: Johan Stenberg, what do you say about all this?

JS: I don't believe it is the role of the military to speculate in questions of theology. [*Looks at RS*] There are others better qualified.

RS: Well, then. If there is a soul it would consist of energy. Some form of energy. The source of this field—which we have all experienced—can't be traced to the brain. No. Why not accept the existence of something outside the body that nonetheless belongs to the body, a transcendent substance that…

JS: Forgive a simple soldier, but I have never heard that the soul is located anywhere but *inside* the body.

RS: When we're alive, yes. But it's accepted that the brain is functioning in a hitherto unknown way in this…state of reliving.

Why couldn't the same be true of the soul? If a large number of souls were hovering, so to speak, outside their bodies, could that not give rise to...how can I put this...

Int: Our time is almost up. To wrap up: why do you think this has happened? Johan Stenberg?

JS: If I had an opinion on that subject I would keep it to myself.

Int: Sten Bergwall?

SB: As I said, we're waiting for the results of the tests.

Int: Runo Sahlin?

RS: A mistake has occurred. Something has gone wrong that has...interrupted the normal order.

Int: And that's something I think we can all agree on. Now for the weather. Camilla?

Camilla: The high pressure fronts that have dominated the Stockholm weather for the past few weeks will give way tonight to low pressure coming in from the west. There will be plenty of rain this evening. In the satellite picture we can see...

[CNN World News, 08.30 Swedish time]
...are now searching for explanations of the bizarre events in the Swedish capital. So far none have been found, but the simultaneous awakenings in different locations hint at a driving force. A military commander said this morning that a connection with terrorist activity cannot be ruled out...

[*Long shot of the Stockholm Forest Cemetery. The fence with the dead behind it, the military among the graves.*]

[Spanish television 08.30]
...mucha gente han esperado por la misma cosa a suceer en pueblos

españoles. Pues, el fenómeno parece aislado a Estocolmo, donde los revividos durante la noche han crecido al total de dos mil personas. Ni los médicosni los sacerdotes tienen explicaciónes a dar al multitud de los parientes que se han reunido al frente del hospital de Danderyd esta mañana...

[*Shot of hundreds of people outside Danderyd, a minister gesticulating dejectedly.*]

[Ard Tagesschau 09.00]
...die Forscher, die heute nacht damit beschäftigt waren, das Rätzel zu lösen. Auf der Presskonferenz heute wurde mitgeteilt, dass einige Enzyme, die in den toten Körpern normalerweise zerstört sind, es in den Wiederlebenden nicht seien. Im Moment untersucht man ob diese Enzyme tatsächlich dieselben sind, die lebendigen Körpern ihre Nahrung zuführen...

[*Stock footage of a Swedish laboratory; a number of test tubes lined up in a stand.*]

[TF1 Journal 13.00]
...qui sont sortis des cimetières et des morgues cette nuit. L'Office du Tourisme Francais deconseille à tout le monde d'aller à Stockholm pour le moment. D'autres villes suédoises ne semblent pas être atteintes de ce phénomène et là il n'y a pas de restrictions. Quand les habitants de Stockholm se sont reveillés ce matin, ils ont vu leur realité changée. Pourtaint la vie à la surface semble être retournée à la normale.

[*Cross-cutting between images of the Forest Cemetery, the dead behind the fence, as well as strolling pedestrians on Drottninggatan.*]

14 August II

The green force that drives the flower

Vällingby 11.55

When Anna had been gone for three quarters of an hour, Mahler started to worry. He walked out onto the balcony and scanned the courtyard, her apartment. A fatherly feeling—*what the hell is holding her up*—gripped him and he immediately suppressed it. Caring was the operative word here. Caring and understanding.

For the past few years he had been more of a co-parent than a grandfather to Elias. Perhaps he was trying to recapture what he had lost when Anna was little, when he was in the middle of his career. His babysitting and daycare pick-ups had allowed Anna to live with a measure of freedom that he thought she did not take full advantage of, but since he knew she resisted his advice—*don't you think it's a little late for that*—he tried not to judge her.

And it was probably all his fault anyway. Anna's inability to settle down, to hold onto a job or complete an education was a learned behaviour. And who had taught her this? Gustav Mahler, the career journalist.

They had moved five times during her childhood, every time he got a better job at a bigger paper. By the time Anna was nine and he finally landed a position as a crime reporter for *Aftonbladet*, Sylvia—Anna's mother—had had enough. She left him. But actually he was the one who had left her, much earlier.

So he had certainly taught his daughter how life should be lived. She had studied psychology for six months and before she dropped out she had learned enough to be able to tell him it was all his fault. He agreed whole-heartedly, although he did not say this to her, since he believed that each person was responsible for his or her own fate. Theoretically, anyway.

His relationship to Anna was marked by ambivalence. He thought that she should stop making excuses, pull herself together and do something. He also thought it was his fault that she made excuses, and neither pulled nor did. Yes. He was entitled to think that it was his fault; she was not.

Mahler lit a cigarette and had time for a single drag before three men emerged from Anna's front door. He ducked down, crushing the cigarette on the concrete floor—

so the enemy won't see the smoke

—and listened attentively to hear if the men were approaching his door. No. They left the courtyard, conversing. He could not hear what they said. He tore off the blackened end of the cigarette and lit it again. Inhaled twice. His fingers trembled. They had to get out of here. Now.

He had unplugged the phone and turned his mobile off for fear that someone would call and say something that he would have to pay attention to. Just as he was plugging the phone back in to check the messages, the front door opened and he froze.

'Daddy?'

His fingers relaxed again. He pulled the cord out of the jack as Anna walked into the room, a suitcase in her hand. She put it down and walked over to the balcony window, peering out.

'They left,' Mahler said. 'I saw them.'

Anna's lower lip was bright red from nervous biting.

'They searched the entire apartment. Pushed away the Legos and looked under the bed.' She snorted. 'Grown men. They said that I should…that I had to let them take care of him.'

'Who were they?'

'Police. And a doctor. They had a notice from the epidemi… something. Told me that it was illegal to…that it was dangerous for Elias.'

'You didn't say that he was here?'

'No, but…'

Mahler nodded, closed his laptop and collected the necessary cords. 'We have to leave immediately.'

'To the hospital?'

Mahler closed his eyes tightly and made an effort to keep his voice calm.

'No, Anna. Not the hospital. To the summer cottage.'

'But they told me…'

'I don't give a damn what they told you. We're going.'

When Mahler had finished packing up his computer and turned to walk into the bedroom, Anna was standing in front of the door with her arms crossed over her chest. Her voice was collected, cold.

'You are not the one who makes this decision.'

'Anna, can you move? We have to go. They could turn up at any moment. Take your bag.'

'No, you're not in charge. I'm his mother.'

Mahler's lips curled and he looked Anna straight in the eye as he said, 'I think it's wonderful that you suddenly feel such a great need to be a mother to him, which you haven't done much about for the past few years, but I intend to bring Elias with me. You can do what you like.'

'Then I'll call the police,' Anna said, and the ice in her voice started to crack. 'Don't you understand that?'

Mahler had the ability to manipulate people. If he had wanted, he could have used a mild voice and subtle accusations to get his daughter where he wanted in a couple of minutes. Out of kindness, or lack of time, he did not do this and instead gave his anger free rein—which he thought was fairer play. He put the bag on the table and pointed toward the bedroom.

'You just said that it wasn't Elias! So how the hell can you be his mother?'

It was like opening a vacuum-pack of coffee. Anna sank into herself a little and began to cry. Mahler cursed himself inwardly. Not fair play at all.

'Anna, forgive me. I didn't mean to...'

'You did.' She amazed him by straightening up and wiping her tears with the back of her hand. 'I know full well that you don't give a damn about me.'

'Now you're not being fair,' Mahler started to lose his grip and back-tracked. 'Haven't I been taking care of you this whole time? Every day...'

'Like a package, yes. Something to do. And now the package is in the way, and you have to move it. You have never done anything out of consideration for me. It's your own guilty conscience you're looking after. Give me a cigarette.'

Mahler stopped his hand half-way to his breast pocket.

'Anna, we don't have time...'

'We have time. A cigarette, I said.'

Anna took it and the lighter, lit up and sat down in the armchair, on the very edge of the seat. Mahler stayed where he was.

'What would you say,' Anna started, 'if I told you that this whole time I really wanted to be left alone? That I think it's been a complete drag to have you running in and out every day. I've been eating at the hot dog stand down on the corner, I haven't needed your food. But I let you do it so that *you* would feel better.'

'That's not true,' Mahler said. 'You mean to say I should have let you lie there alone, day after day...'

'I haven't been alone. Some evenings when I felt up to it I've called someone I know and...'

'Oh you have, have you?' Mahler's voice sounded more taunting than he intended.

'Oh give me a break. Each to their own. At least I've grieved for Elias. I'm not sure what you've been grieving for. Some kind of forlorn hope of atonement. But I'm not doing you any more favours.' Anna put out the half-smoked cigarette and walked into the bedroom.

Mahler stood motionless, his arms hanging at his sides. He was not abashed. What Anna said about him made no impact. It was possible that it was true, but he did not think so. The new information she had shared with him, however...He wouldn't have thought she had it in her.

Elias lay on the bed with his arms outstretched, a helpless alien. Anna sat on the edge with her finger in his curled fist.

'Look,' she said.

'Yes,' Mahler said and pressed his lips together in order not to add, 'I know.' Instead he went and sat down on the other side of the bed and let Elias curl his other hand around his finger. They sat like this for a while, each with a finger in his hand. Mahler thought he could hear sirens in the distance.

'What should we give him?' Anna asked.

Mahler told her about the salt. There was the germ of acquiescence in Anna's question, but he did not want to push it any further. Anna would have to decide now. As long as she didn't make the wrong decision.

'What about sugar?' she asked. 'A glucose solution?'

'Maybe,' Mahler said. 'We can try.'

Anna nodded, kissed the back of Elias' hand, coaxed out her finger and said, 'Let's go then.'

Mahler drove the car to the front door and Anna carried out Elias, wrapped up in the sheet, laid him on the back seat and crawled in after him. The car was a sauna after having been parked in the lot all day. Mahler rolled down both windows and popped the sunroof.

Up by the square he parked in the shade and half-ran to the drugstore. He placed ten packets of grape sugar and four bottles of lotion in a basket. A couple of syringes. He ended up lingering in front of the baby items. Then took several baby bottles as well. Made sure they were the kind with only one hole in the nipple.

He did not want to leave Anna and Elias in the car for too long, but the selection in the drugstore bewildered him. His gaze travelled over the shelves of band-aids, mosquito repellent, anti-fungal cream, vitamins and liniments. There must be something else that could help.

At random, he picked out a number of jars of vitamins and herbal remedies.

The lady at the register glanced at his body, then at the items he was purchasing. Mahler saw the cogs move beneath her business-like mask, trying to see a connection between this amount of sugar, bottles, body lotion—and him.

He paid cash, took his over-stuffed single bag and was wished a nice day.

They were silent the whole way to Norrtälje. Anna sat in the back with Elias, in her lap, staring fixedly out the front with his finger in her hand. As Mahler took the turn-off to Kapellskär she asked, 'Why don't you think they will come looking out there?'

'I don't know,' Mahler said. 'I guess I'm hoping they're not so... motivated. And it is more relaxing out there.'

He turned on the radio. There was no music on the public stations, only the commercial stations carried on as if nothing had happened. He kept P1 on for a while, but it added little to their knowledge. Eight reliving were still missing.

'I wonder what the other seven are doing right now,' Mahler said, and turned it off.

'Something similar,' Anna said. 'How can you really think we're doing the right thing and everyone else is wrong?'

Mahler lifted his gaze from the road in order to turn his head and look at Anna for a couple of seconds. Her question was genuine.

'I don't know if we are doing the right thing,' he said. 'But I know that they don't know either. In my line of work...you would be amazed at how many times the authorities do something without knowing why, without knowing the consequences...only so it will look as if they're doing something.' Now they were on their way he dared to ask something himself. 'Don't you think we're doing the right thing?'

Anna was quiet for a moment. In the rear view mirror Mahler saw that she looked down at Elias and a swift grimace flashed across her face. 'Can you open the window a little more?'

Mahler rolled down the window as far as it would go. Anna leaned back so far that her head tipped back over the neck rest. She spoke into the ceiling, 'Why doesn't he stop smelling?'

Mahler glanced back again. Elias' dark green face with its black spots peeked out of the sheet; it made him look even more like a wrapped mummy. .

'I don't want to give him up,' Anna said. 'That's all.'

The vegetation around the cottage was overgrown and dried up. The enormous honeysuckle vine around the porch had grown tremendously at the beginning of the summer, but was now a ropy tangle, as if the porch had been wrapped in packing materials.

Mahler stopped the car ten metres from the front door and turned off the engine.

'Well,' he said and looked out over the brown grass. 'Here we are at last.'

The cottage lay at the end of the loop that was Koholma vacation area. You had to walk a couple of hundred metres through the forest to get to the water, but when Mahler got out of the car he still felt the seaside quality in the air. He drew a deep breath and the promise of freedom filled his lungs.

Now he knew what he had been thinking.

The cottage felt more secure than the apartment. Of course it was the sea that gave you that feeling. The great blue out there. If they came, there was always the option of...leaving. Out to the islands.

The reason that he had even been able to afford the house fifteen years ago now announced itself: a dull thundering filtered through the forest, made the car body vibrate slightly. He sighed.

Five hundred metres to the south lay the Kapellskär Ferry Terminal. Since ferry traffic to Finland and Åland had increased fifteen or twenty years earlier and the ferries had grown and become a recreation for the masses, the real estate values in the adjacent areas had fallen by almost half. It was not quite as bad as living next to an airport, but almost. The ferries came and went around the clock and it would take almost a week to learn not to hear them.

They started to unpack.

Mahler lifted Elias from the backseat and carried him to the house, fishing the key out of the drainpipe and unlocking the door. The house smelled stale. Mahler carried Elias to his room where the treasures of past summers—feathers, stones and pieces of wood—lay scattered on window ledges and shelves.

He laid Elias on the bed and opened the window. The salty air whirled into the room, inviting a dance.

Yes. It had been the right thing to come here. Here there was space and time. Everything they needed.

Täby Municipality, 12.30

After Flora's late-night call, Elvy had trouble falling asleep. She would have to spend some more time with Grimberg. Fittingly—or not—she had just arrived at Gustav II Adolf's death. The description of the widowed Queen Maria Eleonora's bizarre relationship with his corpse kept her glued to the page.

Maria Eleonora had refused to let go. She visited the body again and again, keeping it company the entire length of the journey from Germany. When she was eventually pried away she had managed to acquire the heart (it irritated Elvy greatly that Grimberg never explained *how* she acquired it) and threatened them with it in order to gain access to the body once again...

'Which she ponders, showers with marks of honour and caresses, with no regard for the fact that it blackens and decays, almost beyond the point of recognition,' as a Swedish diplomat wrote during the funereal journey.

Elvy had lowered the book and reflected on this. The difference of views. If the king had arisen from his coffin the jubilant queen would most likely have taken his rotting flesh into her arms. Why was it so different? Was it Elvy who was heartless?

A kind of explanation was to be found several pages on. Maria

Eleanora had had a double coffin prepared, with spaces for the dead monarch and herself. Her motive for this was that she had 'so little enjoyed' the king during his life. Now that he was dead she wished to take full advantage.

This was a problem that Elvy did not share. She had been able to 'enjoy' Tore plenty during his life. This man ten years her senior who had been kind enough to take a hysterical woman in matrimony, to care for her and lead her through life without ever understanding her—she had simply seen enough of him by the time he gave up the ghost. She harboured little animosity—he had done the best he could—but she was done.

Calmed by this thought, she put the book down and tried to sleep, but it wouldn't come. At half past four she had to get up and sit on the toilet for half an hour and when she lay down again the bedroom was getting light. She let the blinds down, took a couple of sleeping pills and finally managed to nod off. She floated in and out of sleep until it was past eleven, at which point she woke up properly, energetic and full of anticipation.

Until she looked at the news.

Hardly a word was said about anything of significance. It was as if it did not exist. From time to time, some minister or bishop was allowed to say a few words, and what did they speak about?

Anxious relatives, the church hotline, the anguish many people felt in this kind of situation, blah blah.

Elvy felt no anguish. She was furious.

Statistics, images of the night's exhumations. They had dug up almost all of the relevant graves by now, and some extras (people who had been dead longer than two months and had predictably remained dead); the number of reliving was close to two thousand.

The Prime Minister had landed a little while ago and was accosted immediately at Arlanda by the reporters. In order to stress the gravity of the situation, he removed his glasses, stared nakedly into the cameras and said:

'Our nation. Is in a state of shock. I hope that everyone. Will help. Not to make the situation. Worse than it already is. I. And my government. Will do everything. In our power. To give these people. The care. That they need.

'But let us not forget...'

His index finger went up and the Prime Minister looked around with an expression that approximated sorrow. Elvy tensed her entire body and leaned closer to the television. It was coming. Finally. The Prime Minister said, 'We shall all go down this road one day. Nothing separates these people. From us.'

He thanked everyone and a path was made for him to get to the waiting car. Elvy's jaw dropped.

Not even him...

She knew that the Prime Minister knew his Bible, he liked to borrow sayings from it. So the disappointment that now, in this hour of need, he hadn't so much as nodded towards the Holy Book was all the worse. When it was actually appropriate.

We shall all follow this road one day...

Elvy snapped off the TV and spoke out loud. 'What a damned... clown!'

She paced through the house, so upset that she didn't know what to do with herself. In the guest room she took out the copied psalms, spotted with Tore's fluids, crumpled them up and threw them in the bin. Then she called Hagar.

Of all her friends from church, Hagar was most on the ball. Over the past twelve years the two of them, along with Agnes, had done the coffee for the Saturday meetings and taken turns providing the cake. Since Agnes had been stricken with sciatica and become less active, it had mainly been Elvy and Hagar who kept things going these last three years.

Hagar picked up on the second ring.

'612-1926!'

Elvy had to hold the receiver away from her ear since Hagar, who was slightly deaf, was almost screaming into the telephone.

'It's me.'

'Elvy! There has been something wrong with your…'

'Yes, I know. Have you…'

'Tore! Has he…'

'Yes.'

'Come back…'

'Yes. Yes.'

There was silence for a moment. Then Hagar said, a little lower, 'I see. Home to you, then?'

'Yes. But they came for him. It's not that. Did you see the news?'

'Of course. All morning. It's completely incredible. Was it awful?'

'With Tore? Yes, a little in the beginning perhaps, but…it went well. It's not that. Did you…did you see the Prime Minister?'

'Yes,' Hagar said, sounding as if she had bitten into something sour. 'What about him?'

Elvy softly shook her head, forgetting that Hagar could not see her gesture. She stared at a little icon hanging in the hallway, and said slowly, 'Hagar. Are you thinking what I'm thinking about this?'

'About what?'

'About what's happening.'

'The Resurrection?'

Elvy smiled. She had known she could count on Hagar. She nodded at the icon—Jesus as the ruler of the world—and said, 'Yes, exactly. They aren't even talking about it.'

'No,' Hagar's volume went up again. 'It's despicable! To think it's come to this!'

They spoke for several minutes in complete accord and hung up with a vague promise to do something, without having discussed what that was.

Elvy felt a little better. She was not alone in what she was thinking. There were probably others. She walked up to the balcony window and looked out, as if searching for them, the others who realised what all this was about. She caught sight of something else, something she had not seen in several weeks: clouds.

These were not the fluffy summer clouds that serve only to emphasise the blueness of the sky. No, these were strong thunder clouds, gliding so slowly in dark banks that they appeared immobile. She felt a tingle in her stomach. Was this it? Was this how it was going to look?

She wandered around over the house for a while, yawning and trying to prepare herself. She did not know how to prepare.

Let him which is on the housetop not come down to take any thing out of his house: Neither let him which is in the field return back to take his clothes.

There was nothing to do. She sat down in the reading chair and looked up Matthew 24 since she had forgotten the rest of the passage. She became frightened by what she read.

For then shall be great tribulation, such as was not since the beginning of the world to this time, no, nor ever shall be.

She saw concentration camps, she saw Flora.

But for the elect's sake those days shall be shortened.

There was no mention of pain and suffering in a regular sense. Only tribulation greater than what has come before. A way of suffering that we have not yet experienced. But perhaps that was the Swedish translation. The original might speak unequivocally of purely physical, unbearable pangs. Elvy's lids grew heavy.

Perhaps in the original translation...Septuagintan...forty monks in forty rooms...one hundred monkeys at one hundred typewriters for one hundred years...

Elvy's thoughts drifted away in an unruly mishmash of images and she nodded off where she was sitting, her chin on her chest.

She was awakened by the television turning on.

The insides of her eyelids turned orange and when she opened her eyes the light from the TV screen was so blinding that she had to close them again. The television glowed like a small sun and she opened her eyes tentatively, squinting.

As she grew accustomed to the intense light she saw that there was a central figure around which the brightness billowed. Or else the rays were streaming out from the figure itself. The woman. Elvy recognised her immediately; trepidation welled up in her chest.

The woman wore a dark blue shawl over black hair, and in her eyes one could discern the grief of someone who had just seen her child die. Who had stood at the foot of the cross and seen them prise the nails from her son's hands with a crowbar. The curved, stiffened fingers that had once been small, and eager for her breast. The grinding of metal pressed through wood, the hands shredded. And everything lost.

Elvy whispered, 'Holy Virgin…' and did not dare to look. Because suddenly she understood what it meant, *tribulation, such as was not since the beginning of the world.* It was what could be read in Mary's eyes. The suffering of a mother confronted with her dead child—and that child the sum of all goodness. Not simply the pain of watching the child that you have nursed and cherished be tortured and executed, but the suffering, too, that there is a world in which such things happen.

From the corner of her eye Elvy saw Mary spread her arms in a gesture of welcome. Elvy was on her way up out of the chair in order to kneel on the ground but Mary said, 'You can sit, Elvy.'

The voice was light, almost a whisper. No great thundering voice from beyond the heavens; rather a beggar girl's shy plea for a spare coin, something to eat.

'You can sit, Elvy.'

Mary knew her name, and in the words there was a hint of the knowledge that Elvy had been running and working all her life, that she now deserved to sit for a while. Elvy dared to glance quickly at the screen and saw that tiny stars glittered on the tips of Mary's fingers. Or drops of water, tears wiped from her eyes.

'Elvy,' Mary said. 'A task awaits you.'

'Yes,' Elvy whispered, without any sound being heard.

'They must come to me. Their only salvation is to come to me. You must make them understand.'

This had occurred to Elvy, and even in the gravity of the moment she saw her neighbours—people, hard eyes, her approaches rebuffed—and she asked, 'How? How will I get them to listen?'

For one second she stared straight into Mary's eyes and was filled with terror. For in them she saw the suffering that would befall mankind if it did not repent, seek redemption in her arms. Mary held out her hand, said, 'This shall be your sign.'

Something touched Elvy's forehead. The television went off. She fell sideways on the chair and her head exploded.

The edge of the glass table was pressed against her forehead when she opened her eyes. Her head hurt. Dizzy, she straightened up on the chair, looking at the table. There was a smear of red on the corner. Several drops of blood had fallen on the rug.

The television was dark, quiet.

She stood on shaky legs and walked out into the hall, looked in the mirror.

A cut, completely level, three centimetres long but shallow, ran like a minus sign across her forehead above her eyebrows. Blood still welled thickly from the wound and she wiped a drop from her eye.

She blotted the rest of the blood away in the kitchen with a wad of paper towel. She could not bring herself to throw it away, so she placed it in a glass jar, screwed on the lid.

Then she called Hagar.

While the phone rang, she closed her eyes and saw Mary before her. There was one thing she did not understand. When Mary reached out her hand to touch her forehead, Elvy had momentarily glimpsed what it was that glittered on the tips of her fingers. It was hooks. Tiny, thin ones, no larger than ordinary fishing hooks were sticking out of her flesh.

In a way that she could not fully articulate she was convinced that Mary was only an image, created for her human eyes. She was a representation in the form of the Holy Mother. But the hooks? What did the hooks mean?

When Hagar answered, Elvy pushed these questions aside and began to relate the greatest moment of her life.

Koholma 13.30

Anna lifted the bags out of the boot as Mahler disappeared into the house. She carried them across the yard, past the pine tree where Elias' swing was wrapped around the trunk, past the outdoor table that was dry and cracked from having been out in the weather all year. She stopped there and put the bags down. She stood still, taking stock of the situation.

How had this happened? How had she been reduced to some kind of servant while her father took care of what had been her child?

The heat was oppressive in a way that foretold thunder. She looked up at the sky. Yes. The sky was covered with a paper-thin white membrane and from inland a dark mass of clouds was moving toward the coast. It was as if all of nature was trembling with anticipation. The grasses conferenced in whispers about the mercy that was about to pour from the heavens.

She felt dizzy, almost nauseated. For over a month she had lived in a vacuum, restricting her movements, her speech, to a minimum so as not to attract attention from life and allow it to start tearing and clawing at her. For over a month she had been as good as dead.

And then, suddenly: Elias back, the police poking around, flight and action, talk and decisions. She could not decide. Her father made her decisions. She had slipped out of the picture.

Anna left the bags where they were and walked into the forest.

Last year's dried leaves crunched underfoot, the shallow roots of pine trees protruded out of the turf, pressed up into the bottoms of her feet. The rumbling from Kapellskär hovered in the forest like an anxiety. She walked aimlessly down toward the boggy areas closer to the sea.

There was a tangy smell of sun-cooked pine needles and thickly layered sludge when she reached the open, moss-covered expanse. Even the moss, which was normally a bright green from the moisture of the wetland had dried up and become light green, beige in places. When she walked on it, it crackled until her foot sank into the mossy underlayers, as if she was walking on crusty snow.

She waded out toward the centre. The deciduous trees that encircled the bog raised their crowns into a cupola, pierced in places by the sun. She lay down when she reached the centre. The moss accepted her, welled up around her. She stared up at the lazy movements in the lattice of foliage, and disappeared.

How long had she lain there? Half an hour? An hour?

She would have stayed longer if her father's voice had not called her home.

'Anna...Aaannaa!'

She stood up from the bog's embrace, but did not answer. She was too preoccupied with the feeling that had taken up residence in her body, especially her skin. She looked back at the place where she had lain. The contours of her body were clearly visible in the moss, which was now—with an almost audible groan—resuming its old form.

She had changed her skin. That was how she felt. What she was looking for was her old skin which should be lying there wrinkled and used up in the mossy depression.

It wasn't to be found, but the feeling was so strong that she had to pull up the sleeve of her T-shirt and check if the tattoo was still there.

Yes. *Bad to the bone* was still etched on her right shoulder in tiny block letters. Some kind of pride had forced her to keep it instead of having laser removal, even though it was twelve years since she had severed contact with the world to which the tattoo belonged.

'*Aannaa!*'

She walked to the edge of the bog and cried, 'Here I am!'

Mahler stopped where the moss began, as if it were quicksand. He put his hands on his hips.

'Where have you been?'

Anna pointed out to the centre. 'There.'

Mahler frowned and looked out at the depression in the moss.

'I've carried everything inside,' he said.

'Good,' Anna answered and walked past him towards the house. He walked behind her, his hand brushing off her back.

'Look at you,' he said.

She didn't answer. Her steps across the roots were feather light. There was something delicate and precious in her that might shatter if she spoke. They walked silently toward the house and she was grateful that he did not start to explain her own behaviour to her, as he had done when she was younger; that he let her be.

On the table next to Elias' bed there was a packet of dextrose, salt, a jug of water and a measuring cup, two syringes.

Anna could not see any change. Mahler had spread a clean, white sheet over Elias whose old-man hands rested at his sides, two shrivelled bird claws. She was looking at a corpse. The corpse of her son. Maybe something could be changed if only he wanted to open his eyes and look at her. But under the half-closed lids there was only that hint of lifeless plastic, like a dried contact lens. Nothing.

Maybe there was a way back. Her father seemed to think so. But in that case the way was so long that she could not imagine its start, far less its end. Elias had died. A shadow of him lay here, but nothing of the boy she had loved, of whom she held memories she wanted to cherish unspoiled.

Mahler came in and stood next to her. 'I gave him sugar solution with the syringe. He drank some.'

Anna nodded, and crouched down next to the bed.

'Elias? Elias? Your mummy is here.'

Elias did not move one millimetre. Nothing indicated that he heard her. The delicate stuff inside her contracted, became dislodged, and the black grief towered up inside her chest. She quickly got up and left the room. The kitchen smelled of freshly brewed coffee and everything fell back into place.

She would take care of him. She would do what she could. But she was not going to entertain for one second the notion that she was going to get her boy back, did not intend to imagine in any way that her son was buried inside that mummified form somewhere, struggling to get out. That would break her for sure; that would hurt too much.

She poured two cups of coffee and put them on the table. She was calm now. They could talk. Outside, the covering over the sky was turning to grey. A faint breeze rustled the trees. She glanced at her father.

He looked tired. The bags under his eyes were more pronounced than normal and his entire face seemed pained by gravity, pulled down toward the earth in folds and wrinkles.

'Daddy? Don't you want to rest a little?'

Mahler shook his head so that his cheeks wobbled.

'Don't have time. I called the paper and someone's been looking for me: the husband of the woman who...well, they wanted me to write more, but I'll have to see...and we need food and things...'

He shrugged and sighed. Anna took a few sips of coffee; stronger than she liked, as always when her father made it. She said, 'You can go. I'll stay here.'

Mahler looked at her. His eyes were small and bloodshot, almost disappeared into the swollen flesh.

'You'll manage, then?'

'Yes, of course.'

'Are you sure?'

Anna put the coffee mug down, forcefully. 'You don't trust me. I know that. But I don't trust you either. It runs deep. I don't know what you want.'

She got up from the table and went to the fridge to get some milk for the coffee. The fridge was empty. When she came back to the table, Mahler had sunk into his chair.

'I just want everything to be all right.'

Anna nodded, 'I believe you. But you want it to be how you think it should be. How you've planned, in your extremely rational way. Go on. I'll manage here.'

They made a list of items they needed to buy, planning the purchases as if stocking up for a siege.

When Mahler had left, Anna checked on Elias, then walked around the house and shook out the rugs, brushed dead flies from the window sills and vacuumed. As she was wiping the kitchen counter she caught sight of the two unused baby bottles. She put the vacuum cleaner away and went in to Elias. She shook some dextrose into the bottle, filled it with water and shook it until it dissolved. Then she sat there with the bottle in her hand and looked at Elias.

Simply feeling the shape of the bottle in her hand brought back memories. Right up until the age of four, Elias wanted to have a bottle of milk in bed when he was going to sleep. He had never used a dummy or sucked his thumb, but he wanted his bottle.

She had sat like this on the side of his bed countless times as he was going to sleep. Kissed him and said good night, then given him his bottle. Felt that feeling of satisfaction as his little hands took hold of it, his mouth sucked onto the nipple and his gaze grew distant. That he managed.

'Here, Elias...'

She brought the teat to his mouth. Mahler had said that would come later, that Elias couldn't manage to drink by himself yet. But she wanted to try. The dry rubber nudged his lips. He did not move them. Carefully she pushed it in between his lips.

Something happened. At first she thought an insect was crawling on her stomach and she looked down. Elias' fingers were moving slightly. Stiffly, slowly, but they were moving.

When she looked up at his face again, his lips had sealed themselves around the teat. And he was sucking. Tiny, tiny movements in the tinder dry lips, a muscle in his throat faintly working.

The bottle shook in her hand and she clapped her other hand over her mouth so hard that she felt a metallic taste on her tongue.

Elias was drinking from the bottle.

It hurt so much she could not breathe, but when the first wave of pain, of hope, had stilled, her hand reached out and she caressed his cheek as he continued to drink. She bent her head over him.

'My boy...my good little boy...'

Kungsholmen 13.45

Children, children, children...

David stood in the school yard and watched as the children poured out of the school like a liquid. Three, four, ten, thirty multi-coloured little beings with backpacks ran down the stairs. Pieces of humanity, a mass to direct and discipline. Four hundred of them were stuffed into this building six hours a day, four hundred were let out again when those six hours were up.

Material.

But zoom in on one single child and there you had an upholder of the world. A child with a mother and father, grandparents, relatives and friends. A child whose existence is necessary for the proper functioning of many lives. Children are fragile, and carry so many lives on their frail shoulders. Fragile is their world, controlled by adults. Everything is fragile.

All day David had walked around as if in a dream. After the visit to the Medical Examiner he had gone to a pizzeria and drunk a litre of water, then lain down under a tree in the park and slept for almost three hours. When a barking dog woke him up, he opened his eyes to a world that had shut him out. People were having picnics, children were running on the grass. He was no longer part of this life.

The only thing that seemed to have anything to do with him was the black clouds that were slowly approaching. As yet, they were still distant, but they looked to be closing in on Stockholm. He heard a roaring in his ears, felt an itch behind his eyelids. The sunshine did not reach in under his tree, so he curled up against the trunk, picked up the newspapers and read the article again. This too seemed to be about him.

Without really knowing what he wanted to say, what he actually wanted, he took out his cell phone and dialled the newspaper. He told them who he was and said he was looking for Gustav Mahler. He learned that Mahler was a freelancer; unfortunately they could not give out his number, however they would pass on a message and was there anything in particular he wished to say?

'No, I just wanted...to talk to him.'

This would be relayed.

David took the subway back to Kungsholmen. Everyone in the subway carriage who was talking, was talking about the dead. They all thought it was horrible. Someone noticed him, realised who he was and went silent. No condolences this time.

Even on his way toward the school he felt how the threads that usually connected him to the world were severed. At most he was a pair of eyes hovering through the air, avoiding obstacles, stopping for a red light. At the school he grasped a black metal railing, held onto it.

Then the bell rang and the children came pouring out. He opened his eyes and saw the mass of biological tissue that hopped and skipped its way down the stairs and he held onto the railing so that he would not float away.

When the flood had spread out across the school yard and started to gush through the gates, Magnus came out. Pushed open the doors with all his might and ended up standing on the landing, looking around.

David became aware of the railing in his hand. Aware that he had a hand that was holding onto the railing; that the hand was attached to a body that was his. He fell back into his body and became…a father. He was back in the world and he went to meet his son.

'Hi buddy.'

Magnus hoisted his backpack and stared at the ground.

'Dad…'

'Yes?'

'Has Mum become like one of those orcs?'

Evidently there had been talk at school. David had gone back and forth about how to tell him, how he would take it one step at a time, but now that possibility was gone. He took Magnus by the hand and they started to walk home.

'Have you talked about it at school today?'

'Yes. Robin said that it was the same thing as the orcs, that they eat human flesh and stuff.'

'Well, what did the teacher say?'

'Said that it wasn't like that, that it was like…Dad?'

'Yes.'

'Do you know who Lazarus is?'

'Yes. Come on…'

They sat down on the edge of the sidewalk. Magnus took out his Pokémons.

'I've traded five cards. Do you want to see?'

'Magnus, you know…'

David took the cards out of Magnus' hand, and Magnus let him. He stroked the back of his son's head; the thin summery white-blond hair, the fragile skull underneath.

'First of all. Mum hasn't become one of those…orcs. She has just been in an accident.'

The words dried up, he did not know how to go on. He flipped through the cards; Grimer, Koffing, Ghastly, Tentacool; all more or less terrifying creatures.

Why does everything in their world have to be about horror?

Magnus pointed at Ghastly. 'Scary, isn't he?'

'Mmm. You know, it's…you know what you were talking about today. It has happened to Mum. But she is…much healthier than all the others.'

Magnus took back his cards, sorted through them for a while. Then asked, 'Is she dead?'

'Yes, but…she's alive.'

Magnus nodded. 'So when is she coming back?'

'I don't know. But she is coming back. Somehow.'

They sat quietly next to each other. Magnus went through all his cards. Looked carefully at a couple. Then his head pulled down to his shoulders and he started to cry. David threw his arms around him and Magnus curled up into a ball, pressed his face against David's chest. 'I want her to be home *now*. When I get home.'

The tears welled up in David's eyes as well. He rocked Magnus back and forth, stroking his hair.

'I know, sweetheart…I know.'

Bondegatan 15.00

The curved stone staircase to Flora's apartment on the third floor was worn by generations of feet. Like most of the old houses, this building on Bondegatan was aging with dignity. Wood and stone bulged or wore away; there was not the crack and break of concrete. A building with character, and Flora loved it despite herself.

She knew how each one of the forty-two steps looked, knew each irregularity in the stairwell walls. About a year earlier she had drawn an anarchist symbol the size of a fist down by the front door in felt pen. She had been jarred herself by the sight of it each time she walked by, and was relieved when it was painted over.

Her head was spinning when she reached the top of the stairs. She had eaten nothing all day and had only had a few hours' sleep at night. She opened the door and had time to hear a couple of seconds of grinding techno from the living room before it was turned off. Then an agitated whispering and rapid movements.

When she reached the living room, Viktor—her ten-year-old brother—and the friend, Martin, at whose place he had spent the night, were each sitting in an armchair absorbed in a Donald Duck comic.

'Viktor?'

He answered 'Mmm' without raising his eyes from the magazine. Martin raised his comic so she couldn't see his face. She did not waste her breath on them, instead she pressed the eject button on the VCR and took out the tape, holding it out to Viktor.

'What the hell are you doing?' He did not answer. She snatched the comic from his hands. 'Hello! I asked you something.'

'Give it a rest,' Viktor said. 'We just wanted to know what it was.'

'For an hour?'

'Five minutes.'

'That's a crock. I know by the music where you were. You almost saw the whole thing.'

'How many times have you seen it then?'

Flora banged the video—*The Day of the Dead*—into Viktor's head with a judicious amount of force.

'Stay away from my stuff.'

'We just wanted to see what it was.'

'I see. Was it fun?'

The boys exchanged glances and shook their heads. Viktor said, 'But it was cool when they pulled them apart.'

'Mm. Really cool. We'll see what kind of dreams you have tonight.'

Flora did not think they would dip into her video library anymore. She sensed the childish revulsion and fear seeping from their bodies. The movie had made its mark. Probably Viktor and Martin would now be haunted by the images the way she had been after seeing *Cannibal Ferox* at an older friend's house when she was twelve. It had never left her.

'Flora,' Viktor asked. 'Is it true that they've come up out of the graves? For real?'

'Yes.'

'Is it like it is on there?' Viktor pointed to the cassette in Flora's hand. 'That they eat people and stuff?'

'No.'

'So what is it then?'

Flora shrugged. Viktor had been very sad about their grand-father's death, but Flora had intuited that it was less the person he grieved for than the fact of death itself. Death meant that people actually disappeared. That everyone was going to disappear.

'Are you scared?' she asked.

'I was super scared when I walked home from school,' Martin said. 'I kept thinking everyone was one of those zombies.'

'Me too,' Viktor said. 'But I saw one for real. He was totally sick in the eyes. Man, I ran so fast. Do you think Grandpa will get like that?'

'Don't know,' Flora lied and went to her room.

She nodded at Pinhead who was staring at her from the poster on the wall, and then she put the video back on the shelf. She should eat something but did not have the energy to go to the fridge and get it all the together. It felt good to be hungry—ascetic. She lay down on the bed and her body was at peace.

When she'd rested for a while she took down the *Pretty Woman* DVD case and took out the razor blade she kept inside. Her parents had never found it during the phase when she used it.

The scars on her arms were from her amateur period, she had quickly moved on to cutting herself under her collar bones, shoulder blades. There were a couple of scars on the outside of her shoulder blades that were so deep it almost looked like a pair of wings had been cut off. A beautiful thought, but that time she had gotten scared; it wouldn't stop bleeding and it was around that time that the conversation with Elvy happened. Life became slightly more bearable and the wing-scars became the last.

She looked at the knife, unfolding it and turning it between her fingers and…yes. She hadn't been this close to wanting to hurt herself in a long time.

Her gaze ran over the titles in the bookcase to see if she wanted to read anything. There was mostly horror there. Stephen King, Clive Barker, Lovecraft. She had read them all, had no desire to re-read anything. Then she caught sight of a picture book, an author's name, and a little bell went off inside her head.

Bruno the Beaver Finds His Way Home by Eva Zetterberg. She took the book down, looked at the picture of the beaver standing in front of his house: a mound of sticks in the middle of a river.

Eva Zetterberg...

That's right. She had read about her in the paper. She was the one who could talk, the one who had been dead the shortest time.

'Too bad,' Flora said to herself and opened the book. She had the other one as well, *Bruno the Beaver Gets Lost*, which had come out five years earlier, and had been looking forward to the third one that she had heard would soon be out. Of all the books she had been given by her parents, she liked the Bruno books the best, except for Moomin. She had never been able to stand Astrid Lindgren.

What she had liked and still appreciated was the straightforward approach to sorrow, to death. In the Moomin books it had been called Mårran, in the Bruno books it was the Waterman who posed a constant threat lurking in the river. He was death by drowning, he was the force that swept Bruno's house away, the destroyer.

After she had read part of the book she started to cry. Because there would never be another book about Bruno the Beaver. Because he had died with his creator. Because the Waterman had finally got him.

She cried and couldn't stop. Stroked the book and Bruno's shiny fur and whispered, 'Poor little Bruno...'

Koholma 17.00

Mahler drove through the seaside village, his car fully loaded, on his way home. The holiday season was over and there were few people in the cottages. By the weekend there would be even fewer.

The closest neighbour, Aronsson, was standing by the road watering his climbing plants. Mahler suppressed a grimace when Aronsson spotted him, waved him over. He couldn't wilfully ignore him. So he stopped and rolled down the window. Aronsson came up to the car. He was in his seventies, thin and bony and with a denim fisherman's hat on his head. It said *Black & Decker.*

'Hello, Gustav. So you're out here at last.'

'Yes,' Mahler said and pointed at the watering can in Aronsson's hand. 'Is that necessary do you think?'

Aronsson glanced at the sky where the clouds were piling up and shrugged. 'It's become a habit.'

Aronsson was protective of his creepers. Thick, luxuriant strands wound their way around the metal archway that framed the entrance to his property. A wrought iron sign at the top of the frame announced 'THE PEACE GROVE.' After his retirement, Aronsson had made his summer cottage into the tidiest Swedish paradise that could be imagined. There was currently water rationing but to judge from the greenery within the archway, Aronsson had paid no attention to that.

'You know,' Aronsson said. 'I took some of your strawberries. I hope you don't mind. The deer were after them.'

Mahler said, 'No. It's good they didn't go to waste,' even though he would rather the deer ate his strawberries than Aronsson.

Aronsson smacked his lips. 'You got some nice berries. That was before the drought, of course. By the way, I read what you wrote. Do you really think that, or was it just for...well, you know.'

Mahler shook his head. 'How do you mean?'

Aronsson immediately back-pedalled. 'No, I just meant...that it was well-written. It's been a while now, hasn't it?'

'Yes.'

Mahler had been letting the engine idle. Now he turned his face back to the road to demonstrate that he needed to get going, but Aronsson took no notice.

'And now you're out here and you have your daughter with you.'

Mahler nodded. Aronsson had a frightening grasp of everything that went on. He remembered names, dates, events; kept track of what everyone in the vacation village was up to. If a Koholma newsletter ever started up, Aronsson would be a shoo-in for editor.

Aronsson looked in the direction of Mahler's house; it lay beyond the bend and—thank God—could not be seen from here.

'And the little one? Elias. Is he...?'

'He's with his father.'

'I see. I see. That's how it is. Back and forth. So it's only you and the girl, then. That's nice.' Aronsson glanced into the back seat, which was filled with bags from the Flygfyren in Norrtälje. 'Are you staying long?'

'We'll see. You know what, I have to...'

'I understand.' Aronsson jerked his head in the direction of the road behind them, adopting a pitying tone. 'The Siwerts have cancer, did you hear that? Both of them. Got the diagnoses only a month apart. That's how it is sometimes.'

'Yes. I've got to...' Mahler touched the accelerator even though he was idling and Aronsson took a step away from the car.

'Of course,' Aronsson said. 'Home to the girl. Maybe I'll look in on you one day.'

Mahler could not immediately think of a plausible reason to say no, so he nodded and drove home.

Aronsson. Somehow he had managed to forget that there were other people in the area. He had only seen the cottage, the forest, the sea. Not long noses that liked to poke in where they'd no business.

Who called the police as soon as an unknown car was parked a little too long in the area? Aronsson. Who had tipped off social security that Olle Stark, who was on disability, was working in the forest? No one knew. Everyone knew. Aronsson.

And what had he meant by that, *do you really think that?*

They would have to be careful. Damn it. Aronsson was a self-righteous old bugger; why couldn't anyone get it together to burn his house down, preferably when he was asleep inside it?

Mahler clenched his teeth. As if they didn't have enough problems.

He got out of the car and started to unload irritably. When a handle on one of the paper bags broke and a couple of kilos of fruit and vegetables tumbled out he just wanted to swear and kick it all to hell. He managed to control himself—because of Aronsson, which just made him even angrier.

He walked toward the house with the bag in his arms and could not help sneaking a glance over his shoulder, checked to make sure Aronsson was not peeking from up at the bend. He wasn't.

Mahler put the bag down on the kitchen table and called out 'Hello?' When no one answered, he went into the bedroom.

Elias was lying as he had left him, but now his hands were up on his chest. Mahler swallowed. Would he ever get used to him looking like this?

Next to the bed, on the floor, was Anna. She was lying like a dead person, wide eyes staring at the ceiling.

'Anna?'

Without lifting her head, she answered in a weak voice, 'Yes?'

A baby bottle was lying beside Elias' head. A little bit of liquid had spilled out onto the sheet. Mahler picked it up and placed it on the bedside table.

'What is it?'

The feeling of irritation was still there. It had been a lesser form of hell to run around Norrtälje in the oppressive heat, dutifully fetching and carrying. He had hoped to come home to a little peace and quiet. But now there was something new. Anna did not answer. He wanted to poke at her with his foot, but restrained himself.

'Come on, what is it?'

Anna's eyes were swollen, red. Her voice was only a whisper through layers of old tears. 'He's alive...'

'Yes. I know.' Mahler picked up the baby bottle, shook it. There was a pinch of undissolved sugar at the bottom. 'Have you given him this?'

Anna nodded mutely. 'He drank.'

'Yes, well, that's wonderful.'

'He sucked.'

'Yes.'

Mahler knew he should be more enthusiastic about this news than he could manage; his head was a daze of sleep deprivation, exhaustion and heat.

'Can you help me unload the rest?'

Anna lifted her head and looked at him. For a long time. Regarded him as if he were a creature from another planet that she was trying to understand. He wiped his forehead with his sleeve and said, annoyed, 'I have frozen food that will melt if we don't...'

'I'll get it,' Anna said and stood up. 'I'll unpack. The frozen stuff.'

There was something that needed to be said at this point. Something had gone wrong. He did not have the energy to think. When Anna went to the car he locked himself in his room and lay down on the bed. Distractedly he noted that the room had been cleaned while he was gone. Only the tangles of cobwebs in the cornices betrayed the fact that no one had lived here for a while. In a daze he heard Anna come in, the rustle of paper bags as she put things away in the kitchen.

The larger bag says it all...

He wasn't sleeping, but his body sank slowly down to the point where he jerked, a click and he opened his eyes, feeling much more alert than he had all day. He lay in bed for a while, enjoying the fact that he no longer felt as if he had sand under his eyelids. Then he got up and went out into the kitchen.

Anna was sitting at the kitchen table reading one of the books he had checked out of the library.

'Hello,' he said. 'What are you reading?'

Anna showed him the cover: *Autism and Play*, then returned to her reading.

He hesitated for an instant, then walked into the bedroom and stopped short. Elias was lying in bed with a baby bottle that he was holding by himself. Mahler blinked, walked closer.

It was probably only his imagination, sparked by the fact that Elias was doing something that any child could do, but he thought Elias' face looked slightly...more healthy. Not as stiff and hard, not as old man-like. As if a smidgen of light and relief had spread across the dry skin.

The eyes were still closed and with the bottle in his mouth it looked more as if he was...savouring it. Mahler sank to his knees by the bed.

'Elias?'

No answer, not a single movement that indicated that Elias saw or heard. But his lips were moving in a barely perceptible sucking motion and his throat was swallowing. Mahler reached out his hand and gently touched the curly hair. It was soft and smooth under his hand.

Anna had put the book down and was looking out the window on the wall of pine trees and the lone, tall ash tree where the sketch of a tree house—some planks and boards—was attached between the branches. She and Elias had started to build it last summer; Mahler was not one to climb up ladders.

Mahler stopped behind her and said, 'Fantastic.'

'What? The treehouse?'

'No. The fact that he's drinking. By himself.'

'Yes.'

Mahler took a deep breath, and let it out again. Then said, 'Forgive me.'

'For what?'

'Because I...I don't know. For everything.'

Anna shook her head.

'It is what it is.'

'Yes. Would you like some whisky?'

'Yes.' Mahler poured a little in two glasses, then put them on the table. He raised his to Anna and said, 'Truce? For now?'

'Truce. For now.'

When they had each swallowed a sip, they sighed at the exact same time which made both of them smile. Anna told him how she had massaged Elias' hands and fingers for a long time until they felt softer, how she had then put the bottle in his hands.

Mahler told her about Aronsson, that they had to be careful, and Anna made a terrible face, mimicking Aronsson's inquisitorial expression.

Mahler picked up the book that Anna had been reading, asked, 'What do you think?'

'It's good. But this whole…training routine that they describe, it's for…' Anna's voice faltered, 'for healthier children.' She covered her face in her hands. 'He's in such a bad way.' The air pushed out of her lungs in a convulsive exhalation.

Mahler stood up, came up next to her and held her shoulder and head against his stomach. She let him. He stroked her hair and whispered, 'It will be fine…It will be fine…just look at what happened today.' She pressed her head against him and he said, 'We have to have hope.'

Anna nodded against his stomach.

'I do. And that's what's so terribly fucking painful.'

Suddenly she jerked away, wiped her eyes and got up, said, 'Come on.'

Mahler followed her into the bedroom. They sank down onto Elias' bed next to each other. Anna said, 'Hi sweetie. Now both of us are here.' She turned to Mahler. 'Dad. Look at his face. Tell me if I'm crazy.'

Mahler looked. Whatever it was he had seen when Elias was holding the bottle was gone. His face was closed, lifeless. His heart sank. Anna turned down the sheet. Mahler saw that she had dressed him in a pair of his old pyjamas that had been left at the cottage and that only reached to his knees.

Anna placed the index and middle fingers of one hand on Elias' thigh. Then she started to walk her fingers up toward his belly while she sang:

A mouse is coming…it crawls and walks…

She walked her fingers across his hip.

It crawls and walks…and suddenly it says…

She poked Elias' bellybutton.

PEEP!

And Mahler saw. Only a suggestion, like a faint twitch. But it was there. Elias smiled.

Täby Municipality 18.00

Hagar patted her right knee.

'We'll have rain, I think. I've felt it in this old knee all afternoon.'

Elvy leaned against the window and looked out. Yes. She didn't need a psychic knee to know something was coming. The cloud masses were close enough to block the sun and turn the afternoon to evening. The air was loaded with static. To Elvy it could only mean one thing. She rinsed out the empty tea cups and said out loud, 'We have to go out this evening.'

Hagar nodded in agreement. She was prepared. Over the telephone Elvy had told her to wear something decent, in case it turned out that they needed to get started on their task immediately.

The dark blue silk dress with tiny stars that Hagar had chosen was perhaps a little showy for Elvy's taste, but Hagar had said it was a 'momentous occasion' and she could hardly argue with that.

Hagar had no doubts. When Elvy told her about the vision, she chuckled with delight and congratulated her. That Mary would show herself at the End of Days wasn't unexpected; that it was be Elvy to whom she'd shown herself just meant Elvy was enormously lucky, but then people you'd never heard of won millions in the lottery, so...

Truth be told, Elvy was not completely pleased with how lightly Hagar was treating the whole thing. Putting on her party frock, then making this comparison with the lottery.

The encounter with Mary had been a profound shock for Elvy, probably the biggest thing that had ever happened to her. But Hagar only looked at the wound in her forehead, clapped her hands together and said, 'How marvellous! How wonderful!' Elvy nursed a suspicion that Hagar would have reacted similarly if she said she had been abducted by aliens. It was as if Hagar was overjoyed that something was happening, regardless of what it was.

Hagar had been married three times. Since her last husband, Rune, died ten years ago Hagar had done nothing but attend seminars and meetings. For the past three years she had had a *relationship* with a man her own age, but hadn't moved in with him. They had simply had their little 'tête-à-têtes' as Hagar put it. She had ended it when the man started to get senile.

A flighty woman, then; completely different from Elvy. And still they were best friends. Why? Well, for starters she had the same sense of humour. That could get you a long way. And in addition she was educated and still lucid, which was not true of all of Elvy's old friends. And even if they had different opinions most of the time, they understood each other.

But Elvy could not view this matter of Mary with the same levity as Hagar. Did not want to. This was serious. Hopefully Hagar would understand that.

Hagar rubbed her knee, making a face.

'How should we start? You never become a prophet in your own country, you know. Maybe we'll have to go somewhere else with our prophecies.'

Elvy sat down on the other side of the table, pinning Hagar with a look. Hagar's gaze started to flit about. 'What is it?'

'Now Hagar, you have to understand...' Elvy rapped her knuckles on the table for emphasis, 'We are not starting a three-ring circus. You may think this is exciting, like winning the lottery or something. But if you want to be part of this you have to understand...'

Elvy brushed the band-aid on her forehead. The wound had started to itch. She went on, 'what this is about. The Virgin Mary, Holy Mother of God, has personally told me that I should bring people to her. Do you understand what that entails?'

Hagar mumbled, 'That they should believe.'

'Precisely. We are not to get them to grow beards or give away their possessions or anything else. We must give them faith, through the power of our own convictions. And now I ask you, Hagar...' Elvy was almost scaring herself with the tone of her own voice, but went on nevertheless, 'do you believe in the Lord Jesus Christ?'

Hagar squirmed on the chair, looking shyly up at Elvy like a pupil reprimanded by the teacher and said, 'You know I do.'

'No!' Elvy's index finger shot up in the air. She always spoke more loudly when she was talking to Hagar, but now her voice rose even further. It was as if she was possessed. 'No, Hagar! I ask you: do you believe in the Lord Jesus Christ, God's only son?'

'Yes!' Hagar made fists. 'I believe in Jesus Christ, God's only begotten son, who suffered under Pontius Pilate, was crucified, who ascended into heaven and on the third day rose again, yes! I do!'

Whatever had come over Elvy receded. She smiled.

'Good. Then you are accepted.'

Hagar slowly shook her head. 'Goodness, Elvy. What is going on with you?'

Elvy had no answer.

The sky had grown darker, lying like a lid across the earth, when they ventured out. They both had their umbrellas. Hagar complained that it wasn't just a twinge in her knee, it was really hurting. It was going to be one heck of a storm.

But there was no rain yet. The birds sat silent in the trees, the people were inside their houses, waiting. The air pressure made the blood rise to the head in an intoxicating rush. Elvy was happy. It would probably be this very night. Maybe she was only one of many who had been called. She would perform her allotted task.

They started next door at the Söderlunds'. Elvy knew that the man was a mid-level manager at Pharmacia, the woman a librarian who had taken early retirement. They had lived in the area for a long time but Elvy had never had close contact with them.

It was the husband who answered the door. He had a little pot belly, a checked jersey, a bald patch and a moustache.

Elvy had not prepared herself, trusting that inspiration would strike when it was time. The man recognised her and smiled amiably.

'Well, well, Mrs Lundberg, you're out and about...'

'Yes,' Elvy said. 'And this is Hagar.'

'I see. Good evening.' The man's gaze travelled from Elvy to Hagar. 'How may I be of service?'

'Can we come in? We have something important to tell you.'

The man raised his eyebrows, looked back over his shoulder as if to check that he really had a home to invite them into. He turned back to them and appeared to be on the verge of asking something, then simply said, 'Of course. Please come in.'

As Elvy stepped into the hall, Hagar on her heels, the man gestured to her forehead. 'Have you injured yourself?'

Elvy shook her head. 'Quite the opposite.'

The answer did not satisfy him. He frowned and backed up a few paces to give them room, then stood with his hands resting on his belly. The decor in the hall was spare and elegant, seemingly at odds with his personality and probably the work of his wife.

Hagar exclaimed, 'How lovely!'

'Yes, well...' the man looked around and it was apparent that he felt differently. 'I guess you could call it...a certain style.'

'Excuse me?' Hagar said.

Elvy shot Hagar an angry look while the man repeated what he had just said. Then he waited. Before Elvy had decided what she was going to say, the words flew from her mouth.

'We have come to prepare you.'

The man stretched his head out a little. 'I see. For what?'

'For the return of Jesus Christ.'

The man's eyes widened, but before he had time to say anything, Elvy went on, 'The dead have arisen, as you have most likely heard.'

'Yes, but...'

'No,' Elvy interrupted, 'Not But. My own husband came back last night, the same thing has been happening all over. The scientists are at a loss—"impossible, inexplicable" they say. But it is completely self-evident and we all knew it was going to happen. Are you simply going to sit here and act as if this is an everyday phenomenon?'

The woman of the house came out of the kitchen, drying her hands on a tea towel. Elvy heard her and Hagar exchanging greetings. The man asked, 'But...what is it you want?'

'We want...' Elvy held up her hand and without being aware of it, she made the sign of peace, her thumb against the inside of her index finger, the other fingers stretched out. 'We want you to believe in the Lord Jesus.'

The man looked at his wife, a slight panic in his eyes. The woman returned his look with an expression that was closer to saying that this was an offer they had to take a position on. The man shook his head. 'What I believe is my business.'

Elvy nodded. 'Absolutely. But look around you. Can you reasonably interpret all this in any other way?'

The woman cleared her throat. 'I think we have to...'

'Wait a little, Matilda.' The man put up a hand to halt his wife and turned back to Elvy, 'Why are you doing this? What is it you want?'

Before Elvy had time to reply, Hagar said, 'The Virgin Mary

appeared to Elvy and told her to do it. She has no choice. Nor do I, because I believe in her. And Jesus.'

Elvy nodded. For the first time she realised the point of having Hagar with her. Like the Lord Jesus—without making too much of the comparison—had had Peter, the rock.

'We're not making demands,' Elvy said. 'You must do as you wish. We cannot force anyone to do anything. We simply want to let you know that you may be on your way to making a terrible mistake if you turn away from God now that...now that we have all the evidence.'

The woman looked anxiously at her husband as if Elvy and Hagar were offering them a vaccine against a ravaging disease and she sensed that he was about to refuse it.

And sure enough, the man shook his head angrily and walked past Elvy and Hagar, opening the front door.

'I think it sounds a lot like a threat.' He used his hand to indicate that they should leave. 'But good luck to you. There are plenty of lost souls.'

Elvy and Hagar stepped out onto the landing. Before he had time to shut the door Elvy said, 'If you change your mind...my house is open, always.'

The man slammed the door.

When they were back out on the street again, Hagar poked her tongue out at the house and said, 'That didn't go too well.' She glanced at Elvy, who was holding her palm against her forehead, and asked her, 'What is it?'

Elvy closed her eyes. 'My head feels so strange.'

'It's the thunderstorm,' Hagar said and pointed up at the sky with the tip of her umbrella.

'No...' Elvy laid her hand on Hagar's shoulder, steadying herself.

Hagar grabbed a hold of Elvy's arm. 'What is it, dear?'

'I can't quite...' Elvy smacked her hand against her forehead. 'It's as if...something else comes in. Another voice. That thing I said... "my house is open". I hadn't been intending to say that. The thought hadn't occurred to me. It just...came.'

Hagar leaned forward, examining Elvy's head as if she might find some kind of entrance to it, but she saw only the band-aid. She pursed her lips and said, 'Think of the disciples. They suddenly found they could speak in any language. Getting a little inspiration, that's no more extraordinary than Mary appearing to you, now is it?'

Elvy nodded, and straightened up. 'No. I suppose not.'

'Should we keep going then?' Hagar nodded at the house, where the man was now staring at them through the window. 'They were just dry old sticks in there.'

Elvy smiled weakly. 'The Lord has performed greater miracles than bringing buds to dead trees.'

'There we go,' Hagar said. 'That's the spirit.'

They walked on.

Bondegatan 18.30

Flora was sitting at the computer when her parents got home. She had logged onto a Christian chat forum and had presented a satanist's argument on the zombie issue, describing how black masses were being celebrated in her congregation in Falköping in order to hasten Beelzebub's arrival. It had been the most fun in the beginning when the others still believed she was a devout evangelical who had seen the light. Or the dark. Now they were trying to lead her back on track. She had gone too far and lost them, however, by the time the front door opened and Margareta called out, 'Yoo-hoo! Is anyone home?'

Flora wrote, 'Goodbye. See you in hell,' and logged out. Then she sat with her fingers resting on the keyboard and waited for the rustle. There it was. The rustle that always announced her parents' return from a trip. The shopping bags.

'Yoo-hoo!'

Flora closed her eyes, imagining her mother and father submerged in a sea of multi-coloured plastic balls. There was a hiss as their heads disappeared beneath the surface. She would have liked to put on Manson and block out their voices with a wall of guitar, but she was interested to hear how her mother had taken this thing about the dead. Elvy had rung and told her that Margareta had called from London, and had therefore been informed. Flora wondered how she was taking it.

Sure enough, the kitchen floor was covered in plastic bags with English boutique logos. In the midst of it all, Margareta and Göran were unpacking, Viktor waiting with ill-concealed impatience beside them for his battery-powered watergun. Flora crossed her arms over her chest and leaned against the doorpost. Margareta's gaze landed on her.

'Hello darling! How have things been?'

'Fine.'

The question was asked as usual. Bright and perky. No hint that anything out of the ordinary had occurred, so Flora added, 'A little dead.'

A smile flashed across Margareta's face and away, like the lash of a whip as she searched through a bag. In the corner of her eye, Flora saw Göran give her a sharp look. Margareta got hold of a box and held it out to Viktor.

'...and this is for you.'

Viktor frowned and opened the box, taking out an intricate statue of Gandalf and turning it in his hands. His disappointment was enormous. Flora saw the price tag on the box: 59.90. Pounds.

'They only had ones that looked like real ones,' Göran said and held out his hands. 'So it...'

'What ones that looked real?' Viktor asked.

'Rifles. And when you pulled the trigger there were sounds like from a real rifle. And it...we didn't think you should have it. So it was this instead.'

'What do I do with it?'

'You can put it in your room. Don't you want it?'

Viktor looked at the statue. His shoulders slumped.

'Yeah, sure. Course.'

Margareta had started to rummage through a new bag, and said without looking up, 'And what do you say?'

'Thank you,' Viktor said and gave Gandalf a death look.

Margareta got up with a new box that she handed to Flora.

'And here you are. Isn't this something you're supposed to have?'

The thing she was supposed to have was an iPod. Flora handed the box back to her.

'Thanks, but I already have one.'

Margareta pointed at the box without taking it.

'But you can fit...' she turned to Göran, 'was it two hundred?'

'Three hundred,' Göran said.

'...three hundred records in there. Everything.'

'Yes,' Flora said. 'I know. But I don't need it. I have mine.'

Silence fell. A plastic bag crumpled up with a sound like a sigh. Flora savoured it. Not everything can be bought, no, not everything can be bought. Göran smacked his hands together.

'I think,' he said, 'that both of you are incredibly ungrateful.'

'Don't you know what's been going on?' Flora asked.

Margareta shook her head: *Don't talk about it now*, and Flora pretended to misinterpret the gesture.

'Well,' she said, 'last night at around eleven...'

'Have you had anything? To eat?' Margareta interrupted and finally took the box out of Flora's hands. Without waiting for an answer she raised it in Flora's direction. 'Should we sell this then, or give it to someone else, is that what you want?'

Flora watched her mother's compressed lips as they opened for a second, let out a tremor in her lower lip, then closed again.

I could feel sorry for her. But I don't want to.

'Keep it yourself,' Flora said.

'What for?'

'I don't know. Phil Collins.'

Flora went back to her room and closed the door. Her head was sticky with guilt, anger and fatigue, all in a thick mixture. She put *Portrait of an American Family* on the stereo to try to blow it away, air it out. She lay on her bed and allowed herself to be pierced by the vibrations, Manson's voice a salve for what hurt, a pinprick for what had gone to sleep.

When the first song had blown away the worst of it, she skipped forward to 'Wrapped in plastic', lay back down on the bed and closed her eyes.

The steak is cold, but it's wrapped in plastic…

Flora floated away in a vision of all of Stockholm wrapped in plastic. Plastic over the sidewalks, a thin film across the water; when you tried to dip your fingers in the water the only thing you felt was the bulging plastic. Plastic over people's faces, liquid plastic to protect us from bacteria. A little dog rolling along in a bubble of hard plastic.

The volume dropped and she opened her eyes. Margareta was standing at the foot of her bed, arms folded.

'Flora,' she said. 'As long as you live with us…'

'I know. I know.'

'What is it you know?'

Flora knew the routine. The whole program. How you behaved, how *basically every young person we know* behaved. Clean behind your ears, plug yourself into the iPod, listen to Coldplay; let Avril Lavigne whine you into conformity. Take what you're given, be a little grateful. And give something back.

She wasn't going to bite. Not this time.

'Aren't you going to talk about it?' Flora asked.

'About what?'

'About Grandfather?'

Margareta's arms rose…and fell…and rose again as she took a few deep breaths.

'What do you want me to say about it?'

Flora looked into Margareta's eyes and saw terror. Not her problem. She rolled over to face the wall and gave up.

'Nothing. Bring your psychologist,' she said.

'What?'

'I said: bring your psychologist. Leave me alone.'

She felt Margareta's presence behind her for a couple more seconds, then it left her and slammed the door.

The little man...

That was what frightened Margareta.

Six months ago—after coming home from a talk at the Youth Psychiatry Service Margareta had forced Flora to attend—Margareta had suddenly opened up and started to talk about her father.

'I can't take it,' she said. 'I can't handle that vacant stare, the way he doesn't say anything, just sits there.'

At that point she had not been to visit her father for several months.

'And all the time,' she went on, 'all the time, it's like I'm imagining that inside my father, somewhere inside his head there's...a little man...a little man who thinks clearly and looks out onto the world and he's accusing me, he's thinking: Why doesn't my daughter come to see me? He's sitting in there and waiting and...But I can't handle it.'

And Flora sensed that her father was one of the main topics of conversation between Margareta and the psychologist she saw once a week (twice a week when Flora had been doing the most self-cutting).

Even back then, Flora had thought it would have been better if she had just dragged herself out to Täby. But Margareta believed in psychology. She thought it was possible to become whole. That if she worked her problems out conscientiously, one by one, she would finally attain a state of harmony. Possibly also a diploma. Every problem had a solution, except for those that did not.

And what could you do about them? Ignore them! Little men in your head? No such thing. Not worth speaking or even thinking about.

Now the little man had come out. Now he was walking around with vacant eyes. Now the pointing finger of accusation was waiting for Margareta at Danderyd.

But it was an insoluble problem. Therefore there was no problem. It did not exist.

Flora skipped back and raised the volume.

The steak is cold, but it's wrapped in plastic.

Yes. Come to our house. The steak is cold, it may even be rotting, but now we have wrapped it in plastic, we promise that you won't smell anything. Stay a while.

Gladwrap.

The thunder that started rumbling half an hour later interfered with her internet connection. Flora tried to call Elvy but no one answered. When she called Peter, he answered on the first ring.

'This is Peter.' His voice was low, almost a whisper.

'Hello it's me, Flora. What is it?'

'The police. They're cleaning house.'

Even though his voice was electronically flattened, Flora could hear the hatred in it.

'Why?'

There was a crackle on the line as Peter snorted. '*Why*? I don't know. They probably think it's fun.'

'Did you manage to save the scooter?'

'Yes, but they've taken all the bikes.'

'No.'

'Yes. I've never seen so many of them. Eight SWAT units and a van. They're driving all of them away now. All of them.'

'What about you?'

'No. I can't talk any longer. Have to keep quiet. See you.'

'Sure. Good...'

The connection was broken.

'...luck.'

Kungsholmen 20.15

As the first flash of lightning split the sky above Norrmalm, David was standing in front of the freezer staring at a packet of frozen raspberries. The rumble that followed a couple of seconds later stirred him from his trance and he stuffed the raspberries to the back, taking out a bagged loaf of bread.

Roast'n Toast. Best before 16 August. When he bought the bread a week ago everything was normal; life a sequence of great or not-so-great days to pile one on top of the other. He shut the freezer door and lost himself in the bread instead.

How long?

How many days, how many years before even one good memory would be attached to a moment after Eva's accident? Would that ever happen?

'Dad, look.'

Magnus was sitting at the kitchen table, pointing out the window. Fine chalk lines blinked on the blackboard of the sky and the claps of thunder that rolled in shortly afterward did not appear to have anything to do with it. Magnus counted quietly to himself and said that the thunder was three kilometres away. Sheets of water slid down the window.

David took a couple of rock-hard slices of bread from the bag and put them in the toaster for Magnus' evening snack. He had burned the spaghetti sauce for dinner and neither one of them had eaten much. Later they had watched *Shrek* for the fourth time and Magnus had downed half a bag of chips while David drank three glasses of wine. He wasn't hungry anymore.

The house shook with detonations that were drawing closer. David managed to coax Magnus into eating a piece of toast with cheese and marmalade, and a glass of milk. He alternated between regarding Magnus as a machine that had to be taken care of, and as the only other life that existed on this earth. After the wine, it was the latter view that had started to dominate and he had to hold back tears as he looked at his son.

Magnus went off to brush his teeth and at the instant he disappeared from view, panic started to burn in David's stomach. He drank the dregs of the wine straight from the bottle and leaned against the kitchen table, watching the lightning.

After a minute Magnus came back and stood next to him.

'Dad, why does the light move faster than the sound?'

'Because...' David rubbed his hands over his face. 'Because... good question. I don't know. You'll have to...' He broke off. He had been on the verge of saying: *You'll have to ask Mum.* Instead he said, 'You should go to bed now.'

He tucked Magnus in and said he was too tired to tell him a goodnight story. Magnus asked him to read one instead, and he read the one about the leopard that lost a spot. Magnus had heard it many times, but always thought it was funny when they got to the part where the leopard counted its spots and discovered that one was missing.

This evening David lacked his usual storytelling verve. He tried to act out the leopard's consternation, but Magnus' dutiful giggle was so pitiful that he had to stop, and simply read the story as it was written. When it was over they were both quiet for a long time. When David made a move to get up, Magnus said, 'Dad?'

'Yes.'

'Is Mum coming back here?'

'How do you mean?'

Magnus curled up and drew his knees up to his chest.

'Is she going to come back like how she is now and be dead?'

'No. She'll come later. When she is well.'

'I don't want her to come here and be dead.'

'She won't.'

'Are you sure?'

'Yes.'

David leaned over the bed and kissed Magnus on the cheek, and on the mouth. Normally Magnus would make trouble—want to play the Angry Game, make funny faces—but now he just lay still, allowing himself to be kissed. When David stood up Magnus was lying with his brows knit. He was thinking about something, wanted to ask something. David waited. Magnus looked him in the eye.

'Dad? Are you going to be all right without Mum?'

David's jaw froze. The seconds ticked by. A sensible voice at the back of his consciousness shouted at him: *Say something, say something now, you're scaring him.* Finally he managed, 'Go to sleep, buddy. Everything is going to be fine.'

He left the bedroom door open, went to the bathroom and turned on the bathwater, hoping that it would drown out the sound of his sobs.

He had imagined Eva dead many times. Tried to imagine. Wrong. Many times the thought of Eva's death had been forced upon him. Yes. Because things happen, you read about them in the paper every day. Photographs of roads, lakes, some nondescript forest glade. Someone had been in a crash, someone drowned, someone was murdered. And he had thought. A life of emptiness: routines, duties, perhaps eventually a bit of light from somewhere. But now, when it had happened, of course the worst pain came from things he had not been able to imagine.

Dad? Are you going to be all right without Mum?

How could an eight-year-old say that?

David sat on the floor with his head bent over the bathtub where the water was slowly rising. Maybe it was wrong of him to hide his grief from Magnus. But Eva was not dead, he was not allowed to grieve. And she was not alive, so he could not hope. Nothing.

He turned off the water, pulled the plug and walked out to the kitchen and opened a new bottle of wine. Before he had time to pour himself a glass, Magnus came out wrapped in his blanket.

'Dad, I can't sleep.'

David carried him to his and Eva's bedroom, tucked him in again. Magnus almost disappeared in the big bed. He used to toddle in here when he was little and woke in the night. Here was security. David lay down next to him, his hand on his shoulder. Magnus squirmed in and sighed deeply.

David closed his eyes, wondered, *Where is my big bed?*

He had been afraid that his mother would have seen the morning news, but she had not, so when she called in the afternoon and exclaimed about the evening's events he let her talk for a while and then said he had no time. Both she and Eva's father had to be informed, but he couldn't bring himself to do it just now.

Magnus' breathing deepened. His head was wedged in David's armpit.

Where can I go?

The only thing he saw was the kitchen counter where the full bottle of wine was waiting. He would go there as soon as Magnus was fully asleep. Because it was Eva who was his big bed, his only haven, and he could not go there. He lay with his head deep in the pillow, looking at the blue light that occasionally flickered across the ceiling. The rumbling was more distant now, giants mumbling behind the mountains. The rain was fairies tiptoeing across the window ledge.

...and the dead have awakened...

A thought glided past and he took hold of it gratefully.

If everything…if everything impossible starts happening now.

Yes. If vampires came out. If things floated, disappeared. If the trolls came out of the mountains, if the animals began to talk or if Jesus returned. If everything…became different.

David smiled. He smiled at the comforting thought. The continued normality of society—picnics in the park and automated phone systems—was a mockery, and its collapse into the supernatural would be a relief. The attempts of scientists to understand the phenomenon from a biological perspective had nothing to do with him. Come angels, come fairies, it is starting to get cold.

Täby Municipality 20.20

In two hours they managed to visit twelve houses, perhaps twenty people. Some shut their doors as soon as they heard what it was about, but more were willing to hear them out than they had expected. Elvy had herself received visits from the Jehovah's Witnesses several times and treated them with courteous dismissal. Once she had been sitting at the kitchen window and followed their progress, how quickly they were back on the street after visiting each house. It went much better for Elvy and Hagar.

Perhaps it was due to the extraordinary circumstances, or the passion of Elvy's conviction. Even though Elvy had had her vision, had been given her task, she was not naive enough to think she could immediately convince everyone else. Things like that did not even happen in the Bible.

The pressure front of the storm was wrapped around them the whole time like invisible muslin, but it was as if the storm had folded his arms and was waiting for them to finish their task before letting loose.

Most of the people they had managed to interest or convince were women their own age. But there were a couple of men too. The one who embraced their mission with the greatest enthusiasm was a man in his thirties. He was a computer consultant, he explained, and he offered them his services in case they needed help in setting up a web site to spread their message via the internet. They told him they would think about it.

By eight o'clock the storm was no longer able to contain itself. It was already as dark as a winter evening when the wind started to ruffle the treetops, and shortly afterwards the rain came. In a few minutes it had grown to a downpour.

Elvy and Hagar unfurled their umbrellas and the rain streamed down the fabric, creating a curtain of water around them, smattering against the metal roofs of parked cars with such intensity that they could hardly hear each other's voices. Arm in arm, they continued homeward.

'Poor old horses of the apocalypse!' Hagar shouted and Elvy did not know if she was referring to them or their legs, but there was no sense in asking since there was no way Hagar would hear over the din of the rain. They trudged on in silence with the water rushing around their flat shoes.

It was raining so hard that there was hardly any air left to breathe. They proceeded slowly under their buckling umbrellas so as not to exhaust themselves. The first bolt of lightning struck at the exact moment they reached Elvy's house, and the thunder rolled down the street a couple of seconds later like a drumroll of doom.

Hagar closed her umbrella and shook it out. 'Phew!' she laughed. 'Is this the End, do you think?'

Elvy smiled crookedly. 'Your guess is as good as mine.'

'Oh my, oh my...' Hagar shook her head. 'The heavens have opened, as they say.'

Elvy's reply was inaudible; the storm had drawn closer and a blast sent a shudder through the house, rattling the wineglasses in the cupboard. Hagar jumped and asked, 'Are you afraid of lightning?'

'No. Are you?'

'Not really. I just have to...' Hagar tilted her head and turned something on her hearing aid. Then she said, a little louder, 'Now I can't hear so well, but the thunder...it gets too much.'

The thunder came at closer intervals and Hagar shot a frightened look at the ceiling. The part about her not being afraid of thunder was probably not entirely true. Elvy took her hand and Hagar squeezed it gratefully, allowing herself to be led into the living room. Elvy herself felt nothing other than...reliance. Everything was as it should be, and they had done what they could.

When they reached the living room Elvy noted that the ceiling lamp was swaying slightly. Then it went out. All the lamps in the house went out and it became pitch dark. Hagar squeezed Elvy's hand harder and asked, 'Should we pray?'

They made their way onto the floor, easing their stiff legs into place. Hagar grimaced with pain as she got down on her knees, said, 'I can't...my knee...'

Elvy helped her up again and they sat next to each other on the couch instead, hip to hip. They interlaced their fingers and lowered their heads in prayer while the rain continued to run down the roof and thunder filled the world.

When the power had been out for ten minutes and the lightning-strobe of the storm was still playing on the house, Elvy let down the blinds and lit two candles on the coffee table. Hagar, half-lying on the couch, resting her bad knee, was transformed from storm-lit movie monster to dignified saint.

Elvy walked up and down in the room with a rising sense of irritation.

'I don't know,' she said. 'I don't know.'

'What?' Hagar cupped her fingers behind her ear, but Elvy waved the gesture away. She had nothing important to say.

Why is nothing happening?

It wasn't that she had expected an immediate conversion of the masses, but something...something that made this undertaking greater than just two old ladies tottering around together hawking their faith. After all, she had been chosen, personally singled out and marked. Was it like this for all visionaries?

Probably. The thing was to hold onto her vision, not let go.

But for how long, Lord? How long?

She was back in the hall on one of her circuits when there was a gentle knock on the door. She opened up.

Outside stood a sodden likeness of her next-door neighbour. Her hair straggled, her dress spotted with dark patches of moisture. A series of lightning bolts illuminated her and she made an altogether miserable picture.

'Come in, come in,' Elvy said and guided her into the hall.

'Excuse me,' the woman said, 'but you said that...well, that your house was open. And my husband has been very odd since you left. He drank a great deal and then he went out and...if this really is going to be the last night...'

'I understand,' Elvy said, and did. 'Come in.'

While her neighbour was towelling her hair in the bathroom, there was another knock on the door.

Why all this knocking...

But then Elvy remembered that the power cut must also have knocked out the doorbell. Fearing that it was her neighbour come to fetch his runaway wife she opened up, with a speech about freedom of association ready on her lips.

But it was not the neighbour. It was Greta, one of the older women who had appeared to be swayed when they visited earlier. She came better prepared than the neighbour. A vivid green rain poncho was draped over her head and shoulders, and she pulled a basket out from underneath.

'I brought a little coffee and some home-made pastries with me.

So we can keep vigil together.'

It was not long until yet another of the women came. She had brought a box of candles with her, in case they did not have any. Finally Mattias arrived, the young man with the computer background. He said that he had thought about bringing his laptop but that there was no point while the storm was still going.

When they were all assembled in the living room with extra candles lit, coffee poured out and pastries served, there was a general outbreak of explanations. The thunder had died down so Hagar was able to turn up her hearing aid and take part.

It was the storm, they all agreed. It had driven it home. If tonight was going to bring the end of the world, or at least a complete change in life as they knew it, they did not want to sit alone when there was the option of gathering with like-minded people.

When they had spoken about this for a while, everyone's gaze turned to Elvy. She realised they expected her to say something.

'Well,' Elvy said, 'of course, on our own we can do nothing. Faith only lives when it's shared. It was a blessing that you came here. Together we are greater than the sum of our parts. Let us now sit vigil through this night and if it is the last, we will at least meet it together. Hand in hand.'

Elvy finished her speech abashed. It was not inspired. She had simply tried to say what they had been expecting her to say. The others considered her platitudes quietly, until Hagar cried, 'Do you have mattresses?'

Elvy smiled, 'Where there is heart, there is room, and so forth.'

'Should we sing something?' the young man asked.

Yes, of course they had to sing. Everyone scoured their minds for something appropriate. Hagar looked around.

'What is it?' she asked.

'We want to sing something,' Elvy said loudly. 'We're trying to think of something.'

Hagar thought for a second, then piped up: *Nearer My God to Thee...*

Everyone joined in as best they could. They sang at the top of their lungs and the candles flickered in their outgoing breath, as they drowned out the storm.

Bondegatan 21.50

Someone's fiftieth birthday party was in full swing in the party room upstairs. The storm had died down and from her room Flora could hear the partygoers' laughter echoing in the stairwell. In the background, they were singing along to 'Girls Just Want to Have Fun' and Flora could not for the life of her understand how they could play it without feeling ashamed.

She lay still, savouring her contempt for the middle-class world she had been born into. You were allowed to be a little bit of an individual as long as you did it tastefully. Anything beyond that was a job for a psychologist. She was never at home: the tolerance wrapped her up like a straitjacket and she just wanted to wave her arms and scream.

Viktor had been sent to bed at half past nine, and Flora had declined a party invitation issued in a tone of brittle gaiety.

She rolled out of bed and walked into the living room, turned on the television to check the news. She had heard nothing from Peter and she did not dare call and break his silence.

The news was focused almost exclusively on the reliving. A professor of molecular biology explained that what they had at first believed to be an aggressive decomposition bacterium had revealed itself to be a co-enzyme called ATP, the cell's primary energy supplier. The perplexing thing was that it could survive at such a low temperature.

'It's as if you put a batch of dough out in the snow and it still rose,' explained the professor, who also made appearances on popular science shows.

ATP's baffling liveliness also explained how the newly deceased could overcome their rigor mortis, since it is precisely the breaking down of ATP that locks the muscles.

'Let us for the moment assume that we're talking about a mutated form of ATP. However...' The professor pinched his index finger and thumb together to emphasise the point, 'we do not know if it is this enzyme that has caused them to awaken, or if the behaviour of the enzyme is a consequence of their awakening.'

The professor held his arms out and smiled: cause or effect? What do *you* think? Flora did not like his smug way of talking, as if the whole thing was a debate about over-fishing cod stocks.

But the next item made her draw several inches closer to the television screen.

That afternoon a television crew had been allowed into Danderyd. There was vision of a large hospital ward where around twenty reliving were sitting on the floor, on beds, in chairs. At first you could see their faces. The remarkable thing was that every one had the same expression: mute amazement. Eyes wide open, mouths slack. In their blue hospital gowns they evoked a group of uniformed school children watching a magician.

Then the camera tracked out and you saw what they were looking at: a metronome. Perched on a rolling cart, it was ticking back and forth, back and forth before the enraptured audience. A nurse was sitting on a chair next to the metronome, upright, aware of the camera.

Must be the one who starts it again when it stops.

The voiceover outlined how the situation at the hospital had improved now that they'd discovered the thing with the metronome, and that the search was now on for other methods.

The weather would continue to be changeable.

Flora turned off the television and sat looking at her reflection in the screen. Noises from upstairs cut through the silence. They had started to sing a sea shanty, in rounds. When the song was over she heard raised voices, laughter.

Flora leaned back, stretching out onto the floor.

I know, she thought. I know what's missing there. It's death. Death doesn't exist for them, it's not permitted. And for me it's everywhere.

She smiled to herself.

Come on, Flora. Mustn't exaggerate.

Viktor emerged from his room. He looked so thin and frail in his underpants that Flora was overcome by a sudden tenderness.

'Flora?' he said. 'Do you think they're dangerous? Like in that movie?'

Flora patted the floor next to her. He sat down and pulled his knees to his chin as if he was cold.

'The movie…it's all made up,' she said. 'Do you think there really is a basilisk? Like in Harry Potter?'

Viktor shook his head.

'OK. Do you think that there's…do you think there really are elves and hobbits? Like in *Lord of the Rings*?'

Viktor hesitated for an instant, then shook his head and said, 'No, but there are dwarves.'

'Yes,' Flora said. 'But they're not walking around with axes, are they? No. The zombies in that movie are just like the basilisk, just like Gollum. They're just made up. It isn't like that at all in real life.'

'What's it like in real life?'

'In real life…' Flora stared at the black monitor. 'In real life they're nice. At least, they don't want to hurt anyone.'

'Are you sure?'

'I'm sure. Now go to bed.'

Svarvargatan 22.15

The clock on the bedside table said quarter past ten when the phone rang. Magnus had been breathing evenly for a long time and David eased out his tingling arm, walked out into the kitchen and picked up.

'This is David.'

'Hi. My name is Gustav Mahler. I hope I'm not calling too late. You wanted to speak to me.'

'No, it's…nothing,' David caught sight of the bottle and the glass, poured himself some. 'Honestly…' he took a big gulp, 'I don't know why I tried to contact you.'

'I see,' Mahler said. 'That happens sometimes. Cheers.'

There was a click on the other end and David raised his glass, said, 'Cheers,' and took another gulp.

There was silence for several seconds.

'How's it going?' Mahler asked.

And David told him. Whether it was the wine, the bottled-up anguish or something in Mahler's voice—the barriers came down. Not caring whether the stranger on the other end was interested, he told him about the accident, the awakening, Magnus, the visit to the State Pathologist, the feeling of having fallen off the edge of life, about his love for Eva. He talked for at least ten minutes, only pausing because his mouth was dry and he needed more wine. While he poured, Mahler said, 'Death has the capacity to isolate us from each other.'

'Yes,' David said. 'You'll have to excuse me but I don't know why I...I haven't talked to anyone about...' David stopped with the glass half-way to his mouth. A chill shot through his stomach and he put the glass down so violently that wine splashed out. 'You aren't going to write about this, are you?'

'You can...'

'You can't! You can't write about this, there are a lot of people who...'

They lined up in front of his eyes: his mother, Eva's father, his colleagues, Magnus' classmates, their parents...all the people who would find out more than he wanted them to know.

'David,' Mahler said. 'I can promise you that I won't write a single word without your approval.'

'Do you mean it?'

'Yes, I mean it. We're just talking right now. Or more precisely: you're talking and I'm listening.'

David laughed, a short laugh that came out in the form of a snort and pushed mucus into his nose, stale tears. He drew a finger through the spilled wine, forming a question mark. 'What about you?' he asked. 'What's your interest in this? Is it purely...professional?'

The other end grew quiet. David had time to think that the connection had been broken before Mahler answered.

'No. It's more...personal.'

David waited, drank more wine. He was starting to get drunk. He noted with relief that his state of being was starting to lose definition, his thoughts were slowing down. In contrast to earlier in the day this was a state in which he could rest. There was a person on the other end of the telephone line. He was drifting, but he was not alone. He was afraid the conversation would end.

'Personal?' he asked.

'Yes. You trusted me. I'll have to trust you. Or...if you want to put it another way we'll both have something on each other. My grandchild is with me, and he's...' David heard Mahler take a gulp of whatever he was drinking, 'he is...he was dead until last night. Buried.'

'You're hiding him?'

'Yes. Only you and two other people know about it. He's in bad shape. The fact that I called you was mostly because I thought perhaps you...knew something.'

'About...about what?'

Mahler sighed.

'Oh, I don't know. It's just that you were there when she woke up and...I don't know. Maybe something happened that could be useful.'

David replayed what had happened at the hospital in his head. He wanted to help Mahler.

'She spoke,' he said.

'She did? What did she say?'

'Well, she didn't say anything that...it was as if the words were new for her, as if she was testing them. It was...' David heard it again: Eva's metallic, raspy voice, 'it was pretty awful.'

'I see,' Mahler said. 'But it didn't seem as if she...remembered anything?'

Without thinking about it, David had forced that moment at the hospital from his consciousness. Had not wanted to go near it. Now he knew why.

'No,' David said and the tears pricked his eyes. 'It was like she was completely...empty.' He cleared his throat. 'I think I have to...'

'I understand,' Mahler said. 'Let me give you my number in case...well, in case you think of anything.'

They hung up, and David sat at the kitchen table, polishing off the last of the wine and devoting twenty minutes to not thinking of Eva's voice; of her eye, as it had looked at the hospital. When Magnus went to sleep he lay as if crucified in the middle of the bed, his arms thrown wide. David shifted Magnus over to one side, undressed and lay down next to him.

He was so exhausted he fell asleep as soon as he closed his eyes.

Koholma 22.35

'What did he say?'

Anna walked into Mahler's room only a couple of seconds after he hung up. Mahler rubbed his eyes, said, 'Nothing in particular. He told me his story. Horrible, obviously. But nothing that helps us.'

'His wife, was she...'

'No. It was basically the same as with Elias.'

When Anna had gone back to the living room and the television came on, Mahler looked in on Elias. He stood there a long time staring at the little body. Elias had downed yet another bottle of brine, yet another bottle of sugar water over the course of the evening.

It was like she was completely...empty.

But Eva Zetterberg had only been dead for half an hour.

Was he wrong?

Was it true, as Anna said, that nothing of Elias remained in the tiny creature lying in the bed?

When he stepped out onto the patio the air was new. During the long drought he had forgotten that the air could feel so rich, so much like nourishment. The darkness was dense and filled with scents from a landscape that the downpour had restored to life.

Does some…intention exist?

Elias had been dead and withered. Something that was not rain had brought him back to life. What? And what was keeping him alive if he was empty inside?

A seed can lie dormant for hundreds and thousands of years. Dried or frozen in a glacier. Place it in moist earth and it sprouts. There is a power. The green force of the flower. What is the power of the human being?

Mahler studied the stars. Out here in the country they were more numerous than in the city. An illusion. Of course the stars were always there, and in numbers infinitely greater than the sharpest eye could discern.

Something touched him. An insight, inexpressible. He shivered.

In a rapid succession of images he saw a blade of grass break through the seed casing and struggle toward the surface, saw a sunflower strive toward the sky, turning to the light, saw a small child pull itself to its feet, hold its arms out, jubilant, and everything lives and is drawn to the light, and he saw…

It is not inevitable.

The green force of the flower. Not inevitable. Everything is effort, work. A gift. It can be taken from us. It can be given back.

Attachment 2

15 August
Initial Examination: Attempt No. 3 (cure)
[Soc. Dept. Confidential]
The supply of nourishment to patient 260718-0373 Bengt
Andersson was interrupted 2002-08-15 at 08.15.

Catheters for saline and glucose solutions were removed in order
to observe the patient's reaction.

The patient showed no signs of decline by 09.15. ECG blank, EEG
as before.

09.25 the patient experienced a series of spastic cramps. The
contractions lasted for approximately three minutes, whereupon
the patient returned to the earlier state.

No further cramps or other reactions observed by 14.00.

Our conclusion is that the saline and glucose supplements are not
a necessity. The low values that the patients show neither improve
nor decline.

[From Studio One 16.00]
Reporter: ...results that indicate that the reliving do not need
nourishment. Professor Lennart Hallberg, how can this have been
established?

Lennart Hallberg: Well, of course the actual tests have not
been made public at this point, but I assume that they simply
suspended the supply of nutrients in order to observe what would
happen.

Reporter: And you can do that? Is it allowed?

Lennart Hallberg: Firstly, the reliving exist in a kind of legal grey area. It will probably be a while until we develop some medical-ethical guidelines for handling them. Secondly, the flag of pestilence has not been lowered yet, so to speak, and this gives us physicians a certain...leeway.

Reporter: How is it possible to exist without nourishment?

Lennart Hallberg: [*laughing*] That's a good question. A week ago I would have answered it by saying it is physiologically impossible, but now...let us say that there may be a form of nourishment that we have not discovered yet.

Reporter: What would that be?

Lennart Hallberg: I haven't the faintest idea.

[DN Debate]
[Extract from the article 'Can the Dead Help Us?' by Rebecca Liljewall, Professor of Philosophy at Lund University]
...earlier unimagined possibilities to approach the fundamental conditions of life. Should the same ethical criteria be applied to the reliving as to 'normal' patients?

Present laws give a simple answer to this question: No. A person who has been declared deceased falls outside of judicial boundaries, excepting the peace of the grave. It is however doubtful if grave-peace can be invoked in this case.

In all likelihood the laws will shortly be altered to include the reliving. It may sound cynical but in the intervening time the opportunity exists to perform experiments and tests that may later be illegal. My opinion is that the medical experts should be encouraged to take advantage of the situation.

The possible suffering of the reliving must be measured against the benefit it may hold for mankind. In the past two days sixty-five people in Stockholm have died without awakening. In the whole world, around 300 000 people have died during the same time.

It is not too bold to state that a more thorough examination of this small number of reliving would better equip us to prevent a large number of unnecessary deaths in future.

Is it not a price worth paying?

[*Dagens Nyheter*, letter to the Editor]

I am one of thousands of family members who have now waited for two days for a clear answer to the question of what will happen to our dead. Why this secrecy? What is being covered up?

As an old Social Democrat I am very disappointed in the government's actions. I think I speak for many when I say that this will have an impact when I go to vote next month. I have spoken with many people and everyone is saying the same thing: if this government cannot arrange for us to see our loved ones, it has to go.

[*Expressen*, the Daily Bouquet]

I want to offer the Daily Bouquet to all of the doctors and nurses and police officers whose quick action removed the dead from our streets.

I don't think I am alone in feeling that it would have been very disturbing to have them wander freely.

Many thanks!

[From *Reports from the Inside*, SVT 1, 22.10]

Reporter: Vera Martinez, you are a nurse who has been working at

Danderyd these past few days. From what I understand there has been a high staff turnover?

Vera Martinez: Yes. Basically everyone working there now comes from staffing agencies. No one can keep it up. As soon as there is a room full of the dead then it's like...you don't have the energy. It's the thoughts, the feelings—you have to sort of make yourself think nice thoughts the whole time, but in the end you can't keep it up.

Reporter: You brought in metronomes, and the effect appeared to be calming?

VM: There are none left. They picked them all apart. It worked for one day, but then...well, they took them apart. Now we have other things, more durable things...that move.

Reporter: What do you think should be done?

VM: They have to be spread out in some way. They can't be kept together, like they were in the hospital. No one will be able to take it.

Reporter: Karin Pihl, you are an expert at the Ministry of Social Affairs. I believe there are plans to relocate the reliving?

Karin Pihl: As Vera here says, the present situation is untenable. We've been working on a temporary solution since yesterday, but I cannot give out any further details as of yet.

[*Daily Echo* 21.00]
The conservative parties have now united in a declaration of a lack of confidence in the government. It is being called an exceptional move so close to the election, but the leader of the Moderates puts it this way:

Leader, Moderate Party: 'This is exceptional, yes. But the government's handling of this situation has been exceptionally clumsy. Naturally it must be made possible for relatives to see their reliving.'

Parties in coalition with the government have not yet announced any guarantees of their continued support.

Quick investigation: Attempt 5 [Decomposition]
[Min. Soc. Aff. Classified]
Temperature requirements for patient 320114-6381 Greta Ramberg was concluded at 2002-08-15, 09.00 hours.

The patient was isolated in her own room. The climate control was gradually adjusted until it reached 19 degrees Celsius, or normal room temperature.

The patient was kept under constant observation in order to note any signs of an advance in the decomposition of tissue. When none had been noted by 12.00, the temperature was raised to 22 degrees Celsius.

At 15.00 no signs of deterioration were detected. A bacterial analysis of the bowel contents was carried out, and the results showed that all bacterial growth in the body had ceased.

The phenomenon is currently unexplained, but our conclusion is that the reliving do not appear to require the cooling that is otherwise standard practice with cadavers.

[*Daily Echo* 22.00]
...have now confirmed that the man killed in the subway accident at Danderyd Hospital station was Sten Bergwall, chief physician

at Danderyd. According to police, there are no suspicious circumstances...

[Mail to the Br-Toys head office]
...hereby place an order of 5000 (five thousand) copies of item number 3429-21.

We request this order be filled as expeditiously as possible. The transportation costs do not matter. If possible, we ask that the goods be transported by air freight...

[*Daily Echo* 23.00]
All staff have now left Danderyd Hospital. A large number of military vehicles have gathered outside the entrances. For the moment there is no information about what is happening, but the Prime Minister has announced a press conference for seven o'clock tomorrow morning.

16 August

[From the Prime Minister's speech 07.00]

Prime Minister: Military personnel have relocated the reliving during the night. It was a necessary step, for the purposes of being able to provide the proper care...

Journalist: Where have they been taken?

[*Pause*]

Prime Minister: Please save your questions for the appropriate time, otherwise I will have to ask you to leave. [*Pause*] In order to be able to provide the proper care, the reliving have been moved to a facility where they can be kept separated. The mental stress attested to by medical personnel must be taken seriously.

At first the proposed solution was to divide them up among a number of hospitals. This would however have compromised the provision of regular health services. Even the level of service would have been affected.

The solution that we have arrived at is the best at this point in time. The reliving have been moved to the residential area the Heath in north-west Stockholm. The necessary personnel have been dispatched and our aim is for rehabilitation to begin shortly. A place will be made in society for the reliving.

[*Pause*]

Any questions?

Journalist: Is it possible to care for seriously ill people in a residential complex that's only half-completed?

Prime Minister: We have received medical reports to the effect that the condition of the reliving is not nearly as critical as was first thought. Many of the precautionary treatments that were initially provided have turned out to be unnecessary.

Journalist: How can you be sure?

[*Pause*]

Prime Minister: These were questions I was in fact going to refer to Sten Bergwall, who was appointed director of the relocation. I can only say that we had guarantees.

Journalist: Did Sten Bergwall commit suicide?

Prime Minister: I will not dignify that question with speculation. Absolutely not.

Journalist: Isn't this a pretty desperate measure?

Prime Minister: Well, there you are again. How do you expect me to answer that?

Journalist: Why are no relatives allowed into the area?

Prime Minister: Family members will shortly be afforded the opportunity to see their reliving. It is regrettable that it has taken so long.

Journalist: Is this something you are doing in order to avoid a no-confidence motion?

Prime Minister: [*Sighing*] My government and I are fully capable of making decisions without having a gun held to our heads. Up to this point it has not been possible to allow the public to make visits. Now it is possible. Therefore we are now opening for the public.

[Letter found in Sten Bergwall's office]
It is with great regret that I must advise that everything has gone to hell. I cannot assume responsibility for a decision that I know in my heart to be wrong, and one that will lead to catastrophe.

I am exhausted as I have never been before. My hand is shaking on the pen. Thoughts come only with difficulty.

How could it have been handled differently?

The reliving are regarded as vegetables, without will, or thought. This is wrong. They are like jellyfish. Their behaviour is influenced by their environment. They have a will. The will of the person thinking of them. No one is prepared to accept this.

We should isolate them completely. We should destroy them. Burn them. Instead, they will now be released into the uncontrolled thoughts of the public at large. It will end badly. I do not want to be present when this occurs.

If my legs have the strength to get me to the subway, I will leave now.

[*Daily Echo*—lunch edition 12.30]
...spokesperson now says that the situation in the Heath is under control and that relatives who wish to visit their reliving may do so starting at noon tomorrow...

[From *Bruno the Beaver Seeks and Finds* (in press)]

...but with each storey that Bruno added to the tower, the moon slipped further away. He stretched out his paw. His paw was on the moon. He tried to feel if it was rough or smooth. But he only felt air. The moon was still as far away as when he had started to build the tower.

[...]

The tower was now fourteen storeys high, higher than the tallest tree. When Bruno sat at the top he could see the mountains far away. Something was moving in the lake under his feet. Deep down there he saw the Waterman gliding around among the stilts on which he had built his tower. Bruno pulled up his feet and closed his eyes.

[...]

At night Bruno saw that there were two moons. One up in the sky and one down on the surface of the water. The one up there he could not reach, and the one down there he did not dare to take. That was the Waterman's moon.

17 August

Where a corpse lies, vultures gather

Svarvargatan 07.30

David went out to stand vigil in the hall at twenty-eight minutes past seven, right beside the front door. At exactly half past he heard the elevator come up, and then a hesitant knock. The precaution was strictly speaking unnecessary. David had already ascertained that Magnus was asleep, but a certain measure of secrecy was appropriate to birthdays. At least when you were nine years old.

Sture, David's father-in-law, was standing outside the door with a cat carrier in his hand. Sture was rarely seen in anything other than blue trousers and a cardigan, but now he was dressed in a red and orange plaid shirt, and somewhat too-tight dress pants. Dressed up.

'Welcome, Sture.'

'Hello.'

Sture raised the cat box a couple of inches and nodded at it.

'Great,' David said. 'Come in, come in.'

Sture was six foot four inches tall, and broad-shouldered. His presence transformed the apartment from a roomy two-bedroom to a functional prison. Sture needed expanses around him, trees. As soon as he had stepped into the hall, he did something very unexpected: he put down the cat box and hugged David.

It was not a hug intended to give or receive comfort, it was more about taking on a shared fate. Like a handshake. Sture took David into his arms, held him there for five seconds and then let go. David did not even have time to consider laying his head against Sture's chest; only when Sture let go did he think it would have felt nice.

'Well,' Sture said. 'Here we are then.'

David nodded and did not know how to answer. He lifted the lid of the container. A small grey rabbit was curled up on the bottom, staring into the wall. A couple of lettuce leaves were strewn in one corner, some black pellets in the other. He knew the acrid smell that wafted up would soon impregnate the entire apartment.

Sture scooped up the rabbit in his enormous hands. 'Do you have the cage?'

'My mother's bringing it over.'

Sture stroked the rabbit's ears. His nose was redder than when David had last seen him and there was a network of veins under the skin of his cheeks. David caught the smell of whisky, probably from the night before. Sture would never under any circumstances get behind the wheel drunk.

'Would you like some coffee?'

'That would be good, thank you.'

They sat down at the kitchen table. The rabbit was still resting in Sture's hands, secure and vulnerable. The tiny nose was twitching, trying to comprehend the new place that it had come to. Sture drank his heavily sugared coffee with some difficulty, one hand otherwise occupied. They sat quietly in this way for a while. David heard Magnus moving in his bed. He probably had to go pee, but didn't want to get up and break the enchantment.

'She's much better,' David said. 'Much better. I talked to them last night and they say she…there have been great strides.'

Sture slurped some coffee from the saucer.

'When does she get to come home?'

'They couldn't say. They're still working it out and…they have some kind of rehabilitation program.'

Sture nodded, said nothing and David felt dimly idiotic using *their* language to defend *their* actions, becoming some kind of spokesman.

But the neurologist he had spoken with had been vague when David asked the same question: *When will she get to come home?*

'It's too early to say,' he had answered. 'There are still some… problems that we should discuss tomorrow. When you've seen her. It's difficult to convey over the phone.'

'What kind of problems?'

'Well, as I said…it's difficult to understand if you haven't…experienced it. I'll be at the Heath tomorrow. We'll take this up again then.'

They had agreed to meet early. The Heath would open at twelve o'clock and David was planning to be there before that.

There was another quiet knock on the door and David went to let his mother in, with the rabbit cage. She had—to his amazement—taken the news of Eva's accident relatively well, not smothering him with excessive pity as he'd feared.

The cage looked good but there was no sawdust. Sture said that newspaper was just as good and cheaper. He and David's mother set about furnishing it as David stood beside them, the rabbit in his hands.

He and Eva had joked many times about how they ought to fix up their parents, two lonely individuals. The idea foundered on its impracticality; they were far too unlike and both cemented into their respective lives. Now, as he stood watching them whisper and tear up newspaper and fill a bowl with water, it no longer seemed so unreasonable. For a moment their roles were reversed: they were a couple, he was alone.

But I'm not alone. Eva will get well.

The gaping hole in her chest.

David blinked hard, opened his eyes and concentrated on the

rabbit, which was nibbling a shirt button. If it hadn't been for Eva's accident there would not have been a rabbit. Both he and Eva thought it was wrong to keep animals in the city, caged. But now...

Magnus deserved to be happy. At least on his birthday.

'*We are so happy, ha ha!*
That you are born, fallera!
That you were born, fallera!
On just this day!
Hurray hurray!'

David felt a lump in his throat as they entered Magnus' room. Magnus wasn't curled up and sleeping, or pretending to sleep. He was lying ramrod straight on his back with his hands on his stomach, looking gravely at them, and David felt as if he and the others were performing for an audience that was refusing to play along.

'Congratulations, darling.'

David's mother was the first one to reach the bed and the serious look in Magnus' eyes softened when the packages were laid across his feet. For a while he seemed to forget. There were Pokémon cards, Legos and movies. Finally they brought in the cage.

For a while, David had been afraid that Magnus had decided simply to humour them but there was no mistaking his enormous, unfeigned joy as he lifted the rabbit up into the bed, stroking its head and kissing it on the nose. The first thing he said after he had cuddled it for a while was: 'Can I bring it to show Mummy?'

David smiled and nodded. Since the day after the accident, Magnus had hardly mentioned Eva and when David fished a little he had realised that Magnus resented Eva for disappearing. As if Magnus himself saw that this was an unreasonable attitude and was ashamed of it, he refused to talk about Eva at all.

Therefore: if he wanted to bring the bunny, he could bring the bunny.

Sture rubbed Magnus on the head and asked, 'What do you think it's called?'

Magnus answered immediately, 'Balthazar.'

'I see,' Sture said. 'Lucky that it's a boy.'

The cake was brought in. David had bought a ready-made marzipan cake in a bakery and Magnus said nothing about it. Coffee and hot chocolate were poured. The munching of the sugary treat, the silence between the mouthfuls would have been difficult to bear if it hadn't been for Balthazar. He hopped around on Magnus' bed, sniffing the cake and getting cream on his nose.

Instead of talking about Eva, whom they couldn't talk about, they talked about Balthazar. Balthazar was the fifth living creature: Balthazar replaced Eva. They laughed at his antics, discussed the challenges and joys of rabbits.

After David's mother had left, David and Magnus played a couple of Pokémon matches so that Magnus could use the new cards. Sture followed the game with interest, but when Magnus tried to explain the complicated rules he shook his head.

'No, that's too hard for me. I'll stick to snap and gin rummy.'

Magnus won both of the matches and went into his room to play with Balthazar. It was half past nine. No more coffee could be drunk without courting indigestion and they had almost two hours to kill before they could set off. David was about to suggest a game of snap, but felt it would seem contrived. Instead he sat down emptyhanded across the kitchen table from Sture.

'I see you're performing tonight,' Sture said.

'What? Tonight?'

'Yes, or that's what it said in the paper anyway.'

David took out his calendar and checked. *17 August. NB 21.00.* Sture was right. He also saw to his dismay that he had a corporate gig in Uppsala on the nineteenth. Mission: to joke, clown, make people laugh. He rubbed his face.

'I'll have to call and cancel.'

Sture's eyes narrowed, as if he were squinting at the sun. 'Should you really do that?'

'Well you know, standing up there and…prancing around. No. I can't.'

'Maybe it would be good for you to get out a little.'

'Yes, but my routine. It'll be like having a mouth full of rocks. No.'

He could have added that a fair percentage of the audience would know what had happened to him after the story on TV4. The dead woman's husband performing. Most likely Leo had already cancelled him but forgotten to pull the ad.

Sture interlaced his fingers on the table. 'I can watch the boy if you like.'

'Thanks,' David said. 'We'll see. But I don't think so.'

Bondegatan 09.30

Saturday morning the doorbell rang at Flora's apartment. Maja, one of her few friends from school, was standing outside. She was a head taller than Flora, maybe thirty kilos heavier. On the lapel of her army surplus greatcoat there was a button that said, 'I bitch & I moan. What's your religion?'

'Come out for a bit,' she said.

Flora was happy to. The apartment felt breakfast-stuffy, the smell of toast an unhappy reminder of absent harmony. In addition, Flora only really smoked when she was with Maja—and she had a hankering to smoke.

They strolled aimlessly on the street as Maja lit up the first of the day and Flora took a couple of puffs.

'We've been talking about doing something at the Heath,' Maja said, and held out the cigarette.

'We?'

'Yeah, the group.'

Maja belonged to a sub-group of Young Left—mostly girls—who considered themselves creative. When *Café* magazine had their tenth birthday party on a boat, Patricia had poured out ten buckets of wallpaper paste on the docks in front of the gangplank and put up a sign, 'WARNING! SPERM!' The guests had been forced to wade through the grey-white mess until, with some effort, it was scrubbed away.

'What kind of thing?' Flora asked and gave the rest of the cigarette back. She had had enough.

'It's just...' Maja said and pointedly averted her gaze from a girly-girl in white linen pants who was out on a morning walk with a Maltese terrier, 'it's sick what they're doing with them. First they use them as some kind of guinea pigs and now they're going to herd them into a bloody ghetto.'

'Sure,' Flora said. 'But what's the alternative exactly?'

'Alternative? It doesn't matter what the alternative is. This is wrong. Society can only be judged...'

'...by how it treats its weakest members,' Flora filled in. 'Yes, I know, but...'

Maja waved her cigarette impatiently. 'There's never been a weaker group than the dead.' She gave a laugh. 'When was the last time you heard the dead speak up for their rights? They have none. The authorities can do what they want with them, and that's what they're going to do. Did you read that thing in *DN*, what the philosopher-bitch said?'

'Yes,' Flora said, 'and I get that it's wrong. I agree with you, so calm down. I'm just wondering...'

'You can wonder later. You identify the wrong, you do something to put it right. As soon as there's something new, you have to work out who has the power to make use of it. Let's say they do come up with an antidote to death, OK? What do you think they'll use it for? Make sure the population of Africa can live forever? I don't think so. Let every black person die of AIDS first, and we'll see what we can do with Africa after that. You've got to understand that the spread of AIDS is largely controlled by American pharmaceutical companies.' Maja shook her head. 'Ten to one they're out there sniffing around the Heath too.'

'I'm planning to go out there when it opens,' Flora said.

'Where? The Heath? I'll come with you.'

'I don't think you'll get in. Only family...'

'That's the kind of thing I'm talking about. How are you going to prove that you're family, then?'

'I don't know.'

Maja put out the cigarette by rolling it between her index finger and thumb. She stopped, cocked her head to one side and squinted at Flora.

'And what reason do you have to go there, anyway?'

'I don't know. I just...I have to go. Have to see what it's like.'

'You've got a thing about death, haven't you?'

'Hasn't everyone?'

Maja looked at her for a couple of seconds and then said, 'No.'

'Yes.'

'No.'

Flora shrugged. 'You have no idea what you're talking about.'

Maja grinned and sent the butt flying in an arc towards a rubbish bin. Amazingly, it went in. Flora applauded and Maja put an arm around her shoulders.

'Do you know what you are?'

Flora shook her head. 'No.'

'Pretentious. A little bit. I like it.'

They walked around and talked for another couple of hours. Then they parted and Flora took the subway to Tensta.

'We have to take the chance to argue our case when there are this many people gathering.'

'But will anyone listen to us?'

'I'm certain they will.'

'How will they hear us?'

'They'll have loudspeakers.'

'Do you think we'll be allowed to use them?'

'Let me put it this way: when Jesus drove the moneylenders out of the temple, do you think he asked permission? Excuse me, do you mind if I push this table over?'

The others laughed and Mattias folded his arms across his chest, pleased. Elvy was standing with her head resting against the door post, watching them in the kitchen, discussing the day's strategy. She did not take part. The last couple of days she had been feeling weak. It came from sleeplessness and the sleeplessness came from doubt.

She lay awake at night and struggled to hold on to her vision, to stop it from fading and receding into the jumble of images. Tried to understand.

Their only salvation is to come to me...

After the modest success of the first evening, the fishing for souls had stalled. Once the first shock had died down and it appeared that society was in fact capable of handling the situation, people were less willing to come on board. Elvy had only participated that first day. On the second day she was too tired.

'What do you think, Elvy?'

Mattias' round, childlike face turned toward her. It took Elvy a couple of seconds to understand what he was asking. Seven pairs of eyes watched her. As well as Mattias, the only man among them, there was Hagar, Greta, the neighbour woman and the other woman who had come the first evening. Elvy could not remember her name. Then there were two sisters, Ingegerd and Esmeralda, who were friends with the nameless woman. They were the ones who were here for the morning meeting. Other sympathisers would join them later.

'I think...' Elvy said. 'I think...I don't know what I think.'

Mattias frowned. Wrong answer. Elvy absentmindedly rubbed the scab on her forehead.

'You'll have to decide what you think is best and then...that's what we'll do. I think I have to go and lie down.'

Mattias caught up with her outside her bedroom door. He gently grabbed her shoulder.

'Elvy. This is *your* conviction, *your* vision. That is what we are here for.'

'Yes, I know.'

'Don't you believe in this anymore?'

'Yes. It is just that...I don't quite have the energy.'

Mattias put his hand on his cheek, his gaze sliding over Elvy's face. From the cut to her eyes, back to the cut.

'I believe in you. I believe you have a mission, an important one.'

Elvy nodded.

'Yes. It's just that...I don't quite know what it is.'

'Why don't you lie down for a while. We'll take care of this. We're leaving in one hour. Have you seen the flyers?'

'Yes.' Mattias stood there, waiting for something more. Elvy added, 'They look very good,' and went to the bedroom, closing the door behind her. Without undressing, she crawled in under the bedspread and pulled it up to her nose. Her eyes wandered around the room. Nothing was changed. She held her hands up to her eyes.

These are my hands.

She wiggled her fingers.

My fingers. They're moving.

The telephone rang in the hall. She could not be bothered to get up and answer. Someone, perhaps Esmeralda, picked up the receiver and said something.

There is nothing special about me.

Was it always like this?

The saints, the ones who had fought and died in the name of the Lord, Francis dancing eagerly before the pope, Birgitta burning with a holy fire in her cell. Did they have such doubts? Were there days when Birgitta thought she had misunderstood something, that she had made the whole thing up? Times when Francis just wanted to send his disciples away with a 'leave me in peace, I have nothing of value to say'?

There was no one to ask, they were all dead and settled into legend, their humanness long gone.

But she had *seen*.

Perhaps there were others who had seen, thousands through the ages. Perhaps what set the saints apart—the holy women and men—was that they held fast to what they had seen, not allowing their realisation to fade and die, but they *held on, held on* and refused to let go, saw forgetfulness as a tool of the devil and held on. Maybe this was the secret.

Elvy took hold of the bedspread, squeezing it hard.

Yes, Lord. I will hold on.

She shut her eyes and tried to rest. By the time her body finally started to relax, it was time to go.

Koholma 11.00

Elias had made progress. Great progress.

The first day he had not shown the slightest interest in the exercises from the book that Mahler tried to go through with him. Mahler had held out a shoe box and said, 'I wonder what there is in here?' and Elias had not moved, either before or after he opened the lid and showed him the little stuffed dog.

Mahler had put a brightly coloured top on Elias' night stand and set it in motion. The top spun itself out and then fell to the floor. Elias did not even follow it with his gaze. But Mahler kept going. The fact that Elias reached out for the bottle when it was brought to him indicated that he was capable of reacting, if he had a reason.

Anna did not object to the training program, but showed no enthusiasm either. She sat with Elias for hours; slept on a mattress on his floor. But she did nothing concrete, Mahler felt, to improve his condition.

It was the remote-controlled car that broke the ice. The second day Mahler put in fresh batteries and directed it into Elias' room, hoping the sight of the toy he had been so fond of would bring something in him to life. It did. As soon as the car banged into the room something happened to the way Elias held his body. Then he followed the car in its journey around the room. When Mahler brought it to a stop, Elias put his hand out for it.

Mahler did not give it to him, he let it drive around a couple more times. Then what Mahler had been hoping for happened. Slowly, slowly, as if he were wading through mud, Elias started to get up out of bed. When the car stopped, Elias halted for a moment, then continued to make his way up.

'Anna! Come take a look!'

Anna came up in time to see Elias drag his legs over the edge of the bed. She clapped her hand over her mouth, screamed and ran over to him.

'Don't stop him,' Mahler said. 'Help him.'

Anna held Elias under his arms and he got to his feet. With Anna's support he took a tentative step toward the car. Mahler drove it up a few centimetres, then back again. Elias took another step. When he was almost there and held out his hand, Mahler drove the car away, to the door.

'Let him take it,' Anna said.

'No,' Mahler said. 'Then he'll stop.'

Elias turned his head in the direction of the car, turned his body in the direction of his head and walked toward the door. Anna followed, tears streaming down her cheeks. When Elias reached the door, Mahler drove the car into the hall.

'Let him have it,' Anna's voice was muffled. 'He wants it.'

Mahler continued to steer the car away as soon as Elias caught up with it, until Anna stopped, with Elias straining in her arms.

'Stop,' she said. 'Stop. I can't keep doing this.'

Mahler let the car stop. Anna held Elias under his chest with both hands.

'You're making him into a robot,' she said. 'I don't want to be part of it.'

Mahler sighed and lowered the remote control.

'Would you rather he was just a lump? This is fantastic.'

'Yes,' Anna said. 'Yes it is. But it's...wrong.' Anna sank down onto the floor, shifted Elias onto her lap and took the car, giving it to him. 'Here, sweetheart.'

Elias' fingers flew across the plastic details on the car, as if searching for a way in. Anna nodded, stroking his hair. His hair had grown stronger and had stopped falling out, but there were a couple of bald spots from the first few days.

'He's wondering how it can be moving,' Anna said, and drew teary mucus into her nose. 'He's wondering what it is that has made it move.'

Mahler put down the remote control.

'How do you know that?'

'I just know,' Anna answered.

Mahler shook his head, walked out into the kitchen and got himself a beer. There had been several times since they had come here that Anna reported things that she *just knew* about what Elias wanted, and it irritated Mahler that she was using this supposed ability to slow down his training.

'...Elias doesn't like that top...Elias wants me to apply the cream...'

When Mahler asked her how she could know that, he always received the same answer: she *just knew*. He opened the beer, drank half and looked out the window. The tropical rain had not been enough to save the trees. Many were losing their leaves even though it was only the middle of August.

This time he thought Anna was right. Many of Elias' old toys had not stirred the slightest interest, so probably it was the movement inside the car that had awakened him. What use could they make of that?

Anna left Elias on the floor with the car and came into the kitchen.

'Sometimes,' Mahler said, still looking out of the window, 'sometimes I don't believe you want him to get better.'

He heard Anna draw breath to reply, and knew more or less what she was going to say. Before she had time to say it she was interrupted by a sharp crack from the hall.

Elias was sitting on the floor with the car in his hands. Somehow he had managed to break away the entire upper part of the chassis, so that parts and wires were revealed. Before Mahler could stop him he got hold of the battery pack and tore it away, holding it up to his eyes.

Mahler threw his arms out, looked at Anna.

'Well,' he said. 'Are you happy now?'

Elias had taken apart another battery-operated car before Mahler thought of getting a Brio train set with wooden pieces. The engine that came with it was so neatly made, with so few moving parts, that it resisted the attempts of Elias' still-weak fingers to deconstruct it.

That morning he had been in Norrtälje and bought yet another engine. Now he attached a strip of masking tape across the middle of the kitchen table in order to create a demarcation, two zones, and placed a tank engine in one. The first step of the autism training described in the book was a mimicking exercise. He laid three straight track pieces in each zone and then carried Elias out from the bedroom, placing him on a kitchen chair.

Elias looked at the window, toward the garden where Anna was mowing the lawn.

'Look,' Mahler said and held his engine out toward Elias. No reaction. He put the engine down on the table and started it. It made a hollow buzzing sound as it moved slowly across the surface. Elias turned his head toward the sound, reached his hand to it. Mahler took the engine away.

'There.'

He pointed at the identical engine in front of Elias. Elias leaned over the table and tried to get a hold of the engine still buzzing in Mahler's hand. He turned it off and pointed to Elias' engine again.

'There. That one is yours.'

Elias fell back in the chair, expressionless. Mahler stretched out his arm and clicked the on button of the engine in Elias' zone. It droned on across the table until Elias clumsily put his hand over it, grabbed hold of it, lifted it to his eyes and tried to pry off the turning wheels.

'No, no.'

Mahler walked around the table and managed to coax the train out of Elias' stiff hand, and placed it back on the table.

'Look.'

He put his own engine out on the other side of the table and turned it on. Elias stretched for it.

'There,' Mahler pointed to Elias' stationary train. 'There. Now you do that.'

Elias heaved his entire upper body across the table, grabbed hold of Mahler's engine and started trying to take it apart. Mahler did not like standing at this angle; there was a hole in Elias' head where his ear had been. He rubbed his eyes.

Why don't you understand? Why are you so stupid?

The engine made a crunching sound as Elias unexpectedly managed to break it open. The batteries fell to the floor.

'No, Elias. No!'

Mahler grabbed the pieces out of Elias' hand, angry despite himself; he was starting to get so awfully tired of all this. He smashed his own engine into the table and pointed with pedantic precision at the on button.

'Here. You start it here. Here.'

He turned it on. The train inched its way over to Elias and he took it, breaking off one of the wheels.

I can't bear it. He can't. He can't do anything.

'Why do you have to break everything?' he said out loud. 'Why do you have to destroy…'

Suddenly Elias bent his hand back and threw the engine at

Mahler's face. It struck him right across the mouth, splitting his lip, and from behind a red membrane he heard it bounce against the floor as the metal taste rose inside his head. He stared at Elias with a swelling anger. Elias' dark brown lips were pulled back in a grin. He looked...mean.

'What are you doing?' Mahler said. 'What are you doing?'

Elias' head was going back and forth as if shaken from behind by an invisible force and the legs of the chair teetered, hitting the floor. Before Mahler had time to do anything Elias collapsed, completely floppy. He collapsed on the chair and slid down on the floor as if his skeleton had suddenly been transformed into jelly. In slow motion, Mahler saw the chair fall after him, had time to realise that the back of it was going to strike Elias across the cheek before a whining sound pierced his skull like a dentist's drill and forced him to shut his eyes.

His hands went up to his temples and pressed, but the whining noise disappeared, as quickly as it had come. Elias was lying on the floor with the chair over him, absolutely still.

Mahler hurried over and lifted the chair away. 'Elias? Elias?'

The door to the verandah was opened and Anna entered. 'What are you...'

She threw herself on her knees beside Elias, stroking his cheeks. Mahler blinked, looked around the kitchen, and a shiver crawled up his spine.

There is someone here.

The whining returned, weaker this time. Switched off. Elias lifted his hand to Anna and she took it, kissing it. She looked angrily at Mahler, still turning his head this way and that to catch sight of someone he could not see. He licked his lip, which was already starting to swell up, the skin slick as plastic.

Gone.

Anna tugged on his shirt. 'You aren't allowed to do that.'

'I'm not allowed to...what?'

'Dislike him.'

Mahler's fingers flickered, pointing indeterminately toward different areas of the kitchen. 'There was someone...here.'

The perception of a presence was still palpable in the skin of his back. Someone had been watching him and Elias. He stood up, walked over to the counter and rinsed his face with cold water. Once he had wiped himself with a kitchen towel his head felt clearer. He sat on a stool.

'I can't handle this.'

'No,' Anna said. 'I can tell.'

Mahler picked up the half-destroyed engine and weighed it in his hand. 'I don't just mean...this. I mean...' his eyes narrowed, he looked at Anna. 'There is something. There is something I don't understand. Something else is going on here.'

'You don't want to listen,' Anna said. 'You've already made up your mind.'

She shifted Elias to the side so that he was lying on the rag rug in front of the stove. When you looked closely it was unmistakeable: Elias might have made some progress, nearing a kind of consciousness, but his body had shrunk further. The arms poking out of the pyjamas were just bone covered in parchment-like skin, his face a skull, painted and garnished with a wig. It was impossible to imagine a soft, wet, working brain inside.

Mahler made a fist and banged it against his leg.

'What is it I don't understand? What is it. I don't. Understand?'

'That he is dead,' Anna said.

Mahler was about to argue the point when there was the clomp of clogs on the stoop and the front door opened.

'Yoo-hoo in there!'

Mahler and Anna's eyes met and for a second they were united in panic. Aronsson's clogs thundered on into the house and Mahler rushed up from the table, placing himself as an obstacle in the kitchen doorway.

Aronsson looked up and pointed to Mahler's lip. 'Well, well. Been in a fight, have you?' He laughed at his own wit and removed his hat, fanning his face. 'How are you holding up in the heat?'

'OK,' Mahler said. 'It's just, we're a bit busy right now.'

'I understand,' Aronsson said. 'I won't interrupt. I just wanted to hear if they'd picked up your garbage.'

'Yes.'

'I see. But not mine. Not for two weeks. I've called and complained and they say they're coming out, but they don't come. And in this heat. They can't keep carrying on like this.'

'No.'

Aronsson knit his brows. He sensed something. In theory, Mahler could simply have wrapped his arms around him, carried him to the door and thrown him out. Later he would wish that this was what he had done. Aronsson peered past him.

'Fine company, I see. The whole family. That's lovely.'

'We were just going to eat.'

'I see, I see. Well, don't let me interrupt. I just want to say hello...'

Aronsson tried to get past, but Mahler put his hand against the door post so that his arm created a barrier. Aronsson blinked.

'What's wrong with you, Gustav? I just want to say hello to the girl.'

Anna got up quickly, intending to greet Aronsson in the doorway so he wouldn't have to enter the kitchen. When Mahler lowered his arm to let her past, Aronsson ducked in.

'Well, goodness me,' he said and held out his hand to Anna. 'It's been a while hasn't it?'

His sharp eyes scanned the room and Anna didn't bother to say hello; it was too late anyway. Aronsson caught sight of Elias and his eyes widened, locking on like a radar that has finally found its target. His tongue appeared, licking his lips, and for one second Mahler debated whether or not he should hit him in the head with the cast iron pot holder.

Aronsson pointed to Elias. 'What is...that?'

Mahler grabbed him by the shoulders, dragging him into the hall. 'That is Elias, and now you have to go home.' He took the hat out of Aronsson's hands and pushed it onto his head. 'I could ask you to keep quiet, but I know there's no point. Go away.'

Aronsson wiped some spittle from his mouth. 'Is he...dead?'

'No,' Mahler said as he forced Aronsson toward the front door. 'He is reliving and I was trying to help him get better. But that's the end of that, if I know you.'

Aronsson backed out onto the porch with an inscrutable little smile pasted on his face. He was most likely figuring out who exactly he should call to turn them in.

'Well, good luck then,' he said and left, still backing up. Mahler slammed the door.

Anna was sitting on the kitchen floor with Elias in her lap.

'We have to leave,' Mahler said, expecting resistance, but Anna simply nodded. 'Yes. I guess we do.'

They tossed everything in the refrigerator into a cooler and packed Elias' things in a gym bag. Mahler was careful to include the engine and the other toys. The cell phone, some extra clothes. They didn't have sleeping bags or a tent, but Mahler had a plan. The past couple of days, particularly before he fell asleep, he had run through various scenarios, what they would do if this occurred, or this. Now this *had* occurred and in the plastic bag with the clothes he included a hammer, a screwdriver and a crowbar.

Past summers when they had gone out to sea for a whole day, the packing had taken over an hour. Now, when they were going to stay away indefinitely, it took ten minutes and probably they had forgotten about half of what they needed.

So be it. Mahler could return to the mainland at a later point and get provisions if needed. The thing was to get Elias out of the way.

They walked slowly through the forest. Anna was carrying the bags, Mahler had Elias. His heart wasn't giving him any trouble, but he knew this was one of those occasions when he could very well suffer an attack if he did not take it easy.

Elias was a statue in his arms. No sign of life. Mahler trod carefully, unable to look down, feeling his way with his feet over the roots that crossed the path. Sweat stung his eyes.

All this work. For this little scrap of life.

Svarvagatan 11.15

Sture's Volvo 740 was newly washed but a strong smell of wood and linseed oil still clung to it. Sture was a carpenter, and he lived in a hexagonal cottage with an extension at the front, designed by himself for summer guests.

Magnus crawled into the back seat and David handed him the basket with Balthazar, then sat down in the passenger seat. Sture rifled through the maps that he had torn out of the phone book, scratching his head and trying to locate the place.

'The Heath, the Heath...'

'I don't think it's on the map,' David said. 'It's Järva field. Towards Akalla.'

'Akalla...'

'Yes. North-west.'

Sture shook his head. 'Maybe it's better if you drive.'

'I'd rather not,' David said. 'I feel...I'd rather not.'

Sture looked up from the page. A smile flickered at the corner of his mouth and he leaned forward, opening the glove compartment.

'I brought these.' He gave David two wooden dolls, about fifteen centimetres tall, and started the car. 'I'll drive out to the E20 and then we'll see.'

The dolls were silken as only wood sanded down by hands and fingers can be. They were a boy and a girl, and David knew their story.

When Eva was little Sture had worked as a construction carpenter in Norway two weeks on, one week off. On one of his weeks at home he had carved the dolls and given them to his then six-year-old daughter. To his delight they had become her favourite toys, even though she had both Barbie and Ken and Barbie's dog.

The funny thing was that she had given the dolls names: they were called Eva and David. Eva told him this story a couple of months after they met.

'It was inevitable,' she said. 'I've been fated to be with you since I was six years old.'

David closed his eyes, rubbing his fingers over the dolls.

'Do you know why I made them?' Sture asked, his gaze on the road.

'No.'

'In case I died. It wasn't completely without risks, that job. So I thought that *if*...that she would have something left.' He sighed. 'But I wasn't the one who died.' He sounded wistful. Eva's mother had died of cancer six years earlier and Sture was affronted, somehow, that it had not been him, the less valuable person.

Sture glanced at the dolls. 'I don't know. I probably thought... something that would get her to remember.'

David nodded, thinking about what he would leave for Magnus. Piles of paper. Videos of himself performing. He had never made anything with his hands. Nothing worth keeping, at least.

David directed Sture through the city as best he could. Many times people honked at them, since Sture was driving so slowly. But they reached their goal. At ten minutes to twelve they parked on the field close to a hastily erected parking sign. Hundreds of other cars were lined up. Sture turned off the engine and they remained seated.

'We don't have to pay for parking, at least,' David said to break the silence. Magnus opened his door and got out, the basket in his arms. Sture's hands were still resting on the steering wheel. He looked out at the crowds of people outside the gates.

'I'm afraid,' he said.

'I know,' David said. 'Me too.'

Magnus rapped on the window.

'Come *on*!'

Sture took the dolls before he left the car. He held them in tightly clenched fists as they walked toward Eva.

The area was bordered by a newly erected fence that raised the uncomfortable association of a concentration camp, which was what, in the purely literal sense of the term, it was. A gathering place. The perspective was distorted by the fact that the hordes of people were located outside the fence while the area on the inside was empty. Only the grey buildings scattered on the field, fenced in.

There were two gates and at each gate there were four guards. Even if they had not had rifles or even batons, but were placing their trust in the self-control of the masses, it was difficult to see how this could be Sweden. David was tormented less by the repressive aura of the fence or the crowd than the general impression of carnival. An audience agog, eager to see what was concealed beyond the barriers. And that Eva was somewhere at the heart of this circus.

A young man came over and put a piece of paper in his hand.

DO YOU DARE TO LIVE WITHOUT GOD?
THE WORLD WILL CEASE TO EXIST
MAN WILL BE OBLITERATED
PLEASE, PLEASE, PLEASE
TURN TO GOD
BEFORE IT IS TOO LATE
WE CAN HELP YOU

The flyer was well made; an elegantly printed text superimposed onto the pale background figure of the Virgin Mary. The man handing it out looked more like a real estate agent than a fanatic. David nodded thanks and walked on, holding Magnus by the hand. The man took a side step to stand in front of them.

'This is serious,' he said. 'This...' he pointed at the flyer and shrugged. 'This kind of thing is hard to express. We aren't an organisation, no church, but we know, OK? All of this...' His arm swept in the direction of the fence, 'all of this will go to hell if we don't turn to God.'

He threw a pitying glance at Magnus, and if David had been charmed for a couple of seconds by the man's humble words and his *please, please, please*, then this look convinced him that even if the guy was right, he was disgusting.

'Excuse us,' David said and pulled Magnus along. The man made no further attempts to stop them.

'Crackpot,' Sture said.

David thrust the paper in his pocket and saw others lying scrunched up, scattered in the grass. Something was happening in the crowd: a thickening, an increase in concentration. There was a puffing sound that David knew well; someone was testing a microphone.

'One, two...'

They stopped.

'What are they doing?' Sture asked.

'No idea,' David answered. 'Someone must be...going to perform.'

It was starting to look more and more like a festival of some kind. Soon Tomas Ledin would climb up on stage and belt out a couple of numbers. David felt his stomach cramp up, his anxiety spreading to encompass the whole situation. The possibility of the whole thing coming apart; the agony of watching a comedian dying onstage.

The Minister of Social Affairs approached the microphone. There were scattered boos that died down when they received no support. David looked around. Despite the TV and newspapers covering little else but the reliving over the past few days, he had not been able to view this as anything but his own personal drama. Now he realised this was not the case.

Several TV cameras were sticking up out of the crowd, even more were gathered at the front by the podium where the minister was now straightening his suit jacket and leaning forward, tapping the mike—*ladies and gentlemen, boys and girls*—and said:

'Welcome. As a representative of the government I want, first and foremost, to apologise. This has taken far too long. Thank you for your patience. As you understand, this situation took us by surprise and we made a series of decisions that in hindsight can perhaps be judged as not the most enlightened...'

Magnus pulled on David's hand, and he bent down.

'Yes?'

'Dad, why is that man talking?'

'Because he wants everyone to like him.'

'What is he saying?'

'Nothing. Do you want me to take Balthazar?'

Magnus shook his head and gripped the basket more tightly. David thought his arms must be tired, but let it go. He saw that Sture was standing with his arms folded over his chest, scowling. Perhaps David's fears of a disastrous performance had not been so far off the mark. Luckily the minister had the presence of mind to bring things to a rapid close and give the word to a man in a lightweight suit who introduced himself as the head of the Department of Neurology at Danderyd Hospital.

From his first words it was clear that he was critical of the whole carnival atmosphere, even though he did not say as much.

'So to my real point. There has been much speculation and many rumours, but the fact is that people can read each other's thoughts in the proximity of the reliving. I'm not going to dwell on how we have all tried to avoid facing these facts, to rationalise them or soft-pedal the issue. The fact remains…' he pointed toward the enclosed area with a gesture that David felt was unnecessarily theatrical, 'when you pass through these gates you will hear what people around you are thinking. We still don't know how it is possible, but you must be prepared for the fact that the experience is not altogether…pleasant.'

The neurologist went silent for a moment and let his last words sink in, as if he half expected people to split off from the crowd and start leaving, for fear of the unpleasant experience. This did not happen. David, whose profession it was to sense an audience's emotions, could feel a growing impatience. People were stirring restlessly, scratching arms and legs. They were not interested in caveats, they wanted to see their dead.

The neurologist, however, was not finished.

'The effect is less noticeable now that your reliving have been separated—that is one of the reasons that we are here—but it is still present, and I would ask you, as much as humanly possible…' he tilted his head and said in a lightly jocular tone, 'try to think nice thoughts. All right?'

People looked around at each other, some smiled as if to confirm how nice their thoughts were already. The growing pain in David's stomach signalled impending calamity, and he crouched down, his hands clasped around his middle.

'Well, that was all I had to say,' the neurologist said. 'At the gates you will be informed of the exact location of the person you are looking for. Thank you.'

David heard a rustle of clothing as the mass of people started to move forward. If he moved, he would soil himself.

'Dad, what is it?'

'Just a little stomach ache. It'll be fine.'

Yes. The pressure momentarily subsided and he could straighten up, look out over the thousands of heads now dividing into two more compact masses around the gates. Sture shook his head, said, 'It's going to take hours like this.'

Eva, are you there?

Testing, David sent out the strongest thought he could muster, but received no answer. That field they were talking about—where exactly did it start, and why was it only the living could hear each other, not the reliving?

A police officer wandering around, underemployed in the well-mannered crowd, came up to them and said hello. They returned the greeting and the policeman pointed to the basket in Magnus' lap.

'What do you have there?'

'Balthazar,' Magnus answered.

'His rabbit,' David answered. 'It's his birthday today and...' he fell silent, sensing that an explanation wouldn't matter either way.

The policeman smiled. 'Well, congratulations! Were you planning to bring it in? The rabbit?'

Magnus looked up at David.

'That's what we'd been thinking, yes,' David said. He didn't dare lie for fear that Magnus would contradict him.

'I don't think that's such a good idea.'

Sture took a step closer. 'Why not?' he asked. 'Why can't he bring the animal?'

The policeman held up his palms, *Only following orders.* 'There aren't supposed to be any animals in there, that's all I know. Sorry.'

The policeman walked away and Magnus sat down on the ground with the basket on his lap. 'I'm not going in.'

Sture and David looked at each other. Neither of them was going to stay outside with Magnus, and leaving Balthazar in the car was probably out of the question. David stared angrily at the policeman who had wandered on with his hands clasped behind his back, wishing he had been able to pulverise him with his thoughts.

'Let's walk around a bit,' Sture said. They moved around the outskirts of the crowd in a wide quarter circle until they left it and arrived at a forested area where, to his relief, David spotted a couple of portaloos. He excused himself, selected the one with the least graffiti, sat down and exploded with freedom. When he was done he discovered that there was no toilet paper. He tried to use the flyer but the shiny paper was only good for smearing. He removed his socks, used them and tossed them into the hole.

All right...now...

David felt better. Everything was going to go well. He tied his shoe laces on his bare feet and walked out. Sture and Magnus were looking secretive.

'What is it?' David asked.

Sture lifted his jacket a little like a black market dealer and showed the inner pocket with Balthazar's head sticking up. Magnus giggled and Sture shrugged: it was worth a shot anyhow. David had no objections. He was cleansed inside now, unbound and light of heart. Just as the neurologist had requested.

They walked back to the gates. Sture complained that Balthazar was nibbling on his shirt and Magnus laughed. David glanced at Sture, who was struggling exaggeratedly with his jacket, and felt enormous gratitude. It would not have been possible without him. The tension around smuggling Balthazar in appeared to have distracted Magnus completely from the visit ahead of them.

They reached the gates in time for another speech. The crowd had shrunk considerably in their absence, so presumably the guards were not particularly strict about verifying relatives' identities. Before they had reached the queue, something happened up on the podium.

Two elderly women got up on stage and switched on the PA. Before anyone had time to react, one of them approached the microphone.

'Hello?' she called out and was startled by the strength of her own voice, taking half a step back. The other lady put a hand to her ear. The one who had spoken summoned her courage, stepped up again and repeated, 'Hello! I just want to say that all of this is a mistake. The dead have awakened because their souls have returned. This is about our souls. We are all lost if we do not...'

She did not get any further. The PA was turned off and her prescription for how to avoid being lost could only be heard by those closest to the stage. A very large man in a suit, most likely security, got up on stage, ushered the woman firmly away from the microphone and led her to the ground. The other woman followed.

'Daddy?' Magnus asked. 'What is a soul anyway?'

'Something that some people think we have inside of us.'

Magnus felt with his hands over his body.

'Where is it, then?'

'Nowhere in particular. It's like an invisible ghost where all the thoughts and feelings come from, sort of. Some people think that when we die it flies out of the body.'

Magnus nodded. 'I think so.'

'Yes,' David said. 'But I don't.'

Magnus turned to Sture who was holding a hand over his heart as if he was having a heart attack. 'Grandad? Do you believe in the soul?'

'Yes,' Sture said. 'Absolutely. I also believe I'm getting a hole in my shirt. Can we go?'

They got in line. There were still a couple of hundred people ahead of them but the line was moving rapidly. In ten minutes they would be inside.

The Heath 12.15

When Flora reached the Heath and saw the great mass of people and how quickly it was shrinking, her hope of getting in increased. She did not have the same last name as her grandfather and no way to prove her status. She had called Elvy that morning to get a signed document, but as usual she only got to talk with a lady who said that Elvy was busy.

She went and stood in one of the lines snaking up toward the gates. Over the last few days she had spoken several times to Peter, who had avoided discovery during the clear-out and managed to stay in his basement. The evening before, however, his battery had gone flat and he had no possibility of getting out to where there was electricity as long as the feverish activity in the area continued.

Damn, how they must have worked.

Just the feat of putting up at least three kilometres of fence to encircle the area. In two days. One of the few times that Peter had dared to go out he had reported that the area was swarming with military personnel and that the work was continuing round the clock. The press had either been excluded or come to some kind of arrangement, and nothing had been written about the Heath until the Prime Minister made his announcement.

Flora moved slowly forward, straightening the backpack full of fruit that she had brought for Peter. In her head she counted prime numbers—*one, two, three, five, seven, eleven, thirteen, seventeen*—since it was almost unbearable standing here among all these people.

The whiff of fear she could pick up on the streets was nothing to what she found here. Wherever she turned her attention she caught the same signals. People looked as they usually did, possibly somewhat more abstracted in their gaze, a little more purposeful, but there were deep-sea creatures swimming inside them, the terror of confronting the completely unknown; *the other.*

nineteen, twenty-three...

Unlike her, most of the people here had never seen one of the undead. They were here because relatives had awakened in morgues, their dearly departed had been plucked out of the earth by the military and transported to sealed wards. There were good reasons to fear the worst, and that was exactly what people were doing. Flora tried to shut her brain from the ever-present horror and could not understand why people had decided to enact their reunions in this way.

She lowered her head and tried to escape through concentration.

Twenty-nine, thirty-one...thirty-seven...to show they have everything under control...thirty-nine, no...mum rotten face fingers bone...forty-one...forty-one...

'Hello?'

A voice echoed through the fog of thoughts, a voice she knew well. She opened her eyes, lifted her head and saw her grandmother for the first time in four days. On stage, with Hagar standing right behind her.

She was so flabbergasted that she lost control of the Power and was overwhelmed by a wave of jumbled, frightened thoughts that drowned out the sound of her Nana's voice. She caught something about 'souls' before Elvy was forced down from the stage. Flora ran over.

A guard was holding Elvy by the shoulders, but he let go just as Flora arrived, his attention now directed at a besuited man by the sound equipment. The guard raised a finger at the man, at the amplifier, '...get the hell away from those things. You stay right here.'

'Nana!'

Elvy looked up and Flora winced. Elvy had aged so much since they last saw each other. Her face was grey and sunken; she had dark circles under her eyes as if she had not slept in several days. The arms that embraced Flora were slack and thin.

'Nana, how are you?'

'Fine.'

'You don't look well.'

Elvy fingered a scab on her forehead. 'Perhaps I'm a little... tired.'

The guard shoved the younger man over to Elvy and said, 'Now you get away from here, right now.'

Many people had assembled around them, mostly older women who walked over to Elvy, patting her and whispering among themselves.

'Nana,' Flora said. 'What are you doing?'

'Hi,' the younger man held out his hand and Flora shook it. 'Are you Flora?'

Flora nodded and dropped the man's hand. She could not read him through the murmur, which was both an unusual and disconcerting feeling. Hagar came over and patted Flora's arm. 'Hello dearie. How are you?'

'I'm fine,' Flora said and gestured at the stage. 'What was that?'

'What? Oh, sorry,' Hagar fiddled with something behind her ear. 'What did you say?'

'I'm just wondering what you're doing.'

The man answered for Hagar.

'Your grandmother,' he said in a tone that implied that Flora should be proud to be her granddaughter, 'received a message that

266

people need to be saved. That there isn't much time. That it has to be done now. We are her assistants in this struggle. Are you a believer?'

Flora shook her head and the man gave a laugh.

'That's almost comical, isn't it? From what I understand you ought to have been the first to sign on after what both of you experienced that evening in the garden...'

Flora felt creeped out that the man knew about an experience that she herself had not shared with anyone. Elvy was being taken care of by her old ladies and for a moment Flora had a vision that her haggardness was because those helping hands were in fact sucking the life out of her.

'Nana? What is the *message* you have received?'

'Your grandmother...' the man started, but Flora ignored him and walked over to Elvy, laying a hand on her arm. Perhaps because they were so close to the reliving Flora found a sharp image projected into her head: a woman in a television screen, surrounded by a bright light.

...Their only salvation is to come to me...

The television turned off, the image faded and Flora stared into Elvy's tired eyes.

'What does that mean?'

'I don't know. Just that I have to do something. I don't know.'

'But you can't handle it. I can see that.'

Elvy closed her eyes half-way and smiled.

'Oh, I think I can handle it.'

'Why don't you answer when I ring you?'

'I will. I'm sorry.'

One of the women came over and stroked Elvy's back.

'Come along, love. We'll have to think of something else.'

Elvy nodded faintly and allowed herself to be led away. Flora called out to her, 'Nana! I'm going in to see Grandpa.'

Elvy turned around. 'You do that. Give him my best.'

Flora stayed where she was, her arms hanging, unsure what to do. When all of this was over, when she had seen what there was to be seen she would go out to Elvy's and...free her? Well, do something. But not now. Now she had to see.

She joined the line, trying to recall the image that Elvy had sent to her. She did not understand. Was it a television program? She thought she vaguely recognised the woman, but could not place her.

An actress? Daddy all the flowers his hand the lid the earth

It was impossible to think logically with all of these people around. She was forced to put her thoughts in a sealed box, which floated and bobbed around in the others' streams; she could not focus.

In front of her there was a child holding a man by the hand. Next to them was an older gentleman, fidgeting. The incomprehensible image of a rabbit flashed through her head. It hopped around for a couple of moments in the streams and was washed away by coffins, earth, vacant eyes, guilt.

Their only salvation is to come to me.

Yes, Flora thought. People needed some kind of help, that much was clear. She was almost up at the gates now and could see with her normal vision how the people around her were becoming grimmer, more determined; she felt how they tried, and failed, to damp down their fear. Like children on their way into the ghost train for the first time: what *is* it in there, anyway?

Someone pushed her in the back, she heard a woman's voice: 'Lennart, what is it?'

The man's voice was throaty, 'Well, I don't know...I don't know if I...can handle this...'

She turned around and saw a man being supported by a woman. The man's face had a greyish cast, his eyes were wide. The gaze met Flora's and he pointed into the area and said:

'Dad...I didn't like him. When I was little, he used to...'

The woman pulled on the man's arm, shushing him and smiling apologetically at Flora who instantly saw their whole marriage, the man's childhood. What she saw made her turn away from them with a shudder.

'Eva Zetterberg.'

It was the man in front of her who spoke, the man with the child. The guard with the lists asked, 'And you are?'

'Her husband,' the man replied and pointed to the boy and the older man. 'Her son, her father.'

The guard nodded and flipped through to one of the last pages in his packet, running his finger down the column.

The rabbit, the rabbit…

Bruno the Beaver. And a rabbit. A baby rabbit in a pocket. Even the boy, Eva Zetterberg's son, was thinking about a rabbit. The same rabbit. This is what they looked like, her family. And they were thinking about a rabbit.

'17C,' the guard said and pointed into the compound. 'Follow the signs.'

The family set off quickly through the gates. Flora caught a sense of relief and she memorised 17C. The guard looked sternly at her.

'Tore Lundberg,' Flora said.

'And you are?'

'His granddaughter.'

The guard looked appraisingly at her, evaluating her clothing, her black-painted eyes, her big hair and she realised she would not be let in.

'Can you prove it?'

'No,' Flora said. 'Afraid not.'

It was meaningless to engage in a debate; the guard was thinking about cobblestones, youths prying up cobblestones.

She walked away from the gates and followed the fence, letting her fingers trail across the chain links. The streams of thoughts faded away, becoming fainter the farther away she got and it was like coming inside after a storm. She continued until the people inside her died away then sat down in the grass, taking a mental breather.

When she felt OK again she continued along the fence until the angle of the buildings shielded her from the guards at the gate. The fence looked perverse, quite disconnected from the people it was supposed to keep out or keep in. A military neurosis.

There would be no real problem climbing it, the problem was the open area between her and the buildings. It surprised her that there were no other guards on; if it had been a concert, for example, they would have been posted every twenty metres. Maybe they hadn't been counting on people wanting to sneak in.

So why the fence?

She heaved her backpack over, grateful that her favourite sneakers had fallen apart and she'd worn her boots; their narrow points fit perfectly into the wide links and she was over in ten seconds. She crouched down on the other side—pointlessly, since she stood out like a swan on a telephone wire—and eventually concluded that her break-in didn't seem to have triggered any activity. She wrestled her pack back on and walked toward the buildings.

Koholma 12.30

Mahler had been prepared for the situation they now found themselves in. The boat at the dock was bailed out and fuelled up. He laid Elias down, stepped into the boat and took the bags and the cooler Anna held out to him.

'Life jackets,' Anna said.

'We don't have time.'

Mahler saw the vests hanging on the hooks in the shed, saw also that Elias had outgrown his.

'He's lighter now,' Anna said.

Mahler shook his head and stowed the bags. Together they made a bed for Elias on the floor with a blanket and Anna cast off while Mahler tried to start the engine. It was an antique twenty horse-power Penta and as Mahler pulled the cord he wondered if there were any statistics on exactly how many heart attacks troublesome outboard motors had caused through the ages.

...don't av...ight...ack...elker

After eight futile attempts he had to take a break. He sat in the stern and rested his arms on his knees.

'Anna? Did you just say, "You don't have the right knack, Mr Melker?"'

'No,' Anna said. 'But I was thinking it.'

'Ah.'

Mahler looked at Elias. His shrivelled face was unmoving, the half-closed black eyes staring at the sky. During their walk down to the dock Mahler had felt very clearly what he had earlier only guessed: that Elias was lighter, much lighter since that night four days ago when he had risen from his grave.

There was no time to think. How long would it take before Aronsson called, before someone came? He rubbed his eyes; a faint headache was starting.

'Take it easy,' Anna said. 'I'm sure it'll take at least half an hour.'

'Can you please stop,' Mahler said.

'Stop what?'

'Stop...being in my head. I get it. You don't have to prove it.'

Anna said nothing as she crawled down from the bench and sat down on the blanket next to Elias. The sweat ran into Mahler's eyes, stinging. He turned to the motor and jerked so forcefully on the rope that he thought it would snap. Instead the engine roared into life. He eased the choke, put it in drive and they glided off.

Anna sat with her cheek lightly resting against Elias' head. Her lips were moving. Mahler brushed the sweat out of his eyes and felt there was a secret here he was not privy to. He had read about the telepathic phenomena with regard to the reliving but he couldn't read Anna. Why not, when his own consciousness was an open book to her?

The wind, as promised by the shipping forecast, was weak to moderate. The waves clucked against the plastic hull as they zoomed out of the sound. Occasional breakers could be seen out in the bay.

'Where are we headed?' Anna shouted.

Mahler did not reply, simply thinking *Labbskär Island* in defiance.

Anna nodded. Mahler turned the throttle up full.

It wasn't until they reached the Finland ferry route and Mahler had checked that there were no ferries around that he realised he had forgotten to bring the map. He closed his eyes and visualised their course.

Fejan...Sundskär...Remmargrundet...

As long as they could follow the ferry route there were no problems. And he seemed to remember that the radio mast on Manskär would be right ahead of them until it was time to turn south. Then it got harder. The waters around Hamnskär were treacherous and lined with reefs.

He glanced at Anna and received an inscrutable look in return. She knew that they did not have the map and were in danger of getting lost. Probably she also saw the outline of the map he was trying to sketch inside his head. It was unpleasant, like being watched through a two-way mirror. He didn't like the fact that she could read his thoughts. He didn't like the fact that she could read that he didn't like the fact that she could read his thoughts. He didn't like the fact that...

Stop it!

That's just how it is. For an instant when he had started the motor he had heard her. Why only then? What had he done in that moment that had led to...

He looked up and felt his heart lurch. He did not recognise their surroundings. The islands gliding past were nondescript, unfamiliar. A couple of seconds after he thought this, Anna sat up and looked over the railing. Mahler's gaze roved across the blurring landmasses with growing panic. Nothing. Just islands. It was like waking up in an unfamiliar room where you'd passed out drunk: complete disorientation, the feeling of being in another world.

Anna pointed across the port railing and shouted, 'Is that Botveskär?'

Mahler squinted through the sun glitter, saw the white dot at the very tip of the island. Botveskär? In that case the dot straight ahead was Rankarögrund and…yes. The map fell into place. He veered east and within a minute he was back in the main passage again. He looked at Anna, thought *thank you*. Anna nodded and returned to Elias.

After travelling in silence for a quarter of an hour they drew close to Remmargrund. Mahler was looking south, trying to find the inlet where they should turn in, when he heard a sound through the roar of the motor. A deep, bassy thumping sound. He looked around but there was no sign of the ferry he was expecting to see.

Foumfoumfoum.

Was it in his head? The sound was completely different from the whining that had shot through him in the kitchen. He turned back again and this time he managed to glimpse the source of the sound: a helicopter. The instant he formed the mental picture *helicopter*, Anna sank to the floor and pulled the blanket over Elias.

Mahler tried to sift through various courses of action and found there was only one: sit still and do nothing. They were alone in a little boat out at sea. It was not possible to hide or defend themselves in any way. The helicopter—a military helicopter, he now saw—was almost overhead and movie images began to flash through his head: a thumb on the trigger, rockets, cascades of water, the boat shattering, the three of them flying metres up into the air, perhaps catching a glimpse of the earth from another perspective before everything went black.

Sweden, he thought. *Sweden*. That sort of thing doesn't happen here.

The helicopter passed them and Mahler tensed, expecting a voice in a megaphone, *Turn off the engine* or something, but the helicopter continued, turning abruptly southward and becoming smaller and smaller. Mahler laughed with relief as he simultaneously cursed himself.

The islands. Freedom. Indeed. And less than a nautical mile

from the outermost part of the archipelago which housed the large military base at Hamnskär. But did that matter?

Where do you hide the letter that mustn't be found? In the waste basket, of course.

Perhaps it would be an advantage.

He kept his gaze trained on the shrinking helicopter and then spotted the inlet, swerved and followed in the tracks of the enemy.

The water level was so low that many of the most hazardous reefs stuck up above the surface, or appeared as greenish patches over which the waves broke differently. To his amazement, he remembered the way quite well. After another twenty minutes at half-speed they were there.

His biggest concern was that there would be people in the cottage. Mahler didn't think it was likely at this time of year, but he couldn't be certain. He throttled back, gliding through the narrow sound between the islands at a couple of knots. No boat was tied to the dock and that was more or less cast-iron proof that no one was there.

The trip had taken almost an hour and Mahler had become chilled by the wind. He turned the motor off and floated in to the dock. Here between the islands there was almost no wind and the silence was wonderful. The afternoon sun glittered in the still water and everything breathed peace.

They had been here a couple of times before; eaten sandwiches on the rocks and swum. He liked this stark island, almost at the edge of the Åland sea. Mahler had fantasised about one day being able to buy one of the two fishing cottages, the only buildings on the island.

Anna sat up and peered over the railing. 'It's beautiful.'

'Yes.'

The naked rocks down by the water were covered, farther in towards the island, in a blanket of low junipers. Meadows of heath; the occasional alder. The island was small, you could walk around it in fifteen minutes and not find much variety in the vegetation. A little world; one that could be known completely.

They tied the boat up in silence, carried Elias and their things to one of the cottages. Mahler had done most of the talking for the past few days. When he no longer needed to speak, it was quiet.

They laid Elias wrapped in the blanket on a patch of heath and started to look for the key. They checked the pit toilet fifty metres behind the house and noted that the waste at the bottom was dried up. No one had been here for a long time. They looked under the loose stones around the steps, in hollowed-out spaces, under logs. No key.

Mahler laid the tools out on a rock, looked at Anna and received her assent. He jammed the crowbar in the crack of the door, bashed it in deeper with the hammer and applied pressure. The lock gave way immediately. The door frame was somewhat rotten—the mortice was ripped off and the door flew open.

A gust of stale air rushed out, so the cottage was not as drafty as you might have imagined. A good sign if they had to stay here for any length of time. Mahler examined the lock. A large piece of the door post had come away and it would be difficult to repair for whoever owned the place. He sighed.

'We'll have to leave a little money for them.'

Anna looked around, took in the island basking in the afternoon sun and said, 'Or a lot of money.'

It was a two-room house, approximately twenty metres square. There was no electricity or running water, but in the kitchen there was a stove with two hot plates connected to a large propane gas tank. A water container with a tap sat on the kitchen counter. Mahler lifted it. Empty. He slapped his forehead.

'Water,' he said. 'I forgot water.'

Anna was carrying in Elias into the next room to put him to bed. She paused. 'You know, I don't get it.' She nodded at Elias. 'Why don't we give him ordinary sea water?'

'Sure,' Mahler said. 'We probably can. But what about us? We can't drink sea water.'

'There's no fresh water at all?'

While Anna was tucking Elias in Mahler searched the kitchen. He found a number of the things he had expected to, and had not bothered to bring along: plates and cutlery, two fishing rods and a net. But no water. Finally he opened the refrigerator, also hooked up to a gas tank, and found a bottle of ketchup and a couple of cans of sardines in tomato sauce. He hesitantly unscrewed the gas tank and found it was empty.

The tank for the stove hissed forcefully when he tried it and he immediately shut it off.

Water.

He had forgotten it for the same reason that they needed it: it was so basic. There was always water. There is no Swedish house without a well, or a well within walking distance.

Except in the archipelago, of course.

He stood in the middle of the kitchen and saw a troll painting in front of him. A pair of trolls grilling fish over an open fire. He'd had an almost identical picture over his bed when he was a child. Although...no, that wasn't right. The trolls were painted long after his childhood.

His gaze travelled across the kitchen one last time but no water appeared anywhere.

Anna had put Elias in one of the beds and was leaning over it, studying a painting on the wall. The painting depicted a couple of trolls grilling fish over an open fire.

'Look,' she said. 'I had an almost identical one...'

'Over your bed when you were little,' Mahler said.

'Yes. How did you know? I didn't think you ever came to see me and Mum at our place.'

Mahler sat down on a chair.

'I heard it,' he said. 'I hear things from time to time.'

'Do you hear...' she nodded at Elias, 'him?'

'No, that is…' he stopped. 'Do you?'

'Yes.'

'Why haven't you said anything?'

'I have told you.'

'No, you haven't.'

'Yes, I have. You didn't want to listen.'

'If you'd said straight out that…'

'Listen to yourself,' Anna said. 'Even now, when I'm telling you that yes, I can hear Elias, I know what is going on inside his head, even now you don't ask *what it is*, you just try to put me in my place.'

Mahler looked at Elias, tried to make himself empty, receptive; a blank slate for Elias to write on. His head was buzzing, fragments of images flashed by, disappearing before he could grab hold of them. They could just as easily be his own thoughts. He got up, opened the cooler and took out a carton of milk, drinking a couple of gulps directly from it. He felt Anna's eyes on him the whole time. He held the milk out to her, thought: *want some?*

Anna shook her head. Mahler wiped his mouth and put the milk back.

'What does he say, then?'

The corners of Anna's mouth were pulled up. 'Nothing you want to hear.'

'What do you mean?'

'Just that he talks to me, he tells me things that aren't meant for you to hear and therefore I'm not going to tell you, OK?'

'This is ridiculous.'

'Maybe so, but that's how it is.'

Mahler took a couple of steps through the room, picking up the guest book that was on the bureau and turned some pages—compliments about the cottage, thanks for letting us stay—and wondered if they were going to write anything before they left. He turned around.

'You're making it up,' he said. 'There is nothing...I haven't heard anything about the dead being able to...communicate with the living. This is something you're imagining.'

'Maybe they haven't wanted to.'

'Oh for pity's sake, what does he say?'

'Like I said...'

Anna was sitting on the edge of the bed giving him a look that he felt was...pitying. Rage boiled up inside him. It wasn't fair. He was the one who had saved Elias, he was the one who had worked the whole time at trying to make him better while Anna had simply... vegetated. He took a step toward her, and raised his finger.

'You shouldn't...'

Elias sat straight up in the bed, staring at him. Mahler caught his breath, backing up. Anna did not move.

What is this...

A sharp bang inside his temple, as if a blood vessel had burst, made him teeter, almost tripping on the rug. He leaned against the bureau and the raging headache he'd felt coming on immediately retreated, disappeared. Instinctively he held his hands out in front of him, saying, 'I won't...I won't...' He had no idea what he wasn't going to do.

Anna and Elias were sitting next to each other, looking at him. An intense distaste gripped him and he backed out of the room with his outstretched hands protective in front of him. Kept going away from the cottage, over the rocks.

What is happening?

He left the cottage as far behind as possible. His feet ached from the weight of his heavy body on the rock. He crawled out of the wind behind a wall of rock where he could not be seen from the house and sat there looking out at the sea. The occasional gull sailed out there; no prey to dive for. He rested his face in his hands.

I'm...locked out.

They did not want him. What had he done? It was as if Anna

had been biding her time before she let the bomb drop, allowed him to understand that he was not wanted. Took her chance as soon as they got here, when there was no possibility of flight.

He picked up a stone, tossed it at a gull and missed by several metres. A white sail sliced the horizon like a shark fin in the distance. He slapped his hand against the rock face.

Let them try to manage on their own. Let them just try.

He blocked the thought, tried to erase it. Could they hear him?

The insight that, on top of everything else, he had to be careful what he was thinking was even more enraging. He was alone, and could not even be alone in peace.

This was not how he had imagined it. Not at all.

The Heath 12.50

With each step Flora took toward the buildings, she could feel the field grow stronger. If the sensation outside the gates had been of streams running through her head, this was more like wandering into a gradually thickening fog. And just as fog magnifies sound, she could hear single individuals' thoughts faintly but clearly, distant cries. When she reached the area between the buildings she stopped, and took it in.

She had never before experienced anything like this field. It consisted of consciousness, many consciousnesses, but they were simply there: a strong presence, thinking no thoughts. There were thoughts, though. Mental exclamations of horror could be heard within the field, causing it to grow in intensity, just as an electric conductor grows warm when power flows through it.

The more you fear us, the bigger we get.

She leaned against a wall and it was as if there was not enough space for her. There was a micro version of everything happening in the area right now inside her head, and mainly it was terror, despair—the base human emotions, the reflexes of the reptilian mind, and she could feel them everywhere so strongly that she thought the field ought to be visible, billowing in the air like waves of heat rising from the asphalt.

This is not good, this is…dangerous.

She took a couple of steps with her hands around her head and looked in through a balcony window on the ground level. She saw a living room without furniture. Sitting in the middle of the floor there was a figure in a blue hospital gown and pants. A figure, because it was almost impossible to tell if it was a man or a woman. Almost all the hair had fallen from the head, the features had withered away and the yellowing skin was smeared onto the skeleton as though a temporary cover had been applied for the sake of decency. No meat, no muscles. The person on the floor had about as much identity as a head that has spent a couple of weeks on a spike.

Even so the body had not collapsed. It sat rigid, tense, legs jutting out; staring at a point straight ahead. The eyes were too deeply sunk into the skull for it to be clear where the gaze was directed, but the head was turned to the front.

A frog was hopping between its legs. For a moment Flora thought it was a real frog but when she'd watched the mechanical hopping for a couple of seconds she realised it was a toy. Up and down, up and down the frog jumped and the dead person sat with gaping mouth, following its movements. A soft *clicketyclack, clicketyclack* could be heard through the windows.

The movements became slower, the frog's hopping more feeble. Finally there were only small death twitches in its legs, then it stopped completely.

The dead person leaned over and put a hand on the frog, hitting it a couple of times. When nothing happened the frog was lifted to eye level and the dead person studied it, bony fingers working across the frog's smooth metallic surface. Found the key and turned it over and over and over. Put the frog back down on the ground, where it resumed its hopping, observed with exactly the same interest.

Flora turned away from the window and shook her head, which still rang with the anguished cries of a suffering that was in her, but was not hers. She walked into the nearest courtyard, saw the grey facades, the rows of repaired windows, the emptiness between the front doors now that people had gone in to see their own.

Hell. This is Hell.

She had thought this place was creepy before: all the garbage, people quarrelling in bombed-out apartments, but that was nothing compared to what she felt now. Every speck of dirt had been removed from the walkways and a smell of disinfectant hovered in the air. The apartments had been set up nicely, cleaned; the dead had been given somewhere to live and it was simply new graves. Sit still in the grave, staring at an endlessly repeated motion. Hell.

Flora walked out into the middle of the yard where once a play-ground might have been planned, but they had got no further than the swing supports and a couple of benches. She sat down heavily, pressing the heels of her hands into her eyes until she saw exploding suns.

But the field…the presence…

A couple with hunched shoulders walked out of a building. A man and a woman. The man was thinking something about *regard her as dead* and the woman was a little girl, clambering up into her mother's lap.

Flora put her backpack down next to the bench and curled herself up. Peter's building was a couple of hundred metres away and she didn't have the energy to get there. She wished the field would fade back just a little, but there was intense motion everywhere, a cacophony of revulsion and denial that just fed it.

Somewhere behind her glass broke. She looked, but was only in time to see the flash of shards falling to the ground, shattering. There was a scream from somewhere. Oddly enough, she found it calming. The pressure was starting to find release. She smiled.

It is starting.

Yes. It was starting like a distant hum, a swarm of mosquitoes on a summer evening that you can hear but not see. It came closer,

283

slicing through all the other sounds.

Something was coming.

The sharp sound, piercing now, assumed physical form, became a force that was directed at her, pushing her head down and to the right.

Was it her gift? She found she could pinpoint the exact location of the sound; it came from a spot ten metres to the left of her and she understood its significance: she was not allowed to look at that place.

The source changed position, moving away from her.

I am not afraid!

With the muscles of her neck straining, as if she were straightening up under a heavy load, she turned her head up to the left. And saw.

She saw herself moving away from herself.

The girl walking across the yard had a too-large outfit exactly the same as hers. The same backpack, the same straggly red hair. The only thing different was the shoes. The girl was wearing her favourite shoes, the sneakers that had broken; but on her they were intact.

The girl stopped, as if she had felt Flora's eyes in her back. The screech of grinding metal in her head did not let up, and there was no possibility that she could get up and follow the girl when she started moving again, going on down the path to the next courtyard. All the strength in her legs was gone. Flora collapsed on the bench, sobbing and averting her gaze. The screeching stopped.

She closed her eyes, lying down on the bench with her backpack as a pillow, turning her back in the direction she had seen the girl, hugging herself.

I saw it, she thought. *It was here and I saw it.*

The Heath 12.55

It was not easy to find 17C. New hospital-style signs had been put up but no one had removed the old ones. The result was a contradictory mixture of directions to different street names between identical blocks of houses. It was like a maze, with people wandering around like lab rats and no one to stop and ask the way.

It was hard to collect your thoughts, too; hard to concentrate. As soon as David thought he had understood the system, other people's confusion broke into his own—other numbers, other consciousnesses—and it was like trying to do mental arithmetic next to someone reciting random numbers. And if it wasn't numbers, searching, then it was fear, a great trepidation rumbling at the base of it all.

A drink. Alcohol. Calm.

An incredible desire for alcohol sank its claws into him and he did not know if this longing was his own, or Sture's. It was probably a mixture of the two; a conjectural mix of wine and whisky sloshed around in a conjectural mouth.

The disconcerting thing about the telepathy was not so much the fact that he could read Sture's thoughts, Magnus' thoughts, other people's thoughts, as the fact that he didn't know which thoughts were his own. Now he understood why the situation at the hospital had been untenable.

Here, the thoughts of others were mostly fainter, a background murmur of voices, images. After ten minutes of aimless wandering he started to identify his own consciousness in the hubbub. But when the reliving had been closer together it must have been almost impossible, all the 'I' and 'me' flowing in and out of each other like watercolours.

'Dad, I'm tired,' Magnus said. 'Where *is* it?'

They were standing in a passageway between two courtyards. People were walking in and out of buildings, most of them appeared to have found the right place. Sture was looking at the numbers nailed to the wall, wiping sweat from his forehead with his sleeve. 'Idiots,' he said. 'They needn't have bothered with the numbers. Ouch!'

Sture made a fist and raised it to his chest, stopping.

'Should I take him?' David asked.

'Yes.'

Sture looked around and opened his jacket. There was a large hole in his shirt above his heart. Balthazar was writhing inside the pocket, trying to get out. David took the rabbit, now struggling wildly between their hands, and put it into his own inside pocket, where it continued to kick.

'Are we nearly there?' Magnus asked.

David crouched down.

'We'll find it soon,' he said. 'How is everything...' he pointed at Magnus' head, 'in here?'

Magnus rubbed his forehead. 'It's like there's a lot of people talking.'

'Yes. Is it bothering you?'

'Not so much. I'm thinking about Balthazar.'

David kissed him on the head and stood up. Paused. Something had happened. The voices were muted, almost disappeared. Inside his head he saw something he could not at first identify. Tall, yellow bending stalks and a soft warmth. The warmth came from a body right up close.

Sture stood in place, gaping and turning around and around.

He is seeing the same thing, David thought. *What is it?*

Sture looked at David, holding his head.

'Is this...' he said and his eyes widened in terror. David did not understand. What he was feeling was a great sense of comfort, of calm. He could feel the heartbeat of the warm body close by—rapid heartbeats, over one hundred per minute, but nonetheless comforting.

'All these thoughts,' Sture said. 'It makes you crazy...'

Now David saw what the yellow stalks were. He had not recognised them because their size was so distorted. Even though they were as thick as fingers, it was hay. He was lying in hay next to a warm body, and the hay was so large because he himself was so little.

Balthazar.

It was the rabbit's consciousness, making a backdrop to his own. The warm body with the rapid heartbeat was its mother.

Sture came over with his hand outstretched.

'I'm happy to take him again,' he said. 'I'd rather deal with that.'

'What is it?' Magnus asked.

'Come on...'

David signalled to Sture and all three of them crouched down, forming a small circle concealing them from the world. David took Balthazar out of his pocket, holding him out to Magnus.

'Here,' he said. 'Feel.'

Magnus took the rabbit, held him up against his chest and stared unseeing into space. Sture opened his jacket, sniffed his pocket and made a face. A few dark streaks of rabbit urine could be seen on the light lining of the jacket. They sat like that for half a minute, until tears slowly rose in Magnus' eyes. David leaned forward.

'What is it, buddy?'

Magnus' eyes were shiny, he looked at Balthazar and said, 'He doesn't want to be with me. He wants to be with his mum.'

David and Sture exchanged glances and Sture said, 'Yes. But he would not have been able to do that even if he had been wild. The mother drives out the young.'

'What do you mean drives out?' Magnus asked.

'So that they have to manage on their own. Balthazar was lucky he could come to you instead.'

David did not know if this was true, but it soothed Magnus a bit. He pressed Balthazar harder against his chest and spoke as if he were talking to a baby, 'Poor little Balthazar. I will be your mother.'

Incredibly, it seemed that this declaration soothed even Balthazar. He stopped struggling and rested calmly in Magnus' hands. Sture looked around. 'Probably best if I take him anyway.'

Balthazar was put back in Sture's pocket and they continued their search. They caught sight of the number they were looking for in a courtyard, quite by chance. A sign above a door: 17 A–F.

Some minutes had passed as they sat in the passageway. The atmosphere in the area had changed, and as they walked toward the entrance they could hear glass shattering, a door slamming somewhere, isolated cries. People around them were moving more rapidly, looking over their shoulders, and a sound like a swarm of gnats somewhere nearby was growing.

'What is it?' Sture asked, staring up at the sky.

'I don't know,' David said.

Magnus tilted his head, said, 'It's a big machine.'

They could not place the sound, what it was or where it was coming from but, as Magnus had said, it sounded as if a large machine had been turned on. Perhaps a computer, the high-frequency whirring of enormous fans.

They walked through the entrance.

Instead of the usual smells of cooking, sweat and dust there was only a sterile combination of hospital and disinfectant. Everything had been wiped down until it shone and there were letters pasted on the worn doors. A and B on the ground floor. They continued up stairs slick with cleaning fluids.

Magnus moved like a sleepwalker, putting both feet on each step. David felt his fear and adjusted his own steps to match. On the landing between the two floors Magnus stopped and said, 'I want Balthazar.'

Balthazar was handed over and Magnus held him tightly to his chest so that only his little nose was visible, sniffing. The last few steps up to apartment C he walked as if under water.

The doorbell did not work, but before David knocked he tried the handle and found the door was unlocked. He stepped into an empty hallway with Sture and Magnus following behind.

'Hello?'

After a couple of seconds an elderly man appeared, carrying the evening paper. He looked like a caricature of an absentminded professor: short and thin, with tufts of grey hair sticking out above his ears, glasses perched on his nose. David liked him immediately.

'Well, well,' the man said. 'Are you...' He removed his glasses and slipped them into his chest pocket as he stepped forward, his hand outstretched. 'I'm Roy Bodström. We were the ones who...' he held up his index and pinky finger to his ear to indicate a telephone.

They shook hands. Magnus drew back toward the door and tried to hide Balthazar with his arms.

'Hello,' Roy said. 'What's your name?'

'Magnus,' Magnus whispered.

'Magnus, I see. What do you have there?'

Magnus shook his head and David stepped in.

'It's his birthday today and he got a rabbit that he wanted to bring along and show...Eva. She is here, isn't she?'

'Of course,' Roy said and turned back to Magnus. 'A *rabbit*? Yes, well then I certainly understand if you want…I would also want to. Come.'

Without further ceremony he waved for them to follow him and led them into the room from which he had appeared. David took a deep breath, put his hand on Magnus' shoulder and followed.

The room echoed with quiet and the scattering of hospital equipment highlighted the emptiness. There was only a bed with a nightstand on which there was a machine, and next to the bed a simple armchair. On the floor next to the armchair there were a couple of issues of *Journal of American Medicine*. Sitting on the bed, Eva.

The bandage that had earlier covered half of her face had been replaced with a stocking of thick gauze that emphasised the damage beneath. The blue hospital gown curved in on one side of her chest. A number of cables ran from her head to the machine on the nightstand. The bed was raised in a sitting position and both of Eva's hands rested on the institutional blanket, her one eye directed at the door through which they came.

David and Magnus slowly approached the bed. David felt Magnus' body tense: watchful. Eva's eye did not look anything like it had in the hospital—the grey membrane had just about dissolved and the eye looked almost healthy. Almost. On the other hand she looked as if she had lost quite a few kilos in the past few days; the healthy cheek had lost its curve and collapsed toward the oral cavity. When the corners of her mouth pulled up into a smile it looked more like a grimace.

'David,' she said. 'Magnus. My boy.'

The voice still had something of its hoarseness but David would have recognised it anywhere as Eva's. Magnus stopped, David let go of his shoulder and walked up to the bed. He didn't dare hug Eva for fear that her body would break, so he just sat on the edge of the bed, putting his hands on her shoulders.

'Hello, my darling,' he said. 'We're here now.'

He pressed his lips to keep from crying, and waved to Magnus to come forward to the bed, which he did, hesitantly. Even Sture walked up, a step behind Magnus. Eva's eye travelled between them.

'My dearest,' she said. 'My family.'

There was silence for a moment. There was so much to say that they could say nothing. Roy came up with his hands clasped on his stomach as if to show that he was not going to do anything and he nodded at the machine.

'So I'm just measuring EEG,' he said. 'It's nothing dangerous. Just so you...' He backed away again, with yet another unfinished sentence hanging in the air. David looked at the machine, where a number of almost-straight lines floated through blacked space, only interrupted by occasional blips, bumps.

Should it look like that?

He looked at Eva again. Her eye was appraising, calm and not at all frightening. And it sent a shiver through him. It took him a couple of seconds to realise what it was: inside his head he felt Magnus, Sture, Balthazar and Roy all in a messy jumble, but of Eva he felt nothing.

He looked straight into her eye and thought: *Darling, my darling, where are you?* but received no answer. When he really tried he could conjure up a faint image, a contour of what Eva was to him, but it was completely drawn from memory and had nothing to do with the person in front of him. He carefully took her hand. It felt cold even though it was surely the same temperature as the room.

'It is Magnus' birthday today,' he said. 'There was no pancake cake. I didn't know how to make one so I bought a cake instead.'

'Happy birthday, my dear Magnus,' Eva said.

David saw that Magnus made a decision, overcoming what he actually felt, and he stepped up to the bed, displaying Balthazar.

'I got a rabbit. His name is Balthazar.'

'It is very nice,' Eva said.

Magnus put Balthazar down on the bed and he took a couple of tentative hops, sitting between Eva's emaciated thighs and nibbling on the tufts on the blanket. Eva did not appear to take any notice of him.

'His name is Balthazar,' Magnus said.

'Balthazar is a nice name.'

'He's not allowed to sleep in my bed, is he?'

David opened his mouth to reply but realised that the question was directed to Eva and kept quiet. As if stating a fact, Eva said, 'He is not allowed to sleep in your bed.'

'Why not?'

'Magnus...' David put a hand on his shoulder. 'Please stop.'

'So is he?'

'We'll talk about it later.'

Magnus frowned and looked at Eva. Roy cleared his throat, took a step forward.

'Actually,' he said, 'there was a little thing I was wondering about.'

David stroked the back of Eva's hand with his finger, stood up and followed Roy a couple of steps from the bed, making space for Sture. Before he stood up he glanced at the EEG screen and saw that the bubbles on the lines had become slightly larger, spaced slightly closer together.

When they had moved away from the bed David asked, 'Was that what you meant? That she is sort of like a...' David could not bring himself to say 'machine', but that was how he felt. Eva answered all their questions, said completely reasonable things but she did it mechanically, like a rote behaviour.

Roy nodded.

'I don't know,' he said. 'It will probably get better. Like I said, there has been great progress and...' He did not complete the sentence, but started a new one. 'What I'm wondering about is: the Fisher. Does that mean anything to you?'

'The Fisher?'

'Yes. If I ask her about herself then...we always end up back at the Fisher. There's something that frightens her.'

Sture got up from the bed and came over.

'What are you talking about?' he asked.

'The Fisher,' David said. 'It's something Eva says, but we don't know what it is.'

Sture turned to the bed, where Magnus was saying something to Eva as he pointed to Balthazar, who had just crawled up on her belly. 'I know what it is,' he said and sighed. 'Does she talk about it?' Roy nodded and Sture said, 'I see. Yes. That was something that happened when she was little, you see. She was seven and...well, I guess you could say it was my fault for not keeping a good enough eye on her. She came very close to drowning. Very close. It was right on the edge. If my wife hadn't known exactly what to do, then...' Sture shook his head at the memory. 'Anyway. Once we had...brought her back to life, then...'

'Daddy, Daddy!'

David heard Magnus' shriek inside his head one second before it reached his ears. No, the scream inside his head came from Balthazar and just as Magnus' voiced scream died against the walls there was another, a sound more like a bird cry, then a light cracking.

David lunged for the bed, but it was too late.

Balthazar's body was still lying in Eva's lap but she had his head in one hand, moving it up to her eye in order to examine it. She twisted and turned the little rabbit head where the nose still twitched and the eyes stared in terror. In her lap the legs on the headless body were still kicking and a trickle of blood found its way along a fold in the blanket, dropping to the floor.

Balthazar's legs jerked one last time and froze. Eva's eye looked closely at the rabbit's eye; two black pools reflecting in each other.

Magnus screamed, 'I hate you I hate you!' and hit Eva across her arm, her shoulder, his arms flailing, tearing loose the cables attached to her head. David managed to get a last glimpse of the

EEG peaks before they went out: tightly clustered spikes. He took hold of Magnus from behind, locked his arms in a tight hug and carried him out of the apartment, whispering words of comfort to no effect.

'I don't understand...she has never...' Roy was twisting his hands and swaying on his feet, hesitant to approach the bed where Eva was examining Balthazar's head and sticking her finger into the bloody, mucus-filled throat, its lining of tendons and ligaments hanging down in threads.

Sture walked up and gently extracted the head from Eva's dark red hands, placing it on the night stand. He closed his eyes against Magnus' inner screams, took out the two wooden dolls and placed these in her hands instead.

'Here,' he said. 'Your dolls. Eva and David.'

Eva took the dolls, holding them in her hands and looking at them.

'Eva and David,' she said. 'My dolls.'

'Yes.'

'They are very nice.'

The tone of her voice frightened Sture more than what she had done to Balthazar. It sounded like his daughter, and not like her. It sounded like someone imitating her voice. He could not bear to listen to it and he left Eva sitting there with the dolls in her lap.

David was carrying Magnus, Sture what was left of Balthazar. Some tufts of blotchy fur that no longer dreamed of hay. Outside the front door they were confronted by a policeman waving his arms in the direction of the exit.

'I have to ask you to leave the area immediately.'

'What is it?' Sture asked.

The policeman shook his head. 'Figure it out for yourself,' he said and ducked in through the door to continue the evacuation.

They had been so preoccupied by what had happened with Eva

that they had ignored the warning cries from the field. David's mind was filled with Magnus' despair, but when Sture turned his attention to the outside he heard—thought—the sound of a large tree just before it falls to the axe. Sharp cracks, the trunk swaying—which way will it fall?

Thousands of consciousnesses in such panic that no thoughts could be distinguished, an ant-war going on at full volume and through it all that whining, piercing sound. Sture made a face and grabbed David's shoulder.

'Come,' he said. 'We have to get out of here. Now.'

They walked as fast as they could to the gates. Any thoughts of their own were sucked up by the field. More people were pouring out of doors and running toward the exit like they were fleeing from a fire, a war, an approaching army.

The Heath would never again be open to the public.

The Heath 13.15

Flora lay on the bench, curled up like a foetus. She hugged her backpack. Inside the world was coming to an end. Everything was exploding in demented fireworks. She shut her eyes as tightly as she could, as if to prevent her eyeballs from popping out. She couldn't move, she could only wait for it to end, to be over.

Large numbers of dead people were having an effect on the minds of the living, but the large numbers of the living were also affecting the dead. As if through a system of prisms, emotions were being enlarged, reflected in each other, reinforced, and this went on until the force field was unbearable.

After five minutes it started to abate. The horrible thoughts dissipated and ebbed away. After ten minutes she dared to open her eyes, and realised that she had been overlooked. A couple of police officers were just leaving the courtyard. A man was sitting outside a door, weeping. He had scratches in his face and splotches of blood on his shirt collar. As Flora watched, an emergency worker came over to attend to the man's cuts.

Flora lay absolutely still. In her black clothes she was a shadow on the bench. If she moved she would become a human, and humans had to leave.

Once the wounds had been dressed, the paramedic supported the man under an arm and led him away. The man walked as if there was a yoke across his shoulders and he was thinking of his mother, her love, and her nails—polished and painted a cherry red. She had always been particular about her nails, even during her years of illness. When all other dignity was taken from her bit by bit she still insisted that her nails be groomed and painted cherry red. These nails. One of them had been broken off when she scratched him.

Flora waited until they had left the courtyard and then peeked out. The Power told her there was no living being close by, but everything was so strange here she could not be sure.

No person in sight. She crawled out and ran through the passageway to the next courtyard. She had to wait a couple of minutes there for a few more people to leave. One of them was a psychologist or something like that, and she was seriously considering suicide when she got home. Inject herself with an overdose of morphine. She had no family. Neither here nor anywhere else.

It was a quarter to two when Flora gently knocked on Peter's window and was let in. By that time there was not a single living consciousness left in the area.

[*Daily Echo* 14.00]

…have no explanation for the events at the Heath. Police and medical personnel were forced to evacuate the area shortly after one o'clock. Twelve people sustained injuries—three seriously—after having been attacked by the reliving. The Heath will remain closed to the public for the time being…

Summary [Dept. Soc. Affairs; CLASSIFIED]

…in short, it is our conviction that the reliving are using up their intracellular resources at a rapid pace. If the present rate is taken as a guide line, it can be predicted that the resources will be exhausted in at most a week, in certain cases significantly earlier.

That is to say, if nothing is done, the reliving will be burned out in one week—for want of a better terminology.

At present we have no solution.

It may be added that we wonder if such a solution is to be wished for.

[*Daily Echo*, 16.00]

…have placed the Heath under a similar quarantine. A few medical personnel will remain in the area, but at present there are no plans for continued rehabilitation.

17 August II

The Fisher

Labbskär Island 16.45

The shadows had grown long by the time Mahler rose from his bolt-hole and walked back to the cottage. His body ached from the extended period of sitting on rock. He had stayed away longer than it took him to calm down. He had wanted to make a protest, to give Anna a taste of how it would be if he, superfluous as he was, were gone.

On the rocks outside the house there was an old drying rack for nets, three large T-shapes with hooks. Anna was standing under one of them, humming and hanging up Elias' clothes, which she had washed with soap and salt water. She looked thoroughly content, not anxious as Mahler had hoped.

She heard his footsteps on the rock and turned around.

'Hello,' she said. 'Where have you been?'

Mahler waved vaguely with his hand and Anna tilted her head, taking stock of him.

As if I were a child, Mahler thought and Anna chuckled, nodding. The low sun gleamed momentarily in her eye.

'Have you found any water?' he asked.

'No.'

'And that doesn't worry you?'

'Yes, of course, but…' she shrugged and hung up two tiny socks on the same hook.

'But what?'

'I thought you'd go and get some.'

'Maybe I don't feel like it.'

'Well, in that case you'll have to show me how the motor works.'

'Don't be ridiculous.'

Anna shot him a look, *don't be ridiculous yourself*, and Mahler stomped into the house. The largest lifejacket was too small for him, he looked like a giant baby when he pulled the strap across his tummy, so he decided to forgo the vest. Everything seemed to matter less, all of a sudden. He looked in on Elias, lying in the bed under the troll painting. He felt no particular desire to go to him. He picked up the water container and walked out.

'Well then,' he said. 'I guess I'm off.'

Anna had finished hanging up the washing. She crouched down with her hands on her knees.

'Dad,' she said in mild tone of voice. 'Stop it.'

'Stop what?'

'Just stop. You don't have to.'

Mahler walked past her down to the boat. Anna said, 'Drive carefully.'

'Sure, sure.'

When the sound of the engine had died away between the islands, Anna lay on her back on the sun-baked rock, shifting around so the warmth would reach as much of her skin as possible. When she had lain like this for a while she went in and got Elias, putting him next to her on the rock, wrapped in the blanket.

She turned on her side, cradling her head in her hand and focusing on a point in the middle of his black-brown blotchy forehead.

Elias?

The answer she received was not articulated in words. It wasn't even an answer, more of a mute affirmation: *I am here.* It had happened a couple of times recently that Elias had actually talked to her, the last time when she was mowing the lawn as her father was doing his meaningless exercises.

She had been picking a pebble out of the handmower when Elias' clear, high-pitched voice filled her head.

Mummy, come! Grandad is angry. I am going to...

Elias did not get any further before his voice was drowned out by a piercing, whining sound. When she reached the house Elias was lying on the floor with the chair on top of him and the whining sound vanished just as the contact with him was severed.

The time before, it had been in the middle of the night. She was not sleeping much and when she did drop off it was from sheer exhaustion. It was difficult to sleep when she knew Elias was lying in his bed, staring up at the ceiling; that she was leaving him alone when she disappeared into the closed room of sleep.

She had been lying on the mattress next to Elias' bed when she was awakened by his voice. She jerked, sat up and looked at him as he lay in bed, his eyes open.

'Elias, did you say something?'

Mummy...

'Yes?'

I don't want to.

'What is it you don't want?'

Don't want to be here.

'You don't want to be in this cottage?'

No. Don't want to be...here.

They had not been able to get any further before the whining sound had gotten louder. Until it started to get painful, she could feel physically how Elias drew back, disappearing into himself. Something left him for a moment as he talked to her; as soon as he pulled it back they could only communicate without words, weakly.

Another thing.

Every time Elias withdrew, it was from fear. She felt it. What Elias was afraid of was connected with that whining sound.

Out in the sunshine on the rock, with his mummified face sticking out of the blanket, it was clear, terribly clear, that Elias' body was just the shell that people always spoke of. A skin, dried and shrivelled, that enclosed something else, unnameable and not of this world. The boy Elias who had liked the swings and loved nectarines no longer existed and would not come back. She had understood this even in those first minutes in Mahler's bedroom in Vällingby.

And yet, and yet...

She was standing on her own two feet now. She was hanging up laundry and humming songs, which she would never have done a week ago. Why?

Because now she knew that death was not the end.

All those times that she had gone to Råcksta and sat by the grave, lain on the grave, whispered to the grave. At that point she had known that his body was down there but also known that he could not hear her, that nothing of him was really left. That Elias had only been the sum of swings, nectarines, Legos, smiles, grumpiness and 'Mummy, give me another goodnight kiss.' When all that had gone, only memories were left.

She had been wrong. Completely wrong, and that was the reason she was humming. Elias was dead. Elias wasn't gone.

She opened the blankets a little, letting in a bit of air. Elias still smelled bad but not like in the beginning. As if whatever it was that smelled bad had been...used up.

'What is it you are afraid of?'

No answer. She flapped the pyjama top over his stomach and a puff of stale air was released. When the clothes had dried she would change him. They lay on the rocks until the sun sank into the sea of Åland and the cooler breezes began to blow in. Then Anna carried Elias inside again.

The bedclothes smelled mildewed, so she took them out and hung them in an alder tree close to the house. She found an empty kerosene lamp and filled it with fuel for the evening. Checked the fireplace by lighting a sheet of newspaper, placed it on the hearth. The smoke came in. The chimney had probably been closed off. Maybe a bird had built a nest.

Anna made a couple of caviar-spread sandwiches in the kitchen, poured a glass of lukewarm milk and walked out and sat on the rock. When she had finished eating the sanwiches she walked down to the water's edge to examine the large, silver-coloured object, half-concealed in the grass, that had caught her eye a couple of times.

At first she did not understand what it was. A large cylinder covered in holes. Something you tossed into the air, took a picture of and claimed it was a UFO. Then she realised it was the drum of a washing machine, that it had been used as a fish safe.

She walked along the shore, found an empty tube of shaving cream and a beer can. The clouds were starting to get pink and she thought Mahler would be coming soon.

To get a better view of the sunset, as well as her father, she walked to the cairn on top of the hill behind the house. The view was fantastic. Even though the hill was only a couple of metres higher than the house, it gave her a clear view over all of the nearby islands.

Seen from the side, the mass of evening clouds became one big fluffy blanket draped over the low islands, reflected in a sea of blood. To the east there was nothing between the watcher and the horizon. She understood perfectly why people had once believed that the world was flat, that the horizon was an edge beyond which the great Nothingness lay.

She listened. No engine sounds.

When she stood here like this with a view of the whole wide world, it seemed incredible to her that her father would even be able to find his way back here. The world was so infinitely vast.

What is that?

She trained her gaze on a cluster of trees and bushes in a hollow on the other side of the island. She thought she'd seen something moving there. Yes. There was a rustle, and a flash of something white that disappeared again.

White? What kind of animals are white?

Only animals that live where there's snow. Except cats, of course. And dogs. Could it be a cat? Forgotten or inadvertently left behind. Maybe it had fallen off a boat, managed to make its way to land.

She started to walk toward the hollow, then stopped.

It had been larger than a cat. More like a dog. A dog that had fallen off a boat and…gone wild.

She turned and walked quickly back to the cottage. Paused outside the door and listened one last time. It had to be past eight o'clock, why didn't her father come?

She went in, closing the door behind her. It slid open. The lock was gone. She took a broom and threaded it through the handle, jamming the end up against the wall. It was worthless as a lock, but an animal would not be able to get in.

The more she thought about it, the more anxious she became.

It wasn't an animal. It was a person.

She stood at the door and listened. Nothing. Just a lone blackbird trying to sound like a lot of other birds simultaneously.

She could feel her heart, insistent, pumping faster and more emphatically. She was getting worked up over nothing. It was just that she was alone with Elias and couldn't get away from here—it was putting ghosts in her head. There's no problem balancing on a piece of wood ten centimetres wide when it's lying on the ground, but hoist it up ten metres off the ground and sheer terror sinks its claws in. Even though it's the same piece of wood.

It was a gull, probably. Or a swan.

A swan. Yes, of course. It was a swan that had nested on land. Swans are big.

She calmed down and went and checked on Elias. He was lying with his head turned to the wall and appeared to be looking at the troll painting, just a dark rectangle against the wall in the dusk. She sat beside him on the bed.

'Hello sweetheart, how is everything?'

The sound of her own voice filled the silence, chasing it away. The anxious feeling in her chest stilled.

'When I was little I had this kind of painting by my bed. Except it had a troll-daddy and his daughter, fishing. The girl was holding the rod and the father who was—this big—and clumsy, and covered in warts, he was teaching her how she should hold it, holding her arm carefully like this to show her. I don't know if my mum knew how I stared at that picture and how I thought or fantasised that I had a father who would do that with me. Who showed me what to do and who was so close, standing behind me and was big like that and looked kind. All I know is that when I was little I wanted to be a troll. Because everything seemed simple for the trolls. They had nothing, and yet they had everything.'

She rested her hands in her lap, looking straight at the painting— *Whatever happened to it?*—recalling how she had kneeled in her bed, tracing the outline of the troll father's face with her finger.

She sighed, looking at the window. A painted balloon was floating outside. She gasped violently. The balloon was a face. A swollen, white face with two dark slits for eyes. The lips were gone and the teeth exposed. She stared at the face as if turned to stone. The nose was just a hole in spongy, white flesh and it was a face made of floury dough with a lot of big teeth stuck into it.

A hand rose and was placed on the glass. Even this was corpse-white, swollen.

She screamed, deafening herself.

The face drew back from the window, in the direction of the door. She jumped to her feet, hitting her hip against the corner of the table but felt nothing, reached the kitchen—

Mummy?

—and took hold of the door, holding the handle.

Mummy?

Elias' voice, inside her head. She braced herself against the wall, pulling on the handle as hard as she could. Someone had grabbed it on the outside. She was resisting. The thing on the other side was jerking on it.

Dear merciful God, don't let it come in don't let it

Mummy what

don't let it

is it?

It was strong. She sobbed when the door hit against the frame.

'Go away! Go away!'

She could feel the dead, mute power through the handle as the creature monotonously pulled on the door, wanting to get in to her and Elias. Terror made her throat a single tensed muscle. She turned her head stiffly toward the kitchen, looking for a weapon, anything.

There was a small axe under the kitchen counter, but she couldn't let go of the door to grab it. The creature was pulling harder and when the door opened slightly she could momentarily glimpse the whole of the body. It was white and naked, lumps of dough thrown onto a skeleton, and she understood.

A drowned man. It's a drowned man.

She laughed breathlessly as she continued to resist, getting more glimpses of the creature's dissolved, fish-eaten flesh.

The drowned ones. Where are they?

In a flash she saw the whole sea filled with drowned people, all the accidents of the summer months—how many? Floating white bodies, scraping against the bottom. Predatory fish, eels that ate through the skin and gorged themselves on the innards.

Mummy!

Elias' voice was frightened now. She could neither rejoice at the fact that he was speaking to her, nor comfort him. The only thing she could do was resist, stop the thing from entering.

Her arms were starting to feel paralysed by the continuous pulling, the strength required to hold out.

'What do you want? Go away! Go away!'

It let go.

The door banged shut one last time and some slivers of wood broke off, fluttering down to her feet. She held her breath, listening. The blackbird had stopped singing and she heard rapping sounds on the rock outside. Bone on stone. The creature was leaving.

Mummy, what is it?

She answered.

Don't be afraid. It's leaving now.

The whining started, like a fleet of small boats approaching across the bay, coming closer. More than anything Anna wanted to scream, *Stop it, leave us alone, go away* to everything that seemed to want to get at them, but she did not dare for fear that it would frighten Elias. Elias quickly pulled out of her head and the whining died away.

Anna jumped back from the door, grabbed the axe and took up her post again. She listened outside. Nothing to be heard. The axe slid in her sweaty hand. During the whole episode she had not felt the drowned one inside her head for an instant, and that scared her even more. With Elias there was always a shimmer, a presence. The drowned man was silent.

When the blackbird resumed its song, she dared to leave the door and go in to Elias. She stopped in the door opening, dropping the axe.

The drowned man was standing on the rock outside the window, looking in. She carefully lowered herself down and took up the axe again, as though it were an animal that might be startled by the slightest movement. But the drowned one stood still.

What is it doing?

It couldn't look, it had no eyes. Anna sat on the edge of the bed squeezing the axe hard, sitting at an angle so that she could not see the thing outside the window. She'd be able to hear if it moved again, though. It was the most repulsive thing she had ever seen. She could not think about it, was not permitted to think about it—as if there was a finely balanced switch inside her head, poised to flip and catapult her into the darkest insanity.

She stared at the troll picture on the wall, the kind troll-man with his big comforting hands. The little child. And she thought:

Daddy, come home.

Kungsholmen 17.00

They had found a spot in an overgrown thicket along the beach at Kungsholm, halfway between their apartment and the parliament building. David assumed it was against the law to bury animals in the city without authority, but what could they do?

Before they set out they had made a cross from some pieces of string and skirting board. Magnus himself had written BALTHAZAR with a felt pen. David stood guard while Magnus and Sture dug a hole in the thicket large enough for the shoebox.

From this smaller perspective, David thought he could understand the purpose of a burial. Magnus busied himself with the box and the flowers that would be added to it, the construction of the cross satisfied him in a way that words and comforting on their own could not. He had cried a great deal on his way back from the Heath, but as soon as they reached the apartment he had started to talk about the funeral and what they should do.

Even David and Sture had become completely absorbed in the project; they had not yet said a word about what happened. What Eva had done and what it might mean could not be discussed with Magnus there, needing all their attention. But one thing you could say for sure: Eva would not be coming home. Not for a long time.

The hole was ready. Magnus opened the lid of the box one last time and Sture hurried to shift the rabbit's head into place. Magnus stroked the fur with his finger.

'Goodbye little Balthazar. I hope it will be good for you.'

David could not cry anymore. What he felt was rage. A hopeless, compressed rage. If he had been alone he would have shaken his fists at the sky and screamed at it. *Why Why Why?* Instead he sank down next to Magnus and put a hand on his back.

It's his birthday for fuck's sake. Couldn't he have had...just one day.

Magnus put the lid back and placed the shoebox in the ground. Sture handed him the shovel and he shovelled earth and more earth until the box disappeared from view. David sat absolutely still, staring at the shrinking pile of dirt, the hole filling up.

If it...comes back...

He clapped a hand over his mouth, forcing his face not to contort in howls of laughter, as he imagined the headless rabbit digging itself up and crawling zombie-like back to their apartment, dragging itself up the stairs.

Sture helped Magnus put the tufts of grass back, pat them in place and bang the cross into the ground with the shovel. He looked at David and they nodded at each other. It was doubtful whether the grave would stay intact for long, but it was done.

Everyone stood up. Magnus started to sing, 'The world is a sorrow-island...' like he had seen them do in *All of us on Saltkråkan* and David thought:

This is the bottom. Now we have reached rock bottom. We have to have reached the bottom.

David and Sture laid one hand each on Magnus' shoulders and David could not shake the feeling that it was really Eva's funeral they were enacting.

The bottom. It has to be...

Magnus crossed his arms over his chest and David felt his

shoulders draw together, shrinking, as he said, 'It was my fault.'

'No,' David said. 'It was certainly not your fault.'

Magnus nodded. 'I was the one who did it.'

'No, little one, it was...'

'Yes, it was. I was the one who thought, so Mum did it.'

David and Sture exchanged looks. Sture bent down and asked, 'What do you mean?'

Magnus wrapped his arms around David's hips and said into his stomach, 'I thought bad things about Mummy and that was why she got angry.'

'My darling boy...' David crouched down and scooped Magnus into his arms. 'We were the ones who should have known...it is not your fault.'

Magnus body was wracked with sobs and the words gushed out of him.

'Yes, because I thought...I thought that I...because she was only talking so strange like that because she didn't care about...and I was thinking that I didn't like her, I was thinking that she was ugly and that I hated her even though I didn't want to because I thought she was going to be like normal and then she was like that and that's why I thought it and when I thought it...when I thought it, that was when she did it.'

Magnus was still talking as David carried him back to the apartment, did not stop until he lay in his bed, his eyes red and his eyelids heavy.

His birthday...

After a while his eyes closed and he fell asleep. David tucked him in and went out to Sture in the kitchen, collapsing onto a chair.

'He's finished,' David said. 'He's completely finished. These past few days...he hasn't slept much at night and today...it's too much for him. He can't...how's he supposed to handle this?'

Sture didn't answer. After a period of silence he said, 'I think he'll manage. If you do. Then he will too.'

David's gaze travelled across the kitchen and fixed on a bottle of wine. Sture looked in the same direction, then back at David, who shook his head.

'No,' David said. 'But it's…hard.'

'Yes,' Sture said. 'I know.'

Haltingly, with long pauses, they talked about what had happened at the Heath but reached no conclusions. The area had been in uproar since they left. It seemed unlikely that visiting would be reinstituted for a long time. David went and checked on Magnus. He was sleeping deeply. When he came back to the kitchen Sture said, 'This thing that the doctor asked about. The Fisher.'

'Yes?'

'It's…' Sture pulled a finger along the table top as if he was tracing back along a timeline, 'pretty strange. Or completely natural. I don't know which.'

'What is it, then?'

'Well, you know her books. Bruno Beaver. Do you have one here?'

They had a little box with gratis copies of each and David picked out the two books, laying them side by side. Sture turned to a page in *Bruno the Beaver Finds His Way Home* and pointed to the place where Bruno finally found the spot where he was going to build his house, only to discover that the Waterman also lived in the lake.

'This Waterman,' Sture said and pointed at the blurry figure down in the water. 'She met him. I started telling you about it out there, but…' He raised and dropped his shoulders. 'When she almost drowned. Later…quite a few days later she told us that there had been…well, that there had been some kind of creature down there with her.'

David nodded. 'She's told me about that. That it was like that was the thing that had come to take her. The Waterman.'

'Yes,' Sture said. 'But then…I don't know if she remembers, if she's told you, but when she was little…she called that creature the Fisher.'

'No,' David said. 'She never said that.'

Sture idly turned the pages of the book. 'Whenever we've talked about it since she grew up she's always called it the Waterman or just That Thing, so I was wondering if she'd…forgotten.'

'But now she says the Fisher.'

'Yes. I remember that she…We encouraged her, thinking it might be good for her, that she drew a lot of pictures of the Fisher at the time, after it had happened. She was quite an artist even then.'

David went to the hall closet and brought back a box of old papers, magazines, drawings; the objects that Eva had chosen to keep from her childhood. It felt good to have something to do, something to investigate. He placed the box on the kitchen table and they hauled out text books, photographs, beautiful rocks, school year books and drawings. Sture lingered over certain items, sighing deeply at a snapshot of Eva, maybe ten years old, with a large pike in her arms.

'She was the one who got him,' he said. 'All by herself. I just helped her with the net.' He wiped his eyes. 'It was a…nice day.'

They continued through piles. Many of the sketches were dated and it was not hard to see that Eva would one day become an artist. Even as a nine-year-old she was drawing animals and people much better than David would ever be able to.

And then they found what they were looking for.

A single drawing, dated July 1975. Sture quickly checked the papers underneath but there were no others.

'There used to be more,' he said. 'She must have thrown the others out.'

The other papers were pushed aside and David walked around to Sture's side to study the single sketch in the middle of the table.

Eva's style was still childlike, of course. The fish were drawn with a single line, and the little girl who was supposed to be Eva had a disproportionally large head in relation to her body. You could tell she was under water from the wavy line toward the upper edge of the page.

'She's smiling,' David said.

'Yes,' Sture said. 'She is smiling.'

The mouth drawn on the girl's face was so happy as to flout accepted childhood standards of how to represent people. The smile covered half her face. This was a happy child.

Not easy to understand, in view of the character who was right next to her. The Waterman, the Fisher. It was at least three times as big as she was. It did not have a face, there was just an empty oval where the face should be. Outlines of arms, legs and body were drawn with trembling, wavering lines as if the figure was electric or dissolving.

Sture said, 'It wasn't clearly defined, she said. As if it was changing all the time.'

David did not answer. There was a detail in the picture he could not tear his eyes away from. The rest of the body was deliberately drawn to be indistinct, but there was one exception: the hands. The hands had clearly defined fingers, and at the tip of each was a large hook. The hooks were stretched out toward the smiling girl.

'The hooks,' David said. 'What are they?'

'We fished a lot when she was little,' Sture said. 'So...'

'What?'

'Well, at the time she said that it had those hooks to catch her. But it wasn't fast enough.' He pointed to the Fisher's fingers. 'They were not as big in reality, she said. But she saw them very clearly.'

They stared at the picture in silence, until David said, 'But even so she's smiling.'

'Yes,' Sture said. 'She is.'

Gräddö Island 17.45

Mahler moored at the dock in Gräddö at a quarter to six. He walked as fast as he could and got to the store a couple of minutes before they closed. He bought UHT milk, a number of cans and packets of soup and sauces. Macaroni and tortellini. Skogaholm bread, which lasted forever, and soft cheese in a tube.

At the tap behind the store he filled his containers with fresh water. Then he remembered the wheelbarrow down by the harbour with 'Gräddö Island Grocer' stencilled on it. Now he understood why it was there. He tried to decide what was better: go back to the harbour and get the wheelbarrow or try to carry the two containers—now weighing forty kilos—plus the two bags of food.

He decided to carry them.

After twenty minutes he was only half-way there—he had been forced to take a break almost every other minute—so he walked the rest of the way and fetched the wheelbarrow, pushing it back to where his goods were, and was down at the harbour in ten minutes.

It was past seven and starting to get dark. You could still see the bald head of the sun sticking up over the trees, but it was sinking rapidly. He would have to hurry; navigating back to the island in the dark without a map was beyond him. He got the bags and containers in the boat, and had to take another longish break so his heart wouldn't start to race.

Then he said a prayer and pulled on the starter cord. The engine fired immediately. He steered to the pontoon filling station and found that it was closed. He moored the boat but left the engine on, examining the pumps. There was no pump that took cash or cards. The only possibility of getting fuel would be to go back up to the store again. He lifted the fuel container and rocked it side to side. About half full.

He looked up at the road that led to the store. He just did not have the energy.

He was sure he could get back to the island with the fuel he had. The return trip was less certain.

Maybe there was fuel somewhere in the house on the island? He had seen a petrol container under the kitchen counter but had not checked to see if there was anything in it. Admittedly the water containers had been empty, but petrol would keep as long as you wanted.

It was highly likely that there was petrol in the container. Extra fuel for a situation like their own. Yes, of course. It was *guaranteed* there'd be petrol in the container. And if there wasn't, they had oars.

He didn't like this. He should go back up to the store. Without fuel they were at the mercy of...

Of what?

Of nature. Fate.

But there was petrol in that container.

He got back in the boat. Drove away from the mainland and normality.

It was half past nine when he reached the area where he was supposed to turn south. He didn't recognise anything around him. The sun was just a dark red edge at the horizon and dusk gave the islands an altered appearance. He could still see the Manskär Island mast but thought it lay too far to the right.

Must have gone too far.

He turned the dinghy and went back the same way he had come. He could still not tell where he was. In the slowly dimming light it was getting increasingly difficult to judge distances. What was a single large island, and what was a collection of many small ones.

He bit his knuckles.

No map. No extra fuel. The only thing he had to go on was the handful of landmarks he knew, and none of them was in sight.

He turned the throttle as low as he dared without stalling and put the gears in neutral. Tried to calm himself, gazing out over the islands, going over the route he had taken in his head. As long as he had an idea of where the merchant shipping routes were there was no risk that he would get completely lost. He looked around. A Finland ferry, lit up like a fun fair, was approaching from the Sea of Åland. Approaching rapidly.

He did not want to leave the shipping route but the ferry forced him to do so. He puttered in closer to the islands at low power, leaving the passage free. If the ferry collided with him, no shadow of blame would fall upon the captain—you could add lights to the list of things Mahler ought to have but didn't.

The ferry went by. Mahler could see people through the windows who did not have a care in the world. He longed to be with them. Just fly in through the window, land at the bar and order drinks until his wallet was empty; listen to vapid pop music and sneak glances at girls who had slid out of reach thirty years ago. Maybe listen to some lone Estonian tell his sad life story while the alcohol laid a forgiving veil over everything.

The ferry went by. Its lights went by and Mahler was left alone in the dark again.

He checked the time. Past ten o'clock. He felt the petrol tank. Almost empty. When he shook it, the engine sputtered, but resumed its even puttering when he restored the tank to its upright position.

This is no catastrophe, he told himself.

If worse came to worst he could go ashore on some island and wait out the short hours of the night. Motor home the next morning or row, if need be. Maybe it was better to go ashore right now, while there was still fuel for the trip tomorrow.

Anna and Elias would get anxious of course, but they would manage.

And to be honest, would they even get worried?

Relieved, more likely.

He turned and puttered in to the nearest island to spend the night.

The Heath 20.50

It was not until the colour of the little window had faded to dark grey that Flora and Peter talked about going out. There had been no sounds or signs of consciousness for several hours but it was hard to be completely sure.

Flora had winced when Peter opened the door. He had looked undernourished before; now he looked emaciated. As soon as they were in his room he threw himself upon the fruit in her backpack. The room stank. As soon as Flora thought it—that the room stank of human waste—Peter said between bites, 'I know. Sorry. Haven't been able to empty it.'

The rag over the bucket had been reinforced with a blanket, but the odour still came through.

'Peter, you can't live like this.'

What's the alternative?

Flora chuckled. Peter's voice was loud and clear in her head now that everyone else was gone. They did not have to talk aloud as long as they stayed here.

I don't know, she thought.

No. We'll go out tonight, came the answer.

They waited. Amused themselves playing poker for matches, which mostly became a contest to see which one of them was better at masking their thoughts. At the start they both knew each other's cards, but after a while they each had to search for the other's pairs and incomplete straights among the static of numbers and songs they both used as shields.

When they had both become so good at masking that they were getting headaches trying to penetrate the noise, they tried turning off. Making a conscious effort not to read the other's thoughts.

'Which card?' Peter asked, and held out a card with its back to Flora as he looked at it.

It came immediately: the seven of clubs. They tried several times, but it was no good. However hard Flora tried to put different kinds of static between her head and Peter's, she could not block the telepathy. As long as the sender did nothing to deliberately distort their thoughts, it was impossible not to read them.

During the hours they spent in the basement she got to know Peter better than ever before, probably better than he wanted her to know him. He got to know her, too. And she knew what he thought he was seeing, and he knew what she thought of what she was seeing and by eight o'clock it was starting to get unbearable—a kind of torture in the narrow basement. They glanced more and more often out the window to see if it wasn't getting dark enough to go out.

At ten to nine, with the room sunk in darkness and the window a rectangle hovering above them, Peter said, 'Shall we go then?'

'Yes.'

Speaking was a relief. Spoken language had boundaries, the words not so loaded with significance and hidden meanings as the language of thought. By this point they had almost started to hate each other from the sheer saturation of information, and they both knew it. She knew everything about his latent homosexuality, his stinginess towards other people and his contempt for himself. She also felt the work he'd done to overcome his flaws; his longing for and terror of tenderness, of contact with others, which expressed itself in his self-imposed isolation.

It was not a matter of contempt or disdain; it was just too close. When they reached the outer bicycle basement she turned to Peter and asked, 'Peter? Can we forget this?'

'I don't know,' Peter said. 'We can try.'

After checking that there were no people out in the yard, they parted and went their separate ways. Peter went off to empty his bucket and look for water, while Flora walked in the direction of the courtyard where she had seen herself.

Before their telepathic conversation became stifling, they had talked about what Flora had seen. At first Peter had not understood what she meant, but when she sent him the whining sound that accompanied the apparition, he said, or thought, 'I've seen it. But it wasn't you. It was a wolf.'

'A wolf?'

'Yes. A large wolf.'

And as soon as he said it, she received an image that must have come from Peter's childhood.

Cycling unsteadily along a gravel road, between spruce trees. A bend in the road and there is a wolf in front of me. Five metres away. Yellow eyes, grey fur, big. Much bigger than me. My hands squeeze the handlebars, the scream that can't get past my mouth because I am scared. It is standing still, I know that I am about to die. Any second now it will take two leaps and be on top of me. But it looks at me for a while, then goes into the forest. I feel warmth in my pants, I have peed all over myself. I can't move for several minutes. When I do, I go back the way I came, I don't dare go past where it was.

The image came with such force that she felt her own sphincter relax, but her consciousness intervened and took control of the muscles just in time.

For me death is a wolf, Peter thought and Flora realised that something she had thought was only imaginative play was her own fundamental belief: she herself was Death.

Of all the ways it was possible to imagine Death as a human figure—the man with the scythe, the Phantom Charioteer, a leering skeleton or an old African woman—Flora had been drawn to the idea of Death as a twin sister. It stemmed from a couple of years ago when she had been standing in front of the mirror with a candle trying to summon the Dark Lady, and seen only herself. The idea had come to her then.

The courtyards lay silent, empty. Electricity had been brought in with some temporary cables and there were a couple of lights on in every yard. She moved carefully, trying to keep to the shadows, but it seemed that her caution was unnecessary. There was no one in sight, not a glimmer in any window, and the area appeared more like a ghost town than ever.

A ghost town.

Exactly what it was. The dead were in the dark apartments. Sitting, standing, lying, walking around. The remarkable thing was that she was not frightened. Quite the opposite. As her footsteps whispered back to her from the paths, she walked in the tranquility you can feel at a graveyard on a calm evening. She was among friends. The only thing that worried her was if that whining was going to come back.

She had given up on finding her grandfather, but it was almost as hard to find the number she was now looking for: 17C. There were no lights in the passageways where the signs were, and she could not understand the way they'd chosen to number the courtyards. Right now she was in the courtyard where the numbers started, the first one she had come to, closest to the fence.

A door opened. She froze, and shrank back against the wall. At first she did not understand why the Power had not warned her, but it took her only a couple of seconds to realise that the person coming out of the door was one of the dead. Despite the warm glow of camaraderie she had been feeling, her heart started to beat faster and she pressed harder into the wall as if it would help her glide further into the shadows, become more invisible.

The dead man—or dead woman, you couldn't tell—was standing outside the building, swaying. Took a couple of steps to the right, stopped. Took a couple of steps to the left, stopped. Looked around. Another door opened further down and another dead person emerged. This one walked straight out into the courtyard and stopped under a lamppost.

Flora jumped when the door right next to her opened. The dead person was a woman, to judge from the long grey hair. The hospital clothes hung loosely, shroud-like over her bony body. She took a couple of steps from the door, slow tentative steps as if she was walking across black ice in smooth soles.

Flora held her breath. The dead woman turned jerkily. The gaze issuing (Flora supposed) from the empty eye sockets slid toward the place where she was sitting, her presence unnoticed and irrelevant. The woman's interest was drawn instead to the dead man standing under the lamppost; she was lured to the light like a moth. Flora watched, mouth agape; it looked as if the woman had just caught sight of her one true love and was being pulled toward him by a power stronger than death.

More dead people joined the fold. From some doors only one came, from others two or three. When fifteen or so were assembled under the lamp something started that filled Flora with awe, the feeling of bearing witness to an event so primordial that it seemed beyond everything.

She could not see who had started it, but slowly they started to move in a clockwise direction. Soon an irregular circle had formed, with the lamppost in the middle. Sometimes someone bumped into someone else, someone stumbled or fell but quickly resumed their place in the ring. Around and around they moved and their shadows glided across the buildings. The dead were dancing.

Something came to mind that Flora had read about monkeys, or was it gorillas, in captivity. If you placed a pole in their midst it did not take long until the monkeys gathered around the pole, moving around it. The most primitive of all rites, the worship of the central axis.

Tears sprang up in her eyes. Her field of vision narrowed and blurred. She sat as if mesmerised for a long, long time and watched the dead circle, their motion without interruption or variation. If someone had told her at that moment that this was the dance that held the Earth in its rotation, she would have nodded and said, *Yes, I know.*

As the enchantment wore off a little she looked around. In many windows around the courtyard she saw pale ovals that had not been there before. Onlookers. Dead people who were too weak to make their way out, or who did not wish to participate, there was no way of knowing which.

This is how it is.

She formed the thought, and had no idea what she meant by it.

She stood up, intending to move on. Perhaps the same scene was being enacted in all the courtyards right now. She had only taken a couple of steps when she stopped short.

Others were approaching, she could feel it. Other living minds. How many? Four, maybe five. They came from the outside; the same direction she had come from.

As she felt the vivid resonance of other living beings in her head she suddenly understood what she had only suspected earlier: apart from Peter and herself and the ones who were now approaching, there was not a single living person inside the fence. No guards, nothing.

She withdrew to her previous place, concentrating on reading the people approaching. What she sensed dislodged a clump of fear that dropped into her stomach. She read excitement, terror. And just as she managed to disentangle the confused thoughts and identify them as belonging to five people, they entered the courtyard.

Five young men. Too far away for Flora to see properly but they had things in their hands. Sticks or...no. Flora hugged her belly, suddenly sick with comprehension and horror. They were holding baseball bats. Their thoughts were so agitated and mixed up that she could barely isolate any clear images, and she recognised this, knew that it was because they were very drunk.

The dead continued in their dance, apparently unaware of their new audience. One of the guys said, 'What the fuck are they doing?'

'Dunno,' said another. 'Looks like a disco.'

'Zombie disco!'

The guys laughed and Flora thought *They're not going to...they can't...* but knew that they were thinking it and were fully capable. One of them looked around. He was almost as unsteady on his feet as those who had come out of the buildings.

'Hey,' he said. 'There's someone here, isn't there?'

The others stopped talking, scanning the area. Flora bit her lip, sitting absolutely still. It was a completely new situation for her— others reading her thoughts as clearly as she could read theirs. She tried not to think. When that didn't work she used the static she had tried on Peter.

'Fuck it,' one of them said, gesturing at his head. 'It was just something.'

They walked closer to the dead. One of them wrenched off a backpack, said, 'Should we light 'em up right away, or what?'

'Nah,' said another and waved his bat. 'Let's have a feel first.'

'Damn, they're ugly.'

'They're gonna get even uglier.'

The guys stopped only a couple of metres from the dead, who had now stopped their dance and turned towards them. The hatred and terror that had been emanating from the young men grew stronger. And stronger.

'Hello gorgeous!' one of them shouted.

'Aaaaahhhhhh…' another said and an image of a zombie from Resident Evil flashed in Flora's head. When she had caught it, other images linked to it. Zombies from movies, monsters from games. This was what the guys' excursion was about: they'd headed out to get a little live action.

I can't…

Before she had made a conscious decision—it was hard to think with the guys' agitation crackling in her head—she got up and shouted 'Hello!'

It would have been comic under any other circumstances, all of the young men turning their heads in her direction at once. Flora stepped out of the shadows. Her legs shook; no amount of willpower could get them to stop. Trembling, she moved forward half-way to the lamppost, stopped.

'I'm watching you,' she said. 'Just so you know.'

That was all she could say. The only threat she had to brandish. But she knew that her voice, her thoughts betrayed her fear. Their thoughts were set on destruction and human consideration paled.

'A girl!' one of them called out and Flora felt her own body looked over by five minds, picked up twinges of lust, the impulse to fuck her into the ground, before or after they had done what they were going to do. She instinctively backed up a step.

'Go home to bed!' she shouted at the one who seemed to be the leader. He let his bat swing back and forth at her. 'Start thinking with your head instead of your dick, because you can't do this!'

The guy smiled broadly. His hair was combed back and his smile…professional. He was dressed in a light blue shirt and clean jeans. They were all dressed the same way—less like a lynch mob than a social club from the Business School; they'd just wound up a meeting and decided to go out and have some fun.

'Show me the law that...' the guy started and Flora saw an older man, presumably the young man's father, sitting at the kitchen table in a suit, saying *until the laws are changed the reliving are defenceless since they have already been legally determined to be deceased.* The guy didn't get any further, however, because one of his friends shouted, 'Markus! Watch out!'

While the guys were looking at Flora, the reliving had started to move closer to them, nourished and goaded by their hatred. The closest, a stick-thin old man a head shorter than the one they called Markus, stretched out his hands and took hold of Markus' shirt.

Markus jumped back and a low tearing of cloth could be heard. He looked down at the rip and screamed, 'Are you going to tear up my shirt, you bastard?' and swung his baseball bat against the dead man's head.

The blow connected perfectly right above the ear and made a sound like someone cracking a dry branch over their knee, before the force of the blow slung the dead man away a couple of metres, spinning a half-turn in the air and landing on his head. He rolled through another half-rotation in the same direction and collapsed on the concrete.

Markus held his hand up in the air and one of his pals high-fived him. They moved in on their prey.

Flora was unable to move. It was not only the terror that kept her feet nailed to the spot—the blood lust and hatred blazing from the men was intense enough to paralyse her mind. She lost command of her body, her thoughts swamped by theirs. She stood. She watched.

The dead were no match for five young, fit men. They went down one by one, accompanied by shrieks of triumph. Even when they were on the ground the men kept hitting them. It was as if they were demolishing a wall that had to be smashed into little pieces, small enough to be carried away in sacks. The dead made no effort to protect themselves. Even after their legs were broken they just kept crawling towards their attackers, taking more blows. The brittle snapping sounds went on but the dead did not stop, they only moved more slowly.

The young men lowered their bats and moved a couple of paces away from the crawling mass at their feet. One of them took out a pack of cigarettes, offering them round. They smoked and regarded their work.

'Damn,' said one. 'I think one of them bit me.'

He held out his arm and displayed a dark spot on the light fabric. The others recoiled in feigned horror, holding up their hands and shouting, 'Ahhh! He's been infected!'

The guy who had the bite smiled uncertainly and said, 'Oh, come off it. Do you think I should get a tetanus shot or something?'

The others picked up his concern and went on ribbing him about how he'd soon turn into a zombie hungry for human flesh until the guy told them to shut up. They laughed at him and he crouched nonchalantly next to the closest wreck of what had been a person, a little old lady whose one arm was so shattered it lay limply across her neck. He held out his injured arm to her mouth and said, 'Yum, yum. Come on, have a snack.'

The woman's mangled mouth, its few teeth protruding between crushed lips, opened and closed like a fish on a riverbank. The guy smiled and looked up at the others, and at that moment something happened that Flora had been fervently hoping for: the old woman's other arm shot out to grab his, and her teeth sunk into his flesh.

He screamed and lost his balance then quickly regained his feet. The teeth refused to let go and the old woman was dragged up from the ground like a ragdoll, hanging from his arm.

'Someone help me, God damn it,' the young man screamed and shook his arm, but even though the old woman was only a pile of broken bones in a sack of skin, her jaws were locked and she dangled along with his movements.

The man she'd latched onto wrenched his arm and gave an

328

incoherent scream of revulsion as a substantial piece of flesh was torn out of his lower arm. He hopped around stamping his feet as if he could only think of getting away somewhere—anywhere but in this situation.

As the blood ran down the man's arm his friend Markus pulled off his shirt, ripped off the arm that already had a tear and said, 'Come on, we'll have to apply a pressure b...'

His injured friend did not appear to hear him. He frantically ripped open the backpack, produced a couple of plastic bottles, unscrewed the caps and splashed liquid over the heap of bodies still quivering, searching.

'What about this, you bastards!' He ran around the perimeter of the heap, spraying from both bottles until they were empty. 'Let's see you bite now!'

The paralysis that had overcome Flora was wearing off; the other four guys had calmed down, having battered themselves into a state of exhaustion. Only the injured one's hysteria pierced her head like a saw, a saw through metal...

No...

It was the other sound she was hearing. There was nothing she could do to stop the guys, it was too late. She looked around. There, on the other side of the courtyard, she spotted herself on her way toward the lamppost. It was still hard to look, there was a force that told her to look away, but it was as if she was getting used to it—she pushed the whining into the back of her mind and left her thoughts free.

Do something, do something she thought at the figure, so like herself, who had moved, between one breath and another, to the edge of the heap of corpses where the guys were now getting a box of matches out of the backpack. They did not see her, but apparently they heard the sound and spotted her in their peripheral vision because their heads whipped round and they started shouting. 'What the hell is this, what the hell, what the hell...'

Death spread her arms, an invitation to embrace and—as if mesmerised—Flora did the same. She was a mirror image. The guys managed to light a match and Death took a couple of steps into the mass of bodies. She bent down and stretched her hands out, making small plucking movements as if she was picking berries, gathering something.

The match sailed through the air and Flora screamed, 'Look out, get away!'

At the instant the match landed, Death lifted her head and met Flora's gaze. They were identical to one another. There was nothing forbidding or dark in her eyes, they were simply Flora's eyes. For a second they had time to look into each other, share their secrets. Then the petrol exploded into fire and a wall of flames bloomed between them.

The guys stood frozen, staring at the bonfire. The highest flames stretched up almost to the rooftops, but after a few seconds the fumes had burned away and the fire took hold of the fuel itself; a sputtering crackle as hospital gowns and flesh charred.

'Come on, let's get out of here!'

The young men watched the fire a moment longer, as if to imprint it on their memories for good, then turned and jogged away from the yard. The one called Markus, his torso now bare, paused for a moment, looked at Flora and raised his index finger. But if he was planning to say something, he decided against it and followed the others. After a couple of minutes their minds were out of her reach.

The flames died out. Flora knew from the stillness in her mind that Death was gone. She walked up to the bonfire—no more than isolated little flare-ups and a strong, cloying smoke now, billowing up into the sky. Maybe it was because the dead had so little flesh, so little fat, that the fire hadn't really caught.

Everything was black. The doubly dead lay curled up with their elbows against their sides and their fists sticking straight out, as if boxing into the dark. The stench that rose from the heap was nauseating and Flora pulled a corner of her jacket over her nose and mouth.

They were dancing a moment ago.

Her chest filled. Grief, as deep as an abyss. The opposite of that wondrous awe she had felt for the dance of the dead. Grief for all humankind and its paths upon the Earth. And the same thought that had gripped her then returned now, in a different light:

This is how it is.

Norra Brunn 21.00

David had let Sture talk him into this and was already regretting it. As expected, Leo had cancelled him. There was a message on his answering machine that he had not listened to. He got a beer and went to join the others in the kitchen. A condoling silence. The jokes and laughter from just a moment ago died away.

This was not the place for serious conversation. If you couldn't joke about it, it didn't get said. The comedians were all, as individuals, regular people with the same capacity for sadness and joy as everyone else, but as a group they were a flippant lot, unable to handle anything that could not be expressed as a one-liner.

Right before the show was about to start, Benny Melin came up to him and said, 'Look, I hope you don't...but I have some stuff about all this with the reliving.'

'No, no,' David said. 'Do your thing.'

'OK,' Benny said and his face grew lighter. 'It's such a big thing, it's hard not to get into it, you know.'

'I understand.'

David saw that Benny was on the verge of trying out some of his material on him so he raised his glass, wished him good luck and backed away. Benny grimaced faintly. You didn't wish someone good luck, you said *break a leg* or something and David knew it, and Benny knew that David knew. To say good luck was very like an insult.

David went to the bar. The staff nodded to him but no one came up to talk. David downed his beer and asked Leo to pour him another.

'How's it going?' Leo asked as he poured.

'It's going,' David said. 'That's about it.'

Leo placed the beer on the counter. There was no point answering the question in more detail. Leo dried his hands on a towel and said, 'You'll have to give her my regards. When she's better.'

'I will.'

David felt that he was close to tears again. He turned away from the bar, toward the stage, and sank half the glass greedily. Better now. Now that he was left alone and no one had to pretend that they could understand any of it.

Death makes us strangers to one another.

The stage lights went up and via the ghost mike, Leo wished everyone a warm welcome and asked them to put their hands together for the evening's host, Benny Melin.

The place was full and the clapping and whistling that accompanied Benny up on stage gave David a twinge of longing to be back here, in this real world of unreality.

Benny gave a quick bow and the applause died down. He adjusted the mike stand—a little up, a little down—and the microphone ended up in the same place it had been from the start. He said, 'So, I don't know about you, but I'm a little worried about this thing with the Heath. A suburb full of dead people.'

The room was silent. Tense with anticipation. Everyone was worried about this thing with the Heath; maybe there was a new twist to the whole thing that they hadn't considered.

Benny wrinkled his forehead as if contemplating a difficult issue. 'And the one thing I'd really like to know...'

A rhetorical pause.

'Is the ice cream van going to want to drive there?'

Relieved laughter. Not funny enough for applause, but not far off. Benny went on, 'And if it's going to go there, will it sell anything?

'And if it sells something, then what?'

Benny waved his hand through the air, sketching a screen that everyone was supposed to look at.

'Just imagine. Hundreds of dead people lured from their homes by...' Benny started up a rendition of 'Greensleeves' and then quickly switched to being a zombie staggering along with outstretched arms. People giggled and when Benny groaned, 'Popsiiiic-eeeel, Popsiiiic-eeeel...' the applause came.

David downed the last of his beer and slunk out behind the bar. He couldn't handle this. Benny and all the rest of them had every right to joke about something as current as this, in fact they were obliged to, but he didn't have to listen. He walked quickly through the bar and out of the doors onto the street. A new round of applause fired off behind him and he walked away from the sound.

The painful thing was not that they were joking about it. There had to be jokes, jokes were necessary if people were going to keep living. The painful thing was that it had happened so quickly. After the ferry *Estonia* sank, for example, it had taken six months before anyone tried to say anything funny about ferry salvage or bow doors, and then without much success. The World Trade Center had gone much faster. Only a couple of days after the attack someone said something about the new cut-price alternative Taliban Airways, and people had laughed. It had been far enough away to feel like it wasn't really happening.

Apparently the reliving fell into the same category. They weren't real, you didn't have to have any respect. That's why David's presence had been hard for the other comedians to take; he made it real. But in the end that's what the reliving were to them: a joke.

He slunk past the tightly parked cars that lined Surbrunnsgatan, seeing Balthazar's headless body wriggling in Eva's lap, and wondered if he would be able to see the funny side of anything ever again.

The walk from Norra Brunn had exhausted his strength. The hastily downed beer sloshed in his stomach and every step was an act of will. Most of all he wanted to curl up in the nearest doorway and sleep away the remaining hours of this horrible day.

He had to lean up against the wall in the entrance and rest for a couple of minutes before going up to the apartment. He did not want to appear so pathetic that Sture offered to stay. He wanted to be alone.

Sture did not offer. After reporting that Magnus had slept the whole time, he said, 'I guess I should go home now.'

'Of course,' David said. 'Thanks for everything.'

Sture looked searchingly at him.

'Will you manage, then?'

'I'll manage.'

'Sure?'

'I'm sure.' He was so tired, his speech was starting to sound like Eva's; he could only repeat what was said to him. They parted with a hug, instigated by David. This time he let his head drop onto Sture's chest for a few seconds.

When Sture had left he stood still in the kitchen for a while, staring at the bottle of wine, but decided that he was too tired even for that. He went and checked on Magnus, regarding his sleeping child for a long time. He had fallen asleep in almost exactly the position David had left him in: his hand under his cheek, the eyes slowly sliding under thin eyelids.

David crawled gently into bed, slipping into the narrow space between Magnus' body and the wall. Was only planning to lie there for a couple of seconds and look at the thin, smooth shoulder that stuck out of the blankets. He closed his eyes and thought...thought nothing. Slept.

Tomaskobb 21.10

When Mahler stepped ashore on the nearest island he saw the marker. It was fashioned from bleached boards and he had missed it in the dark. The inlet lay straight in. He climbed back into the boat, started the engine. It roared, sputtered and died.

He waggled the tank, pumped in new fuel and this time the engine ran long enough for him to reverse away from the island before it died again. He leaned his arms against his knees and stared in among the islands, velvet blue in the summer night. Lone trees stuck up from low islands, silhouetted against the sky like in documentaries from Africa. The only sound was the distant engine vibration from the passing ferry.

This isn't so bad.

He preferred recognising his surroundings to having fuel. Now he could at least see what was in front of him. With the oars it would take about half an hour to the island, gliding over the still water. No problem. If he just took it easy it would be fine.

He placed the rowlocks in their holes and set to work. He rowed with short strokes, breathing deeply in the mild air. After a couple of minutes he was in a rhythm and hardly noticed the work. It was like meditation.

Om mani padme hum, om mani padme hum…
The oar strokes pushed the sea behind him.

When he had rowed for perhaps twenty minutes he thought he heard the call of a deer. He lifted the oars out of the water, listening. The sound came again. It was no deer, it was more like…a scream. It was hard to determine which direction it was coming from; the sound bounced between the islands. But if he had been asked to guess he would have said it came from…

He put the oars back in the water, and started to row with longer, more powerful strokes. He did not hear another scream. But it had come from the direction of Labbskär Island. Sweat broke out across his back and his calm scattered. He was no longer a meditating person, just a damnably effective motor.

I should have got fuel…

Thick mucus collected in his mouth and he spat at the engine.

'Bloody shit-engine!'

But it was actually his fault. His, and no one else's.

To dispense with mooring the boat, he rowed straight to the shore and crawled out. Water seeped into his shoes and they sucked at the soles of his feet as he walked up to the hut. No lights were on; the house was simply an outline against the deep blue sky.

'Anna! Anna!'

No answer. The front door was closed. When he pulled on it there was a strong resistance until whatever was fighting him gave up. He jumped and put his arm up to shield his face, thinking there was something coming at him. But it was only a loose broomstick that fell forward and clattered to the ground.

'Anna?'

It was darker inside and it took a couple of seconds for his eyes to grow accustomed to it. The door through to the bedroom was closed and on the kitchen floor there was a…heap of snow. He blinked as the snow pile began to take shape, became a blanket and then Anna,

337

who was sitting on the floor squeezing the blanket.

'Anna, what is it?'

Anna's voice was just a hoarse whisper from a screamed-out throat.

'It was here...'

Mahler looked around. The moonlight pouring in through the open door did not help much and he listened for sounds in the other room. Nothing. He knew how afraid Anna was of animals and sighed, saying with irritation, 'Was it a rat?'

Anna shook her head and said something he could not make out. As he turned from her in order to go into the other room and check, she hissed, 'Take this,' and pointed to a small axe lying on the floor at her feet. Then she crawled across the floor with the bedding in her arms, pulled the door shut and sat down with her back against the door post, one hand on the door handle. The room became pitch dark.

Mahler weighed the axe in his hand.

'What is it, then?'

'...drowned...'

'What?'

Anna forced her voice to get louder and croaked, 'A dead man. A corpse. Someone who drowned.'

Mahler closed his eyes, retrieving his memory of the kitchen; visualising the torch on the counter. He groped his way through the dark until his fingers closed around the heavy handle.

Batteries...

He turned it on and a cone of light shot out, illuminating the entire kitchen. He trained the beam on the wall next to Anna so as not to dazzle her. She looked like a ghost; sweat-drenched hair hung in wisps over her face, vacant eyes stared straight ahead.

'Daddy,' she whispered without looking at him. 'We have to let Elias...go.'

'What are you saying? Go where?'

'Go...away.'

'Keep quiet now and I'll...'

He opened the door to the other room a crack, let the light in. There was nothing there. He opened the door a little more, directing the beam of light inside.

Now he saw that the window on the opposite side was broken. Reflected light glittered in slivers of glass spread over the floor and table. He squinted. Something was lying on the table, among the shards. A rat. He took a couple of steps closer.

No, not a rat.

It was a hand. A severed hand. The skin was wrinkled, thin. The flesh on the front of the index finger was gone and only a stick-thin bone remained.

He swallowed, poking the hand with the axe. It rolled over among the glass, lay still. He snorted. What had he expected? That it was going to jump up and put on a stranglehold? He shone the light through the window and saw nothing except rocks sticking up from the creeping juniper.

'OK,' he said to Anna when he returned to the kitchen. 'I'll go out and look around.'

'No...'

'Then what should we do? Go to bed, hope that...'

'...weevil...'

'What was that?'

'It wants to do evil.'

Mahler shrugged, brandishing the axe. 'Were you the one who...'

'Had to. It wanted to get in.'

The adrenaline rush that had kept him going ever since he heard Anna's scream from the boat was starting to abate, and he was faint with hunger. He sank down on the floor next to Anna, breathing heavily. He pulled over the cooler, took out a packet of hot dogs, wolfed two of them and held the rest out to Anna, who made a face.

He ate two more but it felt like the effort of chewing was simply making him hungrier. When he had swallowed the pulpy mass he asked, 'Elias?'

Anna looked at the bundle in her arms and said, 'He's scared.' Her voice was cracked but audible.

Mahler took out a packet of cinnamon buns and ate five. More chewy mass to swallow. He drank a couple of sips of lukewarm milk out of the container and felt just as hungry as before, except that now he also had a heavy mass in his stomach. He leaned back, lying down on the floor to try and get the heaviness to distribute itself more evenly.

'Let's go back,' Anna said.

Mahler shone the flashlight on the petrol container under the kitchen counter and said, 'If there's petrol in it we can. Otherwise it's out of the question.'

'We don't have any *fuel*?'

'No.'

'I thought you were going to...'

'I didn't have the energy.'

Anna did not say anything, which he thought was worse than if she had berated him. Rage slowly kindled in his chest.

'I've been working,' he said. 'The whole time since we...'

'Not now,' Anna said. 'Stop it.'

Mahler clenched his teeth, rolled over and crawled up to the petrol container, lifting it. It was very light, because it was empty.

Fucking idiots, he thought. *The fucking idiots don't have any reserve fuel.*

From the door he heard Anna snort, remembered that she knew what he was thinking. He slowly pulled himself up to his feet, taking the torch and the axe.

'You can sit there and laugh,' he said. 'I'll just go out and...' he waved the axe toward the door. Anna did not move.

'Can you let me out?'

'It isn't like Elias,' Anna said. 'It's been alone, it...'

'Can you please move away from the door?'

Anna looked him in the eyes.

'What do I do?' she said. 'What do I do if...something happens?'

Mahler gave a short bitter laugh.

'Is *that* what you're worried about?' He pulled his cell phone out of his pocket, turned it on and entered the PIN. He gave it to her. 'Nine, one, one. If anything *happens*.'

Anna inspected the phone as if to check that there was reception, then said, 'We're calling now.'

'No,' Mahler said and reached for the phone. 'In that case I'll keep it.' Anna sighed and hid the phone in the blankets. 'You won't call?'

Anna shook her head and let go of the door. 'Daddy. We're not doing the right thing.'

'Yes,' Mahler said. 'I think we are.'

He opened the door and let the beam of light play over the rocks, grass and raspberry bushes. When he raised the beam it lit up a gap in the curtain of alder trees between the house and the water, and he saw a person lying on the shallow jutting rocks in the opening of the inlet. The torch was not really necessary, the moonlight was enough to make out the white shape lying with its torso on the rock, its head by the water's edge.

'I see it,' he said.

'What are you going to do?'

'Remove it.'

He left the house. Anna did not close the door as he had believed she would. When he had taken a couple of steps toward the creature, he turned around. Anna was sitting on the step, hugging the bundle and watching him.

Perhaps it should have made him happy, even touched, but he simply felt scrutinised: Anna did not trust him and was sitting there now to watch him fail, again.

When he reached the shore and passed the boat he saw what the creature was doing. It was drinking. It was lying on its stomach, scooping sea water into its mouth with its one remaining hand.

Mahler turned off the flashlight and crept over the slick seaweed, gripping the axe.

Get rid of it.

That was what he was going to do. Get rid of it.

He was about twenty metres away when it stood up. It was a person, and yet it wasn't. The moon gave enough light to see that large parts of its body were missing. A soft southerly breeze carried the stench of rotten fish. Mahler waded through an area with reeds and then came up on the rock where the creature was waiting for him. Its head was tilted as if it couldn't believe its eyes.

Eyes?

It had no eyes. Its head turned from side to side as if it was sniffing, or listening for the sound of his steps. When Mahler was a couple of feet away from it, he saw that the skin on its chest had been eaten away, and its ribs stuck out white in the moonlight. He saw a movement and caught his breath, thinking it was the creature's heart, pulsating.

He raised the axe and turned on the flashlight. Aimed at the creature, to blind it if it still had eyes to see with. The light made it chalk-white against the sea, and now Mahler saw what was causing the motion: inside the chest cavity was a fat black eel, caught as if in a trap, eating its way out.

Reflexively, from some kind of basic human shame at his own grossness, Mahler turned away before the food he had eaten erupted from his stomach and spurted through his lips. Sausage, pastries, milk poured out onto the rock and ran down into the water. He turned again, so as not to have his back to the creature, even before his nausea had fully subsided.

Vomit continued to trickle down between his trembling jaws,

down over his chin. He saw the eel thrash around inside the chest and in the stillness he heard the sound of its snake-body, gliding over the remnant flesh of its prison. Mahler wiped his mouth but his jaws did not stop chattering.

His revulsion was such that the only impulse in his head was aversion beyond all reason, a command to remove—extinguish—this abomination from the face of the Earth.

Kill it...kill it...

He took a step toward the creature and at the same time the creature moved towards him. It was quick, much quicker than he had thought possible with that wreck of a body. There were a couple of clicks as the bones clashed against the rock and even in his blind rage, Mahler backed up. It was the eel. He did not want that eel, grown fat on human flesh, to come near him.

He backed up and slipped in his own vomit. The axe flew from his hand as his body landed with a wet thud. His neck was jerked back by the blow and the back of his head struck the rock. Bright lights flashed and the instant before they died and dropped him into the darkness, he felt the creature's hands on his body.

Labbskär Island 21.50

Anna saw it happen. She saw her father fall flat on the rock, heard his head meet the unyielding surface, saw the creature throw itself over him. She flew to her feet, still with Elias in her arms.

God, no! The fucking bastard...

The creature lifted its head in their direction and at that moment she heard Elias' voice inside her head.

...nice...think nice...

Anna sobbed and took a few steps. Something rattled near her feet, but she paid it no attention, continuing instead toward the boat, toward the creature whose head tugged and jerked above her father's lifeless body.

Disgusting bloody...

...nice...

She knew. Deep down she knew. As long as she'd sat on the bed doing nothing, thinking nothing, the creature had simply stood outside and looked at them. It was when she had gone up to the window and screamed at it to go away, sent hatred and disgust to it, that it had broken the window. It was her terror that had driven its attempts to get in in the first place.

When her father had started to send hate to the creature, toward the image of the eel in the chest cavity, she had tried to send the same thing as Elias was now doing: *Think nice*, but she had not reached him, and now it was too late.

It's a challenge to reason clearly when someone has just killed your father. Quite a challenge.

Disgusting bloody white disgusting...

She continued into the grass, unable to find any nice words. Everything was being taken from her, bit by bit, person by person. She saw the creature stand up, go down into the reeds and cross the sand toward the boat, toward her.

Her gaze flitted over the ground, looking for a strong tree branch, something to use as a weapon. The branches lying on the ground were all clearly rotten, otherwise they would not have fallen. The creature's feet sloshed through wet seaweed and Anna suddenly spotted the drying rack where Elias' socks still hung. She could break it off, she could use it as...

The creature was level with the boat now and Anna was moving parallel to the shore higher up. If she managed to break off the rack, if she could—Elias squirmed restlessly in her arms, the blanket dragging by her feet—if she could...

What? What? You can't kill someone who's already dead.

But nonetheless she persevered along the hill, laid Elias down on the rocky ground and pulled on the pole, forcing it back and forth. The elements had weathered the wood, but her terror made her strong and the rack broke off at its foot with a creak. Elias' socks were still dangling on their hooks and even as the creature was coming up through the grass, only five metres away, she dashed the rack against the rockface to break off the cross board, make a clean weapon.

Mother's little Olle, walking in the woods...

Elias' little voice penetrated the shell of her terror and she understood. As the creature reached the foot of the boulder right under her and the cadaver stench reached her nostrils she disconnected every other thought and filled her head with:

Roses on his cheek and sunshine in his eyes lips so small, of blueberries so blue

She could not think nice, but she could sing in her mind. The creature stopped. Its legs froze, its arms went limp. A machine suddenly run out of fuel.

If only I did not have to walk here quite so alone.

The tears ran silently down Anna's cheeks as she saw a black substance smeared around the creature's mouth, but she would not think about *Daddy's blood*, nor anything that could lead her thoughts to anger and hatred. Instead she went on reciting:

Brummelibrum, Hark! Who goes there?

The bushes are shaking, it must be a dog.

The irony of the lyrics made her body tremble, but she was no longer in her body. She was standing beside it. Noting its changes, seeing what it saw, but directing: directing the body's brain to keep singing.

The creature turned and walked back the way it had come: toward the inlet, toward the jutting rocks, toward her father's body. She did not reflect on this, simply noted that it was happening.

She waited half a minute until she reached the end of the song, then wrapped Elias in the blanket and walked down to the boat. The yellow moon was reflected in a little pool on the rock face and as the grass whispered over her legs she saw—

Yellow?

—that yellow glow was all wrong. She looked again. The light was coming from the cell phone. She had dropped it. Still singing the same song—she dared not change in case she broke her concentration—she fished up the phone and laid it on Elias' stomach, walked down to the boat.

Teddy he eats almost all that there is...

She settled Elias on the bottom and avoided looking toward the inlet as she pushed the boat out from the edge of the shore, took a couple of steps into the water and crawled in. The boat floated well and they glided out onto the faintly ruffled water. Anna sat in the middle seat, and saw the bags of food, the water. In the silence she heard the moist crunching sounds from the inlet, the sound of a fish being gutted. Her lower jaw started to quiver, she hugged herself.

He tried to...he meant well...he just wanted to...filthy disgusting...Holds out his basket with chubby little hands...

She had to keep singing. The creature could swim.

She unshipped the oars with shaking hands and rowed out into the inlet on the other side. She knew it was in the wrong direction, but she could not stand to get closer, perhaps see...

When she had rowed about fifty strokes and there was only the blue expanse of the Sea of Åland behind her back she let the oars go, let them hang freely from the rowlocks and crept down next to Elias, curled up on the bottom next to him and let everything come. Stopped fleeing, stopped singing, simply stopped.

The southerly breeze was slowly moving them farther and farther out. Gåskobb Island floated past and soon Söderarm's lone blinking eye was the only thing that could be seen between space and the sea.

The Heath 22.00

Flora stood there gazing at the mass of tangled bodies.

That evening in Elvy's garden she had wished—she had known—that something was going to happen. Something that would change Sweden forever. Now it had happened, and what was the change?

Nothing.

Terror gave birth to terror, hatred begat hate and all that was left in the end was a pile of burnt bodies. As everywhere; as always.

Something was moving among the bodies.

At first she thought it was fingers that had managed to survive the blaze somehow and were now struggling to make their way out. Then she saw it was caterpillars. White caterpillars burrowing their way out of some of the bodies. The stench from the bonfire was unbearable despite her face mask and she shuffled back a couple of metres.

Only seven caterpillars had emerged, even though there had been around fifteen people to start.

She took the others.

She knew the caterpillars were people...no, the caterpillars were the human element in the people, given a visible form it was possible to comprehend in this world. Not even her twin was really her twin—she wasn't anything that could be understood in human terms. Flora had known that in the second they had stared into each other's eyes.

The other Flora, the one wearing her best sneakers, was only a force: one that manifested itself in a way that made sense to each individual. The only constant was the hooks, since the task of the power was to catch, to collect. And not even the hooks were anything real, simply an image people could understand.

The caterpillars that had emerged from the black mass wriggled, nowhere to go now that their host had been destroyed.

Lost, Flora thought. *Lost.*

There was nothing she could do. They had turned away in fear and were now lost. As she watched they swelled up, becoming first pink, then red.

Faintly, faintly, Flora could hear screams of anguish as the caterpillar-people realised what she already knew: they were now being pulled inexorably to the other place. The place of which nothing can be said. Nothing.

The caterpillars swelled even more, the thin membrane stretching, and the screams grew stronger. Flora's head spun because she knew that none of this was really happening. Only the fact that she was watching made it visible, it was an invisible drama that was enacted before her eyes, as old as the human race.

With a plop—audible yet inaudible—the caterpillars burst one by one and a viscous, translucent fluid ran out, evaporating in the heat of the scorched bones as the screams faded away.

Lost.

She backed away from the bonfire, sitting down on the bench a couple of metres away, trying to think. She knew too much, much too much. The knowledge that had flooded into her head during that second of eye contact had been too much, she was not able to bear it.

Why? Why has this happened?

She knew. She knew everything. It could not be put into words, but something had happened in the greater order of things. And one of the minor effects, here on our little planet, was that within a certain circumscribed area, the dead had awakened. A hurricane had led to the beating of a butterfly's wings. In the greater scheme it was nothing, one of those things that happens from time to time. A footnote, at most, in the book of the gods.

Suddenly she sat up straight on the bench. She remembered something Elvy had said outside the gates earlier...was it today? Was it still the same day she had gone for a walk with Maja and...yes, the same day.

She took out her phone and dialled Elvy's number. By some miracle it was not any of the ladies or that repulsive guy who answered, but Elvy herself. She sounded tired.

'Nana, it's me. How's it going?'

'Not so good. Things are...not so good.'

Flora could hear raised voices in the background, people quarrelling. The events of the day had caused ructions in the group.

'Nana, listen to me. Do you remember what you told me today?'

Elvy sighed. 'No, I don't know...'

'The woman in the TV, you showed her to me...'

'Yes, yes. All that, it...'

'Wait. She said to you that *they must come unto me*, isn't that right?'

'We are trying,' Elvy said. 'But...'

'Nana, she didn't mean the living. She meant the dead.'

Flora told her what had happened in the courtyard. The gang of young men, the fire, her twin, the caterpillars.

As she was talking, she could feel in another part of her mind that people were approaching the area. These ones were not of a friendly mind-set either. Rage and hatred were approaching. Perhaps the guys had fetched some of their buddies, or there were others with the same idea.

'Nana, you've seen her too. You have to come here. Right now. They...they'll disappear otherwise.'

The other end went quiet for a while, and then Elvy said with an entirely new strength in her voice, 'I'll take a taxi.'

As Flora hung up she realised that they had not arranged a meeting place. Still, that would take care of itself. Their minds were so in tune that it was like having walkie-talkies, at least while they were in this area. More problematic was the question of how Elvy would get in. But that was something they could deal with later.

Flora stood up. Hard people with minds bent on evil were coming.

What do I say, what do I do?

She ran out of the courtyard. She knew that somewhere in this complex there was a reliving whose thinking approximated her own, who thought in the same images. She was looking for 17C.

While she ran, dead people were coming out of the buildings and gathering outside. No dancing now. There were still faces that simply watched from the windows above, but with each passing minute they were getting fewer. The whining, piercing sound of the dentist's drill was growing. In the distance she felt more living people approaching—the gates must have been opened.

She ran with panic in her chest, an approaching catastrophe, a river of terror that she was not capable of damming. She found number 17 and ran in, then paused.

A dead person was on his way down the steps. An old man whose legs had been amputated was dragging himself down, down on his stomach. On each step his chin smacked into the concrete with a thud that hurt Flora's mouth. He was near the surface, she could hear him:

Home...home...home...

When Flora passed him, he reached for her but she twisted herself free and continued up to apartment C, flinging the door open.

Eva was standing in the hallway, on her way out. Her face was simply a pale blotch in the weak light from the stairwell that filtered through the door and illuminated the bandage over half her face.

Without thinking, Flora stepped forward and took her by the shoulders. At the moment the link between them was established Flora knew what to say. She closed her mind to everything going on outside and thought:

Come out. Listen to me.

The body struggled in her grip. What was still Eva in Eva answered:

No. I want to live.

You are not going to live. That door is closed. There are two ways out.

Flora transmitted the two images of souls leaving their fleshly bonds. The ones who were collected, and those that disappeared. The words were not her own, they were simply voiced through her.

Allow it to happen. Give yourself up.

Eva's soul neared the surface; the whining intensified somewhere behind Flora's back. Like a sea swallow that has been searching across the ocean for a long time, the Fisher now let itself swoop down to the glinting flash of silver, toward its catch.

I just want to...say goodbye.

Do it. You are strong.

Before the Fisher had time to take its shape, before Eva's soul had time to take the shape of the Fisher's catch, Eva leaped out of her chest and flew with the speed only disembodied spirit can command. A whisper brushed Flora's skin as a life flitted past her, the flame of a consciousness flickered in her head, and was gone. Eva's body collapsed at Flora's feet.

Good luck.

The whining grew more distant. The Fisher took up the chase.

Svarvagatan 22.30

David slept, and was dreaming. He was locked in a labyrinth, running along corridors. Sometimes he reached a door, but the door always turned out to be closed. Something was chasing him. Something that was always following, just behind a corner somewhere. He knew it was Eva's face, but it wasn't Eva. It was something that had assumed her form the better to get at him.

He tugged at door handles, screaming, feeling all the while the encroachment of something wholly the opposite of love. The worst thing was that he felt he had left Magnus behind; he was back in some room in the dark where the terrible thing could get him.

He ran along an endless corridor, towards a door he knew would be closed. As he ran he noticed something happening to the light in the corridor. All the passages he'd been running through had been lit by cold neon, but now there was another light. Daylight, sunlight. He looked up as he ran. The ceiling of the corridor was gone and he saw a summer sky.

As he laid his hand on the door handle he knew this door would open, and it did. It opened, all the walls dissolved and he was standing on a lawn by Kungsholm shore. Eva was there.

He knew what day it was, felt the moment. A big orange

motorboat was approaching along the canal. Yes. He had looked at it, there was an orange spot on his retina, and then he turned to Eva and asked, 'Do you want to marry me?'

And she said yes.

'Yes! Yes!'

And they tumbled onto the blanket and embraced and they made plans and promised For Ever and For Ever and the man in the orange boat wolf-whistled at them and it was that day now and the boat was approaching and in a moment he would ask his question but right before the words left his lips Eva took his face between her hands and said: 'Yes. Yes. But I have to go now.'

David shook his head. His head turned back and forth on the pillow and he said, 'You can't go.'

Eva's mouth smiled, but her eyes were sad.

'We'll see each other again,' she said. 'It will take a few years, that's all. Don't be afraid.'

He shook off his blankets, held his arms out to the bedroom ceiling, he reached out his arms for her on the lawn and a piercing cry came between them.

The lawn, the canal, the boat, the light and Eva were sucked up, shrinking to a single point and he opened his eyes. He was lying in Magnus' bed with his arms outstretched. From his right he heard a whining sound almost loud enough to deafen him; he was not permitted to look in that direction. A white caterpillar lay curled up on his stomach.

The scent of cheap perfume filled the room and he knew it, he recognised it. He saw a hint of pink out of the corner of his eye. His head was locked, he could not turn it to see his own image of Death, the woman in the grocery store. A hand reached into his field of vision. Colourful bracelets hung from the wrist and at the tips of the fingers there were hooks.

No! No!

His hands flew out, cupped over the caterpillar. The hooks

halted, some ten centimetres from his hand. They were not permitted to touch him, he was a living. The caterpillar wriggled, tickling the palm of his hand and through the skin of his hand, in through the flesh and into his bones, there came a plea:

Let me go.

David shook his head, he tried to shake his head. He wanted to jump out of his bed with the caterpillar cupped in his hands, escape the house, get away from the Earth, the very world where things must be this way. But he was paralysed with fear as Death stood by his bedside. And he refused to let go.

The caterpillar swelled under his hand. The hooks slowly pulled back out of sight. The plea grew weaker, Eva's voice faded away, layer upon layer of darkness was coming between her and the part of him that could hear her. Only a whisper:

If you love me...let me go...

David let out a sob and lifted his hands.

'I love you.'

The caterpillar on his stomach was swollen now, pink. It looked sick. Dying.

What have I done, what have I...

The hooks were there again, the hook on the index finger drilled into the caterpillar, lifted it up and David's mouth shaped around a scream but before it came something happened.

Where the hook had entered the caterpillar, a crack opened. The hand lingered before his eyes, as if to show him what was happening now. The crack widened and he saw that the caterpillar was not a caterpillar but a pupa. A head was emerging from the crack, no bigger than the head of a pin.

The butterfly made its way out of the pupa and the dry shell fell away, dissolving. It sat motionless on the hook for a moment, as if to dry its wings or display itself, then it lifted, flying upward. David followed it with his eyes and saw it disappear through the ceiling.

When he looked down again the hand with the hooks was gone and the whining noise had abated. He stared up at the ceiling, toward the point where the butterfly had disappeared.

Disappeared.

Magnus moved next to him. In his sleep he said, 'Mummy...'

David got up out of bed, careful not to wake Magnus. He closed the door behind him so he wouldn't hear. Then he lay down on the kitchen floor and cried until the tears dried up and he was empty. The world was empty again.

I believe.

There is a place where happiness exists. A place, and a time.

The Heath 22.35

Flora had changed her mind.

She found it natural, now, that the body must require a soul even for a simple act like standing up. Even more remarkable, the soul required a body. What remained here of Eva was something that could be burned, or buried like so much rubbish.

Why are we born? What is the point?

That was the great mystery and of this Flora knew nothing. It was not included in the science of Death. Flora remained kneeling for a couple of minutes beside the vacated body and heard the whole area in uproar around her.

I can't go on...

It was absurd. This morning she had been smoking and chatting with Maja as usual, now she was supposed to be saving souls.

Saving?

She didn't know anything about it. The only thing she knew about the Place they were going was that it was a place you couldn't know anything about unless you were there. And that there was Another Place, about which nothing could be said, ever.

Why her? Why Elvy?

Nana...

It was at least twenty minutes since she had called Elvy. She might already be standing at the gates. Even though Flora was afraid to go out, she ran down the stairs. All at once she felt like a little girl again. Nana would tell her, Nana would know what had to be done.

But I am the one who knows...

Life would never be the same after this.

The courtyard was deserted. No. The man without legs, the one she had encountered on the stairs, had got no further than the main entrance and was still dragging himself along by the arms. All around her there was calm, but the clamour inside her head was indescribable. An insane cacophony of cries, prayers, anger, pleas for help, howls of hatred.

She ran over to the man, crouched down and put her hand on his back, sent her knowledge into him, but the man resisted. He did not want to leave his wreck of a body. Instead he turned around and struck out at her hand, tried to grab her, baring his teeth.

Come on, you idiot. Don't you get it...

Impotent rage bubbled up inside her; she jumped back as the man's wrath and bitterness clicked in with her own, each feeding the other's. She measured a kick at his face but managed to control herself; she left him there.

She reached the other side of the courtyard entrance and stopped abruptly.

All of the dead had left their yards and were moving toward the fence. The field was boiling with people. The gates were wide open and a number of police SWAT teams had already driven in, more arriving as she watched. Police officers jumped out with weapons drawn. The dead were trying to move toward the gates but were being held at bay by the police. As yet no shots had been fired but it was only a matter of time. There was maybe one police officer for thirty dead.

Have to...

Flora ran toward the seething mass. When the legless man had turned to her and bared his teeth she had seen something inside him. Hunger. He had used up his own flesh and needed more to sustain his non-existence. It was possible he would have let himself starve to death if he had not been met by this anger from the outside, driving him to satisfy himself. Now he was crawling as fast as he could toward the source of the anger.

Flora reached a young police officer surrounded by the dead and threw herself forward—a second after she felt his consciousness give way—to avoid the gunfire he was pumping into the bodies around her.

He might as well have been using a cap gun. The effect was the same even if the bangs were louder. There were small tugs at the flesh of the dead as the bullets hit, but they didn't miss a step. Within a couple of seconds the policeman had disappeared in a mass of thin arms, legs, blue clothes.

Now there were shots from several directions. Flora reached the gates and ran past a SWAT unit where a policewoman in the front seat was shouting something about back-up into her radio. Flora ran on down the road and after a hundred metres saw Elvy hurrying along the muddy path.

The pistol shots were now distant, muffled cracks as if there was a New Year's Eve party somewhere far behind her. She caught up with her grandmother, took her hand and said, 'Come.'

As they walked quickly, hand-in-hand, back toward the gates an insight blossomed up inside Flora: *It's too late.*

Elvy pressed her hand harder, said, 'Someone. If only we can... how could I...I...'

We didn't know, Flora sent.

Yet another couple of SWAT vehicles came bouncing along the field in the direction of the gates. One pulled up next to them, and the front window wound down.

'Hey you! You're not allowed to be here!'

Flora stared at the gates. The dead were pouring out now, in the direction of the road, toward the city.

'For Chrissake,' came a voice from inside the vehicle. 'Jump in. Now!'

Flora looked at Elvy and for a couple of seconds they were able to share each other's thoughts. Elvy's great shame that she hadn't understood, that she hadn't done what she was supposed to. She didn't care what happened to her, she was old and this was her last chance to put something right. As for Flora, she knew that she would never be able to return to a normal life after that second inside Death.

They had to try.

They took a step away from the SWAT vehicle toward the dead, but at that moment a side door opened and a couple of officers jumped out and grabbed them.

'Are you deaf? You're not allowed here!'

They were manhandled onto the bus, turned over to more waiting arms that received them, held onto them. The door was pulled shut and locked. The armoured vehicle backed up a couple of metres, until the police officer next to the driver said, 'Take it once around.'

The driver asked what he meant and the man next to him gestured in a circular motion at the horde of dead people approaching the car. The driver understood what he was getting at, gave a snort and stepped on the gas.

There was a clang of metal as they hit the dead, who were thrown wide by the vehicle ploughing through them. Through the side window, Flora saw the ones who had been hit stand up again.

She held her hands over her ears, sagged into Elvy's lap, but she felt the thud through her body whenever the car hit dead flesh.

It is over, she thought. *It is over.*

The Sea of Åland 23.30

Anna didn't care where they were. There were no islands in sight; even the Söderarm lighthouse had disappeared below the horizon and they were floating down a silvery moon-river on an endless sea. The island of Åland was out there somewhere, and Finland beyond that, but these were names without significance. They were at sea; just at sea.

Light waves were clucking against the hull. Elias lay by her side. Everything was as it should be and if it was not, it no longer mattered. They were beyond, outside. They could go on floating for ever.

The sound that broke the silence was so wrong that at first Anna took it as a cosmic joke bestowed by the night: *Eine kleine Nachtmusik*, in an ugly electronic tone. She dug the cell phone out from under the blanket. Even though she had brought it in case of a situation like this, it seemed impossible that anyone could reach her out here: there was nothing here.

For a moment she was about to throw it overboard, the sound was so irritating. Then she came to her senses and pressed the talk button.

'Yes?'

A voice buzzing with tension on the other end. Or else it was simply that the reception was bad.

'Hello, my name is David Zetterberg. I'm trying to reach Gustav Mahler.'

Anna looked around. The light from the display had disturbed her night vision and she could no longer distinguish the line between sea and sky; they were hovering in space.

'He's...not here.'

'You'll have to excuse me, I have to talk to someone. He had a grandchild who...there is something I have to say.'

'You can say it to me.'

Anna listened to David's story, thanked him and turned off the phone. Then she sat there for a long time looking at Elias, pulled him up into her lap and laid her forehead against his.

Elias...I'm going to tell you something...

She felt that Elias was listening. She related what she had just been told.

You don't have to be afraid...

His voice echoed in her head: *Are you sure?*

Yes. I'm sure. Stay here until...until it's time. Inside of me.

Through the blankets she felt his body slump together, becoming dead weight. He went into her.

Mummy? What's it like there?

I don't know. I think you are...light.

Do you think you can fly?

Maybe. Yes, I think so.

A whining sound, intensifying, carried over the water, as if a ferry were approaching, but the only light came from the moon and the stars. The whining grew stronger, drawing closer, and Anna changed her mind. She had Elias with her, he was inside her again as he had been when he began, and she was no longer willing to give him up. At the moment she thought this, she felt Elias start to pull away from her.

No, no, my love. Stay. Stay. I'm sorry.

Mummy, I'm frightened.

Don't be afraid. I'm here with you.

The whining was in the dinghy now. From the corner of her left eye she saw a shadow slide across the moon. Something was sitting on the thwart. She could not look there.

Mummy, will we see each other again soon?

Yes, my love. Soon.

Elias was about to say something else, but his speech was going, becoming weaker as a white caterpillar broke free from his chest and a clump of darkness reached out from where it was seated. At the very end of the clump there was a hook.

Anna cupped her hand around the caterpillar and picked it up, holding it there for a couple of seconds.

I will think of you always.

Then she let him go.

The thought, so delicate, as hopeful

as the northward journey of the

light across the sky

in soft streaks

like snail trails

or mussels sensing the bottom of the sea

in the chest, mouth, hands

the heart, the beating heart

the cry of the brain.

MIA AJVIDE
Cries of Flight

Turn the page for a sneak peek at
John Ajvide Lindqvist's new novel

HARBOR

Available October 2011

Gåvasten (February 2004)

'What a day. It's incredible.'

Cecilia and Anders were standing by the window in the living room, looking towards the bay. The ice was covered with virgin snow, and the sun shone from a cloudless sky, eating away the contours of the inlet, the jetty and the shore like an over-exposed photograph.

'Let me see, let me see!'

Maja came racing in from the kitchen, and Anders barely had time to open his mouth to warn her for the hundredth time. Then her thick socks skidded on the polished wooden floor and she landed flat on her back at his feet.

In a reflex action he bent down to comfort her, but Maja immediately rolled to one side and wriggled back a metre. Tears sprang to her eyes. She screamed, 'Stupid stupid things!' then tore off the socks and hurled them at the wall. Then she got up and ran back into the kitchen.

Anders and Cecilia looked at each other and sighed. They could hear Maja rummaging in the kitchen drawers.

Whose turn?

Cecilia winked and took on the task of intervening before Maja tipped the entire contents of the drawers on to the floor, or broke something. She went into the kitchen and Anders turned back to the glorious day.

'No, Maja! Wait!'

Maja came running in from the kitchen with a pair of scissors in her hand, Cecilia right behind her. Before either of them could stop her, Maja had grabbed one of the socks and started hacking at it.

Anders seized her arms and managed to get her to drop the scissors. Her whole body was trembling with rage as she kicked out at the sock. 'I hate you, you stupid thing!'

Anders hugged her, holding her flailing arms fast with his own. 'Maja, that doesn't help. The socks don't understand.'

Maja was a quivering bundle in his arms. 'I hate them!'

'I know, but that doesn't mean you have to . . .'

'I'm going to chop them up and burn them!'

'Calm down, little one. Calm down.'

Anders sat down on the sofa without loosening his grip on Maja. Cecilia sat down next to him. They spoke softly and stroked her hair and the blue velour tracksuit that was the only thing she would consent to wear. After a couple of minutes she stopped shaking, her heartbeat slowed and she relaxed in Anders' arms. He said, 'You can wear shoes instead, if you like.'

'I want to go barefoot.'

'You can't. The floor's too cold.'

'Barefoot.'

Cecilia shrugged her shoulders. Maja rarely felt cold. Even when the temperature was close to freezing she would run around outdoors in a T-shirt unless somebody said something to her. She slept eight hours a night at the most, and yet it was rare for her to fall ill or feel tired.

Cecilia held Maja's feet in her hands and blew on them. 'Well, you need to put some socks on now. We're going out.'

Maja sat upright on Anders' knee. 'Where to?'

Cecilia pointed out of the window, towards the north-east.

'To Gåvasten. To the lighthouse.'

Maja leaned forward, screwing her eyes up into the sunlight. The old stone lighthouse was visible only as a vague rift in the sky where it met the horizon. It was about two kilometres away, and they had been waiting for a day like this so they could make the trip they had been talking about all winter.

Maja's shoulders drooped. 'Are we going to *walk* all that way?'

'We thought we might ski,' said Anders, and the words were hardly out of his mouth before Maja shot off his knee and raced into the hallway. She had been given her first pair of skis on her sixth birthday two weeks earlier, and on only her second practice outing she had done really well. She had a natural talent. Two minutes later she was back, dressed in her snowsuit, hat and gloves.

'Come on then!'

They ignored Maja's protests and made a picnic to eat out by the lighthouse. Coffee, chocolate and sandwiches. Then they gathered up their skiing equipment and went down to the inlet. The light was dazzling. There had been no wind for several days, and fresh snow still covered the branches of the trees. Wherever you turned there was whiteness, blinding whiteness. It was impossible to imagine that there could be warmth and greenness anywhere. Even from space the earth must look like a perfectly formed snowball, white and round.

It took a while to get Maja's skis on because she was so excited she couldn't stand still. Once the bindings were tight and the straps of the poles wrapped around her hands, she immediately slid out on to the ice, shouting, 'Look at me! Look at me!'

For once they didn't need to worry as she set off on her own. Despite the fact that she had travelled a hundred metres from the jetty before Anders and Cecilia had even got their skis on, she was clearly visible as a bright red patch in the middle of all the whiteness.

It was different in the city. Maja had run off on her own several times because she had seen something or thought of something, and they had joked about fitting her with a GPS transmitter. Not that it was all that much of a joke, really; they had given it serious consideration, but it felt like overkill.

They set off. Far out on the ice Maja fell over, but she was back on her feet in no time and whizzing along. Anders and Cecilia followed in her tracks. When they had travelled about fifty metres, Anders turned around.

Their house, generally known as the Shack, lay at the edge of the point. Plumes of smoke were rising from both chimneys. Two pine trees, weighed down with snow, framed it on either side. It was a complete dump, badly built and poorly maintained, but right now, from this distance, it looked like a little paradise.

Anders struggled to get his old Nikon out of his rucksack, zoomed in and took a picture. Something to remind him when he was cursing the ill-fitting walls and sloping floors. That it was a little paradise. As well. He put the camera away and followed his family.

After a couple of minutes he caught up with them. He had intended to lead the way, making it easier for Maja and Cecilia as they followed in his tracks through the thick covering of snow, but Maja refused. She was the guide and group leader, and they were to follow her.

The ice was nothing to worry about; this was confirmed when they heard a roaring sound from the direction of the mainland. A car was heading for Domarö from the steamboat jetty in Nåten. From this distance it was no bigger than a fly. Maja stopped and stared at it.

'Is that a *real* car?'

'Yes,' said Anders. 'What else would it be?'

Maja didn't reply, but carried on looking at the car, which was on its way towards the point on the opposite side of the island.

'Who's driving?'

'Holidaymakers, probably. Wanting to go for a swim.'

Maja grinned and looked at him with that supercilious expression she sometimes wore, and said, 'Daddy. Wanting to go for a swim? *Now?*'

Anders and Cecilia laughed. The car disappeared behind the point, leaving a thin cloud of whirling snow behind it.

'People from Stockholm, then. I expect they're on their way to their summer cottage to . . . look at the ice, or something.'

Maja seemed satisfied with this response, and turned to set off again. Then she thought of something and turned back.

'Why aren't we people from Stockholm, then? We live in Stockholm, after all.'

Cecilia said, 'You and I are from Stockholm, but Daddy isn't, not really, because his daddy wasn't from Stockholm.'

'My grandad?'

'Yes.'

'What was he, then?'

Cecilia made a vague movement with her lips and looked at Anders, who said, 'An old fisherman.'

Maja nodded and set off towards the lighthouse, which had now become an extended blot against the bright sky.

'Hang on a minute!'

Anders waved to Maja and Cecilia to get them in the right position and took a picture, two pictures, three pictures with different degrees of zoom. Maja was struggling to get away the whole time, but Cecilia held her close. It looked fantastic with the two small figures in the snow and the lighthouse towering up behind them. Anders gave them the thumbs up and stowed the camera in his rucksack once again.

Maja and Cecilia headed for the bright red door in the lighthouse wall. Anders stayed where he was with his hands in his pockets, gazing at the twenty-metre-high tower. It was built of stone. Not brick, but ordinary grey stone. A building that looked as if it could withstand just about anything.

What a job it must have been. Transporting all that stone here, lifting it, putting it in place . . .

'Daddy! Daddy, come on!'

Maja was standing next to the lighthouse door jumping up and down with excitement, waving her gloves in the air.

'What is it?' asked Anders as he walked towards them.

'It's open!'

Indeed it was. Just inside the door were a collection box and a stand containing brochures. There was a sign saying that the Archipelago Foundation welcomed visitors to Gåvasten lighthouse. Please take an information leaflet and continue up into the lighthouse, all contributions gratefully received.

Anders rooted in his pockets and found a crumpled fifty-kronor note, which he happily pushed into the empty collection box. This was better than he could have hoped for. He had never expected the lighthouse to be open, particularly in the winter.

Maja was already on her way up the stairs, Anders and Cecilia following. The worn spiral staircase was so narrow that it was impossible for two people to walk abreast. Iron shutters fastened with wing nuts covered the window openings.

Cecilia stopped. Anders could hear that she was breathing heavily. She reached out behind her back with one hand. Anders took it and asked, 'How are you doing?'

'OK.'

Cecilia carried on upwards as she squeezed Anders' hand. She had a tendency towards claustrophobia, and from that point of view the lighthouse was an absolute nightmare. The thick stone walls rising up so close together swallowed every sound, and the only light came from the open door down at the bottom and a fainter source of light higher up.

After another forty or so steps it was completely dark behind them, while the light above them had grown stronger. From somewhere up above they could hear Maja's voice, 'Hurry up! Come and see!'

The staircase ended at an open space in a wooden floor. They were standing in a circular room where a number of small windows made of thick glass let in a limited amount of light. In the middle of the room was another open door in a tower within the tower, with light pouring out.

Cecilia sat down on the floor and rubbed her hands over her face. When Anders crouched down beside her she waved dismissively. 'I'm fine. I just need to . . .'

Maja was shouting from inside the tower and Cecilia told him to go, she would follow shortly. Anders stroked her hair and went over to the open door, which led to another spiral staircase, this one made of iron. The light hurt his eyes as he climbed the twenty or so steps up to the heart and the brain of the lighthouse, the reflector.

Anders stopped and gazed open-mouthed. It was so beautiful.

From the darkness we ascend towards the light. He made his way up the dark staircase, and it was a shock to reach the top. Apart from a whitewashed border right at the bottom, the circular walls were made entirely of glass, and everything was sky and light. In the middle of the room stood the reflector, an obelisk made up of prisms and different coloured, geometrically precise pieces of glass. A shrine to the light.

Maja was standing with her nose and hands pressed against the glass wall. When she heard Anders coming, she pointed out across the ice, towards the north-east.

'Daddy, what's that?'

Anders screwed his eyes up against the brightness and looked out over the ice. He couldn't see anything apart from the white covering, and far away on the horizon just a hint of Ledinge archipelago.

'What do you mean?'

Maja pointed. 'There. On the ice.'

A gust of wind made the powdery snow whirl up, moving like a spirit across the pristine surface. Anders shook his head and turned back to face the room.

'Have you seen this?'

They examined the reflector and Anders took some pictures of Maja through the reflector, behind the reflector, in front of the reflector. The little girl and the kaleidoscope of light, refracted in all directions. When they had finished Cecilia came up the stairs, and she too was amazed.

They ate their picnic in the light room looking out across the archipelago, trying to spot familiar landmarks. Maja was interested in the graffiti on the white wall, but since some of it required explanations unsuitable for the ears of a six-year-old, Anders took out the information leaflet and started reading aloud.

The lower parts of the lighthouse had been built as early as the sixteenth century, as a platform for the beacons lit to mark the navigable channel into Stockholm. Later the tower was added and a primitive reflector was installed; at first it was illuminated using oil, then kerosene.

That was enough for Maja, and she was off down the stairs. Anders grabbed hold of her snowsuit.

'Just hang on, sunshine. Where are you off to?'

'I'm going to look at that thing I said I could see.'

'You're not to go too far.'

'I won't.'

Anders let go and Maja carried on down the stairs. Cecilia watched her disappear.

'Shouldn't we . . . ?'

'Well yes. But where can she go?'

They spent a couple of minutes reading the rest of the leaflet, and learned that the Aga aggregate had eventually been installed, that the lighthouse had been decommissioned in 1973 and had then been taken over by the Archipelago Foundation, which had put in a symbolic hundred-watt bulb. These days it ran on solar cells.

They looked at the graffiti and established that at least one instance of sexual intercourse must have taken place on this floor, unless of course it was just a case of wishful thinking on the part of the writer. Then they gathered their things together and set off down the stairs. Cecilia had to take her time because of the palpitations, the pressure on her chest, and Anders waited for her.

When they got outside there was no sign of Maja. The wind had started to get up and the snow was swirling through the air in thin veils, glittering in the sunlight. Anders closed his eyes and inhaled deeply. It had been a fantastic outing, but now it was time to go home.

'Maaaja,' he shouted. No reply. They walked around the lighthouse, looking out for her. The rock itself was only small, perhaps a hundred metres in circumference. There was no sign of Maja anywhere, and Anders gazed out across the ice. No small red figure.

'*Maaaja!*'

This time he shouted a little more loudly, and his heart began to beat a little more quickly. It was foolish, of course. There was no chance that she could have got lost here. He felt Cecilia's hand on his shoulder. She was pointing down at the snow.

'There are no tracks here.'

There was a hint of unease in her voice too. Anders nodded. Of course. All they had to do was follow Maja's tracks.

They went back to where they'd started from, by the lighthouse door. Anders poked his head inside and shouted up the stairs, just in case Maja had come back and they hadn't heard her. No reply.

The area around the door was covered in footprints made by all of them, but there were no tracks leading off to the right or left. Anders took a few steps down the rock. He could see their own tracks leading up towards the lighthouse from the ice, and Maja's footprints heading off in the opposite direction.

He stared out over the ice. No Maja. He blinked, rubbed his eyes. She couldn't have gone far enough to be out of sight. The contours of Domarö merged with those of the mainland, a thicker line of charcoal above a thinner one. He turned to face the other way, catching Cecilia's expression: concentrated, tense.

There was no sign of their daughter in the opposite direction either.

Cecilia passed him on her way out on to the ice. She was walking with her head down, following the tracks with her eyes.

'I'll check inside the lighthouse,' Anders shouted. 'She must be hiding or something.'

He ran over to the door and up the stairs, shouting for Maja but getting no reply. His heart was pounding now and he tried to calm himself down, to be cool and clear-headed.

It just isn't possible.

It's always possible.

No, it isn't. Not here. There's nowhere she can be.

Exactly.